The Secret of Orchard Cottage

Alex Brown is the bestselling author of five books and launched her career with the hugely popular Carrington's series, set in a seaside town department store. Alex now writes warm, witty and heartfelt novels centred on the cosy community spirit of village life.

Alex began her writing career as a weekly columnist for *The London Paper*, before trading in the rat race for the good life. *The Secret of Orchard Cottage* is Alex's sixth book.

When she isn't writing Alex enjoys knitting, watching Disney films with her daughter and going to Northern Soul nights, and she is passionate about supporting charities working with care leavers, adoption and vulnerable young people.

Alex lives in an oast house in a rural village in Sussex with her husband, daughter and a very shiny black Labrador. She loves hearing from her readers, so please visit her website – www.alexbrownauthor.com – or join her for chats on Facebook at www.facebook.com/alexandrabrownauthor and Twitter @alexbrownbooks.

Also by Alex Brown

The Carrington's series
Cupcakes at Carrington's
Christmas at Carrington's
Ice Creams at Carrington's
Me and Mr Carrington: A Short Story

The Tindledale series
The Great Christmas Knit Off
The Great Village Show

The Secret of Orchard Cottage

Alex Brown

HARPER

Harper
An imprint of HarperCollins*Publishers*
1 London Bridge Street,
London SE1 9GF

www.harpercollins.co.uk

A Paperback Original 2016
2

A catalogue record for this book is available from the British Library

ISBN: 978-0-00-759742-0

Set in Birka by Palimpsest Book Production Limited,
Falkirk, Stirlingshire

Printed and bound in Great Britain by
Clays Ltd, St Ives plc

MIX
Paper from
responsible sources
FSC C007454

For all the ordinary women everywhere,
doing extraordinary things

'Treasure this book always, for it will stand the test of time'

— Winnie Lovell, 1941

and straightened the collar, proud to be a part of the First Aid Nursing Yeomanry, or FANY as everyone said, and cast one last glance around the rose-print-papered bedroom in the eaves of the honey-stoned cottage that had been her home for all of her twenty years. She really would miss this old place, Orchard Cottage, a special place on the outskirts of Tindledale, the village where she had grown up. With its tiny school with the clock tower on the roof and the cobbled High Street, flanked either side with black timber-framed, white wattle-walled shops with mullioned windows, surrounded by lush, undulating fields full of hops, hay, lambs, cows, strawberries, buttercups and delicate pink cherry blossom in springtime that swirled all around like confetti in a breeze. All the familiarity, and there was a certain beauty, comfort even in the predictable, seasonal routine of a life lived in a rural village. But constraint too, and as much as she loved Tindledale, Winnie knew there was a whole new world waiting for her beyond the bus stop in the village square. Adventure. That's what this was. She had waited her whole life, or so it seemed, for this very moment. She had already fulfilled her duties in the Women's Land Army, teaching the city girls how to work the land. Luckily the base hadn't been that far away so she had been able to hop on the bus home when she had leave, but this time it was different. As soon as the next part of her training was completed, she would go into the field and then who knew when she might next come home? But Winnie was determined to give it her all. Do her bit for the war effort. Her patriotic duty. And her parents had been so proud when Bill the postman had cycled up to the apple barn door to deliver the letter requesting her to report to the special FANY training centre located over two hundred miles away. Before war had been declared, the furthest Winnie had been was to Market Briar, the market town on the other side of the valley, and she had certainly never travelled on a train, which reminded her – she looked at the alarm clock on the cabinet beside the bed – it really wouldn't do to be late! The next bus, *on the hour every hour*, left the village square at ten sharpish, and it was already nearly nine o'clock.

Winnie folded her new hand-knitted cardy into her suitcase – made especially for today with some wool unravelled from an old blanket. Make do and mend! That's what all the women in the village were chatting about, along with 'beauty is your duty'. So she checked her hair and make-up then applied a little more lipstick in Scarlet Pimpernel – having swapped a stick of liquorice and a book for a selection of tester sticks and a block of mascara with a couple of younger girls in the village. (Hettie and Marigold; one had an aunt who worked on the Yardley make-up counter in a department store.) She then gathered up her hat, gloves, handbag, suitcase and, lastly, the ugly gas mask in its square cardboard box with a length of string for a handle, and closed the bedroom door behind her. Winnie made her way down the rickety old staircase and into the kitchen where the homely aroma of a traditional fry-up greeted her.

'Eggs *and* bacon for you, Winifred?' her mother

Delphine asked, with the hint of a French accent, lifting the edge of her apron to wipe her hands as Winnie slipped into the chair next to Edith, whose cheeks were flushed red like a pair of plum tomatoes from having been outside in the fields since the crack of dawn. As little sisters went, Edith – or Edie, as she liked to be called – wasn't too bad. And Edie loved working in the orchards, crating up the apples and pears and tending to the horses, which was just as well now that it all came down to their father, George, and their neighbour, seventy-year-old Albert from three fields over, to keep things going, since both of their brothers had left the farm at the start of the war, having enlisted right away. Which was even more reason why Winnie was determined to do her bit. Yes, the Land Army had been fun, hard work too, but she was quite used to that, having grown up helping her father in the orchards. But now she wanted to do more; properly support the war effort like her brothers and saw no reason not to just because she was a woman. So after using every shilling she had, and with some help from her parents, she had managed to buy her uniform and was now ready to show what she could really do to help stop the Nazis in their tracks.

'Ooh, yes please Mum,' Winnie said, knowing better than to refuse, given that the rationing of bacon had come into force last year. Nerves and anticipation had seen to her appetite, but Winnie knew that her mother had saved the rashers, cut as generously as could be afforded during war time by Bessie up in Cooper's the butchers' shop in the High Street, especially for her farewell breakfast, just as she had for each of her brothers. So it would be churlish to turn it down and risk the wrath of her father who was a stickler for citing that old adage of 'waste not want not' and gratitude really was next to godliness, as far as he was concerned.

Winnie poured herself some tea from the knitted tea-cosied pot before smoothing a starched white linen napkin into her lap – her mother always liked to look her best and to keep an immaculate home too, and certainly saw 'no reason to let standards slip just because Hitler has seen fit to turn our lives upside down', as she frequently reminded them all. Their father begged to differ, and said that it was Delphine's chic French ancestry that made her a perfect petal amidst the 'ruddy-cheeked horrors' that he had grown up with toiling the fields surrounding Tindledale. Talking of which, both parts of the kitchen stable back door burst open and George appeared, stamping the mud from his boots on to the mat before pulling Delphine towards him for a hearty morning kiss.

'Ew! Enough of that,' Delphine shooed him away, pretending to chastise. 'You'll make my face all mucky and that really won't do when we venture up to the village square later on.'

'Don't worry about that – handsome woman like you. You're the best looker in Tindledale!' George puffed out his chest as he reluctantly let go of his wife. Delphine patted her neatly prepared pin curls back into place.

'You always were a charmer, George.' Delphine pecked his cheek, before bringing proceedings back to the importance of the day. 'Now, there's a fresh shirt hanging

in the wardrobe next to your good suit. But first . . .'
Delphine delivered two perfectly poached eggs on to a
plate, 'eat your breakfast up!' And she smiled contentedly.
Delphine was in her element and at her happiest when
feeding and fussing over her family.

'Right you are,' George replied, doing as he was told.
He sat at the kitchen table and popped the filmy yolk
of an egg with the corner of a hunk of home-baked crusty
bread. 'Want to look my best too for waving off our
Winnie,' he added, winking at his eldest daughter. 'It's
been smashing having you home again for a bit love, and
so grown up you are now.'

Winnie smiled; she wasn't the naïve girl she used to
be. Not like she was when she first went off to the Land
Army at the start of the war. But so much had changed
since then . . . courting for starters, that had come as a
pleasant surprise. And quite unexpected too. She smiled
at the memory of that morning when she first met him
– she'd just finished showing the girls how to crate the
apples correctly, when someone from the nearby army
base at Market Briar had requested a volunteer who
could drive.

'And it's not every day one of our own gets chosen for
driving duties,' George went on. 'For the top brass no
less. I knew my showing you how to drive would come
in handy one day.' He punctuated the air with the prongs
of his fork. 'You didn't even know how to switch on the
apple lorry's engine before I showed you.' He took
another big bite of his bread.

'Daaad.' Winnie gave him a pretend exasperated look.

'It's hardly the same – an open-back truck crammed full of apples bobbing all over the place every time the tyres hit a pothole. No, the "top brass", as you call them, enjoy a very smooth ride in a proper car, thank you very much.' Winnie took a sip of her tea and pondered again on her good fortune in having spent the last couple of months in and out of the army base where she had been noticed, something that never would have happened if she'd stayed milking cows and digging for victory in the fields with the other girls.

'You'll be driving ambulances now though!' Edie blithely chipped in, before turning her attentions back to the infinitely more interesting dollop of homemade blackberry jam that she had just let plop from a knife on to her toast. Winnie turned to study her little sister, half wishing that she still possessed Edie's innocent view of the world. But there was a war on, and already Winnie had seen first hand the real effect it was having on the country. What her parents didn't know was that one of Winnie's driving duties had taken her to Brighton – she hadn't wanted to alarm them with accounts of what she saw there, preferring they enjoy their still near-idyllic lives out here in the countryside – but the devastation that the German bomb had caused when it landed on the cinema in Kemp Town would stay with Winnie for always, especially the four children amongst the fifty-five people who were killed.

'And doesn't she look a picture in her uniform?' Delphine joined in, smoothing a proud hand over Winnie's right shoulder with a formidable look on her face, as if warning the tiniest speck of fluff to so much as dare go near her daughter's immaculate jacket.

'Indeed she does,' George nodded, equally proud.

*

As the emerald green and cream split-window Bedford bus chugged away from the village square, Edie dashed after it, along with several other girls from the village, all waving white cotton hankies with stoic smiles fixed firmly in place as they treasured last glimpses, potentially, of their soldier sweethearts. But it was different for Edie: she loved her big sister, of course she did, but she'd be lying if she said she wasn't a tiny bit gleeful that Winnie had signed up to join the FANY, driving ambulances and doing first aid, and it wasn't as if she was going somewhere really dangerous like her brothers. No, Winnie would be having the time of her life at the training centre, and it wasn't for ever. Winnie would be back before they knew it, which was why Edie didn't feel *quite* so bad for having already boxed up all her belongings ready to move into her big sister's bedroom for the duration. After their parents' room, which was set at the front of the cottage overlooking the single-track lane, Winnie's attic bedroom, with its very own pastel-pink vanity unit and dual-aspect windows with views of the surrounding fields, really was the perfect place to be in Orchard Cottage.

Present day . . .

In the bedroom of a 1930s bungalow in Basingstoke, April Wilson slipped off her pink hand-knitted cardy and placed it back on the padded hanger before putting it away inside the wardrobe – managing, as she had become accustomed to doing, to avoid making eye contact with her late husband's shirts still hanging neatly on his half of the hanging rail.

Graham had died eighteen months ago. Motor neurone disease. Ten years her senior, but with a zest for life befitting a far younger man, Gray had been the proverbial life and soul of the party until the cruel disease had taken hold, and then when his breathing muscles had degenerated so severely, he had slipped away one night in his sleep. And April would always be grateful for that. Having given up her nursing career to care for Gray, it had been his wish right from the start, on that sad, drizzly autumn day in the consultant's room at the hospital when the diagnosis had first been given, to be at home in his own bed when the end came.

'Only me,' the effervescent voice of April's stepdaughter,

Nancy, cut through her reverie as the door opened slowly. 'Sorry, am I disturbing you? Only these arrived a few minutes ago addressed to Mrs Wilson.' And a gorgeous array of vibrant red and orange roses appeared in the gap between the door and the frame.

April quickly closed the wardrobe doors and pulled on a polka-dot towelling robe, before smoothing down her curly brown hair, which had got mussed up from tugging the dress off over her head.

Gray used to help her with the zip.

April stopped moving.

Instinctively, she inhaled sharply and squeezed her right hand, pressing the fingernails hard into her palm to stop herself from going there. It was the best way. And it was always the little things that still managed to catch her off guard. But she'd get out her sewing machine and alter the zip, build in a small ruched panel on either side of the waist to create a looser fit and the problem would be solved. No more tugging at the dress and her heartstrings while yearning for Gray to be there beside her. Of course, that feeling would never completely disappear, but for now, April needed at least some of her waking hours to feel normal, to be free from the near-physical pain of her battered heart.

'No, I was just getting changed, come on in sweetheart.' April smiled, tying the belt as she walked across the room to take the roses from Nancy. 'Oh they're absolutely lovely, thank you so much.' She pressed her nose into the highly scented flowers, figuring they must have cost quite a bit by the looks of the gorgeous white wicker trug and elaborate puff of scarlet tulle ribbon wrapped all around it.

'Oh, don't thank me,' Nancy grinned. 'The cookery book and that melt-in-the-mouth steak were your birthday treats from me – flowers are a waste of money in my opinion,' she added in her usual matter-of-fact way before bouncing down on to the end of April's bed. Just like her dad, thought April; Gray had been a prag-matist too. 'Here, see who they're from,' and Nancy plucked an envelope from a wire stem and handed it to April.

After placing the trug on top of the chest of drawers, April opened the envelope and pulled out a gold-embossed cream card.

To my amazing and beautiful wife on her birthday. Seize the day my darling, wherever or however that may be, as life really is too short.
Bye for now.
Love always.
Gray xxx

April pressed the card to her chest and gasped. Trust him to have remembered, even from beyond the grave, but then Gray always was so thoughtful, and they had joked about this bonkers idea years ago – it was over Sunday lunch in the local pub, shortly after the diagnosis, when they'd all been keen to keep spirits up and put on brave faces. Gray had said he was going to pay his sister, Jen, a florist, up front, to send roses every year on April's birthday. Gray had then teased April, telling her, 'But just don't be living until you're a hundred years old or the money will have run out by then and you'll end up getting a measly bunch of dandelions.' They had all laughed, and then later Jen had taken April aside and explained that she intended on honouring Gray's wishes no matter what. April would have roses on her birthday. It was the least she could do after all the love and care she had already shown her brother. And April had smiled and shrugged, for she liked taking care of people, loved it in fact; it gave her a purpose and made her feel like she was making a difference. It was the reason she had trained to become a nurse in the first place.

And then so much had happened since to keep her busy: there had been the funeral to arrange, sorting out his financial affairs and the memorial service – Gray had been a renowned research scientist, involved in pioneering work developing cures for a number of life-limiting illnesses, which Gray had often said was actually very ironic really, given the fate of his own health. And of course there was the grieving process to work through. That had hit April hard and somehow all the brave facing and wry jokes while Gray had still been alive had made it even harder once he'd gone. Back then it had been easy for April to occupy her thoughts and time by caring for Gray as he deteriorated: making sure all his needs were met; showing him she was strong and would be OK without him. It had been important for April to give Gray that, to ease the burden of worry for him, as she knew his biggest fear after the diagnosis was for those he loved and was used to looking after, and would ultimately leave behind – his family. Twenty-two-year-old twins, Freddie and Nancy, how would they cope? Their mother lived on the other side of the world in New Zealand, having emigrated there with her new husband when they were teenagers. But the twins had coped remarkably well, in that robust, resilient way that many young people seemed able to do. Of course, there had been ups and downs, but April admired them, their strength, and having spent some time with their mother they now seemed OK and were starting to normalise . . . which was more than could be said for her.

Gray had worried so much about April; often confiding in Jen, asking her to look out for his wife and to support her through his demise and when he was no longer here. Because, although Gray and April had been together for a while, they had only been married for a year when the diagnosis came, and Gray had said he would completely understand if April wanted to end things with him then and move on. Make a life for herself with somebody new. Somebody fit and vibrant. Instead of 'saddling herself with a sickly, older, and quite often grumpy git like me' (Gray could be quite self-deprecating at times). It was a lot to expect of her to stick by him, but April was having none of it. In sickness and health. That's what she had vowed, and gladly so. She wasn't a quitter, never had been.

And caring for Gray had given April a purpose, something to live for, and God knows she had needed it, because if the truth be told, her world had fallen apart that day in the consultant's office. April had hidden it well of course, put on a brave face, stoic, and she was good at that, having trained at Great Ormond Street hospital where nursing seriously ill children required an ability to protect one's self, close off emotions when required – maintain an emotional distance, if you like. It really wouldn't do for a nurse to cry. No, that was for other people. April's job was to be strong so that everyone else around her could cope. Hence, she hadn't cried once in front of Gray or the twins. Or burdened any of her friends from the knitting group or gym classes that she used to do in the local leisure centre before Gray became seriously incapacitated. And April used to love knitting: sitting next to Gray on the sofa of an evening, they would watch TV together and he'd tease her about the chunkiness of her size 12 needles for a cosy Aran jumper that had been her last project. It was the simple, everyday 'doing nothing' stuff that April missed most. But now, well . . . it just wasn't the same on her own. The happy association of knit one purl one and laughing along to *Gogglebox* wasn't there any more.

'Are you OK?' Nancy asked, leaning forward to stroke April's arm.

'Yes, sure. Sorry darling, I was miles away.'

April shook her head as if to clear her thoughts, and then smiled at Nancy.

'Don't apologise,' Nancy smiled back. 'We all knew today would be extra tough for you. Another birthday without Dad.' She shuffled her bottom backwards over the duvet and then patted the bed, indicating for April to sit beside her.

'Actually, today has been better than I anticipated,' April replied, conscious that underneath the veneer of being OK, Nancy was still grieving too, and she didn't want to upset her stepdaughter by appearing to be 'getting over her father's death' too quickly. But deep down April knew that she most likely would never really 'get over' Gray. Yes she'd learn to live without him, be happy again perhaps, a different kind of happiness, she hoped, one day, but still . . .

'Good,' Nancy stated. 'You know, Dad would never have wanted you to be "moping" all over the place.' She paused to do quote signs in the air and April winced. 'Especially on your birthday.' A short silence followed. 'Um, sorry, not that you are,' Nancy added. 'Gosh, sorry, I didn't mean it like that, you aren't . . . um, haven't been "moping" at all, in fact you've been amazingly strong and kind and lovely as always to me and Freddie, putting everyone else before yourself. Sorry, me and my big mouth. I really must engage my brain before opening my gob and just letting words blurt out.' Nancy pulled a face and shook her head, making her fiery red hair swish around her shoulders. 'I just meant that . . . well, you know how practical Dad was about stuff, being a scientist and all. I didn't mean to be so insensitive, God no, but somehow it always comes out that way.'

'It's OK,' April replied. 'Like father like daughter, eh?' and she nudged Nancy with her elbow, before both women exchanged glances and a smile.

'Hmm, I guess so.' Nancy pressed her hands together as if to break the moment and lift the mood, buoy them both back up. 'I know! How about we watch an old film together? *Mamma Mia*, you *love* that one.' April's smile widened. 'Whaaaat? What's so funny?' Nancy lifted her shoulders and pulled a face.

'*Mamma Mia!*' April laughed. 'It's hardly an *old* film . . .'

'Hmm, weeeeell . . . it is to me. Or would you prefer to watch something *really* ancient, like *Dirty Dancing* perhaps?'

'Or how about *Some Like It Hot?*' April couldn't resist, and Nancy creased her forehead.

'Sounds like filth to me.' Nancy folded her arms. 'April, you fox! Never had you down as a porn fan,' she teased.

'Noooooo!' April protested, her cheeks flushing. 'Oh gosh no, nothing like that. It's a classic, starring Marilyn Monroe. With Tony Curtis and Jack Lemmon – they dress up as women and—'

'Cross-dressing! Hmm, guess that could be cool.' Nancy raised her eyebrows.

'Hmm, it's a bit more than that,' April said.

'Well, I've never heard of it!'

'Ha! Now why doesn't that surprise me?' April gave her stepdaughter's thigh an affectionate pat. 'You know, I feel *reeeeeally* old now.' She shook her head and let out a long sigh.

'Oh don't be daft! You're still young. A million miles away from the menopause.' April shook her head; trust Nancy to be so blunt. 'Tell you what . . . why don't I do your hair and make-up this afternoon? I could do your nails too; we could have a girly makeover party. I'll get us some chocolate and maybe a cheeky bottle of bubbles . . . what do you say?'

'That sounds lovely, are you sure though?' April said, surprised, as it wasn't really Nancy's thing.

'Yep. It's your birthday and I want to make it nice for you. And you love all that beauty and pampering stuff.' A short silence followed. April swallowed, hard. And then Nancy added, 'Weell,' she hesitated, 'you used to before Dad died, and I know it's hard, I really still miss him too, but he'd want us to make an effort on your birthday and you made an effort on mine, even though I bet you didn't really feel up to it.' She pulled herself off the bed and went in search of April's beauty paraphernalia. She opened the top drawer of a chest. It was full of underwear. 'Sorry,' she said, closing it again. 'Nail polish?'

'No problem,' April replied, 'it's in the basket on the shelf in the ensuite.' She paused and fiddled with the belt of her dressing gown. 'And I say that a pamper afternoon is a very lovely idea, thank you sweetheart.'

'Great!' Nancy chimed. 'But I'm sensing a big *but*!' She stopped moving and turned to look at April.

'It's just that I thought my hair looked OK! Why didn't you tell me *before* we went out for lunch?' April pretended to admonish, but knew seriously that she hadn't really bothered with all of that since Gray went, often wondering what was the point. Of course, she always made sure her hair was brushed and that she looked presentable and had clean clothes on, that sort of thing (well . . . under-wear at least), but she had found it hard to muster up much enthusiasm for applying make-up or painting her nails. To be honest, the last eighteen months had seen her operating as if on autopilot, going through the motions really.

'April, your hair looks lovely. Honestly. I just thought it would be something nice to do for the rest of your birthday.'

'Ahh, OK. Then thank you, and sorry, ignore me, I'm just being oversensitive. Come on, you grab the chocolate and champagne and I'll sort out what we need up here,' April chivvied, seizing the opportunity to busy herself and be in her preferred state.

'Perfect.' Nancy walked towards the door. 'Ooh, before I forget – this came too. It's addressed to "Miss W. Lovell", no idea who that is, but it looks like a birthday card and Lovell was your surname before you married Dad so I'm guessing it's for you.' She pulled out a crumpled lilac envelope from the back pocket of her jeans and gave it to April. 'Sorry for squashing it.'

'Thank you. Ooh, it's from Edie,' April said, taking the envelope and recognising the old-lady spidery writing on the front.

'Your great aunt?'

'That's right.' April opened the envelope and slipped out the card, drawing in the faint, but evocatively familiar scent of her childhood summer holidays spent in the quaint little village of Tindledale with her grandfather's sister. This was before her parents had died in a car crash shortly before her sixteenth birthday and her life had changed for ever. April, an only child, had gone to live with her mum's parents at the other end of the country and the strong connection with her great aunt Edie faded until she was able to visit more frequently as an adult. And then her grandparents died, leaving Edie as April's last living relative.

April wafted the card in front of her nose. 'Ahh, lavender mingled with mothballs. Takes me right back – I used to get told off for fiddling with the mothballs hanging in the little muslin bag in the back of her wardrobe whilst playing *The Lion, the Witch and the Wardrobe* game, thinking I was on my way to Narnia.'

'Really? I can't imagine you getting told off for anything, April,' Nancy grinned. 'I always imagined you as a polite, well-behaved child . . . much like you are now.'

'Trust me, I had my moments.' April rolled her eyes before opening the card. 'Ooops!' She bent down to retrieve a five-pound note that had fluttered from it, while simultaneously reading.

Happy birthday Winnie
   Treat yourself to a nice dinner somewhere fancy.
   Lots of love
   Your Edie xxx

April frowned.

'What is it?' Nancy asked, sounding concerned. April sighed as she realised what this meant, showing the card to Nancy. Her great aunt Edie must be getting forgetful and somewhat confused. And a fancy dinner for a fiver? Oh dear.

'Ahh! Well, it's nice that your aunt remembered your birthday, eh? Probably just got into a muddle with names, that's all, no need to worry. How old is she?' Nancy asked, folding her arms.

'You know, I'm not sure exactly,' April said, feeling a twinge of guilt as she racked her brains trying to recall when she had last visited her great aunt Edie or indeed sent her a birthday card. 'I reckon she must be ninety at least.'

'Wow! And did she come to Dad's funeral? I don't remember seeing her there, but then it was all such a blur . . .'

'No, she wasn't up to it – was getting over a fall, I think she said, I can't really remember either, as it was, like you said . . . all a bit of a blur for me too. But I do know that I promised to—' April stopped talking.

'What's the matter?' Nancy asked gently. 'You look like you're about to cry. What's up?'

'Nothing.' April dipped her head and busied herself with putting the card and the money back inside the envelope.

'Something clearly is.' Silence followed. 'Come on, out with it,' Nancy cajoled.

'I feel dreadful,' April eventually said.

'Why?'

'OK.' April inhaled and let out a long breath. 'When Great Aunt Edie wrote to apologise for not coming to

Gray's funeral, I said I'd visit her soon, and well, that was over a year and a half ago . . .' April's voice dwindled, knowing that it was eighteen months, two weeks and three days to be precise. She crossed off the days in her diary. At first, it had been a comfort, well, more of a life-raft, something to cling on to, because every day ticked off was a day closer to shedding the cocoon of numbness in favour of feeling something again – she had hoped. But now it was just a habit, because April had learnt over the months that grief really wasn't as kind as all that. It came in peaks and troughs like a giant rollercoaster with no predictability; it was not a set process to be worked through at all, despite what people had assured her.

'Oh April, come here.' Nancy pulled her in for a big hug. 'I'm sure she'll understand – your husband had just died! I'd say that's extenuating circumstances, wouldn't you?'

April knew that Nancy was trying to make her feel better, but it had to be at least a couple of years since she had visited her great aunt in Tindledale. The last time had been with Gray, when he was still fairly mobile. They had driven down one sunny Saturday afternoon, stopping on the way at a quaint old black and white Tudor-framed pub with a lovely garden full of pink hollyhocks and a couple of goats in a pen for children to pet. Gray had surreptitiously fed them his salad – never having been a fan of 'rabbit food', as he called it. They'd had a wonderful time relaxing, and for a few precious hours it had seemed like the old days, carefree and fun, before the diagnosis changed everything.

'I guess so. But I've still neglected her,' April said.

'Then do something about it. Go and see her.' Nancy stepped back from April and put her hands on her hips. 'Go on! It'll do you good – get away from here for a few days, give yourself some space, and you know what they say, a change of scenery and all that.' Nancy looked April in the eyes. 'A mini break is exactly what you need.' She nodded.

'Hmm! Are you trying to get rid of me?' April asked, instantly wishing she didn't sound quite so needy. It really was unlike her, but it was something she had noticed creeping upon her more and more since Gray had died. She felt exposed, vulnerable even, and she wasn't really sure why, preferring not to think too much about it, hoping the feeling would go away if she ignored it.

April coughed to clear her throat. 'But I can't go and leave you here on your own.' She wasn't sure it was right, certainly not so soon after the memorial service – the twins might need her.

'Of course you can.'

'But what about Freddie?' April knew how hopeless he was at getting himself up for his job as a car mechanic every morning. And hadn't she promised Gray that she'd be here for the twins no matter what?

'What about him?' Nancy shook her head. 'No. It'll do Freddie good to look after himself for a day or two. He's a lazy arse and relies on you too much. And you really must stop doing his washing!' She wagged a finger in the air.

'But it's no trouble to put it in with my stuff, I quite

like doing it in fact,' April said, always happy to help out.

'Oh April, pleeeeease, go and visit your great aunt. If only to remind her that your name isn't Winnie! And you never know, you might even solve the mystery!'

'Mystery?' April raised her eyebrows. 'What do you mean?'

'You know . . . find out who this Winnie woman is,' Nancy joked.

'Ahh, yes, indeed. And I could very well have her fiver here,' April smiled, waving the note.

'Exactly! And Freddie is perfectly capable of seeing to his own washing and I'll be here to make sure he pulls his weight around the house,' she laughed.

'Hmm. But joking aside, the name Winnie does seem to ring a bell. I'm sure I've heard it before . . . a relative perhaps. I think there was an old black and white picture of her on my aunt's sideboard in the sitting room . . . in a uniform during the war . . . It used to fascinate me as you don't often see that, it's mostly men, the soldiers.' April creased her forehead, casting her mind back trying to remember more.

'Sounds intriguing, what happened to her?'

'I'm not sure – you know how family history gets lost in the mists of time – but I'd like to see if I can find out before it's too late. My aunt is getting on now and once she's gone that'll be it, I suppose, for my family, my flesh and blood. It'll just be me left.'

'Then you must go right away, before, as you say . . . it's too late.'

'Yes, I should do that. And I *am* concerned about Aunt

Edie.' A short silence followed, leaving April deep in thought.

'And it can't be easy for her on her own at that age. Has she got a husband? Any children? I can't remember . . .,' Nancy asked.

'No. She never married,' April replied, then pondered, casting her mind back. 'She used to joke that there was a shortage of men around after the war, and the only eligible ones in the village were either daft, or already spoken for . . . And that she much preferred the company of horses in any case.'

'Oh dear.'

'Indeed. She always had a good circle of friends though, but I guess most of them have probably died by now.' April shook her head.

'I guess so. Ninety is a ripe old age. And definitely more reason why you should go and see her.'

'But are you sure?' April checked, but now that all the practicalities following Gray's death had been completed, she was actually starting to feel a tiny bit brighter each morning. Gone was the dreadful split-second gear change on waking, that glorious moment before the synapses of her brain kicked in and it was as if Gray was still alive and still well, only for the grief to come hurtling back all over again when her memory was restored. Yes, April was definitely on the way to feeling a little bit more like her old self, less wobbly, and it would certainly keep her busy for a couple of days. All this sitting around doing nothing very much really wouldn't do. And hadn't Gray said on his card for her to seize the day?

So, April made a decision. Nancy was right: she could do with a break, time to gather her thoughts, dust herself down and figure out what next. And it was a pleasant, pretty drive through the countryside to get there, which would give her plenty of time to do just that. Yes, first thing tomorrow morning April would go to Tindledale and visit her great aunt Edith in Orchard Cottage.

2

April's blue Beetle bounced around the corner of the pot-holed country lane, the top of her head very nearly making contact with the little lever that opened the sunroof. She slammed her right foot on the brake, just in time! Gripping the steering wheel, April held her breath as a resplendent gingery-brown feathered hen dawdled across in front of the car followed by a row of fluffy yellow chicks.

'Awww, so sweet,' April said to herself, before picking up the concertinaed paper map nestled next to Gray's trug of roses on the passenger seat beside her. Nancy had said it would be a shame for April not to bring the flowers with her, as she was on nights for the rest of the week so would most likely forget to water them and they'd end up dying from dehydration. So April had loaded them into the car along with a lovely bunch of late blooming pastel-pink peonies picked earlier this morning from the back garden, and a tin containing a magnificent cherry madeira cake, with the perfect crack running across the top, for Great Aunt Edie. April had remembered that madeira cake was Edie's favourite so had baked one last night especially, using a recipe from

The Great British Bake Off book that Nancy had kindly surprised her with for her birthday. And everyone loved peonies.

April unfolded the map, thankful to the man in the petrol station situated just outside Market Briar, the nearest big town. After asking where she was heading, he had reminded her that most of the country lanes in and around Tindledale were simply single-track 'unnamed' roads so April really needed to 'do herself a favour and take a good old-fashioned map'. And he had been right. April had done this journey more than once with Gray, but it all looked so different now. Although Great Aunt Edie's postcode was on the sat nav, it covered such a vast rural area that April had reached her destination point supposedly fifteen minutes ago so was now reliant on reading the map to make her way down to the valley and right through the middle of fields, or so it seemed. At one point, after taking a wrong turn, the Beetle had to go along little more than a dirt track with enormous black-and-white-splodged cows on either side chewing and staring at April, before arriving at a tiny derelict church in the middle of nowhere, which was a bit eerie if she was honest. April had then had to do at least a ten-point turn, being careful not to topple the crumbling gravestones, before making her way back along the dirt track and on to what constituted a proper road around these parts.

Once the last of the chicks had safely made it to the other side of the lane, April tentatively continued on her way, turning another corner, but still not entirely sure that she was going in the right direction as there weren't any signposts to guide her. A few metres later and she was facing a five-bar gate with an empty field behind it. Although on second glance, April saw a very large black bull eyeing her from under a tree in the far corner. Wasting no time, and remembering as a child the very close encounter she and a friend had experienced when a similarly intimidating bull had charged at them whilst they were picking blackberries on the other side of Tindledale, April quickly and quietly reversed back on to the lane. She had seen first hand how a raging bull could trample a wooden gate, given enough ground to gather enough speed. Even now, the sight of a blackberry brought back that moment when she had hurled her Tupperware box into a bush and legged it over a stile to safety – a well-placed farmer had then grabbed her and her friend and hurled them up on to his hay tractor before dealing with the bull.

After finding a layby, April pulled over, switched off the engine and sat for a while to weigh up her options, wondering if she should head back to the main road and start again in her quest to find Orchard Cottage. It all looked so different somehow, or perhaps it was because she hadn't really paid attention on any of the previous trips over the years, when her parents had brought her here in the school summer holidays, or Edie had arranged for a taxi to pick her up from the station located down the bottom of the hill, or Gray had driven and she would have been busy chatting and laughing along with him.

Ahh, April spotted a van in the distance. She'd flag

it down and ask for directions. Stepping out of the car, she waved an arm and the green van slowed down until it was stationary in front of her. The diesel engine was still chugging away as the window was rolled down. April glanced at the side and saw 'Only Shoes and Horses. Matt Carter & Daughter – Farrier' written in white signage. *Nice touch mentioning his daughter.* And then she saw the man. With curls the colour of treacle, prominent cheekbones, full lips and the greenest eyes that April had ever seen. Wearing a chocolate-brown leather waistcoat over a checked shirt, he had the look of a Romany gypsy about him, or as if he had just stepped out of a Catherine Cookson saga – all windswept and mysterious, moody, brooding angst. And he was definitely 'hot for an older guy' as Nancy would say, while most likely elbowing April in the ribs and nodding her head slowly with a cheeky smile set firmly in place like she used to when they went out shopping together, in the carefree, fun days, before Gray got ill. *And on second thoughts, was there something vaguely familiar about this man?* April wasn't sure. Had she seen him somewhere before? *Hmmm. Maybe in the village on a previous visit. That'll be it! He is very striking so it's entirely possible that our paths have crossed and his face and those green eyes have just stuck in my mind. And he's not that old, but then Nancy is only twenty-two – anyone over thirty-five is practically ancient as far as she is concerned.*

'Um, hello . . .' April ventured a few seconds later, after Matt (she assumed) still hadn't spoken, having busied himself with pushing up the sleeves of his shirt, revealing part of a sleeve tattoo, before taking an enormous swig of water from a plastic bottle which, now empty, he had thrown into the footwell of the passenger seat beside him. 'Er, sorry to bother you . . . but, er . . .' April was feeling self-conscious; his eyes really were quite mesmerising and they were fixed on her. She hesitated and then managed a some-what meagre, 'I'm lost!'

Still silence.

Then Matt gave April an up-and-down glance as if mulling over whether to help her or not, although it was difficult to tell for sure what exactly he was thinking as his face hadn't moved at all except to drink the water. He stared intently, making April feel a little hot as she wondered what was going on. Why wasn't he saying anything? It was as if he was in some sort of trance. And then, as if someone had found the cord in the back of his body and given it a good yank, Matt started talking.

'Where you heading?'

'Oh, um thanks. I'm trying to find Orchard Cottage, it's—'

'I know it. Get in your car and follow me. I'm going past the top of the lane.' And before April could get another word in, if only to say thank you, Matt wound up the window and drove off, but then waited in front of the Beetle while April raced over to it, leapt in and started the engine up as fast as she could. Ten minutes later, Matt stuck his right arm out of the van window and pointed to a gap in the hedgerow before disappearing around a bend further on. April assumed this meant she should turn right . . . so she did.

*

Matt watched her go. Glancing again in his wing mirror as the blue Beetle disappeared out of sight, he gripped the steering wheel a little tighter before pulling into a layby and switching off the engine. He couldn't believe it. Of course, he had recognised her right away. But she had no idea who he was. And why would she? He looked very different now. Unrecognisable, it seemed. April Lovell. Even her name was lovely. And she really had been so lovely back then. When he had first spotted her, cycling along the stream down near the Blackwood Farm Estate, it had been the school holidays and he had been fishing on the other side of the water with Jack, his brother, who had teased him for gawping at the girl down from London. Everyone in the village knew who she was; she came every year in the school holidays to stay with her aunt.

Matt must have been about twelve – bottle-top glasses and crooked teeth – and with typical pre-pubescent boy hormones racing through him, but still, he had never seen a girl like her. A vision she was. With her long curly brown hair flaring out behind her as she sped along, her white cotton skirt puffing up in the breeze, allowing him a glimpse of her suntanned thighs. And to cap it all, she had turned her freckled face and actually grinned at him as she had gone by. He thought he had died and gone to heaven. And he had never forgotten that moment.

It had been a few summers later when he had seen her again, part of the group that met on the village green every morning with their bikes, bags of sweets and cling-filmed sandwiches and instructions to be home by sunset for their tea. More confident by now, thanks to the braces straightening his teeth and the new, decent glasses, he hadn't wanted to miss his chance a second time around and had plucked up the courage to talk to her. He had made her laugh and in turn she had made him feel on top of the world. They had spent the whole week of her holiday together that summer. Cycling, fishing, swimming in the stream, they had even made a den in the woods together. And that was where it had happened. April Lovell was the first girl Matt kissed. Properly kissed. Pulling her into him, pressing his body against hers in the buttercup field. Soft and curvy, he had been nervous of crushing her. Later, they had lain on the grass in the sunshine together. Him with his arms wrapped around her, his fingers entwined in her hair as she rested her head on his chest and twirled a buttercup underneath his chin, making jokes about liking butter or something. He couldn't remember the words for sure, but he'd never forgotten the scent of her, like a bunch of lovely fresh flowers it was.

Matt pushed a hand through his hair, shocked at the effect the sudden memory of that intense summer was having on him all these years later. Even though he had never seen her again until today in the lane. He rubbed a hand over his stubbly chin and glanced in the rear-view mirror, knowing he needed to pull himself together. And fast. Everything was different now. He was a dad with responsibilities for starters, so there was no point mooning over the past like some lovestruck teenager. He switched the engine back on and carried on driving.

*

Orchard Cottage was at the end of a private, single-track lane, April remembered that much, and last time she'd been here the lane was pristine with beautifully mani-cured herbaceous borders running the length on either side. But now, there was just a mass of higgledy-piggledy brambles and nettles, some so long they were practically meeting in the middle like an arch covering the lane and tapping the top of the Beetle as April nudged gently on. And she didn't dare risk going over five miles an hour for fear of driving into one of the gigantic craters (and that really wasn't an exaggeration) littering the tarmac. Or worse still, the hen and her chicks that were dandering along, weaving in and out of the undergrowth and bringing a whole new meaning to the term 'free-range'. From what April could see, these chickens had the run of the whole place, and there were at least six hens now – she'd lost count of the number of chicks – all pecking away and squabbling with one another.

April came to the end of the lane. Ahh, this looked more like it. With rolling green fields all around her, there was a patch of dandelion-covered tarmac that she reckoned constituted a turning point. And what was that? A tiny opening in between two giant bun-shaped blue hydrangea bushes.

April got out of the car and looked around, drawing in the sweet honeysuckle mingled with wood-smoke scent that filled the air, feeling baffled that Aunt Edie's cottage looked so overgrown. It hadn't been like this at all the last time she had visited. April walked over to the opening and saw a narrow, winding footpath to the left leading up to the cottage's front door that was barely visible now, given the glorious red, yellow, pink and green rainbow assortment of geraniums tumbling down from two hanging baskets, almost touching the red tiles surrounding the porch.

After retrieving her handbag, the cake tin and the bunch of peonies – figuring she could pop back to the car for the rest of her stuff in a bit – April made her way along the footpath, flanked either side by tons of tall buttery-yellow hollyhocks, and up to the front door. Placing the bunch of peonies and the cake tin on the tiles, she found the rope attached to the brass bell hanging from the wall and gave it a good jangle. Nothing happened. April waited for what felt like a respectable length of time before giving it another good jangle, a little louder and longer this time. Perhaps Great Aunt Edie was having a nap. April checked her watch. It was nearly two o'clock and she knew that her great aunt liked a little lie-down in the afternoon after her lunch, which was always at one p.m. sharpish; but then she *was* in her nineties so it only seemed right for her to be taking it easy at her time of life.

April took a step back and looked up at the two upstairs windows nestling in the eaves of the thatched roof, with their black paint surround and criss-cross ironwork, and saw that the curtains were still closed. She opened the white picket fence side gate and stepped tentatively through the thigh-high grass – trying not to imagine what the soft, sluggy-like feeling was that had just squelched along the side of her right Birkenstock sandal – and across to the sitting room window.

Taking in the flowery wallpaper, the mahogany sideboard with dusty bottles of alcohol on a silver tray for guests – Cinzano, Vermouth, Campari and of course the creamy yellow Advocaat – ahh, April smiled, fondly remembering the potent snowballs with a glacé cherry on a cocktail stick that her great aunt used to mix into a big highball glass tumbler for her as a young teenager, telling her in a naughty whisper-voice not to tell her mum. On the other side of the room was a Dralon settee with white lace covers protecting the arms. There was a rosewood display cabinet in the alcove next to the log burner, crammed with various keepsakes gathered over the years – lots of black and white framed photos, a sprig of lavender wrapped in silver foil, a lucky rabbit's foot, a collection of china thimbles and postcards sent from her soldier brothers during the Second World War – April remembered being allowed to look at these when she was a child. And, still there, was the picture of the woman in the uniform. Winnie perhaps.

But where was Great Aunt Edie?

Wading through the grass, across the footpath and

around to the back of the cottage, April wondered what was going on. When she had phoned her aunt to thank her for the birthday card and to ask if she could visit, Edie had sounded delighted.

'Oh yes, dear! I had been wondering when you would come back. It'll be very lovely to see you. And I'll bake your favourite cinnamon apple crumble and custard for your tea. I'll use the Carnation evaporated milk, just the way you like it,' she had said – getting a little confused after mistaking her for Winnie again, April had assumed, as she couldn't stomach evaporated milk. But once she had gently informed Edie that it was April, her brother Robert's granddaughter, who would be visiting today . . . well, April was surprised that her father's aunt wasn't in. It was very unlike her, Edie was always quite fastidious when it came to receiving guests. April remembered one time as a child, she had been staying for the weekend while her parents went to a wedding, and the Tindledale village vicar had been due to pop by, just to collect some jars for the church fete (Great Aunt Edie was famous for her homemade apple sauce, using sweet Braeburns from the orchards) – Edie had spent the morning dusting the cottage and had changed into her best dress at least an hour before the vicar arrived. So how come she wasn't at home now?

Admittedly, it was a little later than April had predicted arriving, damn sat nav, but Aunt Edie wouldn't have just gone out, surely? And where would she go in any case? The last time she had visited, April had got the impression her aunt never went very far at all; being a home bird, she preferred pottering around her country cottage.

April made her way around to the back of the cottage where the grass was just as tall – and what was that? As she ventured nearer to the back door, she felt her Birkenstocks sinking into something slippery and wet. A bog of some kind, or a blocked drain overflowing, perhaps. April went to lift her bare foot, to no avail. It was sinking into the foul-smelling puddle that seemed to be seeping from a mildew-covered mound, the septic tank. Oh God. With her hand over her face, April shook her head when a shot of guilt darted right through her. Clearly her aunt was struggling, had let things go and if April had visited more often then she would have known about this before now! The once tidy lawn was now almost a meadow, left to nature and full of wild flowers, which she was sure would be eyed with envy in some of the trendier London suburbs, but knowing her great aunt, April was certain the rustic charm was not intentional.

Gingerly, April tried to lift her left foot, but nothing happened. She tried again, but it was well and truly submerged in the quagmire. Instead, she shoved her other foot forward, but lost her balance and skidded back-wards, and ended up planting both palms in the mess to stop her whole body from getting covered. Ugh. She wiped the worst of it off down the front of her jeans, but then without thinking, touched her cheek so she now had a streak of the stinky stuff on her face. There was nobody around, so April quickly lifted the front of her top to use as a cloth to clean her face as best she could. She was a muddy mess, and the sooner she got into Orchard Cottage to clean up properly, the better. Although it was highly likely that her aunt might mistake her for some kind of vagabond living off the land in the depths of the woods, given the now disgusting state of her. Even her hair was a sight, the curls conspiring to form an unruly big bale of hay, having been buffeted about in the summer breeze.

April persevered, making a conscious effort to breathe in through her mouth in an attempt to avoid the smell wafting all around her, as she waded towards the cottage. Then, after batting away a tangle of blackberry bushes, she made it to the kitchen window and with her filthy hands up to the side of her head, but not quite touching her skin, she used the sleeve-covered part of her forearm to push her bushy hair back and pressed her nose up close to the window.

And gasped.

Oh God!

How on earth had things got so bad that it had come to this?

Aunt Edie was slumped on the quarry-tiled kitchen floor with her snow-white curly-haired head inside the big oven part of the sunshine-yellow Aga. And her left arm was draped in the top of the two small adjacent ovens.

3

April's pulse raced as she took in the scene. Not one to normally panic, she pushed up the sleeves of her top as a call to action, dumped her handbag in the long grass (not giving the gunk a second thought) and hammered hard on the window.

'AUNT EDIEEEEEEE!' April hollered as loud as she could, her voice slicing through the silence of the rolling green fields all around the cottage. 'ARE YOU OK?' She banged again and inwardly berated herself – clearly her great aunt was not OK, far from it, so why had she asked such a daft question? But with no time to ponder on the nuances of everyday niceties, April yelled some more before crouching down to rummage inside her handbag in search of her mobile phone.

She'd call an ambulance.

No signal.

April waggled her phone around in the air hoping to magic up at least one bar, but no luck. Oh well, she dialled anyway in the hope of getting through on another network. Still nothing. Ahh, one bar, she tried again, but as soon as she pressed on the nine key, 'No Service' flicked up on to the screen. Damn. So April went to plan B and shoved the phone in the back pocket of her jeans. She had a Swiss Army knife in her bag somewhere. It had been Gray's and for some reason April had taken to carrying it around with her, sort of like a comforter, a talisman that made it seem like Gray was still with her, by her side. And thank goodness she had, as it was just the thing to prise open a rickety old wooden window frame. In haste, April turfed out the contents of her bag – purse, book, three opened packets of tissues, a ripped yarn label, a variety of lip balms, a diary, a ridiculous assortment of pens and half a packet of wine gums.

A-ha! Found it.

April flicked open the knife and pushed the sharp end into the side of the frame just underneath the catch and tried to yank open the window, but it was no use, it seemed to be painted shut. She tried again, pulling harder this time with her fingertips, but the window definitely wasn't budging.

'AUNT EDIE, CAN YOU HEAR ME?' April shouted again, but still no response. Well, there was nothing for it; she'd have to smash the window. There was no other way. The front door was solid oak and about six inches thick so April was never going to be able to force it open, even if she pressed her shoulder against it or attempted to karate kick it in as she had seen people do in films.

After desperately scanning the garden looking for a suitably heavy object – there was nothing – April pulled off her bog-caked right Birkenstock and lifted it in the air and, after swinging it back behind her as far she could, she was just about to throw it hard into the window when a man's voice bellowed right behind her, nearly making her jump right out of her skin.

'WHAT THE BLOODY HELL DO YOU THINK YOU'RE DOING?'

April swivelled on her heel, the Birkenstock, like a brick at first glance, still high up in the air, the other hand pressed to her chest in shock, and saw a tall, well-built man wearing a tweed deerstalker hat over wavy blond hair with a furious look on his suntanned face. And a shotgun hanging from a leather strap over his shoulder.

April gulped, and then quickly pulled herself together. There really was no time to waste. Aunt Edie could be dead for all she knew. Oh please no. April wasn't sure if she could cope with any more loss right now.

'Um. Thank God you're here. Come on, you can smash the window! Hurry!' she ordered, before hopping forward to hand him the Birkenstock brick.

'Er, I don't think so!' The man's eyes flicked towards the sandal, before he gave her an up-and-down look, practically recoiling in horror at the state of her. His nose even wrinkled when the stench hit. 'I'm calling the Old Bill. Stay right where you are.' And he actually clasped a hand around the end of the shotgun and tilted it upwards as if to apprehend her in case she tried to abscond before the police arrived.

'Well good luck with that,' April quipped, stepping back as he lowered the gun and pulled out a big black phone that looked like it should be on display in a museum; it must be at least twenty years old. 'There's no signal in this place.' She nodded, folding her arms around her body as if to protect herself.

'Don't need one.' The man flashed her a look. April narrowed her eyes and held his stare, masking the panic that was mounting inside her. She needed to get to Edie, and quickly. This really wasn't the time to be dealing with the local eccentric (must be – who went around tilting shotguns at people?) busybody, gamekeeper, rambler, or whatever he was. 'Walkie-talkie,' the man retorted, going to lift the handset to his ear. 'This'll go straight through to my pal, Mark, in the police house up in the village,' he informed her, before doing a supercilious smile that made his conker-brown eyes crinkle at the corners in satisfaction.

April had heard enough, and with no time to waste she didn't bother explaining – seemed the busybody had already drawn his own conclusions about her – so she turned back to smash the window and get to her aunt.

'Yep! Mark? Is that you?' A short crackly silence filtered into the quiet, rural, countryside air. 'Got a nutter down here trying to burgle old Edith's place . . .'

SMAAAAASH!

Glass went everywhere.

Using the sole of her Birkenstock, April carefully cleared the glass debris away as safely as she could and then reached her hand through the remaining shards to deftly lift the latch on the window.

'Okaaaayyyy . . . got a live one here, she's going in!'

The man with the shotgun continued commentating with a mounting urgency in his voice. 'Bold as brass she is, right in front of my eyes. And covered in crap too by the looks of her.' Another silence. 'Whaaaat? Mark, you're cracking up. Just get down here sharpish or I'll have to execute a citizen's arrest. She's clearly a pro. And armed with a brick. Probably on drugs looking for a way to fund her next fix.' And April felt the man's hand on the top of her arm. 'I'm arresting you for breaking and entering, you do not, um, er . . . well, you probably know the rest. A seasoned crook like you,' he bellowed at the back of her head.

April managed to wrench her arm free.

'Get off me, you idiot,' she yelled back over her shoulder whilst attempting to pull herself up and over the windowsill. 'It's a sandal. See!' April deftly attempted to wipe the Birkenstock as best she could with her sleeve, before waving it in his direction. 'And *Old Edith*, as you call her, is my great aunt, and if you had bothered to investigate first . . . *Sherlock Holmes*,' April flashed a disparaging glare at the silly deerstalker hat, 'then you would know that she's currently on the kitchen floor with her head inside the oven! Now get back on your walkie-talkie and tell Mark to send an ambulance,' April instructed in the best staff-nurse voice that she could muster before pausing to catch her breath and adding, 'SHARPISH!'

The man fell silent momentarily, his jaw dropped, he stared with a fleeting glimmer of admiration in his eyes, he closed his mouth, and then it registered.

'Then why the bloody hell didn't you say so?' And he jumped into action. April instantly felt two large hands cupping her bottom, propelling her forward like a bowling ball hurtling towards a row of skittles, and she was immediately able to fling her right knee up on to the windowsill. Balancing carefully, she gripped the window frame with both hands and managed to hoist herself through the gap and on to the top of the tall, old-fashioned boiler directly in front of her. Crouching in the confined space – the beamed cottage ceiling was so low she could barely lift her head, let alone stand up – April contemplated just letting herself tumble on to the quarry tiles, but her great aunt's surgical stocking-clad legs were right there in front of her on the tiny patch of empty kitchen floor, so she couldn't risk doing that. What if she misjudged and landed splat on top of Edie and hurt her?

April managed to shuffle sideways on to the draining board and was just about to crawl on all fours towards the end of the counter, where she could see a tiny gap next to the pantry door that she could easily slip her body down on to, when the man with the shotgun appeared in the kitchen doorway with the cake tin in his arms and the peonies perched on top. He dumped his load on the table and after taking one long stride towards Great Aunt Edie, he bent down to place two fingers at the side of her neck to check her pulse.

'Still going!' he pronounced, as if checking on a snared rabbit in the woods. 'And the oven isn't even on, not that it matters, no gas around here if that's what you were panicking about! Plus you can't even gas yourself in an oven these days anyway – we might be out in the sticks in Tindledale, but this isn't the 1920s.'

April's mouth fell open as she sagged a little in relief at this news – thank God her aunt was still alive and hadn't deliberately tried to kill herself. But that still didn't explain why she was sprawled like this in her kitchen in the middle of the afternoon.

'Um, well . . . I knew that!' April said, her cheeks flaming.

'No you didn't.'

'Yes I did.'

'Why did you panic then?'

'I didn't panic! Anyway, I don't have time for an interrogation; I need to see to my aunt. How did you even get in here?' April asked as she scanned the scene and tried to work it all out. To the left of Edie was a dustpan and brush on the floor alongside a cloth.

'Through the front door!' he replied, glancing up at her and casually raising an eyebrow. April could see the corners of his mouth resisting the urge to smirk.

'But how?' she asked as he swiftly sprang up and swung her from the draining board before plonking her into a standing position on the tiles next to him.

'Er, the usual way. You know, I pushed it open with my hand.' And he actually laughed and waggled his hand in air as if to demonstrate the action before giving April a big wink. Cheeky.

'So it was open all along?' April shook her head as she bent down to tend to her aunt.

'Of course! Old Edith never locks her front door . . .

nor do I, come to think of it. Not sure anyone does here in the valley. Apart from the ones moved down from London.' He paused to shake his head, clearly not enamoured by newcomers. 'No need. This is Tindledale,' he explained, as if the village was some kind of crime-free oasis leftover from bygone times.

'Hmm, well, you could have mentioned it before I broke the glass and hauled myself in through the window,' April bristled, carefully unbuttoning Edie's crocheted waistcoat so she could push it back over her shoulders and loosen the collar of her blouse.

'You never asked! You were too busy breaking in.'

April opened her mouth to reply, but thought better of it. He was clearly enjoying winding her up, and besides, Edie let out an extremely loud snore at that precise moment. The old lady then fluttered her eyelids and tried to move, seemingly having forgotten that part of her body was still inside the Aga, so she ended up nudging the top of her head on the roof of the oven.

'Ewwwwwwww,' Aunt Edie groaned.

'It's OK. I'm here,' April started in a soothing voice, and the busybody coughed. 'Um, *we* are here,' she corrected, flashing him a look. 'What happened, Aunty?' She stroked Edie's forehead as she contemplated the best way to get her aunt out of the oven and up and on to a chair.

'Oh hello dear. There you are. No need to fuss, I was just having a lovely little nap.' Aunt Edie smiled like it was the most normal thing in the world to have forty winks while cleaning the oven.

'A nap? Inside the oven?' April stuttered, her mind boggling. And then saw her aunt had a tea towel folded up like a little makeshift pillow underneath her cheek, but still . . . and how on earth had she got down on to the floor in the first place?

'I'm very nimble,' Edie stated as if reading April's mind. 'I keep my joints well oiled. It's the dancing. And the stout, dear – a bottle a day! But the cleaning takes it out of me sometimes, although it's important to keep the Aga nice. My mother was a stickler for it and I see no reason to let standards slip. Will you help me up please? I usually use the chair but someone has moved it,' she said, giving the man a disparaging glance.

'Um, yes, of course,' April replied, quickly trying to get her head around all that her aunt was telling her, and regretting all over again that she hadn't made more of an effort to visit more frequently. A ninety-year-old lady really shouldn't be cleaning the oven, even if she did think she was nimble! 'Here, lean on me.' April swiftly manoeuvred herself into position to properly lift her aunt, as she had first been trained to do back when she was a fledging nurse, and placed her hands around the old lady's body. And then up and under her armpits so she could clasp them together to form a sturdy support.

'No need for all that carry on, my love.' Edie shook her head and April smiled. Her great aunt always had been a fiercely independent woman, which might explain the state of the garden – she couldn't imagine Edie would willingly ask for help even when it was so obviously needed. 'Just give me your arm,' Edie said, and gently lifted April's hands away from her chest. 'There we go. Bob's your uncle!' April tried not to look concerned as her elderly great aunt deftly pulled herself up into a standing position with a very determined look on her face. But then her papery skin crumpled into a frown.

'What's he doing here?' Edie pointed a bony finger towards the guy with the shotgun. April turned to look at him.

'Hello Edie,' the man said pleasantly enough, but the old lady looked confused, so he swiftly added, 'It's me, Harvey from the fruit farm. Your neighbour. You remember me.' But Edie still looked blank, and April wondered what on earth was going on.

'He, um . . . Harvey.' April glanced at the man and he nodded and shrugged as if he was quite used to Edie being forgetful. 'He helped me get into the kitchen, Aunty. I was worried about you—'

'What for? I'm fine,' Edie immediately admonished, looking even more puzzled now. April spotted a dart of fear flicker in her aunt's eyes. 'And you better get going before my father returns from the orchards! He'll have your guts for garters coming in here with flowers before you've been introduced.' The old lady looked at the bunch of peonies and then lifted a gnarled index finger and remonstrated in Harvey's direction. But before April or Harvey could say any more, a police officer burst into the tiny cottage kitchen with a baton at the ready, followed by an exuberantly plump woman muscling her way to the front with, April was astonished to see, a ferret wearing a little high-visibility vest nestled in the crook of her elbow. And April felt as though she had been plunged into a parallel universe where nobody really knew what was going on.

4

Later – it having taken almost an hour for Harvey, whose fruit farm was a few fields over and was actually very charming once he knew that April wasn't a drug-fuelled, crap-covered burglar, to fix a wooden board at the broken window as a temporary repair – April persuaded Edie to put her feet up on the Dralon settee with a nice cup of Earl Grey tea and a generous slice of April's exceedingly good madeira cake (according to Mark, the policeman, who enjoyed a quick slice too). It seemed that the old lady had indeed nodded off while attempting to clean the Aga, so April, who'd had a good wash and changed into a clean top and jeans, having also made a note to get the blockage by the back door seen to right away, was finishing the job while Aunt Edie pottered around in the sitting room looking for a pack of playing cards that she swore were just there on the sideboard. But after searching everywhere, even looking under the settee in case Edie had dropped them and then shuffled them underneath it with her slipper-clad foot, April still hadn't been able to find them.

She had figured it best to leave her aunt to it, because Edie had been delighted by the offer of having her Aga cleaned, even though April wasn't convinced it needed doing as it already looked immaculate to her. But it was a small thing to do to make an old lady happy, and if the truth be told, April still felt guilty for not having visited her aunt in over three years. Edie clearly wasn't keeping on top of things and was finding it difficult to ask for help, not to mention her memory loss, and April felt as her only living relative that it was her responsibility to rectify that. And pronto. She may only be here for a couple of days but at least she could get the garden into some sort of tidy state, and perhaps tackle the hedgerow in the lane, before her great aunt got completely blocked in when the road became impassable. She'd see about getting a cleaner to come in and help out too, if Edie would agree to it – April was under no illusion that her aunt might take some persuading to allow a stranger into the cottage, especially to keep the place nice; Aunt Edie was old school and might very well take issue with having a cleaner. What if people thought she was lazy?

There was a brief knock on the front door and the woman from earlier appeared in the kitchen doorway.

'Just thought I'd pop in and see how you're getting on? I'm Molly by the way, don't think we were properly introduced, what with all the commotion that was going on.' The woman chuckled and pushed out a hand towards April. 'You must be Winnie. Old Edie often mentions you. We always have a little chat when she calls up with her meat order – I'm Cooper's wife, we own the butchers' shop in Tindledale High Street,' Molly finished explaining.

'Oh, um pleased to meet you again!' April smiled and pushed her hair off her face with the top of her forearm. 'But no, I'm not Winnie. I'm April. Edie is my great aunt.'

'Ahh, that's nice and a turn up for the books – I didn't think Old Edie had any relatives left . . . apart from Winnie of course and from what I gather she looks just like you – dark curly hair, handsome and petite, is what Edie says. Well there you go, just goes to show.' Molly lifted her eyebrows. 'And it's very nice to meet you, April.' She nodded resolutely. 'You gave us quite a scare before . . . when we thought you were a burglar.' Molly chuckled heartily, making her shoulders bob up and down and her ample bosoms jiggle around.

'Um, yes!' April grinned as she stood up. 'And I really am so very sorry to be the cause of such a drama in the village . . . it's unlike me, I'm usually quite calm in a crisis but I guess, well, I panicked and . . .' April paused to shrug. 'I certainly shouldn't have smashed the window, not when the door was open all along and my aunt was only sleeping, even if it was inside her oven . . . I feel like a prize fool now.' She peeled the rubber gloves off her hands to reciprocate Molly's handshake, pleased to see that the ferret wasn't in attendance this time. It did have quite an acquired scent, which April was still being treated to a whiff of from time to time. But, thankfully, in the ferret's place was a large white enamel pie dish covered with a navy striped tea towel from which a deliciously cosy aroma wafted.

'Oh, don't be daft, no need to apologise, love. Honestly, you did me a favour to be fair . . .' Molly smiled as she took a place mat from the pile next to a fruit bowl and carefully set the pie dish down on the kitchen table.

'I did?' April asked, keenly eyeing the dish.

'Steak and ale, just warm it through for your tea, and it'll be lovely with some runners and mash,' and Molly rummaged inside a reusable shopping bag looped over her left arm before producing a handful of super-sized runner beans followed by two large Maris Pipers which she placed on the table next to the pie. 'Freshly pulled from my patch in the garden – thought you could do with a decent meal after your long journey, and then what with all that broken window shenanigans . . .' She shook her head as she lifted the towel before instantly getting back to the conversation – leaving April with not even a second to acknowledge the kind gesture (instead she made a mental note to call into the butchers' to return the dish and say a proper thank you, before she went back to Basingstoke). 'Oh yes. Mark, he's the policeman,' Molly continued, 'well, he came into the shop to pick up some pork and leek sausages for his tea . . .' she paused to catch her breath. April nodded, liking Molly right away. 'Anyway, I was up to my elbows in chicken giblets when the call came through to Mark on his radio and then, well, I just couldn't help myself.' Molly's cheeks flushed. 'I can't remember the last time we had a bona fide emergency in Tindledale and it's not every day that you get to see a crime unfolding right in front of your eyes so I hot-footed it down here . . .' Her voice petered out and silence followed. 'Blimey, I sound dreadful don't I?' Molly added a few seconds later. 'What must you think of me?'

'Not at all,' April replied graciously to spare Molly's obvious embarrassment – her neck was now covered in a myriad of red blotches. 'Anyway, I'm glad you've come back to the cottage.'

'You are?' Molly looked relieved and the redness immediately started to diminish.

'Sure. Because I can't remember the last time someone brought me a homemade pie, so thank you.' April beamed. 'And I'm curious to know more about Winnie . . . what else has Edie told you about her?'

'Oh, it's my pleasure, I love baking,' Molly said. 'It's so satisfying, and you can't beat a good pie, don't you think?' April nodded. 'And as for Winnie, um, well I don't know very much, not in terms of where she lives and stuff. Only that Edie is very fond of her . . . I get the impression she's a much younger relative, a niece or daughter perhaps. That's why I assumed you were Winnie – Edie always says stuff like, "Our Winnie loves a nice rasher of bacon for her breakfast", you know, when I bring down her order. I always pop in an extra few slices for Old Edie.' Molly paused and lowered her voice. 'Poor dear doesn't have many pleasures in life, and I guess I feel a bit sorry for her . . . think she gets lonely, probably why she likes to go for a wander,' she mouthed, indicating with her head towards the sitting room next door, 'and that's no way for a lovely old lady to end her days.'

'A wander?'

'Yes, you know, it's happened a few times . . . I found her once in her slippers at the top of the lane. Driving past I was when I spotted her, and thank God I did as she only had a cotton sundress on and it was perishing outside.' Molly shook her head. 'Soon got her warmed up though after I popped her in the car and brought her back home, so disaster averted.' And Molly chuckled like it really was no big deal . . . or, and April's heart sank at the thought . . . maybe Molly, like Harvey, was just used to Old Edie's muddled ways and impromptu jaunts around the village in her slippers!

'Thank you,' April said quietly.

And now it was her turn to feel embarrassed. It really was no excuse not to have visited her great aunt – since the funeral was fair enough, but that was over eighteen months ago as it was. April felt that she should have mustered up more effort and made herself come to Tindledale before now. Whilst it was wonderfully community-spirited of Harvey and Molly to be looking out for her aunt, it shouldn't be that way. April flicked her eyes away and then pretended to busy herself by putting the rubber gloves back in the cupboard under the sink. When she had finished, she grabbed her bag from the counter and found a tube of hand cream. She squirted a dollop on to the back of her right hand while Molly continued talking, moving on to another topic.

'So I see you're married?' She gestured to April's left hand where her wedding band was. 'Is your husband visiting too?'

April froze.

Silence shrouded in awkwardness hung in the air between the two women.

After what seemed like an eternity, but in reality was

probably only a few seconds, April managed to shake her head, initially taken aback at the directness of the question, but then quickly came to the realisation that, actually, she felt OK. A bit wobbly, she hadn't been prepared, that was all, but . . .

She took a deep breath and replied.

'Um, no. No he won't be doing that,' April started, wondering how to explain . . . as so far she hadn't had to. Everyone she had spoken to since Gray died – friends, his colleagues, utility companies, people at his squash club (Gray had loved playing squash before he was no longer able to swing a racket), the library, bank, etc. – already knew. April was suddenly conscious that this would be her first time explaining from scratch to a person who didn't know Gray and she had no idea where to begin – in fact, she wasn't sure she wanted to share this information about her husband with someone she had just met. It might seem strange, but by keeping the motor neurone disease and Gray's death to herself while she was here in Tindledale, April felt as though his memory, indeed his life, could be just hers, and hers alone, and therefore protected. Whole. And not diluted by having to share him. At home, she had no choice but to share him with Nancy and Freddie and, whilst April knew that he was never hers alone, today and tomorrow he could be – selfishly so, and right now, she really wanted that.

So she added, 'It's just me,' and pulled her bottom lip in over her teeth and bit down hard as she worked the cream into her hands, masking the sudden tremble that had engulfed them. Molly studied April momentarily before continuing.

'Don't worry, love. Happens to the best of us! My Cooper, and the boys – I've got four of the wee bastards, God love them – but they drive me bonkers sometimes and I have to take off to a spa for a day or so just to gather my thoughts and gear up for round two hundred trillion.' Molly puffed in sheer exasperation. 'Well, you've come to the right place for some R&R, fresh rural air and hearty country food, and you'll have made up in no time . . . give him a few days to miss you and see how he likes lying next to a cold section of the bed—'

'He died!' April blurted involuntarily, despite her earlier decision to not mention Gray, and then instinctively pressed a hand to the top of her chest. 'Sorry, I um . . . er, I shouldn't have shouted it out like that.' The hand moved to her earlobe to twiddle a silver stud as she wondered what on earth to say next. Molly was staring at her, her mouth still open in an O shape and her eyebrows furrowing underneath her fringe.

But then, quite unexpectedly, Molly had her arms around April.

'Oh God love you,' she said, patting April's back before letting her go and taking a couple of steps backwards into her own personal space. 'I am so bloody sorry. Me and my massive mouth . . . and don't you dare apologise,' Molly admonished harshly, although her eyes were soft and full of warmth.

'It's OK. It was a year and a half ago now . . . don't know why it still gets me like this,' April fidgeted.

'Crikey. That's no time at all. And who said there was a time limit on your feelings in any case? If it gets you, *it gets you*, and that's the end of it!' Molly shook her head and then looked as if she was trying to work out what to do next for the best. April waited, wondering if she should explain, indeed *could* explain . . . without breaking down. She had become so accustomed to keeping all her feelings stashed away inside her and was getting pretty good at it to be fair. But then this was big, a first, having to tell someone what had happened to Gray – her wonderful, witty, vibrant husband, best friend and lover – and would Molly really get it? Could April do Gray justice? Convey exactly how amazing he was to someone who had never known him, or even met him? And somehow it made it all seem so raw again. But April was saved from having to fathom out how she felt exactly in this precise moment in time, because Molly came right out with it and asked a very direct question. A question so direct that many other people may have avoided it for fear of upsetting the bereaved person.

'How did he die?'

And April surprised herself by suddenly feeling relieved, relaxed even, especially when Molly bustled across the kitchen to where the kettle was on the Aga and, after lifting it up, added, 'If you've got time, I'd love to hear all about him. Shall I make us a brew?'

April nodded and smiled, before glancing through the little serving hatch in the wall into the sitting room to check on Edie. Ahh, her great aunt had given up on her search for the playing cards and was having her

An hour or so later, as April said goodbye to Molly, she closed the front door behind her new friend and smiled to herself. She felt as though she'd known Molly her whole life, which it turned out was pretty near true, as Molly remembered cycling around Tindledale one summer as a child with the 'girl down from London'. April couldn't remember this exactly, it seemed so long ago, but she did have fond memories of those carefree days in the school holidays with a big group of children from the village, so it had been lovely to reminisce with Molly. A rare treat for April, as apart from Aunt Edie, there wasn't anyone else in her life who shared those memories from years back. When she had gone to live with her grandparents, after her parents died, April had lost contact with her school friends. It was as if the rug had been pulled from under her, and she'd been left dealing with a massive thing when she should have been concentrating on exams and filling her time with reading *Jackie* magazine and such like. But instead the grief took over and since then she had always found it hard to connect with that period before her parents died. It was often too painful to remember the happy, good times, only for the reality of not having them in her life to then come crashing back all over again. And later, when April had finished her nurse training, she had immersed herself into working as many shifts as she could in the hospital, until she met Gray. It had been easier that way, especially after her grandparents died and she had felt so very alone.

Yes, she had friends now, but was conscious that she had retreated into her shell again after losing Gray, and even though her friends had made such a tremendous effort to re-engage her in life since his death – taking it in turns to visit on a Saturday night with a bottle of wine and ideas for fun nights out, bowling, ice skating, cinema, etc. – she just hadn't felt up to it. Preferring instead to curl up on the sofa in her pyjamas staring at her wedding video, and then the honeymoon weekend in Venice on the flatscreen TV. No lights on, no volume, just silence and Gray waving and pulling a silly face at the camera. It had been a comfort. But April knew it wasn't right, she couldn't carry on like that for ever. Even Nancy, when she returned from her nights out, wouldn't come into the lounge, probably couldn't bear to; instead she had crept upstairs to bed and left April alone with her memories.

This had made April very self-conscious, often feeling whenever she left the house for essential trips, such as the bank, supermarket and such like, that everyone was looking at her, as if she had a big sign hanging around her neck that said, 'My husband died and now I'm turning into a very sad and lonely recluse'. It was an utterly awful way to be. But slowly, it had subsided and her confidence was starting to return – just driving to Tindledale had already given her a boost, something she wouldn't have even contemplated doing a while ago. Although, she reflected, some of those friends had drifted away . . . maybe it was too late and they had run out of patience already, moved on. After all, they had their own life ups and downs to deal with, so she couldn't blame them for that. April chewed the inside of her cheek, and resolved to make more of an effort when she got back home. She'd neglected her aunt, and it wouldn't do to neglect the few friends that she had left as well. Yes, a change of scenery sure had given her a different perspective on things. And maybe she'd go back to work, find a nursing job again – she'd thought about it on and off since Gray had died, but somehow hadn't managed to actually put herself forward, get a plan in place and be proactive about it. It had felt, somehow, in that time, that going back to work meant the part of her life with Gray was properly over, and she hadn't been sure she was ready for that . . .

April went back into the kitchen and was pleasantly surprised to see that her aunt was laying the table for dinner. Humming to herself, Edie seemed perfectly sprightly as she nipped around the table making sure everything was just so. Knives, forks, pudding spoons, napkins and even a jug of iced water with two glasses. It was nice to see, and gave April a warm glow, a sense of having come home, belonging, just like she had felt as a child during those trips to Tindledale . . .

'You're just in time. Dinner won't be long, dear. Sit down and I'll dish up.' Edie smiled, reaching for a very faded, holey tea towel with which to open the Aga to check on the pie. April hesitated, unsure whether to intervene or not as the tea towel really wasn't up to the job of protecting an old lady's hand from getting burnt. But April was conscious that she was in her aunt's home and didn't want to be seen as interfering – and, besides, her aunt seemed to be managing just fine, as she then flung the tea towel over her shoulder and pushed a masher into the saucepan of potatoes and started mashing, so April sat down. On second thoughts, maybe not! Hot water was splashing everywhere. April jumped up and gently took the masher from Edie as she winced when a droplet landed on her bare arm.

'Oh dear. I forgot to drain the potatoes,' Edie said, wiping her arm on her apron before clasping her hands together.

'It's OK. Easy mistake to make,' April consoled, care-fully lifting her aunt's arm to check that she wasn't hurt. Thankfully, she was fine. 'How about you sit down and let me wait on you for a change? Think of me as your waitress for this evening. Dinner will be served in five minutes, Madame.' April did a little bow and laughed, remembering the game they always played in the past when she had visited as a child. Aunt Edie would let her carefully bring the plates to the table, reminding her to use two hands, and April had felt so grown up. Sometimes, the game had started earlier with April pulling out a piece of paper from her letter-writing set on which to write a menu, and then Aunt Edie would pretend to choose her favourite dish – naturally it was always the meal that they were actually having. April wondered if her aunt would remember – probably not, it was such a long time ago – but to her delight Edie's face broke into a smile of recollection.

'Well, that would be marvellous, my dear. But aren't you forgetting something?' April raised an eyebrow, mentally crossing her fingers. 'The menu? We must have a menu.' And as if by magic, April instantly felt transported back in time. Just like the old days, before her parents died and her whole world changed, to a simpler section of her life, halcyon, where nothing bad ever happened, or so it had seemed back then. And it really was rather lovely to relive the memory . . . if only for a few minutes. And Aunt Edie looked calm and relaxed too, her eyes had come alive and gone all sparkly, but then there was a certain safety in the past, a comfort. April had seen it with Gray, especially towards the end when she knew he had been feeling frightened, and Aunt Edie had seemed fearful earlier too when she couldn't remember who Harvey was. Gray had coped by cosying up with a blanket and watching all the old *Monty Python* shows with Nancy – something they had done together when she was a child – the pair of them nodding along to that upbeat 'Always Look on the Bright Side of Life' song. Gray, with a very content smile on his face, cocooned almost in a bubble of familiarity and happy memories that this simple pastime recreated.

'Coming right up!' Keen to see if reconnecting with

the past would have a positive effect on Aunt Edie, April darted off to the sitting room to retrieve her handbag – there was a notepad inside, but she needed something to write with. She popped her head through the hatch. 'Do you have a pen, Aunty?'

'Look in the sideboard, dear.'

'Thanks.' April pulled open the door and immediately inhaled. Mothballs and lavender. Ahh, she really was ten years old all over again. She selected a pencil from an old, washed-out Del Monte peach tin, then went to close the door, but paused to run her finger over the red felt lining inside the sideboard, just as she'd loved to do as a child. Then, after closing the door, she stood up and quickly glanced again at the framed photos: her parents – Dad with his arm around Mum, her long hair blowing out in the breeze – and April in her Brownie uniform with a big gappy smile after losing two front teeth. There were also photos of various people she didn't recognise – although on closer inspection, the one of a teenage girl standing under an apple tree looked just like Edie, only much, much younger, with lovely long dark plaits (it was hard to be sure with the picture being black and white) and a gorgeous smile that lit up her whole face. Next to this was a picture of the woman in the uniform, only this time she was wearing a lovely, floral tea dress and had a beautiful, sunny smile, and there was definitely a family resemblance. Molly was right, because if this was Winnie, she did look a bit like April with her dark curly hair and petite frame.

Having polished off Molly's scrumptious pie, runners and mash, April went to clear the plates away, but Aunt Edie stopped her by placing a hand on April's forearm.

'What is it, dear?'

'Um, what do you mean?' April, her hand still clasped around a plate, hesitated.

'Well, you've been awfully quiet, and that's not like you.' Edie's voice softened. 'What is it, Winnie?' April blinked. And sighed inwardly, as she had already corrected her aunt three times over dinner, but to no avail. So, deciding on another approach, April tackled the issue head on.

'Aunty, I'm not Winnie. But I'd love to know who she is. Can you tell me about her?' April smiled and waited, eager to hear more about Winnie, the relative she had never known.

Silence followed.

Edith stared at April. She blinked a few times, frowned and then glanced away with a doubtful look on her face. Suspicious almost. And then attempted to cover up her muddle by saying, 'Oh, now you're just teasing me. Shall I put the kettle on?' And she stood up and turned her back.

April's heart sank with disappointment; she was so keen to know more about her family, but she decided to leave it for now. She didn't want to put pressure on her aunt, make her feel alarmed by bringing attention to her failing faculties, and maybe there was a valid reason why Aunt Edie was being evasive, confused, or whatever it was that was going on for her.

'Yes please, that would be lovely. And there's some cherry madeira cake left if you fancy another slice?' April offered.

'Ooh, don't mind if I do.' But then Edie hesitated, and changed her mind. 'But I really shouldn't, don't want to ruin my figure.' And she patted her perfectly tiny tummy with both hands, while a disappointed look darted across her face.

'I'm sure a second slice won't hurt.' April busied herself with opening the tin, and after pulling a knife from the block on the side, she cut a couple of very generous slices, figuring it a crying shame if an elderly lady couldn't have two slices of cake in one day if she really wanted to, and served them on to plates. 'There, I'll finish the tea while you tuck in.' April put the plates on the table.

'Well, if you insist, my dear.' Edie wasted no time in breaking off a corner of cake and popping it into her mouth.

'I most certainly do,' April grinned, preparing the tea in a china tea pot, with cups on saucers, just the way she knew her aunt liked it.

'You always were a persuasive child,' Edie chuckled, licking crumbs from the tips of her fingers, thoroughly enjoying the treat.

'Was I, Aunty?' April asked, seizing the moment to talk about the past.

'Oh, yes, very much so. Spirited! That's what we used to say . . . your parents and I.' April placed the pot of tea on the table and sat down, allowing herself a moment of contemplation while she remembered her parents.

Their smiles. Her mum's perfume – one whiff of Rive Gauche and April was in her childhood bedroom being kissed goodnight. She swallowed, hard, and rearranged her thoughts, not wanting to go there right now. It was at least twenty years ago and she had only happy, albeit faded, memories of her mum and dad, but she knew from experience that train of thought inevitably led to Gray. But his death was different. Raw. And he had suffered, been forced to be brave and face up to his end of life. At least her parents had gone quickly, most likely went out with a bang – literally, if the newspaper reports at the time were anything to go by with their unnecessarily graphic details about the crash. She had read them online, several years later, out of curiosity mainly, but had regretted doing so ever since.

'And what did they say about you when you were a child?' April asked, pouring her aunt some tea.

'Cheeky!' Edie shook her head. 'But I got away with it you know.'

'Oh, why was that then?'

'I was the youngest. The apple of my father's eye. Spoilt, my brothers and sister would say . . .'

'Your sister? What was her name?'

'Winnie.'

Bingo! April leant forward and the faded memory of her dad chatting to Aunt Edie in the sitting room, years ago, flooded into her head. She had been playing with her Tiny Tears doll on the carpet and Dad had picked up the photo of the woman in the uniform. April suddenly felt overwhelmed with joy, figuring it was very lovely

dressed quite inappropriately for another afternoon of pottering around her rural country cottage, or indeed cleaning her Aga . . . again, as she had mooted earlier this morning over their scrumptious breakfast of freshly laid eggs. Edie had asked April to check the hen house, and amazingly there were ten feathery, mud-splattered eggs waiting in the straw for them, which they enjoyed boiled with soldiers slathered in salted butter, made from bread from the baker in the village, whose sister lived in the cottage at the top of the lane, so 'it's no trouble for him to drop a loaf in when he's passing by', apparently. April had heard all about it from Edie over breakfast.

'There you are, Winnie, my dear! I looked all over for you,' Edie said in a very chirpy, singsong voice. April went to correct her, but didn't get the chance before the old lady carried on talking, and besides, April wondered if it really mattered. Especially as she had lost count of the times now that she had reminded her great aunt that her name wasn't Winnie. And when April had taken the opportunity again over breakfast to find out more about the elusive Winnie, her aunt had given April a baffled look, just as she had last night, before swiftly changing the subject. Not to mention the fact that Edie still hadn't said a word about Gray; it was as if she really had forgotten he had died, and that in itself was worrying as April knew that her aunt had been very fond of him. Until his death she'd always asked after him when they spoke on the phone and she had never missed his birthday. In fact, when they last visited Edie together, it had been Gray that her aunt had seemed most keen to chat to, even taking him around the orchard and regaling him with stories of how she had enjoyed many summers playing in the fields, running in between the apple and pear trees with her brothers, paying special attention to Robert, April's grandfather. Gray had said she was very lucid for a woman of her age – she had remembered the tiniest of details, such as the time Robert had found a baby starling with a broken wing and nursed it back to full health before setting it free.

'That'll be where your compassion comes from, April,' Gray had said later in the car on the way home, and April had liked the thought of having inherited something of her grandfather. It was comforting, knowing that a genetic part of him lived on in her. It seemed important to April, with her not having any living relatives left apart from Edie. And April and Gray hadn't been blessed with babies, despite them both wanting a family – they had tried at the start, soon after the wedding, but then when Gray became ill . . . it hadn't seemed important any more. Although still young enough to have a baby, April doubted now that she'd ever be a mother, but she felt very lucky to have Nancy and Freddie in her life. Being their stepmum was a wonderful next-best thing . . .

'Now, I shan't be gone for very long – will you be all right without me for a bit?' Edie smiled sweetly as she patted the sprig of cherry blossom.

'Er, um . . .' April managed before nodding her head, curious to know what this was all about. 'You look amazing, Aunty. May I ask where you're off to?' she ventured, making a mental note to see if she could have a chat to her aunt's GP before she went back home – just to see if she, or he, had any concerns too about Edie's mental health. But her aunt didn't answer. Instead, she did a blank stare before busying herself by plucking dead leaves from a nearby rhododendron bush. Perhaps she hadn't heard – maybe Edie's hearing was diminishing, and April could ask the GP about that too.

April had a little bit of experience of caring for elderly patients, having worked a summer, many years ago, on a geriatric ward as part of her training, but no real first-hand knowledge of dementia. Or memory loss. Perhaps that's all this was – with the obsessive Aga-cleaning thing, and wandering out and about in her slippers, forgetting to put on her shoes, and of course continually forgetting April's name – and Edith was in her nineties so it was to be expected . . . she guessed, hoped. Full-blown dementia could be a very cruel thing. Debilitating, just like Grey's motor neurone disease was, which had progressively robbed him of the man he used to be. He had kept his independence for as long as was possible though – going to work in a wheelchair with oxygen piped directly into his nostrils, wearing an elastic strap around his head to keep the plastic tube in place. April had admired him for that as he had always hated wearing stuff on his head, ever since childhood when his mum had said she could never get him to keep a hat on even in winter. April hadn't known this until later in their relationship when she had knitted him a lovely red wool hat as a stocking filler for their first Christmas together. And, to give him his due, Gray had worn the hat a couple of times before stuffing it into his coat pocket, later admitting that hats just drove him mad. She could still see his face now – apologetic but exasperated too, followed by silliness when he had made light of it all by suggesting several ludicrous alternative uses for the hat, culminating in April crying with laughter at the 'cut in two leg holes to turn it into a pair of woolly pants' option.

April smiled at the sudden memory before focusing her attentions back to her aunt who was still busy inspecting the rhododendron.

'Aunty, is everything OK?' April started.

'Of course my dear, why wouldn't it be?'

'Well, I . . .' April paused to take a breath, and changed tack. 'You look marvellous, where are you off to this afternoon?'

'To the tea dance of course! My escort will be here soon, and a very dashing chap he is too,' Edie smiled, making herself look much younger as she pulled a powder compact from a sparkly evening bag that was swinging on a delicate silver chain from her elbow.

'Oh! I see,' April said, watching her aunt pat powder across the bridge of her nose. 'Well, perhaps I can drive you there, where is it?' she asked, thinking on her feet, for she didn't want to alarm her aunt by going in gung ho and telling her that a dance on a Tuesday afternoon was very unlikely and perhaps she should go inside and take the ballgown off. What if it just added to her confusion? There had been no mention of her going to a dance over breakfast so it was obviously a spur of the moment thing. Or what if Edie got upset or cried with disappointment?

It could happen – April vaguely recalled watching a documentary about Alzheimer's where an elderly lady had sobbed like a little girl and it was heartbreaking, distressing, pitiful and poignant and there was no way she was going to put her aunt through that unnecessarily. Right now, Edie could very well be thinking she was young again, waiting for a suitor to arrive to escort her to the ball, so to burst that bubble of joy was the last thing April wanted to do. But how long should she let her aunt stand on the path waiting for the imaginary man to not show up? April had no idea, and ordinarily would have rung Gray and said, 'Guess what . . .' and they would have chatted about it and worked out the best course of action between them, but . . .

April pressed her fingertips into her palm and was just about to put an arm around her aunt to gently guide her back into the cottage when a woman's voice trilled out from the turning-point piece of tarmac where April's Beetle was parked.

'COO-EEEEEEEEE. Only me!' April swivelled on her heel. 'Ooh, Edie, you do look a picture!' a vivacious, sixty-something woman chuckled as she swept a glittery pink pashmina around her shoulders and practically skipped on up the path towards them, her super-strong perfume permeating the air. 'The general is going to be so *very* pleased to see you.'

April marvelled at the transformation in her aunt. She was absolutely glowing at the mention of the general, whoever he was, but there was something more. A sort of luminance radiating from within Edie now, as if she had suddenly come alive. And clearly wasn't imagining there to be a suitor after all! April was now even more fascinated to see how things were going to unfold.

'And I'm so looking forward to seeing him,' Edie cooed, popping the powder compact back inside her bag. 'But where's the bus?' she asked, leaning forward as if to scan the lane.

'Oh, not to worry, the general had to park it a bit further back near the main road,' the woman said brightly, and then turned to April with a saucy look on her face and added, 'it's getting *very* bushy down this end!' before doing an extremely filthy laugh.

'Yes, I really should—'

'I'm Audrey by the way,' the woman said, letting the pashmina slip down into the crooks of her elbows, revealing a tight, low-cut bodycon dress, before April could offer to get the hedgerow sorted out too before she returned home – maybe a local gardener? April made a mental note to ask Molly later if there was someone she could pay to keep on top of her aunt's garden and the section of the single-track lane that was her responsibility, as she was quite sure Edie didn't have the means to pay for help around the home. And April had some funds, a third of Gray's modest life insurance money (she hadn't thought it fair to keep it all, so had split it with Nancy and Freddie), not very much, but certainly enough to help her aunt get the garden straight. 'I run the weekly speed-dating tea dance . . .'

'Ooh, sounds intriguing,' April said, fascinated that such things went on in rural villages where she had assumed the elderly residents spent their time making jam and watching *Countdown*.

'Oh, it's just a bit of fun. It's not full-on dating, or looking for . . .' Audrey paused, did furtive sideways eyes and after leaning into April she clutched her arm and mouthed, '*seeeeex*.' April had to press a hand over her mouth to stifle a giggle. 'No, it's more companionship for the . . .' she paused again as if searching for the right words before settling on, 'our more "*young at heart*" villagers.'

'Ah, I see.'

'And just call me Deedee, everyone does,' the woman continued. 'My daughter, Meg, is the headteacher at the village school,' she added proudly.

'Lovely to meet you, Deedee,' April replied, feeling a little foolish for doubting Edie. Seemed there was a tea dance here in Tindledale on a Tuesday afternoon after all. Weeeeell, fancy that!

'You too. And I've heard all about you . . .' Deedee made big eyes.

'You have?' April asked tentatively.

'Yes, that's right. You're April. Molly mentioned that you were here visiting your aunt, our lovely Edie, and the star of the weekly tea dance in the village hall.'

'Oh, yes, um . . . that's right,' April replied apprehensively, wondering if Molly had mentioned their conversation about Gray too. But then Deedee said, 'Are you here on your own, or have you got a gorgeous husband hidden about the place?' in a breezy voice, as she scanned around the garden as if searching for him. So Molly clearly hadn't gossiped, and April was pleased that she had been discreet, remembering that news usually travelled fast in a small village like Tindledale. Whenever April had arrived to stay with her aunt in the school summer holidays, within an hour or so the local children would be down to the cottage to see if she was coming out to play in the fields after someone had spotted her parents' green Morris Minor Traveller pulling into the village store on the way to get a box of chocolates to go with the flowers as a present for Edie. Everyone always knew everyone else's business. Tindledale was just that kind of place.

April took a breath and felt much more prepared for the question this time.

'No, just me – here to spend some time with my aunt . . .' April said as cheerily as she could muster.

'Lovely. Well, if you're at a loose end this afternoon and fancy a bit of a *booooogie*,' Deedee paused to do an enthusiastic shoulder shimmy, making her boobs wobble around like two jellies, and April laugh, 'then you are more than welcome to join us. The more the merrier. Isn't that right, my love?' And Deedee tucked her arm through the crook of Edie's elbow, giving the top of her hand a little pat.

'Ooh, yes,' Edie agreed. 'And don't be put off by it being called a tea dance. It's not a load of old dears shuffling around the dance floor in pairs because all the men in the village have already popped their clogs. Certainly not. There's the raffle to think about too. And the general does a *veeeeery* good quiz.' Edie nodded her head several times as if to emphasise this fact. 'And there will be sandwiches and cake. *And* champagne!' she continued marvelling, all the while making big eyes.

'Yes, that's right. My Meg makes it – homemade fizzy elderflower champagne,' Deedee confirmed. 'Goes lovely with the buffet – a smashing spread of cold cuts and healthy salad options, courtesy of my Meg's other half, Dan – he's a famous chef you know, on the telly and everything . . . well, used to be, he's retired now. Not that he's old or anything, oh no, very fit and vibrant in fact. He just doesn't need the pressure of the high life any more so he sold his Michelin restaurant in London for an absolute fortune and can afford to take it easy now.' Deedee paused to take a quick breath and puff her hair up a little more, clearly captivated by her daughter's partner. 'And we always have a beautiful selection of pastries and fairy cakes from Kitty's café. It's called The Spotted Pig. Can't miss it, it's on the corner of the High Street. You must try it if you get a chance . . . the Battenberg is TO DIE FOR!' Deedee shook her head and fluttered her eyes as if being transported to her very own personal nirvana, while April felt breathless on her behalf just taking it all in.

Then Edie smiled brightly and added, 'And my niece loves a little tipple, don't you April?'

April instantly flicked her attentions on to her aunt. Ahh, a moment of clarity! And suddenly, April felt very thrilled to have her aunt back again, even if she was making her sound like some kind of lush.

'*Weell*, I'm not sure I'd put it quite like—' April started.

'Do you remember those snowballs, April?' Edie interjected and April nodded, fascinated that her aunt now seemed able to remember this minutiae – they'd had those snowballs over thirty years ago! 'I'll have to make you one before you go home. You loved them as a teenager. We could make a night of it just like we used to – play a few hands of rummy while we are at it too – if I can find the blasted pack of cards that is.' Edie shook her head and turned to Deedee. 'I've searched high and low and they've disappeared. April had a look too but no luck . . .'

'Ooh, I'm so sorry, I should have said – I have them in my handbag in the bus for you. I picked them up by accident after last week's tea dance. Do you remember, Edie? I helped you into your sitting room and plonked my pashmina on the sideboard only to scoop up the pack of cards with it when I left.'

'Ahh, well that solves that mystery – thank heavens you did, dear!' Edie smiled kindly at Deedee. 'For a moment there I thought I was losing my marbles.' And both women chuckled to themselves before proceeding down the garden path to the waiting bus, leaving April wondering why she had ever worried about her aunt. Clearly her memory wasn't *that* bad, and she was having the time of her life, whooping it up at the weekly tea dance with her 'date', the general. And in a strange moment of role reversal, April felt quite eager to meet the general, if only to assure herself that he was indeed a suitable suitor for her dear old great aunt Edie.

As she waved the two ladies off, April couldn't resist grinning. Deedee was certainly a bon vivant, a breath of fresh air, and April admired her zest for life and the ease with which she had brought 'Old Edie' to life, practically transforming her into a much younger woman in the blink of an eye. It was infectious. And April felt spurred on by it, in addition to the wave of confidence she now had after reconnecting with her past last night, and so in a rare, but quite welcome moment of spontaneity, she decided to get in her Beetle and go to the High Street.

But first, she would pick a selection of pretty wild flowers from Edie's back garden as a little thank-you gift for Molly. (April was quite sure her aunt wouldn't mind; there were hundreds to choose from in any case so April wondered if she would even notice.) April could ask about a gardener too while she returned the pie dish, and it would be a chance to have a look around Tindledale and see if it had changed much since her last visit. She might even treat herself to a nice slice of Battenberg in The Spotted Pig café. Yes, April thought this sounded like a very nice thing to do.

And for the first time in a very long time, April didn't feel wobbly at the prospect of going out alone, without at least having someone she knew by her side, supporting her as they had for the last eighteen months – Nancy, Freddie, her friends from the knitting club or the girls from the gym . . . the ones that had stuck around, that is, the ones who, despite April's lack of desire to socialise, had still visited and taken her out for the occasional coffee. Well, now she'd have something to talk to them about, something other than how she was coping, or how she felt, or if she'd had a good day . . .

On arriving in Tindledale, April parked the Beetle right outside the village store, pleased to have found a space – well, on closer inspection there were several in fact. The heart of Tindledale with its cobbled High Street lined on either side with tiny Tudor-framed shops with even tinier mullioned windows wasn't exactly a bustling metropolis, April noticed as she closed the car door behind her and went to walk off. Smiling, she looked around and saw that the village hadn't changed at all since her last visit, indeed it was almost the same as when she used to visit as a child in the school holidays. The only difference now was a jaunty polka-dotted length of bunting bobbing in the breeze linking the lampposts, and on the corner opposite the village green was an extremely exotic-looking Indian restaurant. Wow! Double-fronted with a selection of brightly painted tables outside with gold and white parasols. Gray would have loved it – he was very partial to a chicken balti with all the trimmings.

April swallowed hard and adjusted her thoughts; now was not the time. *Focus, this was supposed to be fun, not maudlin!* Something else caught April's eye. A bench. She made a beeline towards it, grateful to have a focal point to concentrate on, and remembered sitting on it with her mum and dad to enjoy a bag of chips from Moby Dick's, the mobile fish and chip van that came to Tindledale every Friday evening. April wondered if the van still came, and made a mental note to ask her aunt later. But the bench was no longer made of boring wood, no, it had been transformed into a yarnbombed extravaganza of loveliness – a myriad of colours made up of hundreds of granny patches all stitched together by hand – it was amazing. A real labour of love – she ran a finger over the knitting and wondered if she might be ready to pick up her needles some time soon, but the thought was immediately followed by a pang of panic and April knew it was too soon. Another day hopefully. April thought about sitting on the bench instead and allowing herself ten minutes just to think about Gray, but a shrill voice filled the air and the moment vanished.

'Excuse me!' A woman wearing a dowdy beige mac and a flowery headscarf, with an old-fashioned wicker basket looped over her arm and a determined look on her face, came beetling towards her from the door of the bookshop opposite. April stopped moving and smiled at the older woman.

'Hello,' April said, shifting the flowers into her free hand so she could swing her handbag over her shoulder and tuck Molly's pie dish under her arm, wondering what the woman wanted. Maybe she was a friend of her aunt's, on the way to the tea dance, and had heard that April was visiting too and wanted to welcome her.

'We like to keep this space clear for the disabled villagers!' the woman announced, emphasising the 'we' as if verbally holding a placard above April's head with 'outsider' emblazoned on it to make her feel unwelcome. Circumventing any pleasantries, the woman then pointed a disdainful finger to the blue Beetle with its jaunty plastic sunflower in the air vent on the dashboard.

'Oh!' April replied, taken aback. 'I didn't know . . . I, um, didn't see a disabled sign anywhere or even on the road,' she added, feeling like a naughty schoolgirl all of a sudden as she did a quick scan to check a nearby lamppost too. The woman continued to glare at the Beetle. And then April twigged. This woman, aka the village parking warden, surely, was clearly waiting for April to move her car to one of the other numerous patches of free parking space. But April felt ruffled and not in the least bit inclined to move her car. She hadn't broken any laws as far as she could fathom, but it was just as well that Mark, the policeman from yesterday, happened to cycle past at this precise moment. He gave April a pleasant wave before bringing his bike to a halt at the kerb.

'Not interrupting, am I?' he smiled at both women, who politely shook their heads. 'Great. How's Edie doing today, April? Not decided to have another little snooze on spec . . .?' he laughed.

'No, thankfully,' April smiled back. 'She's absolutely fine. And sorry again for the confusion, but thank you for your help,' she added, clocking the woman giving her a cautionary glance. Ha! The woman looked baffled now and a little apprehensive at having waded into somebody the village police officer appeared to know by name.

'No problem, better safe than sorry, eh? Best be getting on. And good day to you, Mrs Pocket.' Mark gave the woman a courteous nod and pushed his boot down on the pedal.

'But before you go—' Mrs Pocket called out after Mark, but it was too late and he was already pedalling off down the High Street. April took her chance to escape and, after a quick glance around, she spotted a hanging sign saying 'Cooper's' so stuck her head down and made a beeline for the butchers' shop as fast as she could.

'April! Lovely to see you – what are you doing here? Here, let me help you with that.' Molly was arranging some joints of clingfilm-wrapped beef on a tray in the window when April arrived.

'Thanks so much,' April grinned, attempting to push open the door with her right hip as she juggled the pie dish and flowers in her arms – she had got a bit carried away in her aunt's garden and ended up with an enormous bunch of brightly coloured blooms which she had tied up in the length of scarlet ribbon taken from Gray's trug of roses.

Inside, April presented Molly with the flowers.

'I'm here to give you these.'

'For me?' Molly looked flabbergasted. April nodded.

'A little thank you for being so kind to me yesterday. And your steak and ale pie was truly scrumptious – Aunt Edie thoroughly enjoyed it too.'

'Oh, you daft mare. Come here.' And after handing the bouquet to a big teddy bear of a man in a white butcher's coat whom April presumed must be Cooper, Molly enveloped April in one of her enormous hugs. 'You didn't need to do that,' she laughed.

'I know. But I wanted to,' April grinned.

'Well I'm pleased that you did – can't remember the last time anyone got me flowers.' Molly gave her husband a teasing look before popping her nose into the bouquet to draw in their delicious scent.

'Now don't be starting all that,' Cooper pretended to chastise. 'That bunch on Mother's Day cost me an arm and a leg, my petal.' And he plopped a kiss on Molly's pouting lips.

'Hmm, and I'm worth every penny,' Molly replied cutely before squeezing his cheek. 'Come on,' she turned to April, 'let's go out the back for a minute while I put these in water. Cooper can cope without me for a while, can't you, my love?'

Cooper nodded his agreement and went to come back with a fresh retort, but the door opened and another customer came in to take his attentions away.

April followed Molly through a door and into a little kitchenette area next to the office. After rummaging in the cupboard under the sink, Molly managed to find a bucket which she filled with water. She untied the ribbon and handed it to April.

'You should keep this,' Molly smiled.

'It's OK.' April returned the smile but lowered her eyes. 'It's from the trug, isn't it? I remember it from the kitchen table yesterday when we were drinking tea. You said Gray's sister had sent it on his behalf.'

'Yes, but—'

'Here. Please keep it. It's a lovely thought, but you may regret it later . . .' And after carefully rolling the length of ribbon up, Molly slipped it into April's handbag before she could say anything more.

'Thank you,' April said. 'And, ahh, I nearly forgot, here . . .' she added to move the mood on to a lighter note, realising that the pie dish was still gripped under her elbow.

'Oh thanks, just leave it on the side please and I'll put it away later. Now, have you got time for a quick cuppa?' Molly asked, having finished sorting out the flowers.

'Um, yes please,' April glanced at her watch, wondering what time The Spotted Pig café closed, 'unless you fancy . . .' she started but then stopped, figuring she really should make the visit on her own – it felt like a milestone somehow. Earlier, she had been up for venturing out for cake by herself, a little bit excited even at this new flourish of courage and independence, a step towards getting her old confidence back. Before Gray got ill, April wouldn't have thought twice about going out on her own for a coffee and cake if that's what she really fancied, so why now was she stalling and about to ask Molly to join her?

'Go on . . .' Molly encouraged.

'*Weell*, you're probably busy in any case – but I was going to try some cake in the café and . . .'

'Ahh, April, that would have been lovely, but I have to go for one of my boys in a bit, he's got the dentist after school and if I'm not there at the school gate waiting for him, I just know he'll scarper off home with one of his pals to avoid facing the dreaded dentist's drill.' Molly shook her head with an exasperated look on her face. And April smiled to mask the mixture of emotions – fear, relief, she wasn't quite sure. 'Another time though for sure. When are you off home?'

'Great. I'd really like that,' April said before adding, 'tomorrow morning.'

'Oh that's a shame – you'll be back though, right?'

'Yes, for sure, which reminds me . . . I don't suppose you know any gardeners? Someone reliable that I can arrange to keep on top of my aunt's garden and the lane leading down to Orchard Cottage. And most likely the old apple orchards surrounding the cottage. I've not ventured into them yet, but I'm guessing they'll be just as overgrown.'

'Hmm, you're going to need a specialist landscaper I reckon – or how about one of the farmers with a ride-on mower and one of those big hedge trimmers? Hang on a sec . . .' And Molly bustled off back into the shop. A few seconds later she returned with a piece of paper. 'Here, this is Pete's number, he's a dairy farmer, and his farm is not far from your Edie's place. He's a lovely bloke and I'm sure he'll be happy to help out. Especially if you treat him to a few beers in the Duck & Puddle pub next to the village green,' she laughed, 'his preferred method of payment I've heard.'

'Thank you. I'll give him a call,' April said, pushing the piece of paper inside her bag.

'Yes, do. I've popped my number on the back too in case you need anything else while you're here.'

'Thank you,' April said, thinking how kind and welcoming Molly was, unlike that spiky Mrs Pocket.

Molly finished making the tea and handed a mug to April.

'I love your cardy by the way. Knit it yourself?' she said, admiring April's white lace-weight shrug.

'Yes. Thank you. Several years ago now, but the wool seems to wash really well . . .'

'Wonderful,' Molly grinned. 'And you know, I was thinking last night about your question. About Winnie.'

'Oh yes?' April nodded hopefully, and then added, 'I found out that she's my aunt's sister!'

'Well I never! In that case you really must talk to Hettie.'

'Hettie?' April's interest was piqued. Molly nodded.

'That's right, she's about the same age as Edie and has lived in Tindledale her whole life, so she's bound to know more. You could call in and have a chat to her, she lives in the oast house next to the haberdashery shop on the road leading down to the Blackwood Farm Estate. Do you know it?'

'Hmm, yes . . . I think so.' April paused, creasing her forehead as she tried to remember. 'Was that where we rode our bikes in the school holidays? In and out of the grove of oak trees and then along the stream, it was glorious in springtime with a carpet of purple violets as far as you could see. Is the Country Club still there too?'

'Yes that's right. And it sure is, and is thriving – they've got a flash new swimming pool and spa with a sauna and Jacuzzi and beauty treatment rooms, the works! It's where I go to escape when Cooper and the boys are playing up. Nothing realigns my chakras like a lovely hot stone massage followed by a spot of lunch, eaten along to the blissful sound of silence, without my boys hollering and fighting over second helpings of cottage pie or whatever,' Molly chuckled.

'That's good to hear, I remember going there with Aunt Edie when it was just a golf club with a members' lounge bar and restaurant. She used to let me have my favourite – scampi, peas and chips! And I thought I was the epitome of sophistication.' Both women laughed in between taking sips of their tea.

'I should get going and leave you to your window display . . .' April grinned, having finished her tea. She retrieved her bag from a nearby chair and looped it over her shoulder. 'And thanks for the tip re Hettie. I really would like to find out more about my mysterious other great aunt, Winnie.'

'Ahh, you're welcome. It's quite a mystery, but I reckon, if anyone is going to know more about Winnie, then it'll be Hettie for sure! Let me know how you get on please, and do come back soon. I reckon you and I are going to be good friends. We could even do a spa day together at the Country Club some time, if you fancy it?'

April turned to look back over her shoulder.

'Um . . .' She instinctively hesitated, still used to considering Gray's care plan out of habit. April hadn't had any free time of her own for such a long time and since the funeral would never have even considered going to a spa just for pleasure. But determined to look forward, to the future, she took a deep breath, smiled and then said, 'Yes please. You know . . . I think I'd *really* like that.'

8

April was enveloped in a great big hug of welcoming warmth when she walked into The Spotted Pig café and tea room. With its vintage Formica tables – some set in booths around the perimeter, the others dotted all around the space – and the windows covered in steam from the hot air rising from the bread oven in the kitchen, it was like stepping back in time to another world where nothing bad ever happened, or so it seemed.

'Hello.' A woman with aqua-blue eyes and curly blonde hair wearing a ditsy-print apron gave April a welcoming smile. 'Would you like a table? Or I can do takeaway if you like . . .'

'Ooh, I'd love a booth please, if that's OK?' April replied, breathing in the tantalising scent of cinnamon mingled with macaroons. Talking of which, she was drawn to an extensive selection of the delicate French fancies – pistachio, lemon, raspberry and salted caramel to mention a few – all arranged on paper-lace doilies in a three-tiered floral china cake stand on a counter beside an old wooden piano. April could feel her mouth watering already. And would it really be too greedy to have a macaroon after her Battenberg cake?

'Sure. I'm Kitty by the way. Don't think we've met before . . .'

'Oh, hi,' April replied, relaxing a little after such an inviting welcome. 'Lovely to meet you, I'm April, and no it's my first time here in The Spotted Pig,' she added as she was led to a lovely booth beside an old-fashioned wooden cake trolley crammed with every one of her favourites, including the recommended Battenberg cake: a giant, marzipan-covered brick with pink and yellow checked sponge inside, stuck together with a generous slather of strawberry jam.

'Well, thank you for coming in. I'll give you a few minutes to look at the menu,' Kitty said, handing April a card with today's selection of sandwiches, salads, soups, puddings and cakes on, 'unless you already know what you'd like?' She tilted her head to one side.

'I heard the Battenberg cake is delicious so I'd love a slice of that please.' April eyed the trolley. 'Aaaaaand . . .' she paused to scan the drinks section on the back of the menu.

'The honey and almond hot chocolate is a winner,' a friendly-looking woman on an adjacent table suggested. She was breastfeeding a baby under a pretty butterfly-print scarf draped from her left shoulder and looked so content and happy with her lot. 'Sorry, I wasn't trying to intrude or anything – it's just that it was recommended to me on my first visit here and it really is truly scrump-tious. I'm addicted to it now,' she smiled.

'In that case, I'll give it a go.' April grinned at the woman and relaxed some more. 'One honey and almond hot chocolate please,' she requested, looking back to Kitty.

'All the trimmings?' Kitty raised an eyebrow as she whipped out a little notepad and a pencil from the pocket on the front of her pinny.

'Um?' April wasn't sure.

'Whipped cream, sprinkles – I can do hundreds and thousands, or Smarties, Maltesers, grated chocolate, coconut shavings, someone even had a crushed pink wafer biscuit the other day . . . so whatever you fancy really, you can have the lot if you like. Lots of my customers do . . .' Kitty laughed as she counted the options out on her fingers. April felt quite overwhelmed by all the possibilities and faltered.

'Ooh, I'm not sure . . .' She glanced at the woman with the baby to help her out, who pondered before kindly obliging and offering:

'Grated chocolate! Simple but so very satisfying. That's my favourite.'

April nodded and Kitty wrote it down. 'Good choice,' she winked before making her way over to the kitchen.

'And thank you,' April said to the woman as she slipped her handbag from her shoulder and shuffled into place on the red leatherette banquette.

'Ahh, not at all – I'm happy to help out. I'm Jessie by the way,' the woman said before tending to her baby.

'Nice to meet you, Jessie. I'm April.'

'Uh-oh. This little guy needs changing. Sorry. I better see to him and then get going – see you around next time, hopefully . . .' And Jessie grabbed a big flowery changing bag and headed towards the bathroom at the back of the café, leaving April feeling upbeat and optimistic, and pleasantly pleased with herself for having ventured out for cake. It didn't feel so bad being on her own after all, and she was sure that the more she did this the easier it would become. Yes, April was determined to get some of her old self back. Seize the day, that's what Gray had said, and she fully intended to honour his wish. And then something occurred to her . . . 'seize the spa day' as Molly had kindly invited her to do . . . Gray would have laughed at that!

Kitty arrived at the table with the hot chocolate and the biggest wedge of Battenberg cake that April had ever seen.

'Thank you,' April couldn't wait to get stuck in – for the first time in a very long time, she felt relaxed. She really did. And she grinned to herself as she looked around the café, intrigued by a picture on the wall of a young, good-looking man in a sandy desert, wearing a khaki soldier uniform and kneeling down next to a very handsome black Labrador. A relative of Kitty's perhaps? Oooh, what was that? April felt something vibrating against the side of her thigh. She glanced at her bag. And then realised. It was her phone.

'We've got a new mast. Only covers the village square and this end of the High Street though,' Kitty explained from over by the counter on seeing April's surprise; having had no signal at all since arriving in Tindledale, she clearly wasn't expecting her phone to ring.

'Ahh, well that explains it!' April grinned, lifting her phone up to her ear. 'Hello.'

'April. How are you?'

'Nancy! How are you doing, darling?'

'I'm fine thanks, but worried. I've been calling and calling and calling you and was starting to think something terrible had happened. Did you drop your phone down the loo or something?'

'Oh no . . . I'm so sorry, it must be the signal. Or the lack of it at Aunt Edie's cottage, and well, much of Tindledale to be precise. I didn't mean to worry you – I should have called you though, sweetheart. But I didn't want to wake you up, what with you being on nights and all . . . I know you have to sleep during the day.' April smiled to herself and hoped that Nancy was looking after herself properly, no early morning pizzas on returning home after her shift at the fire station or sitting up till lunchtime listening to her favourite rare Northern Soul dance songs from the sixties and seventies on YouTube because she was too wired to sleep. As a firefighter, Nancy had a very active job, so even more reason for her to get her full eight hours. 'Are you all right?'

'Ahh, well, it is the countryside – I imagine all the little lambs and cows in the fields don't have much call for . . . *calling* each other, boom boom!' Nancy joked, and April laughed, pleased to hear that she was on form as usual, but noticed that she hadn't actually answered the question. 'Just expect to get, like, a trillion messages come through now, all from me.' Nancy laughed. 'Anyway, are you OK? I was getting worried and you didn't leave the number of your aunt's landline.'

'I'm sorry, love, I should have done, but honestly, I'm

fine. Better than I've been in ages. It's been a real tonic coming to Tindledale.'

'Good-o! And such a relief. When I didn't hear from you, I was half tempted to hop on my scooter and come there too, just to check on you.' April laughed, and felt quite touched by her stepdaughter's concern for her well-being, but sensed there was something more; Nancy seemed overly anxious.

'Oh, no need to do that,' April quickly replied, keen to allay Nancy's fears.

'But you could have gone AWOL on the way there on some sort of mad mission brought on by delayed shock over losing your husband.'

'Pardon?' April said, not paying proper attention, as the guy in the van, the farrier with the gorgeous green eyes, walked past the window, so she smiled and did a little wave with her free hand. He did a double take, hesitated, and looked as if he was about to smile back, but then changed his mind, bowed his head and crossed over the road. *Charming!* April wondered what his problem was.

'Yes, I read an article about it in an online magazine where bereaved people do strange things, stuff that's completely out of character. Like join a commune or go skydiving. One woman got on a plane and went to stay a whole month in Disney World, Florida, and none of her family had a clue; they thought she was staying with an old school friend until one of them called to check. That's when they found out she had blown her savings on flying first class and was staying in a deluxe villa in the Animal Kingdom with the full-board meal plan option.' Nancy paused, and April laughed but couldn't help noticing there was a slight edge in her stepdaughter's voice.

'Oh dear. Well you have nothing to worry about, darling, I'm really not about to disappear to Disney World,' April reassured again. 'I'm fine, honestly. And I'm really sorry for my silence – I didn't mean to make you anxious. But it's like another world here where it's very easy to lose track of time. It's sort of like a bubble, or a cocoon, and then a neighbour popped by yesterday and we got chatting, and then I had a lovely evening with my aunt, so to cut a very long story short . . . I've just popped into the village for cake,' April explained, deliberately leaving out the part where she'd found Great Aunt Edie having a snooze in the oven. Even though she could kind of see the funny side now, it wasn't enough to erase the worm of guilt that was still niggling inside her. What if she hadn't arrived when she did? Would Edie have been lying there on the cold hard kitchen floor until she woke up? And when would that have been? The following morning with her age-addled body so stiff she was barely able to stand upright without assistance? No, Edie needed taking care of, someone to watch over her.

'Oooh, good for you!' Nancy said, sounding pleased.

'How's Freddie? Pulling his weight I hope . . .' April ventured, picking at a piece of marzipan from the corner of the cake. She couldn't resist. It tasted divine – sugary and of almond paste.

'Yes he's the same as always. I'm making him do his

share. You know I even saw him putting something in the washing machine earlier. Not sure if he knows how to actually turn it on, but it's a start at least. It's a fact, my twin brother is bone idle around the house, always has been, and it's a wonder that he ever manages to pull himself out of his pit to go to work. It was Mum's fault, she pandered to him and now you do the same,' Nancy laughed.

'Oh dear, but you'll show him though?' April asked. It was true, she had looked after Freddie, but was happy to.

'Yes. Don't worry. I'm happy to hand him the instruction manual, but that is it!'

'Ahh, that's a start and I'm sure he'll appreciate your help,' April said. She knew Freddie wouldn't ask for any assistance – he had become very withdrawn since Gray died, spending a lot of time in his bedroom and only appearing at meal times where he didn't say very much at all. April felt a sudden surge of guilt; maybe she should go back home today and make sure the twins really were all right? But what about Edie? She needed April too, if only to sort out the garden and fix the massive potholes in the lane. Yes, Nancy was full of bluster, but what was really going on for her? Was she handling her father's death as well as she appeared to be? April couldn't tell, not for sure, as Nancy seemed to be carrying on like normal most of the time – she had cried a lot at the start when Gray was first diagnosed and again on the day he died, but since the funeral she appeared to have bounced back, although she seemed still anxious too. *Guess everyone copes with grief in different ways . . .*

'So, how is it in Tindledale? How's your aunt?' Nancy said.

'Yes, Tindledale is still the same, as I remembered it,' April started, casting a glance around the café to make sure she wasn't annoying anyone by being on her phone, but it was nearly empty now – Kitty was behind the counter sorting out the till, and Jessie had returned from the bathroom and after strapping the baby into his buggy had left, giving April a cheery wave through the window as she crossed the road. 'Everyone here is so friendly,' she added, forgetting about Mrs Pocket.

'Wonderful. And your aunt Edie? How is she?'

'Yes, she's OK, I think. She's gone off to a tea dance this afternoon . . .'

'Ooh, get her, can't remember the last time I went out dancing and I'm a quarter of her age.' A short silence and then, 'I'm such a saddo . . .' Nancy laughed, but April had heard the wobble in her voice.

'No you're not!'

'Yes I am. Nothing exciting ever happens to me.'

'You go out, you have a great social life, what about all those Northern Soul weekends you go off to on your scooter? You love them and always have a fantastic time,' April reminded her.

'Maybe, but that's only a couple of times a year if I can get a whole weekend off work. Otherwise it's cut-price beer in the social club with the blokes from the station, which really isn't the same . . .'

'And your job is pretty exciting . . . not that a house fire is a thrill of course, but it beats the ordinary office nine-to-five, surely?'

'I suppose so,' Nancy agreed, and April wondered where this was all coming from. She really didn't want Nancy to go on a downer about herself. She had done that in her teens; soon after her mum went off to New Zealand, Nancy had become very withdrawn, down and continually criticised herself – it had taken Gray months to lift her out of it. He had told April all about it, saying how he'd found out she was being bullied at school and had been that worried, he'd even considered an appointment for Nancy with a psychotherapist at one point. April felt that she really needed to be back at home, taking care of the twins, but Edie needed her too . . . Suddenly she was torn and felt very confused as to where her priorities were best placed. 'Anyway, did you find out any more about Winnie?' Nancy continued, changing topic and sounding marginally brighter.

'Only that she's my aunt's sister.' April decided to let it go for now, figuring it best to try to talk to Nancy when she got back home. 'But the worrying thing is – Edie keeps on calling me Winnie,' April explained, before elaborating further, telling Nancy all about Edie and the memory loss, and the state of the garden and the obsession over cleaning the Aga.

'Well, she is ninety-odd . . . so she's bound to be a bit forgetful. And so what if she likes to clean her Aga? I can think of worse things she could be doing . . . you wanna be grateful she isn't gambling your inheritance away on that Foxy Bingo thing or whatever it's called.' Nancy sighed. 'And as for the garden, I would come and give you a hand with it, but I've promised to help out a bit more at work this week, one of the guy's wives is about to drop so he'll be off on paternity leave soon.'

'Ahh, not to worry. Molly, she's the butcher's wife, has given me a number for a farmer who might help out. And I can always pop back again to Tindledale to see how she's getting on . . .'

'Sure. But you're not coming home already, are you?'

'Yes, I was going to come back tomorrow, that's what we agreed, a mini break for a couple of days,' April said before spooning off some cream from the top of her hot chocolate. It tasted delicious, warm and with a hint of nutmeg which paired perfectly with the chocolate shavings.

'But what about Edie? Your aunt needs you, April, you can't just leave her to muddle through on her own.'

'Um, er . . . well, I wasn't going to just leave her to it, I'll make arrangements before I return . . . but she's very independent you know,' April replied, wondering what this was really about. It sounded as if Nancy was trying to be strong, to get rid of her, make her redundant. 'But what about home, and you and Freddie . . .?' And the neediness that had crept up on April over the last few months, but had then seemed to diminish since arriving in Tindledale, made a hasty return.

'April, the house is spotless, Freddie is fine. I'm fine. Please, stay a bit longer – a couple of weeks if you have to. More. It's fine, honestly.'

'But I can't just do that!' April said, her mind racing at the possibility. And she felt thrown, not having even considered it an option.

'Why not? You can do whatever you like . . . you're a free agent now.' An awkward silence followed. 'Sorry.' More silence. 'I didn't mean it like that, it's just that you can't—' Nancy stopped talking.

'Go on darling . . .' April coaxed kindly, used to Nancy's bluntness, but keen to find out what was on her stepdaughter's mind.

'I want you to be happy . . .'

'I am happy, sweetheart, honestly, please don't worry about me.'

'Are you sure?'

'Quite sure,' April said, figuring a little exaggeration wouldn't hurt, and she sensed that Nancy needed to know that she was OK. And right now, sitting in the café drinking hot chocolate and eating cake, April did feel happy. Maybe that was the key to moving on with her life – moment by moment, until all the moments joined together.

'So no more sitting in night after night watching your wedding video?'

'I can't promise that I won't ever watch it again, but getting out of the house to come here has made a big difference.'

'That's settled then. You'll stay for a bit.'

'Oh, um . . . but what about clothes? I brought some extra things just in case, but not enough for a few weeks . . .' April knew she was stalling. Her aunt had a washing machine. And Tindledale wasn't like Basingstoke, where her friends rotated outfits so they wore a different one each day of the week for fear of appearing to have not made an effort. No, here in Tindledale they didn't seem bothered by all that and wore a uniform of jeans, T-shirts and wellies. April had remembered to throw her wellies in the boot of the Beetle so she really had everything she needed for an extended stay. And she could always pop into the gorgeous-looking vintage dress shop that she could see through the window, over the road. Yes, she fancied that, it would cheer her up and do her good to get some new clothes. Perhaps a lovely 1930s floral tea dress, like the one Winnie was wearing in the picture on the sideboard.

'Look, why don't you give this dairy farmer guy a call and see if he can help out with the garden and I'll come down soon, in a couple of weeks if I can and bring you some more clothes? What do you say?' More silence followed. 'And it will give you a chance to find out more about your great aunt Winnie. I'm intrigued to know what happened to her, aren't you?'

'Well, yes . . . I really am, she looks so lovely in the picture, and very brave in her uniform. But are you sure?' April asked, wondering if Nancy really would be OK for a while. 'Do you promise to pop to Tindledale soon?' At least then they could have a heart-to-heart and Nancy might open up.

'I promise. Plus I want to see if you've managed to keep your birthday roses alive!' Nancy laughed.

'Of course I have, cheeky!' April relaxed a little.

'Although if I'm going to stay on for a bit then I really should plant them in the Orchard Cottage garden – if I can find a space . . . you wait until you see the state of it!'

'Ahh, I'm sure there'll be a nice spot somewhere. So you're definitely staying then?'

'Hmm, but what about Freddie?'

'I'll look after him. I'm going now, April. You're staying in Tindledale and that's the end of it! Give me a call when you're next up in the High Street having cake, and text me the number of the landline at Orchard Cottage and I'll call in a day or so to see how you are and find out what you've managed to discover about your aunt Winnie. In fact, Miss Marple, that's what I'm going to call you from now on. Byeeeeee . . .' April could hear Nancy laughing before she hung up.

Stirring the hot chocolate with one hand, while using the other to deliver delicious Battenberg cake to her mouth, April pondered on the phone call. Maybe the twins *would* be OK without her for a while and it would be good to get her aunt's garden sorted out, not to mention having a chat to Edie's GP to see if there might be some help available for her – someone to call in and check on her, a home help or something for when April eventually returned home. And to be honest, April did feel different here in Tindledale. Somehow it was easier here being away from home and all the memories there, like the sight of Gray's shirts in the wardrobe every morning – which reminded her, it really was time to pack them up and see about giving them to a charity shop. Yes, being in Tindledale gave April a different perspective. Maybe it was time. Time to let the twins grow up. April knew deep down that they could manage, they didn't need her like they had at the start of her relationship with Gray. Whereas Aunt Edie did need her, if only to clean her Aga and fetch the eggs from the hen house.

So, feeling like she had reached a milestone of some kind, April finished up her truly scrumptious cake and hot chocolate treat and paid Kitty for a box of eight macaroons, one in each flavour. Then she left The Spotted Pig café to make her way back to Orchard Cottage where she was looking forward to making a night of it with her great aunt Edie – they would drink snowballs and eat macaroons while they played a few rounds of rummy, and it would be just like the old days. April almost had a spring in her step as she walked along Tindledale High Street towards the Beetle.

But what was that?

April couldn't believe her eyes.

And her mouth actually dropped open because around the wheels of her car on the tarmac was a white painted box. April hurried over the cobbled pavement and saw to her dismay that a sign had been erected too. Admittedly a makeshift one, but still, Mrs Pocket was obviously a woman of influence in the local community as the hand-written notice covered in polythene and drawing-pinned to a wooden post read:

PARKING FOR DISABLED BADGE
HOLDERS ONLY

Well, April didn't know whether to cry or laugh out loud at this, quite frankly, absurd eccentricity of rural, country life.

*

Matt pushed his hands further into his jean pockets as he reached the end of the High Street and walked across the village green. He'd finished work for the day, shoeing a couple of stud horses over on the Blackwood Farm Estate – they always took the best part of a morning, needing special care and expert handling or they would get skittish and inclined to rear up. And now he could really do with a nice pint and a ploughman's lunch in the Duck & Puddle pub.

But April Lovell was going to think he was a right rude bugger now. Why had he blanked her like that, when she had waved and smiled from the window of the café? He felt like an overgrown schoolboy and it was doing his head in. His marriage had been a disaster, and though it had been over years ago, and he'd had a few girlfriends since, he still felt inclined to steer clear of getting involved with someone new. In his experience, having a love life only led to problems . . . and it wasn't just about him any more. Plus, he knew nothing about April. She wasn't the young girl he had rolled around in the buttercup field with all those years ago. Definitely not. She could be happily married with a load of kids and a husband in tow and he'd make a fool of himself. No, he wasn't going there.

Matt pushed open the door of the pub and went through to the snug and over to his usual spot at the end of the bar.

'You all right, mate?' Cher, the landlady, asked from behind the bar.

'Yeah, been better. How are you?'

'Good thanks,' Cher smiled, going to retrieve Matt's silver tankard from behind the bar. 'Your usual?' He nodded. 'What's up?' Cher asked as she flicked the beer tap up and tilted the tankard to pull the perfect pint. 'You look like you've seen a ghost!'

'Hmm, something like that . . .' Matt replied, reaching for his wallet, thinking Cher had inadvertently hit the nail on the proverbial head. April Lovell was a ghost from his past, a lovely, happy reminder of a time in his life when everything was so straightforward, fun and easy. Shame it couldn't always be like that . . .

9

When April arrived back at Orchard Cottage, Aunt Edie wasn't home – most likely still foxtrotting herself around the village hall with the general – so April fetched her wellies from the boot of the Beetle and waded through the long grass towards the rickety old ramshackle shed in the far corner of the garden in search of gardening gloves and secateurs. And if she was really lucky, a lawnmower would most definitely come in handy. Now that her mind was made up – she was staying in Tindledale for the foreseeable future – there was no time like the present to get cracking, and whip this garden into shape.

As she reached the shed, April spotted a weather-worn wooden stile to her left, almost concealed by a large overhanging tree, an abundance of bramble bushes and some fierce-looking stinging nettles. Intriguing. So, after managing to find some rusty shears and a pair of old, cobweb-covered gloves behind a big, old-fashioned, cumbersome bicycle that was so rusty it looked as if it had been in the shed since the war, she decided to explore. Leaving the shears underneath the bottom wooden step, April brushed off the cobwebs and pulled on the gloves, slipped her sleeves down to protect her arms from the nettles and stepped up and over the stile.

And . . . *wow*!

A shard of sunshine bathed the view before her, making the air hazy and giving the field an almost magical, fairytale feel. It was so vibrant, April had to shield her eyes with a raised hand. Stretched out before her was an undulating orchard reaching as far as she could see. Overgrown, the trunks of the trees gnarled and with branches nearly touching the ground where they were so laden with fruit, but still . . . just glorious. And quite unlike the much smaller orchard that April remembered playing in as a child on the other side of the house. This one had rows and rows of apple trees that had been left to nature with some old dried-out stumps dotted around with broken branches strewn on the ground, the bark of which was near white from exposure to the sun. April felt as though she had stepped back in time as the orchard must have been here for over a hundred years, most likely longer given the age of the trees – the stump of the nearest one had at least a trillion rings it seemed, one for every year of its age. There was an etherealness in the orchard, spiritual almost, evoking the ghosts of apple pickers past perhaps, but not scarily so . . . no, the field felt pleasant, happy and welcoming, restorative even. A place of secrets too, sown over years and years and years – April imagined her aunt as a child with her sister Winnie, and brothers Sidney and Robert, running in and out of the trees, scrumping apples – relatives before them also. Perhaps Edie's parents, George and Delphine, had come here when they were courting. April remembered years ago her dad mentioning them and had thought that her great grand-mother's name sounded very romantic indeed, French and chic. She'd love to know how Delphine met George, as it wasn't every day that a French woman came to be living in Tindledale, a tiny, traditional English village. George and Delphine could have wandered through the orchard together, holding hands and whispering words of love, swapping secrets . . . April took a moment to daydream, letting her mind drift to a simpler time when life was so much easier, or so she liked to think.

But if the orchard hadn't been touched in so long, how come then that the grass was so short? Surely it should be as long as the grass in Edie's garden. Knee-high at least. April walked on over to the still fertile part of the orchard, and down the middle, in between an aisle of apple trees, trying to avoid stepping on the fallen fruit on the ground, but it was impossible, there were big, rosy-red ripe apples everywhere. April wondered if she dare try one and crouched down to take a better look.

After searching through a pile at her feet, she selected the best-looking apple and polished it on the knee of her jeans, figuring a little bit of the soil's earthiness wouldn't hurt. This was an apple fallen straight from the tree – not picked, packaged and packed off to a super-market, having most likely been sprayed with pesticide too, like the ones she was used to eating. April was just about to take a bite when she heard a noise. A rustling at the end of the row. She jumped up and threw the apple back on the ground.

Was there someone here?

She looked around, before walking as fast as she could, almost jogging now to the end of the row, but nothing. Then the noise again. April stood stock still. There it was again. Sort of like a swooshing noise. Low and calm. Breezy and melodic. Wind perhaps, whistling through the trees. And for some unknown reason, April held an index finger up in the air – she had seen her dad do it as a child when checking the weather before loading up the car with a picnic for a day out, and well . . . the habit had somehow stuck. But no, it wasn't windy, quite the opposite in fact, it was a lovely, sunny clear day with a perfect blue cloudless sky. Maybe April had imagined the noise, it was entirely possible as shortly after Gray had died she had gone through a phase of thinking that she heard him moving around the house, his footsteps on the stairs, the familiar sounds he made.

April pushed her hair off her face and put her hands on her hips. Then, after surveying the field, she turned to her right and walked up the next row of trees, pleasantly surprised to see pears this time. Plump green pears hanging like fat droplets ready to spill on to the ground at any moment.

And then she saw the sheep.

Ahh, well that explained the length of the grass. Five exceedingly woolly sheep, their bottoms covered in mud – or perhaps, she wrinkled her nose, it was poo – were busy mooching in between the trees, scoffing the grass and snaffling the abandoned fruit. April smiled as she stood and watched the sheep, fascinated, and enjoyed being so close to them, not something that had ever happened back home in Basingstoke. There, the closest she had been to an actual sheep was waiting to be served a slice from the leg of lamb at the Sunday roast carvery in the local Toby Inn. And on that thought, April now felt quite guilty; standing here watching the sheep minding their own business in this idyllic and peaceful location put an entirely different perspective on the prospect of a lovely Sunday roast lunch. And when one of the sheep turned to give her an inquisitive look, its cute white face studying her intently, April was almost certain she could go without ever eating lamb again.

About to head back to the cottage, April heard the swooshing noise again and knew this time that she definitely wasn't mistaken as three more of the sheep stopped chewing and cocked their little woolly heads over in the direction it came from. Determined, April ran towards the noise, down the next row of pear trees until she reached the end. She spotted something in the corner of her eye, a flash of green, or was it navy? It was hard to tell with the sunlight dazzling in her eyes. Whatever it was darted in between two of the plumpest trees. April couldn't be sure, it might be a trick of the light, but it really looked like a person, but before she could get any closer something else caught her eye and she swivelled on her heel in the opposite direction.

And stopped.

Standing square in front of her against a tall, nettle-covered fence were two horses. One chestnut, the other a dappled grey and white. Both had their heads bowed, nuzzling as if to comfort each other. Their manes so matted and long they could barely see from under the hair. April took a step closer and then hesitated as the horses shied their heads away. After waiting a few seconds, she tried again and very slowly edged nearer to them. They kept still this time, heads bowed, and she saw that the chestnut horse had a nasty sore on her shin and was struggling to stand on it, intermittently lifting her hoof as if to ease the pain before setting it down, only to repeat the pattern all over again. Poor thing. April wondered what she could do. Both horses desperately needed a vet, as the other one had a series of large scabs across his back and down over his bottom. But who did they belong to? The orchard was still Edie's, April knew that from her last visit here with Gray, but he hadn't mentioned anything about seeing two neglected old horses, or indeed five sheep roaming free . . . or how overgrown and abandoned this field and the fruit trees were. Maybe the horses belonged to somebody else, a nearby stable perhaps, and they had somehow broken loose and wandered in here.

April picked up a couple of unbruised apples and tried to feed them to the horses while she pondered the best course of action, but neither of them would take the fruit, only sniffing and opening their mouths as if to try before backing away. No wonder their ribs were visible, the poor horses looked half starved; maybe they were wary, having eaten some of the rotten apples previously and now didn't trust them, or perhaps they were nervous of her? April had read somewhere about how complex horses were when it came to trusting humans, so she silently backed away, vowing to get help for them right away.

Maybe Molly would know who the horses belonged to – after the disabled parking debacle, April wasn't sure if she should just go ahead and call a vet without at least checking. The last thing she wanted to do as the newcomer to Tindledale was to step out of line and make a mistake again. Mrs Pocket was bound to have told all the locals about how she parked in the wrong place and they wouldn't take kindly to her interfering if the horses belonged to one of the villagers. Vet bills were very expensive and the horses' owner may not thank her for it. And as for the sheep, weren't there special farming laws about livestock in the English countryside? Surely they weren't allowed to roam whenever they liked, they must belong to someone too, a local farmer. Maybe they'd escaped from a nearby field as well. Perhaps the farmer, Pete, would know.

April turned her head to look at the horses over her shoulder and then with a sense of purpose headed back to the cottage. She'd call Molly and Pete right away, certain that between them they'd know what to do for the best.

'Oh there you are, love.' It was Deedee with a conspiratorial look on her face, standing on the path next to an older man with a very impressive moustache, wearing a paisley cravat and a navy blazer with two rows of gold buttons down the front.

'Hello Deedee. I was just in the orchard . . .' April said, feeling a sudden need to explain. Deedee and the gentleman exchanged looks before simultaneously stepping towards her. 'Is everything OK? Is my aunt all right?' She glanced at the cottage.

'Oh yes, Edie is fine,' the man assured her. 'And she had a wonderful time dancing . . . but is having a little rest now on the settee. At her age, the waltz rather takes it out of her . . . especially after the seventh dance!' He nodded, linking his hands behind his back and looking to Deedee to get to the point of whatever it was they really wanted to say. April inhaled through her nostrils and fixed a smile on her face as she had a feeling she might not like what she was about to hear.

'Dear, I, er um . . . well, *we* wondered if you had a moment for a little chat?' Deedee started, fiddling with her pashmina while giving the man a surreptitious side-way glance.

'Sure, what's the matter? Are you worried about the state of the garden? Because I'm going to be staying with my aunt now for a while to help out and just as soon as I've got organised I'll make sure the land around the cottage and also the lane is tidy, the hedgerow too, even the orchards – I've just been to have a look and had no idea how overgrown it had got. I'll be taking care of everything.' April figured it best to cut to the chase as there was clearly something wrong. The stab of guilt about having neglected her aunt made a rapid return. She folded her arms and then quickly unfolded them, realising it made her look defensive, which wasn't her intention at all. April was here to help and these people had been very kind in taking her aunt to the weekly speed-dating tea dance.

'Oh no darling, don't be worrying about all that stuff, the bushes and everything – I'll get one of the farmers to sort them out.'

'Thank you. Molly mentioned that Pete might help, I was about to call him,' April offered, keen to show that she was already on the case.

'Ooh, yes, good idea, and Pete owes me a favour in any case . . .' Deedee batted her pashmina about for a bit and giggled like a hormone-fuelled schoolgirl, making April really *not* want to wonder what Deedee had done to warrant such a favour being owed. 'Leave it with me . . .'

'Well, that's, um . . . very kind of you,' April said.

'My pleasure. I'll get on to it right away and Pete will be here soon to clear the lane and plough the fields or whatever it is he does with that *enormous* tractor of his!' Deedee said, her voice coated in innuendo. 'Now, the matter we need to chat about is more troubling I'm afraid . . .'

'Go on,' April coaxed. And for the first time in their exchange, Deedee looked uncertain and hesitated before speaking.

'Dear, it's your aunt. I'm afraid she's going a bit, er . . . well, not to put too fine a point on it . . .'

'What Deedee means is that your aunt is going doolally . . .' The man stepped in to take over and had now adopted a grave expression. '*And* hysterical!' April winced at his use of the old-fashioned derogatory term. Her aunt was certainly struggling with her memory but she was very far from 'doolally' or 'hysterical'.

Then Deedee, her face all flustered now, quickly jostled the man out of the way with her elbow.

'What the general is trying to say, *badly*, my love, is that your aunt is getting muddled . . . confused, and she was very upset at this afternoon's dance,' Deedee explained rather more tactfully. So, April realised, this was the much-mentioned general. However, with that attitude April didn't think he was a very suitable suitor for her aunt. Besides, he seemed at least twenty years younger than Edie. She hoped he wasn't a gold-digger – you read about these things happening to little old ladies . . . April gave him a look before fixing a smile on her face.

'What happened?' she said, keeping eye contact with Deedee, and hoping the general would go back to his bus, which she presumed was parked further up the lane somewhere.

'Your aunt was confused, she was saying something about Winnie having returned, but that now she's gone again . . .'

'Ahh, I see . . .' April started, glancing at the ground.

'Actually it's not quite as simple as that,' the general butted in again, only to be told:

'Shush, let me explain please, sweetie,' Deedee insisted, firmly.

The general seemed happy to bow to her authority. 'As you wish, my flower. I'll potter by the barn,' and he put a bristly, moustachioed kiss on Deedee's cheek before swiftly escaping down the path to the almost derelict old apple barn by the back orchard.

'Don't mind him, he means well – a retired military man you see, he can be *very* blunt, it comes from years of running around with a rucksack on his back in the blazing desert and then having to survive on those titchy little powdered meals that come in a packet!' Deedee indicated the size with her thumb and index finger. 'Survival of the fittest and all that.' She paused while April's mind boggled at her logic . . . 'I'll have a word with him later. We're trying the new Indian restaurant this evening, the one up overlooking the village green, do you know it?' Deedee inquired.

'Um, yes . . . I saw it earlier when I was in the village,' April said, wondering if this meant that Deedee and the general were a unlikely couple – they seemed like polar opposites, her vivaciousness to his staid pomposity – but if that was the case, then where did Edie fit in? April immediately felt protective of her aunt.

'Your aunt has a soft spot for the general and, well, he's very fond of her too, she reminds him of his dear old mother . . . so he always escorts her into the tea dance, that is OK, isn't it? Only he's been doing it for quite some time now so it would be a shame for our lovely Edie to miss out.' Deedee seemed to sense April's anxiety, 'But if you'd rather he didn't any more . . .?'

'Oh, yes. Of course he must . . . that's very kind of him.' April breathed an inward sigh of relief that her aunt's relationship with the old-school, bordering-on-rude general wasn't anything more than an innocent arrangement. Edie clearly enjoyed the attention from him, so where was the harm?

'Jolly good.' Deedee patted her arm before adopting a serious face again. 'Now, let me tell you what happened this afternoon, but before I do, please know that we all care and nobody was judging . . . we don't do that.' She shook her head so vehemently that it made her softly layered hair swish around her face. 'If we did, then most of the tea dance attendees would have been locked up by now. Honestly, they're all blooming bananas. And I'm the worst! You know, I put my best bubble bath in the freezer instead of the bathroom cabinet the other day . . . well, it was actually my Meg's, Dan bought it for her for her birthday, *very expensive*, and she went berserk, but anyway, can you imagine? ROCK SOLID it was when we realised. I'm losing my mind, going *doolally* as the general would say.' Deedee rolled her eyes and whirled an index finger round in a loop at her temple as she patted April's arm with her free hand. 'Anyway, to cut a long story short, your aunt has been talking about someone called Winnie, whoever she is, for quite some time now, months in fact, and has become somewhat obsessed. And today, right after the rumba she started crying and wringing her hands . . . it was truly pitiful, poor dear.'

'Oh no! Really? That's so sad, poor Edie. Do you have any idea why?'

'Not really, dear. It just seemed to come out of the blue. One minute she was all glowing cheeks from all that hip-shimmying . . . but then she just seemed to crumble.'

'Thanks for letting me know,' April said, remembering the sobbing old lady in the Alzheimer's documentary. She was keen to check on her aunt right away and went to walk up the path but then stopped when Deedee added:

'And then she said that now you were here, Winnie would never return because if she did, then you would send her away! She was inconsolable at one point, crying like a young girl she was. I'm so sorry, April.'

'Really? But it doesn't make sense . . . Winnie is her sister, my other great aunt.' April shook her head, racking her brains trying to work out what to do for the best. 'And why would I send Winnie away?'

'I've no idea, darling, she did seem very confused and

muddled. But the strangest thing is, when we got your aunt calmed down and had given her one of her favourite Garibaldi biscuits to dunk in her Earl Grey, she had a perfectly lucid moment and said that Winnie left Tindledale on a bus in 1941 and never came back. She could even remember what she was wearing when she waved her off in the village square: "a smart new uniform". And it was a gloriously warm day and therefore too hot for her coat which she took with her anyway, folded over her arm, Edie said. She recalled it all in such detail,' Deedee said, shaking her head again.

'Wow, that's fascinating,' April said, making a mental note to see if she could engage her aunt more on this topic later. Maybe if she mentioned the bus and the uniform, she might remember more. 'It really is something that she can recall such events from decades ago, but then struggle with present-day detail,' April said, thinking about Edie's snowball recollection from earlier but then getting muddled over April's name.

'I know darling. Heartbreaking!' Deedee pressed a hand to her chest. 'Then Bill piped up, he's our oldest dancer – holding out for his telegram from the Queen next year, and he's not really a dancer as such, he's in a wheelchair now, but he manages to bob along to the beat, nonetheless – anyway, he said that Winnie joined the FANY!'

Silence lingered as April took in the news.

'Ahh, that explains the uniform.'

'Yes, Bill may have dementia, but when it comes to details from years back then he's sharp as a pin. He was the village postman for years and years and all the way through the war, he had a medical exemption apparently but that didn't stop him from doing his bit on the home front. He told us all about it – said it was his duty to keep a keen eye on all the Tindledale residents when delivering their letters. Loose lips and all that! Fascinating it was, listening to him telling us who had lived where. Generations of families still in the same house, rather like your aunt – she's lived here at Orchard Cottage for donkey's years. Anyway, Bill said he remembers delivering the official letter to Winnie from the War Office. And the whole family had been ever so excited and proud that she had been accepted into the FANY. But she never came back.' Deedee paused and lowered her voice before continuing. 'And then one of the other old dears said there was some tittle-tattle at the time, something to do with Winnie and a married man, and then it all went a bit hush-hush she said . . .'

'Fascinating. And I wonder how I could find out more . . .' April said, making a mental note to visit Hettie as Molly had suggested; perhaps she would know about the married man. Maybe that's why Winnie didn't come home . . . April imagined being involved with a married man would have caused quite a scandal in those days. Perhaps she felt ashamed? But April didn't want to speculate, no, she wanted to know the truth. This gem of information was like finding a crucial piece of a puzzle. Very intriguing. And April wanted to know more.

'Tell you what, sweetheart, I'll get the general to do

some more digging – he's a keen historian. His father was awarded an OBE, you know, so I'm sure he'll get to the bottom of it and find out where Winnie is. And then we can all put it to rest and Edie won't get distressed any more. At her time of life she shouldn't have to shoulder such a concern,' Deedee offered.

April nodded, still deep in thought, but then a bizarrely abstract thought popped into her head: how on earth could having a father with an OBE possibly help in the search for a woman who went missing during the war? Connections maybe? Who knew? It was a mystery, but one thing April did know was that she was determined to get to the bottom of this particular mystery and find out exactly what happened to her great aunt Winnie, the woman in the tea dress with the beautiful, sunny smile. And more importantly, Deedee was right . . . Great Aunt Edie really shouldn't be so concerned to the point of tears, but April was here to look after her now. And that was exactly what she was going to do!

11

After saying goodbye to Deedee, April went into the cottage to find her aunt sitting on the settee watching TV. April sat down beside her and put an arm around her tiny frame before gently pulling her in close. Edie let her body relax into April and the two women sat in silence for a while.

And then April had an idea.

Ten minutes later, she had set up the card table, arranged the macaroons from The Spotted Pig café on to a plate, found the Advocaat and a dusty bottle of lemonade and a jar of glacé cherries in the pantry (they'd have to do), poured them both a snowball and they were playing rummy . . . just like the old days. And that's when Edie started talking. All the while fiddling with the cards in between her age-gnarled fingers.

'I'm ever so sorry, my dear . . .'

'What on earth for, Aunty? You have nothing to apologise about . . .' April kept her voice soft and encouraging the way she used to when on the ward with a vulnerable patient.

'For making a show of myself. I heard Deedee through the open window telling you all about my making a scene at the tea dance.' April swivelled her head to the side of the sitting room and sure enough the window was wide open. Damn! She sincerely hoped her aunt had been dozing when the 'doolally' comment was made. 'What must you think of me?' Edie twisted the tissue some more.

'That you're a lovely, caring lady who misses her sister and wants to know what happened to her. There's nothing wrong with that . . .' April soothed, leaning across the table to touch the top of her aunt's hand.

Edie's tense shoulders relaxed in relief.

'Oh, you've always been a kind girl, April, and after all the heartache you've been through – losing your parents at such a young age and then dear Gray, I always had a soft spot for him. He was such a character . . .' *Ahh, so she hadn't forgotten about him after all!* 'Life can be wretched sometimes – and there's many folk that would be quite jaded and bitter by the experiences you've had, but not my April. Always bonny in the face of adversity, aren't you, my love?' Edie smiled, sounding very lucid indeed as she scrutinised her hand of cards.

'I do try. And thank you, Aunty.'

'What for?' Edie asked sharply, glancing up.

'You know, I'm not entirely sure,' April smiled, and then, after contemplating momentarily, added, 'for coming back to me I guess.'

She shrugged and nodded slowly. 'I'll always be here, maybe not in body one day, but certainly in spirit. And in the meantime you must make the most of your stay here. Promise me that you will?'

'I will, I promise.' April gently squeezed her aunt's hand by way of confirmation.

'That's a girl!' Edie nodded and took a big sip of her snowball. 'Because we really can't have you being so quiet like you have been since you arrived.' April went to talk, but her aunt interjected. 'I know dear, it's the loss and it takes time, but let me tell you something, darling – this place, Orchard Cottage, is special, and it's been my home my whole life. I was born right up there,' Edie stopped to point a bony finger at the ceiling above their heads, 'my parents' bedroom! It's my room now of course.' April waited politely, having heard before all about the numerous home births over the years at Orchard Cottage. 'And this might sound a bit cuckoo, but the cottage will heal you. Help you come to terms with your loss, give you a new life if you let it. That's its magic. Have faith, my dear, and it will make you whole again. They say that some houses have spirits and this one most certainly does. It's been the one constant in my life, always here to comfort me, see me through the bad times, and trust me . . . like lots of people I've had my share . . .' Edie's voice tailed off.

'Have you?' April asked, delicately, hoping to engage her aunt.

'Oh yes! I've suffered loss too, dear . . . everyone's gone now. My parents. My brothers, not to mention poor Bobby.'

'Bobby?'

'Bobby was very nearly my husband.'

'I never knew . . .' April smiled, placed her cards on

the table and waited patiently. 'What happened to Bobby?'

'It was the nerves, my dear.' Edie shook her head and picked at the corner of the green baize on the card table. 'Bobby was my sweetheart from school days . . . his father owned the ironmongers in the village, it's not there any more, but, well . . . he was never the same after the war. The last time I saw him . . .' Edie paused, took another sip of her drink and then added, 'Bobby said it wouldn't be fair to burden me with his night terrors. And then he went off to London. Next I heard, he had joined the merchant navy and then fell overboard several years later.' Silence followed. Edie closed her eyes momentarily, deep in thought, and then added, 'Well, that's what they said, but his parents heard from one of the other men that poor Bobby's night terrors had overwhelmed him to the point where the bottom of the cold, dark sea seemed a more preferable place to be than the one inside his head, and he jumped.'

'Aunty, I'm so very sorry.'

'I was too. But it was a very common thing in those days, and is it any wonder with the horrors they witnessed . . . Bobby was a country boy, not a soldier,' she said, pragmatically. 'But you know the thing I missed most about not marrying?'

'What's that?'

'Having babies. I would have liked to have had a little girl or boy of my own. And then there would have been someone to keep you company too . . . look out for you. Will you be OK when I'm gone?'

'Oh please, Aunty . . . I'll be fine. Please, please don't worry about me,' April just about managed, her bottom lip quivering with the effort not to cry, as she couldn't bear to think of her aunt worrying about such stuff. And she felt so touched by Edie's compassion, even though April had neglected her aunt for far too long. 'It's my time to look after you . . . and Orchard Cottage.' She paused, and then decided to go for it. 'And I thought I'd see about getting some help—'

'Help?' Edie asked, alarmed.

'Yes, with the garden.' Silence followed and seemed to go on for ages, broken only by the intermittent sound of an owl terwit-terwooing in the distance, while Edie appeared to be mulling it all over until she eventually mumbled:

'As you like, dear.' April took this as her aunt's acceptance of help, but figured it best to build up to the topic of a cleaner.

The two women carried on playing rummy, sipping snowballs, popping glacé cherries into their mouths and enjoying each other's company for a while without the need for words – just as with any longstanding, loving relationship . . . until Great Aunt Edie won the last game.

After gathering up all the cards, she said, 'I know the last few years have been tremendously tough for you . . .' Edie's voice broke off and the two women sat in silence some more. 'And that's why I haven't mentioned Gray – I didn't want to add to the obvious burden you were carrying when you arrived here with your shoulders laden down with woe. And I'm sorry for going "doolally" . . .'

Oh dear, she hadn't been dozing at that point in the conversation after all. Poor Edie, I hope she isn't offended. 'I get forgetful and muddled sometimes. Brain fog I call it. The doctor wanted to give me pills – thyroid problem he said, but I've never been one for all that stuff. They make it in factories you know! Mix it up with all sorts of ingredients that nobody has ever heard of.'

Edie shook her head as if to gain some clarity and April wondered if her aunt's impaired thyroid function could be contributing to her tiredness – falling asleep in the oven for example, and brain fog and confusion could very well be down to untreated hypothyroidism and not dementia at all. April really did need to have a word with the village GP or, better still, see if she could arrange a house visit for her aunt as she may be reluctant to take a trip to the surgery given her suspicion of modern medicine. Yes, Edie would be more relaxed seeing the doctor in her own home.

'It's tricky to know some mornings where my mind is at. It could be this month . . . or any month for that matter, it can be quite problematic you know. I started writing my Christmas cards a few weeks ago. That was before I checked the date on the wall calendar in the kitchen and saw that we were still in summertime . . . now that is *very doolally*!' Edie did a small chuckle and April instantly felt full of admiration for her aunt that she was able to laugh at her own predicament. It reminded her of Gray; he had found comfort in humour too, sometimes in the darkest moments of his demise, like when he was no longer able to go to the toilet by himself . . . he had made every joke in the book about having his arse wiped for him!

'It's OK, Aunty. Please don't apologise – getting ahead with your Christmas cards is no bad thing, not when you have a list of people to send one to as long as yours. And besides, I'm here now to help out and we can "muddle through" together,' April smiled.

'Thank you, my dear. Having you around the place is such a tonic. And the cottage really could do with some . . . er, maintenance.' Edie glanced away, and April knew it wasn't easy for her aunt to acknowledge the need for some help. 'It's such a wonderful home, a special place. Like I said, it will heal you . . .'

'Yes, I know,' April contemplated. 'It healed me once before . . . do you remember that summer?' she asked with a faraway look in her eye.

'Yes dear. I remember. Your parents. Terrible business that was. They didn't stand a chance when their car rolled on that wet, windy night.' Edie shook her head, her face folding in concern at the memory.

'It was a long time ago,' April muttered, remembering that it was the end of the half-term holiday, Halloween, when her parents were on their way to collect her from Orchard Cottage. And April had been devastated, but Aunt Edie had looked after her here for a few months until it was decided she'd live with her mum's parents who were devastated at having lost their daughter. *You've lost your only child, your daughter, it's the least I can do* . . . April remembered being here in the sitting room, overhearing her aunt, through the hatch, talking in a hushed voice with all the other grown-ups in the kitchen. And as an adult, she realised now how selfless, but incredibly hard, it must have been for her aunt to let April go, meaning she'd be all on her own with a yearning to be a mother. Feeling a sudden rush of affection for her aunt, April got out of her chair and went to give Edie a cuddle.

'What's this for?' Edie's watery blue eyes sought out April's as she looked up.

'Because I love you. And I'm going to take care of you, do my best by you . . . just as you did for me.' April rubbed her hand across her elderly aunt's back, breathing in the familiar scent of lavender, fully intending to hold on to this moment for always like a permanent picture inside her head to cherish long after Edie was gone. Pictures were one thing, but scents and moments were what really lasted for ever. And April was under no illusion that just being here with her aunt, talking about old times was a true tonic for her too. Her elderly great aunt was continuing to look after her, look out for her as well, if not in a physical sense, but certainly in an emotional sense, providing an anchor of familiarity, family, belonging – a perfect recipe to make April feel steadfast and strong again.

'I love you too,' Edie said and more silence followed until she added, 'And I need to ask you something,' in a soft, but quite serious voice.

April, back in her seat now, looked at her aunt, and her heart went out to her – the mature lucidity that Edie had displayed only moments earlier had been replaced with an almost childlike vulnerability.

'What is it, Aunty?'

'Will you help me, please?'

'Of course I will,' April assured her. 'I'm staying here with you . . . if that's OK?' Edie blinked as if taking it all in. 'And, there will be someone coming to help sort out the hedgerow and the garden . . . and I thought a cleaner would be . . .' April stopped talking. Her aunt's eyes were pooled with tears.

'Thank you,' Aunt Edie managed as a solitary tear trickled down the side of her wrinkled nose. She quickly pulled a hanky from her sleeve and dabbed it away while April averted her eyes, pretending to be busy drinking the last of her snowball; instinct told her Edie would prefer it that way – she came from a generation where emotion was kept contained, and crying could be perceived as a weakness of character. 'But what I meant was . . .' Edie ploughed on, having swiftly pulled herself together, 'please will you help me find out what happened to my sister Winnie? I need to know where she is.'

'Yes,' April immediately promised. 'Yes, of course, I certainly will. I want to meet her too,' she added, knowing that, while not impossible, it was highly unlikely that Winnie was still alive; however, Edie was upset enough as it was, so April thought it best to go along with things for now.

'Oh but you can't!' Edie said, sounding panicked all of a sudden.

'Why not?' April's forehead creased in concern. The change in her aunt's demeanour was quite startling, as if she had somehow regressed to another time in her life and was now not fully present. It was quite extraordinary. Even the blue colour of her eyes had an altered hue.

'You'll be ashamed.' Edie stared at the hanky still in her hand.

'Why is that, Aunty?'

'Because she ran off with a married man!' The elderly woman's voice dropped almost to a childlike whisper. 'And had his baby . . . that's what they all said in the village. Shocking it was. I think she started courting when she was in the Land Army, she was a driver for the big wigs, you know. My big sister was the woman who went off to do her bit for the war effort and wrecked a marriage instead.' Edie shook her head. 'We are a close-knit community here in Tindledale and there's a lot to be said for that, but the villagers do love to dissect other people's business . . . seeing Winnie with an older man in uniform would be enough to set the tongues wagging,' she explained, sounding more like her mature self again now. 'And it's so unlike Winnie to have been carrying on . . . she was always the sensible one. And my parents never said anything about the rumours, but I heard the girls in the village talking about it.'

Silence followed as April digested this information, wondering if it was true because if so then it would have been an enormous scandal back then. A secret the family may have wanted to hide from the rest of the community. And most likely why Edie had commented, in the midst of her confusion at the tea dance, that April would want to send Winnie away . . . but things were different nowadays. April vowed to get to the bottom of this, because surely, if Winnie had indeed run off with a married man and had his baby, wouldn't she have heard about this somehow? Yes, family stuff got skewed and indeed lost over the course of time, but wouldn't her dad have known? Had some kind of inkling . . . surely? April thought it sounded very odd indeed.

'But what about the FANY? Deedee mentioned that Bill remembers delivering the special letter to Winnie . . .' April ventured, unsure if she was going over old ground that Edie may not want to discuss, or worse still might feel offended by if she thought people had been gossiping again.

'FANY?' Edie said vaguely, and April's heart sank . . . her aunt was fading again.

'Yes, that's what Bill remembers,' April persevered, figuring it had to be worth at least trying to prompt Edie for more information.

'Yes dear, but she didn't come back home . . . stopped sending letters.' Edie rallied, fixing her watery cobalt-blue eyes on to April and then added, 'I think Mum wrote to the War Office after my father died, but it's all so vague.' Edie shook her head, getting more and more agitated as she twisted the hanky around her fingers, over and over. 'But Winnie could have told me . . . if there was a man and a baby. I would have kept the secret. And I still have the letters that she sent during the war so you can see for yourself – lovely letters from the start of the war when she was in the Land Army, but then later, when she went away, there is hardly any mention of what she was doing at the FANY training place, very formal they were and not at all warm and friendly like her letters at the start. It could have been for security reasons of course, there was a war on after all! But then the letters stopped coming and I can't remember what happened . . . and then Dad died, and well, it's just all so hazy. Blasted memory!' Aunt Edie closed her eyes tightly, as if inwardly chastising herself.

'You have letters?' April's heart lifted at this unexpected piece of information.

'Oh yes, dear. They're in the biscuit tin on top of the wardrobe in her bedroom – it was my bedroom after she left . . . and now it's yours, the room you're sleeping in while you're here.'

'Ooh, I didn't notice. I could get them now and we can read through them together if you like? Maybe we can see if there are some clues as to what actually happened to Winnie.' April went to stand up, eager to get started as quickly as possible, keen to find a way to put her aunt's mind at rest. It seemed that not knowing for sure was causing the most distress.

'Right you are, dear.' Edie managed a smile. 'Although my eyesight isn't what it used to be so you may need to read them aloud.'

'I can do that. No problem!'

'Good girl. You see, I really need to know why she never told me about the man, or indeed the baby. If it is true then I understand that she would have felt ashamed, but there could be a person, a relative, a niece or nephew that I've never met! Wouldn't that be marvellous?' April nodded, enthused by her aunt's seemingly open heart

– there was no judgement there. Just concern and love for a sister who went off a very long time ago to do her bit for the war effort and didn't come home.

'And there are records we can check, Aunty – you know, it's all online now these days – birth certificates, marriages and deaths, it's all there,' April said.

'Fancy that! But if she died, then where is she? Why can't I visit her grave? Sidney died and there's a plaque in the graveyard next to the church in the village.'

'Sidney?'

'My brother. Killed in action over Cologne in December 1941, I remember it so clearly as it was the week before Christmas. He was an air gunner in the RAF,' Edie said, with crystal-clear clarity.

'Oh dear. That must have been so very sad for you all.'

'It was. My mother was never the same after that. But what about Winnie? Why don't I know? Why did nobody tell me?' Edie said, the break in her voice palpable, and sounding much younger, like a young girl. It was as if the distress of not knowing for sure, of not having tangible evidence, a gravestone, an official letter or some such thing, was making her regress back to the girl she had been when Winnie left and never came home again. Poor Edie.

'I don't know, Aunty. But I'm sure we can find out,' April assured, wondering how hard could it be to see if a person had died . . . and then she had a thought. 'When was Winnie's birthday? Can you remember?' She got up and gestured for her aunt to move on to the settee where it might be more comfortable for her. They had been sitting in the hardback chairs at the card table for quite some time now and April's back was getting stiff . . . and she was less than half Edie's age. Once settled, Aunt Edie looked deep in thought before figuring it out.

'1920! Winnie was twenty years old when she went off on the bus. The seventh of July was her birthday and she left in June. It was a hot, sunny day and I went swimming in the stream after waving her off.'

'Wonderful.' April did a quick sum in her head to calculate that Winnie would be ninety-five now, if by some miracle she was still alive. April thought it highly unlikely, but surely the family would know if she had died? Weren't the next of kin informed? Especially during wartime! And even if, years later, a person was estranged from their family – say the rumours in the village were true and Winnie had run off to have a secret love child with a married man and then died – surely the coroner, a friend, someone, would have tracked down the relatives. April had watched a TV programme about something similar. Awfully sad it was: a man died all alone in his flat and the people from the council who were called to sort everything out found photos of him in a uniform, with relatives at the seaside, a wedding picture – he had a life, the whole lot – and they then managed to track down a distant nephew living in Canada who came right away to organise the funeral. It had made April cry. Gray had put an arm around April to comfort her, making a wry joke about being 'blooming grateful I'm not that poor bugger', before resolutely pointing the remote at the TV to flick over to 'something more cheerful'.

But perhaps Aunt Edie had forgotten what actually happened to Winnie, blocked it from her mind perhaps? It was entirely possible given her deteriorating mental health. Either way, even if Winnie was still alive, neither sister was getting any younger . . . so time really was of the essence. April needed to start researching right away if she was to find out the truth. She really wanted to, her curiosity was piqued and it was important to do this for her aunt before it was too late.

'I'm going to write it all down and then I'll get the letters, Aunty. No time like the present for us to get started on taking action.' April smiled, and after giving her aunt's arm a reassuring pat, she quickly popped next door into the kitchen to make them each another snowball, and to retrieve her pad and pen.

Minutes later, April handed her aunt her snowball and then sat down next to her, thinking about how she could get online and search stuff, ancestry sites, etc. – she could sit in The Spotted Pig café on her mobile if it came to it, just to access the free Wi-Fi. And there might even be a special FANY database that she could contact for help. Anything was worth a go. Maybe Facebook! And then a thought occurred to her.

'Aunty, do you have any more photos of Winnie?' April thought she could post a selection of pictures online, see if anyone recognised Winnie, old friends perhaps. Obviously, if she was actually still alive, she'd look completely different now, but somebody might remember her. Or if there ever really was a baby, he or she would be an adult, older than April, and there might be a family resemblance. April's head was buzzing with all the possibilities, especially if she could create a Facebook post that could be shared over and over to help widen the search. And for the first time in a very long time, she felt focused, alert and alive and thinking and caring about something other than Gray's demise.

'Yes dear, only a few pictures, mind you, they're in the tin with the letters. Plus those two of course.' Edie pointed to the woman in the uniform and the tea dress. 'It wasn't like it is now with all the cameras and pictures people have on their phones. Back when I was a young girl, a photo was what you held inside your head . . .'

'Thank you.'

'And there's one of when she qualified as a St John's Ambulance cadet. They ran a course in the village hall and Winnie signed up right away – she was only a schoolgirl, but already knew then that she wanted to be a nurse, to look after others . . . a bit like you, dear.' April smiled as she wrote all the details down, already loving the parallels between her and her great aunt Winnie.

'Why didn't she become a nurse?' April asked.

'Well, when she finished school at fourteen, she had to help out in the orchards for a few harvests. She had filled in all the paperwork and persuaded our parents to let her go to London to start her nurse training, but then when the rumours of war started, and well . . . my mother got extremely anxious about the bombs dropping. So that put paid to that!'

'But, I guess she followed her heart eventually, by signing up to join the FANY. It was a nursing corps

146

from what I know . . .' April said vaguely, casting her mind back to a trip to the Imperial War Museum several years ago.

'Yes. Winnie was a very headstrong girl. And once she set her mind to something she was quite determined, and fearless . . . you know, she told me once that she went to visit a bomb site! In Brighton. With some big wigs from the army!' Aunt Edie's eyes widened. 'And saw a mountain of rubble where a cinema once stood,' she added covertly, lowering her voice and leaning into April, as if all these years later, things that happened in wartime must still be kept secret. Loose lips and all that!

'*Really?*' April marvelled, making another note. It was incredible how her aunt's memory came and went like this.

'Yes. But how could she have? Winnie was in the Land Army at the time, working in the fields, and I was just a young girl, so I may have been mistaken. Not very likely is it?' Edie chuckled as she took a sip of her second snowball. And then, 'I better not have too many of these, or who knows what I'll end up thinking actually happened?' And both women laughed, as they finished their drinks, thoroughly content in each other's company.

As bedtime approached, Edie turned to April.

'I'm getting on a bit you know, dear.' She paused, and April glanced at the red patterned carpet, smiling politely and wondered if she would make it into her nineties and, if so, how would she feel? Would she have the energy for tea dances and consider herself to be merely 'getting on a bit'? She really hoped so . . . And suddenly, the attraction of wearing an organza ballgown on a Tuesday afternoon seemed very appealing indeed. 'So I really must find out what happened to Winnie before it's too late . . .' Edie continued, all the while patting the back of April's hand as she drained the last of her second snowball, and then tottered off to bed.

12

Midnight, and April was still sitting up in bed and reading through all of Winnie's letters to Edie, written in violet-blue ink on cream-lined Basildon Bond notepaper with matching envelopes. Unable to wait a moment longer, she had found the biscuit tin and got stuck in right away, and now the bed was strewn with envelopes and a selection of photos.

April picked up another letter, written while Winnie was in the Land Army.

Dearest sister Edie,

I do hope you are keeping well.

The weather here was wretched today, windy rain and dreary skies, which didn't bother me, yet the city girls kicked up the most dreadful hullabaloo. They're not used to it you see, certainly not being outside in the fields. But they're a good bunch on the whole and I think you'd rather like them. Rita is a card, and keeps us amused with the most shocking jokes, quite blue at times, but she's a cockney from Whitechapel in the East End of London, and far more worldly than the rest of us girls.

One of the other girls, Doreen, had never seen sheep

before! Isn't that extraordinary – and tell Father he wouldn't care for Maud, as it took her the best part of half an hour to pick two crates of apples!

How are Mum and Dad? Do give them my love, dear girl, and say I'm keeping Robert and Sidney safe in my thoughts.

See you in two weeks' time.

Your sister Winnie x

PS – if you want to wear my dresses then that is O.K. But not the blue, floral tea dress as I shall want to bring that back with me next time I'm home on leave. I've been invited to a dance in Brighton at the end of the month, which I'm awfully excited about. There are going to be boys from the base there. Rita says she will ask one to dance with me, if it appears that I'm to be a wallflower. She's very forward . . .

Ahh, April took a sip of her tea and felt quite emotional as she read the words of her twenty-year-old great aunt Winnie. The innocence and optimism of a dance to look forward to – a chink of light in the dark days of war. And the old-fashioned, formal dialogue, it really was like stepping back in time. But no mention of a man, and by the sounds of it, Winnie wasn't a worldly-wise type of girl whatsoever, certainly not if she thought asking a man to dance was forward. Mind you, it was very different then, which was why Winnie having anything to do with a married man would have been highly scandalous.

April shuffled through the letters and picked up another one sent from the FANY training base . . . April paused to check her pad. Yes, she had made a note: in one of the earlier letters, Winnie had said the Oxfordshire countryside was very similar to Tindledale. She took another sip of her tea and got comfy against the head-board of the bed to read the next letter. Dated 1942, it was far more formal.

Dear Edie,

The weather here is certainly changeable. Much like the food, today it was chicken and dumplings for lunch, yesterday cold ham and potato, but I mustn't grumble.

I'm learning so very much, and keeping well. Do tell Mum and Dad I'm continuing to keep Robert and Sidney safe in my thoughts . . .

Hold on. April sat upright and put down her mug on the bedside cabinet. She checked the date. 1942. But Sidney was killed in 1941! That's what Edie had said . . . with crystal-clear clarity! It was the week before Christmas. April grabbed her pad again and flipped through the pages.

Sidney – December 1941.

It was right there. Circled several times. Surely Winnie would have been told that her brother hadn't made it? April thought it very strange indeed. Mulling it all over, wondering if Aunt Edie had got the year wrong perhaps – that would explain the discrepancy – April looked inside the envelope again, as if it might contain some kind of clue. But nothing. She looked at the front with the Orchard Cottage address on. And the postmark. And her pulse quickened further.

London?

But that wasn't right. April sifted through all of the envelopes spread out across the old-fashioned eiderdown on her bed, checking each one. Perhaps this letter had got muddled up and then put back inside the wrong envelope. But after reading through every letter again, April couldn't find any mention at all of Winnie ever being in London . . . so how come this letter had been posted from there? It just didn't make any sense.

Even more determined to unravel the truth of what happened to her great aunt Winnie, April gathered up all the letters and photos, put them back in the biscuit tin and turned off the lamp and lay in the dark, silent countryside night letting all the information she had collated so far swirl around inside her head. Maybe her unconscious mind would work out the truth as she drifted off to sleep.

13

A week later, and with Pete's help, April had already transformed the garden, having planted Gray's roses in a perfect spot near a particularly flourishing apple tree over in the meadow section packed with wild flowers. It had been Edie's idea; in another one of her lucid moments she had said that now a part of Gray would always be here at Orchard Cottage. And April liked the thought of that. It was interesting too, how since being here in Tindledale, April's feelings had started to change – she felt more relaxed and far less panicky whenever Gray entered her thoughts. And she had enjoyed the best sleep in years here. The stillness and calm at night were a stark contrast to the traffic and hollering in the streets of Basingstoke. She had woken up every morning feeling refreshed and raring to go without a whiff of that god-awful gear change thing on remembering that Gray wasn't here any more. But now she woke up already armed with this know-ledge and was grateful to no longer have such a cruel reminder to contend with.

April had also sorted out the leaky septic tank and Pete was here today, busy putting a small fence around it so that nobody else would have the displeasure of inadvertently wandering through the boggy patch that was still lingering.

'You could get the waste removal boys down with the truck and motorised suction hose to suck it all up if you like?' Pete offered, taking a break from hammering the last fence post into the ground.

'Good idea, does it cost very much?' April asked.

'Nah, not too bad,' he started, pushing his hair away from his face with his forearm. He was a good bloke, thought April, only young, early thirties or so, and had really helped her out and she was well aware that he wasn't charging her the full going rate for the work that he was doing. April had tried to insist, but he'd said he wouldn't dream of it, and besides, he was happy to help out . . . Old Edie had let him and his mates play in the orchards as kids, had even brought pitchers of cold apple juice out to them in the summer, so it was the least he could do. 'But it stinks to high heaven when they switch the motor on.' Pete pulled a face as he swigged some water from a bottle that he kept in the back pocket of his heavy-duty farmer jeans.

'Ahh, in that case, maybe it's best to let sleeping muck lie,' April said, eyeing the patch of grass inside the fence.

'Sure, and it'll disappear over time in any case now that we've cleared the drain of all those dead leaves . . .' Pete assured. 'I'll put the garden hose over it too to help it on its way.'

They both turned on hearing footsteps.

'Hiya.' It was Molly, laden with food, as always. 'Here,

had one left over, pulled pork, apple and cider. I know how partial Edie is to one of my pies,' she beamed, handing April a cloth-covered pie dish.

'Ooh, thank you. But you must let me do something in return this time,' April said, taking the pie.

'OK. You're on.' Molly glanced at Pete. 'How about a nice cup of tea and a chat, if Pete can spare you for a bit?' she chuckled. 'My boys are doing my head in, so it would be nice to have some "me time", without one or all of them yelling "Muuuuuum" at me continuously.' Molly rolled her eyes, despite it being quite obvious that she absolutely adored her boys.

'Sure,' Pete grinned, nodding. 'As long as you bring me out a mug of tea and a couple of biscuits to dunk in.'

'Coming right up,' April smiled, and the two women walked around the fence and into the cottage via the back door.

After setting the pie on the kitchen table, April put the kettle on and turned to ask Molly how she was, and also to see if she knew anything about the horses.

'Ahh, yes they actually have names. Darby and Joan. And they belong to Old Edie,' Molly said, settling down in a chair at the table. 'She inadvertently adopted them a number of years ago. From what I can remember, they were abandoned in the orchard several years back, when the recession first bit and the upkeep costs of looking after ponies were most likely deemed a luxury that their previous owners couldn't afford.'

'Gosh, I had no idea,' April said, popping a tea bag into each of the mugs.

'Yes, your aunt told me all about it during one of her telephone calls to the shop. Apparently, an apology note was left pinned to the wooden stile. Edie discovered it one morning, alongside a huge hole in the far corner of the orchard's perimeter fencing where two panels had been removed to let the horses in, but then hastily abandoned flat on the grass when the previous owners had seemingly left in a hurry. It's a wonder the horses didn't wander back out into the lane!'

'It sure is.'

'It's become quite a problem over the years, in and around Tindledale and the surrounding villages, with horses being left in fields during the night.' Molly shook her head. 'Here, call the vet.' She grabbed her bag and rummaged around before pulling out an old dog-eared business card. 'He's very good and he'll come out right away to take a look at Darby and Joan. This afternoon most likely, if you explain . . .' Molly handed April the card.

'Thanks Molly, I'll do that right after we've drunk our tea.'

'Good. And what are you up to tomorrow?'

'Sorting out more of the garden and pottering around the cottage, why?'

'I thought I'd take you over to Hettie's House of Haberdashery and introduce you to Hettie to see if she can shed any more light on Winnie's disappearance. I've become quite intrigued myself now,' she laughed.

*

Later, having waved goodbye to Pete, April was going to drive up to the village to pick up something nice for her and Edie's pudding that evening, to have after Molly's pie – a couple of cakes from Kitty's Spotted Pig café perhaps – but just as she opened the door of the Beetle, she heard footsteps on the gravel behind her.

'Hope you're not breaking in to steal that car!' It was Harvey, with a carrier bag in one hand, a muddy black Labrador on a length of rope in the other and a big grin on his face.

'Ha-ha, very funny!' April laughed. 'Can I help you with anything or are you just passing by?' she asked, reaching into her handbag on the car seat to retrieve her sunglasses. The hot July sun was dazzling today.

'I come bearing gifts,' he said, walking towards her. Harvey handed her the carrier bag. 'Early season plums from my fruit farm. Lovely, big, juicy plums!' April took the bag and looked inside. They sure were 'lovely, big, juicy plums' . . . but was Harvey flirting? It seemed like it! April felt her cheeks flush and was grateful to have the Labrador as a distraction. She gave his shiny black head an enthusiastic stroke, managing to avoid the mud, and he repaid the gesture with an affectionate nuzzle against the side of her jeans.

'Thank you,' she said, lifting the carrier bag up a little awkwardly. It was a long time since she had been flirted with and she wasn't entirely sure how it made her feel . . . But before she could analyse further, Harvey moved in close. Close enough for April to catch a whiff of his lemony-fresh scent.

'Fancy a drink with me in the village pub – the Duck & Puddle – one evening? Or dinner. We could have dinner at the new Indian restaurant . . .'

Wow! Now April knew for certain that he was flirting. Well, he sure didn't waste any time. She took a small step backwards.

'Oh, I, um . . .' she paused, taken aback. She fiddled with her hair, feeling so out of practice. And a little bit guilty to be honest. What would Gray think? Just because he was no longer physically here . . . April still felt his presence all around her, and she still loved him. Was still *in* love with him. And Nancy and Freddie, come to think of it, what would they think if their late dad's wife went out for a . . . what was Harvey even offering? *A dinner date?* April smiled and certainly felt flattered, but had no idea if she wanted to go for a drink or have dinner with Harvey or not, so settled on 'I'm not sure' as an answer. But Harvey wasn't fazed in the slightest.

'Well, have a think about it, and let me know when you are sure! No strings. You're a great-looking woman and I'd be a fool not to get my offer in first. Unless Pete's already beaten me to it?' Harvey eyed her curiously before turning his attentions on the dog as he nudged April's hand, wanting another stroke. 'Looks like Oscar has taken a fancy to you too . . .' He laughed.

'Oh, no! Pete is doing . . .' April paused, 'it's nothing like that . . .' She gave Oscar another stroke and then fiddled with the carrier bag feeling even more flattered now as Pete was quite a bit younger than her. She imagined he had his pick of the young, single women for miles around, although Deedee had seemed very coquettish when she had spoken about him, so perhaps Pete did have a thing for older women . . .

'Hmm! I saw he was here tidying up Old Edie's garden.'

'Um, yes, that's right,' April said, quickly focusing her thoughts back on the conversation.

'Has he sorted out the orchards yet?'

'No, just the garden. And the nettles and hedges in the lane.' April hadn't wanted to take advantage of Pete's generosity (he was already doing the work at a discount as a favour to Deedee) and she figured access down the lane to the cottage and the garden was the priority. The orchards could wait.

'Well, I can get the orchards tidied up for you. No problem.' Harvey nodded and smiled, making his eyes crinkle at the corners again and his messy, blond hair flop over his forehead. April thought that he was actually quite attractive, in an earthy, fruity fruit-farmer kind of way, and she hadn't really paid much attention to his physical features during their first encounter. Not really her type. But then she wasn't totally sure what her type was any more.

'Er, thank you!' April willed her cheeks to stop flushing, she could feel the blood pulsing in them now, which was ridiculous she knew, but she certainly hadn't been expecting this when she decided to visit her aunt in the sleepy little village of Tindledale. To be asked out on a date! Besides, it felt far too soon to even be contemplating meeting someone new.

'So, where are you off to?' Harvey asked, quite casually, as if it was an everyday occurrence for him to ask women out on dates . . . on second thoughts, April had an inkling that it probably was. Or maybe that's just how it was out here in the countryside, people cut to the chase, didn't bother with Internet dating and all that malarkey. Nancy would be pleased if she came to visit, as she was always bemoaning the perils of Match and Tinder and suchlike, or grumbling that the men she met at her Northern Soul nights were more interested in the music and their scooters than getting an actual girl-friend. April turned back towards the car to hide her grin. She had to admit, she was flattered by Harvey's audacity.

'Just up to the village – to the café. And then I've got the vet coming this afternoon . . .' she replied, keen to chat about something other than her potential date with the audacious Harvey.

'The vet? What for?' But before April could explain, Harvey carried on talking. 'You wanna watch old Patrick . . . sure knows how to charge, he does! *And a home visit?*' Harvey shook his head and drew in a long sharp breath to indicate that this afternoon could prove very costly indeed. April's heart sank – she had already paid out rather more than she had envisaged on getting the garden and the lane sorted out. Her modest funds were dwindling rapidly.

'Oh, it's not Patrick. It's a new vet . . . Molly said he's very good. And he looks after the horses at the military base on the other side of Market Briar. The dogs too!' April replied brightly, wanting to remain upbeat.

'Ahh, yes I know. But he still works for Patrick. There's only one vet practice around here . . . What's he coming for? Edie doesn't have any pets, does she?'

'Not in the house, she doesn't – he's coming to take a look at the two horses in the orchard. Darby and Joan.'

Harvey laughed. 'Those two old knackers?' He indicated with his head towards the back orchard. 'You'd be better off sending them to the glue factory. Or what about Cooper? Molly's other half. Can't he take them off your hands? Horsemeat is quite something I've heard. Don't they eat it in posh Parisian bistros? You never know, there might be a couple of decent rump steaks left on Darby and Joan's respective backsides.'

April shook her head and rolled her eyes, unsure if Harvey was kidding or not.

'Only joking!' he then confirmed. 'Are they really that bad? Last time I saw them over the back of the orchard by the hedgerow – I was driving past – they looked all right. A bit scruffy but not worth calling the vet out for.'

'Well, they're in a terrible state now. I've been keeping an eye on them every day. But they won't eat any food that I offer them, and I even took some fresh carrots into the orchard, but they only shy away whenever I go near, so I'm worried. They're practically skin and bone and covered in sores.'

'That doesn't sound good at all. Come on. Show me,' Harvey said, sounding concerned now, and wasting no time, he marched off towards the stile with Oscar trotting obediently by his side. 'And I'll talk you through the fruit trees too – depending on the variety, they might be ready to harvest soon . . . you could sell the fruit to pay the extortionate vet bills that are going to be coming your way very soon.'

'Oh, er . . . OK. Thank you,' April replied, grabbing her wellies from the boot of the Beetle, kicking off the Birkenstocks and slipping her feet in, figuring it best to just dash after him. She hadn't even considered the possibility of actually doing something with all the apples and pears . . . so if there was a chance of utilising the fruit to make enough money to help out with the upkeep costs of running Orchard Cottage, then she was definitely keen to give it a go. Aunt Edie would agree too, April was convinced of it: only last night, over what had become a regular routine for them now after dinner – a few rounds of rummy with a snowball or two – Edie had shared her worry over the leak in the thatched roof. A damp patch had appeared on the ceiling above the wardrobe in April's bedroom, Winnie's old room, and April had made the mistake of mentioning it to Edie at the time. Only to ask if it had ever appeared before, but her aunt had said definitely not . . . and they had both come to the conclusion that some of the thatching must have worn away and with the weather having been so warm and dry of late, it hadn't mattered until now. But it had rained yesterday – typical temperamental British weather in summertime – and everyone knew that new roofs cost a small fortune. And April didn't know for sure, but imagined that thatched ones were probably even more costly, requiring a specialist thatcher. But, more worryingly, April knew that her aunt most definitely didn't have the money for a new roof, or even enough to patch it up, so she would need to come up with a plan, especially as the septic tank had already cost a small fortune to replace. And there were the potholes in the lane to think about as well . . .

14

In the orchard, and after Harvey had attempted another bottom-cupping exercise as April went to climb over the stile (she had been prepared this time and swiftly batted his hands away), he let Oscar off the lead. The Labrador darted off, his body wiggling from side to side in excitement at having the whole run of the huge orchard.

'He'll lead us to the horses. Sniff them out, he will. What did you say they're called?' Harvey asked, not even fazed by April's rebuttal.

'Darby and Joan.'

'Ha-ha! Like an old married couple. God help them! Wonder how long they've been saddled together . . .' Harvey shook his head in mock despair. 'Get it? Saddle. Horses.' He shrugged his shoulders and grinned at the joke.

'Hmm, I guess so . . .' April replied, looking at the still-wet grass below her wellies, then added, 'but not all marriages are the proverbial prison sentence, you know . . .'

'If you say so!' he came back with, turning to hold April's eye contact as she looked up. 'Come on, let's follow the dog.' And Harvey actually looped April's arm through his and practically marched her off down to the end of the first row. He was so confident and in a strange way it made April feel rather relaxed . . . in that she didn't need to be in charge at this precise moment. Harvey was making all the decisions, taking the lead and leading her . . . literally. It was nice not to have to be the decision maker for a change. When Gray had been alive and still functioning fully they had made most decisions together – stuff to do with the home, holidays, Nancy and Freddie, as well as everyday things like what takeaway to have on a Saturday night and whether to try some new bulbs in the hanging baskets that summer, etc. But since his decline and ultimate death April had had to do it all alone, and it was draining sometimes, scary too, knowing the buck stopped solely with her now.

Harvey stopped walking and turned to look at April. He twisted a particularly rosy red apple from a nearby tree and bit into it.

'Mmm, it's good. Try it.' And he moved the apple towards April's lips.

'Oh, um . . . sure.' And once again April figured it best to just get on with it. She bit into the apple and then promptly wiped her chin with the back of her hand when the sweet juice inadvertently trickled out from the corner of her mouth as she chewed.

'See?' Harvey said, his eyes twinkling with enthusiasm. April nodded and chewed some more, wishing she hadn't bitten off such an ambitious chunk. She felt self-conscious with Harvey standing so close; she could almost feel his breath on her cheek. But what was more disconcerting was that she found herself quite liking it. It was comforting. To have a man in such close proximity again. And for a split second, as she closed her eyes to blink and look away, it could have been Gray. Close. Warm. And right beside her. 'You're sitting on a gold mine here.'

'Pardon?' April said, in between chews and snapping back to the moment.

'This lot.' Harvey stretched an expansive arm around the orchard. 'There's a bumper crop here. You'll need to get some pickers in to harvest it all, but that's no problem – there's a very efficient team over from Poland at the moment, at another farm I know. Reckon they'd jump at the chance to box this lot up for you before heading home. Need paying of course . . .' And he handed the rest of the apple to April and walked on to another row. Pears this time. Harvey twisted one off and took a bite. 'Perfect too! I know just the man who will rip your arm off for all this fruit.'

'You do?' April was intrigued.

'Yep. He's an organic cider producer. They go mad for it in London apparently, the hipsters. Slap "organic" on the bottle and Bob's your uncle, he says. Ker-ching!' They both laughed. 'I could call him. He'll pay you a fair price . . .' Harvey finished with a flourish.

'Yes please.' April didn't hesitate. She picked another pear and took a bite. 'Mmm, organic pear cider. I bet it tastes delicious.' *And who would have thought it? Aunt Edie has an abundance of fruit, ripe for the picking, literally! And thank goodness she does, as the proceeds from the fruit will make all the difference to the running of Orchard Cottage, and ease her anxiety over the roof and suchlike too. Money worries for a lady in her nineties is just not right.*

'Sure does. I've tried a few complimentary bottles and it was the best cider I've ever tasted.'

'Really?' April was excited at this unexpected turn of events. 'And if there are some apples and pears left over then I could make some jars of apple sauce. Aunt Edie used to be well known around Tindledale for it.' She took another bite. 'And pear chutney. Yes, I'm sure I could make pear chutney!' she finished, really getting into it now. Maybe Kitty would be interested in some chutney for her sandwiches in The Spotted Pig café . . . and how about the Duck & Puddle pub? They'd be bound to get through loads of apple sauce with their Sunday roasts. And Aunt Edie was sure to have the recipe for her fabulous apple sauce somewhere. Or maybe she'd remember it with a bit of luck, she did seem to have a knack for recalling details from far back. They could make the sauce together, just like they used to when April came to visit as a child. And it would keep her aunt occupied, stimulate her, which seemed to have an enormously positive effect. April had noticed how her aunt went downhill very quickly, seemed more forgetful and vague when she had been sitting in front of the TV for any length of time, so wanted to limit her screen hours as much as possible. No wonder some elderly people faded away when they went into a home if all they were doing was watching the telly all day long. And the same thing had almost happened to April in the first few weeks after Gray's death, she had watched far too much TV, finding it cathartic to start with. Meditative almost. Until she became near vegetative – physically and mentally numb from inactivity. It was Nancy who made her get up and get dressed. A fire-fighter's lift all the way upstairs to the bathroom with instructions to not come down until she had showered and put clean clothes on. April felt as though she had come a long way since then.

'But hang on a minute . . . don't I need to get proper certification of the apples' and pears' organic status?' she asked, spotting an immediate flaw in Harvey's ingenious plan, and her heart sank.

'Yes, but that's easily sorted too. You get an inspector in from the Soil Association . . . it'll be fine, I can put you in touch with someone there. These trees have been here for donkey's years. And in their natural state – no pesticides, antibiotics, genetic modification going on here, unless Old Edie has been running around with a spray gun in her spare time?' Harvey raised his eyebrows and pulled a face. April shrugged.

'Not that I know of,' she grinned, her heart lifting again at the prospect of business being back on with the organic cider producer.

'Of course not,' he shrugged.

'But how much will it cost to pay the pickers?' April had no idea, but given the size of the orchard, she envisaged it being a tidy sum; what if her funds weren't enough to cover their wages? Maybe she could get a loan or borrow some money . . . April's mind went into overdrive. Not one to give up easily, she'd find a way to make it happen for her aunt.

'Don't worry about all that. Jimmy – he's the cider producer – will give you a part payment up front. An advance if you like. Or he'll send his own pickers over here.'

'Well, this sounds like a wonderful way to do business. Thank you very much,' April said, feeling very thrilled indeed. Focused and raring to get to work. Turning Aunt Edie's orchards back into a working fruit farm felt like just the thing April needed to utilise her time and indeed her thoughts during the day, and then she could spend her evenings trying to figure out what had happened to Winnie while making sure Edie was happy and looked after. Yes, coming to Tindledale was a tonic, the most perfect recipe to help move her grief for Gray on to a different place in her head and her heart. 'You're very kind.'

'Ahh, call it an apology.'

'Apology?' April creased her forehead.

'You know, that naughty business when you first got here . . . I shouldn't have called you a criminal. Not a very nice welcome to our lovely little village of Tindledale now, is it?' He tilted his head to one side and grinned.

'Oh, it's fine. And funny come to think of it now.' April waved a dismissive hand in the air. 'And it's not my first time here in Tindledale, I spent many happy holidays here as a child.'

'Did you?' Harvey frowned.

'Yes, that's right. Most summers, until I went off to nursing school in London.'

'So you're a proper nurse, eh?'

'Yes, that's right.'

'With a little white uniform and all?' he asked cheekily.

'Stop it!' April quickly told him off. 'You're incorrigible, Harvey,' she laughed.

'Sorry, but you can't blame a guy for trying.' He shrugged and then changed tack. 'So how come we've not met before now?'

'I don't know. Have you always lived in Tindledale?' April asked.

'Ah, that will be why our paths have never crossed . . . I only bought the fruit farm about fifteen years ago. Makes me a relative newcomer compared to the other villagers . . .'

'Ha-ha, yes! I know exactly what you mean. Don't you have to live here for a hundred years or so, and your grandparents before you, to be officially confirmed as a proper Tindledale villager?' April laughed.

'Yep, something like that.' He shook his head and grinned. 'So why did you stop coming to Tindledale? I've not ever seen you here and I know I would remember spotting you in the High Street or in the pub.' He winked and April shook her head, finding herself enjoying his harmless flirtation.

'Well, I did still visit my aunt when I could, and I wrote to her regularly, and then . . . well, I guess life took over.' April busied herself with picking a leaf from a nearby tree and studying it. She knew full well what

171

Harvey was really asking, but she had chosen to omit the part about Gray being ill and circumstances making it more difficult to come to Tindledale. It was nice though, to feel normal, to not have to explain, or to talk about death and grief and all the sad stuff. Surely there was nothing wrong with wanting to move on from that? If only for the pocket of time she was spending with Harvey today. He was a new friend, admittedly one that wanted their friendship to be more, but for now, April was enjoying being 'just April, the nurse visiting her elderly aunt' and not 'April, you know (nudge nudge) . . . the one whose husband died of motor neurone disease, poor cow, and so young he was too, barely fifty, that's no age at all', as she had overheard one time on her way out of the library when she went to return Gray's books shortly after his death – he'd been two-thirds of the way through reading one of them when he died. The poignancy of Gray never knowing the book's ending had made April sob in bed, alone, for most of the previous night. And then again the following afternoon in the safety of her Beetle when she had made it back to the car park after that awful trip to the library.

April folded the leaf in half before absent-mindedly slipping it into her jeans pocket and shook her hair back as if to clear her mind.

'To be honest, Harvey, I'm actually pleased that you did apprehend me . . .' she said. 'It's nice to know my aunt has neighbours that actually care. Where I come from, I'm not entirely sure anyone would bat an eyelid if they had seen me trying to smash a window with a mud-covered Birkenstock that could very easily have been mistaken for a brick.'

'Blimey!' Harvey shook his head and pulled a face of disbelief.

And they carried on walking.

As they turned at the end of the row and walked down in between the next row of apple trees, Oscar came bounding back to them with what looked like a green baseball cap in his mouth.

'Hold up!' Harvey stopped striding and let go of April's arm. 'Stay there,' he quickly instructed, taking a step forward and sticking a chivalrous arm out in front of April as if to protect her. 'I'll deal with this.'

'What is it?' she asked, ignoring his command and stepping forward too.

'Nothing for you to worry about . . .'

'Oh don't be daft. Tell me . . . it can't be that bad,' she said, tactfully removing his arm. Just because she had relaxed for a brief moment and let him take charge, and enjoyed doing so, it didn't mean she was now a feeble damsel and couldn't look after herself.

'Well, all right then . . . there might be someone here. A poacher or something. Bloody typical I didn't bring my shotgun with me . . .' he said, picking up the hat after ordering Oscar to drop it.

'But you can't just shoot them!'

'True!' Harvey had his hands on his hips now and an outraged look on his face. 'But I can give them a blooming good scare. Flaming trespassers! In fact, I bet it's a rambler. Or one of those fake new-age hippy types with their pretend dreadlocks and rainbow-coloured jackets made from hemp seed or whatever.'

'What do you mean fake?' April tried not to smile.

'You know, aristocrats who try to live in trees and shit,' Harvey puffed, 'they're the worst with their "right of way" bollocks.' He did sarcastic quote signs in the air and pulled a face. 'Don't want to know though when it comes to forking out to fix broken gates or clear fallen trees from the public footpaths, oh no! But somebody has to pay for all that. Muggins, that's who, as the council rarely coughs up.' April swiftly looked away so he wouldn't see her desperately trying not to laugh. He really was a 'wade in first and think later' kind of guy, and set in his ways, and it was amusing . . . She could tell that he wasn't really angry, just disgruntled, which made it even more comical as he went to storm off in search of the poor ramblers with the rainbow-coloured jackets. April had always thought they looked rather cheerful. 'Come on, let's find 'em.'

April went after him, figuring she may need to step in to defuse the situation if he got too irate.

'How are we going to do that?' she called out, already lagging behind. Harvey sure could walk fast.

'By sniffing them out of course.' He pointed to Oscar who was spinning round in circles with excited anticipation just waiting for the 'find' command. Harvey stopped walking. He bent down and held the hat at Oscar's nose. The dog nudged his nose into it, drawing in the scent, while all the time listening for Harvey to click his fingers to signify the start of the search. When it came, Oscar shot off at full pelt and Harvey immediately ran after him, with April doing her best to bring up the rear.

Half a mile later, or so it seemed, of weaving in and out of the rows of trees, April felt as though her chest might burst open from sheer exertion. She really did need to get back to the gym – she hadn't been in over a year and it most definitely showed. She could barely breathe and there was a stinging stitch-like pain in her left side, which never would have happened when she was doing regular Pilates and spin classes. She made a mental note to make a concerted effort to do some proper exercise while she was here and then see about going back to the gym when she went home.

'Shuuuuuush.' Harvey looked back at her over his shoulder after stopping abruptly. April almost fell into him as she came to a sudden halt. Oscar was sitting on the grass beside another wooden stile surrounded by head-height brambles leading into what looked like another orchard, and swishing his tail from side to side with a very gleeful look on his face.

'What is it?' April whispered.

'He's found something . . .'

April followed Harvey towards the stile. Oscar leapt up on to all four paws and then hunched down and practically commando-styled his way underneath the stile, before sitting again in the grass and staring intently at Harvey, who took a step up, and after bashing the brambles out of the way, was just about to climb over the stile when he looked up and promptly stopped.

Silence.

Then.

'FLAAAMING HELL.'

'What? What is it?' April pulled herself up on to the stile and then leant around Harvey to get a good look.

And gasped.

'WOW!'

There was an old wooden gypsy wagon in the field. And part of the arched roof was covered in glorious striped yellow-and-orange knitting! Yarnbombed. And it was beautiful. And April couldn't wait to take a closer look, having always wanted to go inside a proper gypsy wagon, ever since watching *The Diddakoi* on the telly as a child.

'What are you doing?' Harvey's face was a picture.

'Going in to take a look of course.' April beamed. Harvey gave her a sideways look of incredulity. And then he was outraged all over again.

'Are you mad?' he expostulated. 'I'll call Mark. He knows how to deal with squatters!' And Harvey went to pull out his walkie-talkie. 'It's one thing abandoning horses in fields but moving your whole gaff in is a bloody liberty.' He was off on one again . . .

'Oh don't be ridiculous.' And April hopped down off the stile and walked over to the wagon, keen to see inside.

15

After stepping up the little wooden ladder propped outside the gypsy wagon, April was just about to duck down to go through the arched entrance when a figure in a green hoodie and black jeans shoved her sharply aside – April landed face first in the alcove seated area – and then leapt over the ladder, landed on the grass and went to run off.

'OH NO YOU DON'T. COME 'ERE!' Harvey hollered, rugby-tackling the person to the ground. A yelp resonated around the field.

'Get off me. You're hurting me!'

Harvey grabbed the person's wrists and attempted to wrestle them into submission. April hurried down the ladder and darted forward to intervene. The person pinned underneath him on the grass was a young girl of about thirteen, with a petrified look in her eyes.

'Harvey stop it! That's enough. YOU'LL HURT HER,' April yelled, yanking his shirt.

'*Her?*' Harvey immediately stopped wrestling and leapt to his feet.

'Yes. *Her!* Didn't you hear the girl screaming?' April admonished, helping the girl up and giving her a cuddle.

'Poor thing is terrified and is it any wonder with you going in so gung ho again? You're damn lucky Mark isn't here or it would be you facing arrest right now for attacking and scaring the living daylights out of a teenage girl.'

'I, er . . . Jesus! I didn't realise.' And to give him his due, Harvey did look horrified as he pushed a shaky hand through his hair. 'I'm really sorry, I . . . um . . .' He stopped talking.

'What's the matter?' April looked first at the girl and then at Harvey.

'Please don't tell my dad, he'll go mental.' The girl went to bolt again, but April took charge this time and managed to get her hand and hold on to it.

'Hey, it's OK,' April soothed, putting her hand on the girl's back. She was horrified to feel her thin frame trembling all over. 'Surely it's not that bad . . . look, why don't we all calm down and see if we can sort this out.'

Harvey and the girl exchanged glances, and then he nodded his support for April's suggestion.

'Fine by me. But your dad will be worried, love . . . Why aren't you at school?' he asked the girl, and April was surprised by the tenderness in his voice. Harvey then turned his face to April and said, 'This is my mate's girl. Bella.' He shook his head, concern etched on his face.

'I came to see the horses! That's all. Nobody cares about them and they're hungry . . . and ill. What if they die?' Bella was crying now as she stared at the grass curled around her trainers.

'That's OK,' April said brightly, 'and that's why we are

here too. I've got a vet coming later to take a look at poor Darby and Joan . . . you see, we do care.'

'Then how come you've let them get so bad?' Bella accused.

'Well, I didn't know about them until recently . . . and my great aunt – this is her orchard – she's getting forgetful and things have got on top of her a bit . . .' April's voice faded under the furious teenager's scrutiny.

'Look, Bella, you really shouldn't be here on your own, it's not safe,' Harvey walked towards the wagon. 'Could be an axe murderer hiding in here.' He put his hand on the side of the wagon. 'Have they hurt you?' Harvey pulled out his walkie-talkie, not even waiting for an answer from Bella. 'Right, that is it! I'm calling your dad.'

'No, please don't. Nobody else comes here. Only me. The wagon was empty when I first found it. I swear,' Bella cried. 'I didn't do anything wrong.'

'Then how do you explain the giant . . . er . . .' Harvey paused, searching for a suitable word, '*jumper* that's draped all over the roof?' and he grabbed a corner of the knitting and gave it a good tug. 'Ahh, I bet there's one of those hippies in here, isn't there?' He stomped up the wooden ladder and went inside.

Bella was full on sobbing now.

'No. There isn't. There's nobody in there. Only me. I did it!' she stammered in between sobs. 'I like knitting and wanted the wagon to look nice. I've cleaned it inside too, and I . . .' She stopped talking and buried her head into April's shoulder.

April felt baffled and utterly in awe of the young girl

and the marvellous yarnbomb. It really was an achievement. But what on earth was going on in her life that made her want to hide out in a decrepit old gypsy wagon in Aunt Edie's orchard?

'Come on. Let's see if we can find the horses and then you can tell me all about it,' she said, letting go of Bella and giving her a cheery smile. 'Here, wipe those tears away. It's going to be fine.' April handed Bella a clean tissue from her jeans pocket. 'You're not in trouble. And I think a yarnbombed gypsy wagon in my aunt's orchard is a wonderful thing.' April gave Harvey a surreptitious look as if to say, 'Probably best if I handle this situation from here on after the blithering mess you've made of it so far, so make yourself scarce for a bit.' He immediately got the hint, a look of relief spreading all over his face, and wandered off in the opposite direction.

April had managed to calm Bella down enough to walk for ten minutes or so with her telling April that she had decorated the inside of the wagon too, with new flowery printed seat covers using some old fabric she had bought from a charity shop in Market Briar, and had been busy knitting the next section of the yarn-bombed roof when they had discovered her. Seemed Bella liked spending time in the wagon most afternoons when she should have been busy learning lots at school . . .

'I hate everyone at school, and they all hate me,' Bella blurted out as if she couldn't keep it inside herself any longer, all the while sniffing and wiping her nose with the tissue that April had given her.

'Oh dear, I'm so sorry to hear that,' April said gently,

conscious of saying the wrong thing, and rather taken aback by the girl's desperation to tell her all about it. In the short time they had been talking, Bella seemed so volatile and anxious – almost as if she was in a constant state of hyper-alert, continuously looking for signs of danger – things, or people, that might hurt her. April's heart went out to her, what a sad existence for such a young girl. But she seemed to want to talk, to open up . . . maybe because April was a stranger, it was easier for her, but whatever it was, April figured it best that she just let the girl tell her what was troubling her.

'The other girls are such idiots with their make-up and big hair and rolled-over skirts and smartphones. And the boys are disgusting . . . you know one of them went to grab me down there . . .' Bella motioned with her head towards her pelvis. 'It was in the sports field. When nobody was looking. And I decked him. But then I got suspended when he told the Head of Year that the split lip I gave him was totally unprovoked. They took his word over mine 'cos he's a prefect and so they be-lieved him.'

'But that's shocking! Isn't there anyone . . .' April paused to pick the right words as she was now raging inside on Bella's behalf. The poor girl was clearly desper-ately unhappy from being bullied at school. No wonder she came here to the orchard to escape from it all – school kids could be so cruel. '. . . That you like at the school?'

'No. Would you, if they slut-shamed you on social media?' Bella blurted out, before scrubbing the tears away again.

'Um, er . . . no, I'm pretty certain I wouldn't,' April started, shocked by her outburst, and not entirely sure what 'slut-shaming' was, but she could hazard a guess and now felt a mixture of anger and utter hopelessness on Bella's behalf. 'And what does your mum say about it all?'

'Nothing. She's gone. And I answered the email from school to my dad, before he even saw it. I deleted it right after of course, I'm not totally dumb,' Bella said in a monotone matter-of-fact voice, as if she regularly managed this kind of stuff for herself and it was really no big deal.

'Oh dear. And your dad? Have you talked to him about school? Told him what's going on? I could chat to him for you, or be with you when you explain, if you like. It might help to have . . .' April offered tentatively, conscious of not wanting to be seen as interfering in matters that were none of her business, but she couldn't just stand by and do nothing. And Bella had been hiding out in her aunt's orchard, and had chosen, for whatever reason, to confide in her so that made April involved, whether she wanted to be or not.

They had reached the far corner of the orchard where a hedge separated it from the lane on the other side, when Harvey reappeared.

'I'm sorry, Bella. But your dad would never forgive me if I didn't . . .' And before he could finish, a vehicle screeched to a halt in the lane. With the engine still running, the door slammed and someone practically hurdled over the hedge and into the field, landing with a giant thud on the grass in front of April and Bella.

Matt.

It was the guy driving the Only Shoes and Horses van. The one with the romantic gypsy curls and the mesmerising eyes and very few words. The man who had helped April when she had lost her way.

'But why?' Bella yelled, and instantly went to bolt again, but it was Matt who caught her this time.

After wrapping his arms around Bella and pulling her in close to him, he then gently pushed her to the ground and sat down beside her keeping one arm, firmly but tenderly, around her shoulders.

'What's going on, sweetheart? Harvey here says you've been hiding in the field . . .' Matt's voice was soft and kind and April was about to walk away, not wanting to intrude on their father–daughter time, when Bella sprang back up and stood adjacent to her.

'No I haven't.'

'Then what are you doing here? Why aren't you at school, Bells?'

'Don't call me that!' Bella folded her arms and kicked the toe of her left trainer into an extra-tufty clump of grass, over and over. Matt stood up, unfazed, or so he appeared on first glance, but April spotted the vein pulsing at the side of his neck and the now underlying look of fear in those intoxicating eyes.

'Sorry,' he said, and April bit her bottom lip, unsure of what to do. She felt so sad for them both. Matt looked crushed, with his shoulders sagged and his head bowed, as if he was carrying the whole weight of the world. And Bella was doing a wonderful job of being furious to cover the excruciating pain that she was enduring. And

Harvey was no use; he was fiddling with his walkie-talkie, pretending to be trying to switch it off or whatever, clearly out of his depth, or oblivious, or most likely both, when it came to handling sensitive situations.

'She knows!' Bella blurted furiously.

'Who does?' Matt asked.

'Her.' Bella indicated sideways with her left thumb. And April felt them looking at her, including Harvey. Even Oscar stopped pottering around in the grass and stood squarely in front of April with his little furry head tilted to one side as if to say, '*Come on then, tell us all what you know.*'

'Oh, I, um . . .' April started, desperately trying to gauge whether Matt was going to be OK with his teenage daughter opening up to a complete stranger when she had clearly kept him in the dark. 'Well, we chatted, that's all. I found Bella in the wagon . . . which is no problem at all by the way, she's very welcome to come here any time. Well, not during the school day obviously, that's not what I meant, I'm not encouraging . . .' April stopped talking, cleared her throat and then started again, cutting to the chase. Now was not the time to babble on offering niceties; Bella needed her help. 'What I meant was, that Bella was telling me about school, about the bullying and—'

'Bullying?' Matt interjected, running a hand through his curls. And then, 'Why didn't you tell me?' in a far quieter voice, and April saw his shoulders sag some more, if that was even possible.

'Because you don't understand . . . you never listen.

All you do is tell me what to do. I hate you,' Bella screamed. Silence followed. April looked at Bella and then at Matt, his green eyes several shades darker now, or so it seemed, and fixed intensely on April like a laser, with a mixture of bewilderment and fury. April held eye contact until she could bear it no longer, feeling slightly dizzy on realising that she was holding her breath. She drew in an enormous gulp of air before exhaling hard. It was extraordinary the effect Matt was having on her.

'I guess it's just easier sometimes to chat to a stranger,' April offered. Matt blinked and went to speak, but Bella bolted again. And this time she ran so fast and hard that neither Harvey, Matt or indeed April were quick enough to catch her. The three adults looked at each other.

'I need to go after her,' Matt said, and went to go, but then hesitated. He looked back at April. 'You were lost,' he nodded, locking his emerald-green eyes on to her again. A moment's silence. April opened her mouth to reply, but hesitated too. Harvey leapt in as always, striding towards April to stand alongside her and opposite Matt as if they were a team, together in agreement. But before April could speak, Harvey jumped in.

'Yes! Matt, you should go after her.' And he slapped Matt on the arm as if to pack him off right away. Matt looked at Harvey and then at April. He seemed to want to say more to her, but stayed silent, and then, just as he had in the van, he appeared to refocus.

'Er, yes. Yes I should.' And he ran off. 'OK if I come back later to sort things out? Repair any damage, that kind of thing . . .' he then called out over his shoulder.

Harvey went to reply, but April gently but firmly touched his arm as if to say, 'He's talking to me, thank you very much.'

'Yes, of course. Any time. No damage in any case. As I said, Bella is welcome here whenever she likes, it'll be school summer holidays soon . . .' April called out and Matt waved a hand up in the air to signal his thanks.

As soon as Matt was out of earshot, April turned to face Harvey square on.

'What did you do that for?'

'*Whaaaat?*' He feigned ignorance.

'You know very well what. Tell her dad she was here. Bella was talking to me about all her problems. How she comes here to escape. That her mum isn't around. And my guess is that she doesn't have many people to confide in, poor girl. Why else would she talk to me, a complete stranger? She's desperately lonely, and is being bullied at school,' April said. 'And now she's in trouble with her dad too.'

'Ahh, Matt will sort it out. We go back years. He's my pal and he's had it tough with the girl, bringing her up on his own since the missus buggered off without so much as a goodbye. A single dad. But he does his best. Bella is a handful. Like most teenagers.'

'She seemed lovely to me. Kind and creative. She was genuinely concerned for the horses and the knitting was amazing. She's having a very tough time . . . so is it any wonder she's angry?' April said, instinctively protective of the girl she had just met, who had reminded her of herself a bit as a young teenager. Sixteen, her parents had gone, she was living in a new town up north where nobody talked like her, she had been going to a new college where the other teenagers hadn't particularly welcomed her into their established friendship groups . . . Yes, April knew how it felt to be lonely, the odd one out that didn't fit in. And had then had to deal with the same thing all over again when she had moved to the hospital in London, and then Basingstoke as part of her nurse training.

'Maybe so. But she can't be staying in a gypsy wagon in the middle of a field. It's not right. What if something had happened to her and Matt didn't even know where she was?' Harvey shook his head vehemently. 'Nah, I for one wasn't taking a chance. Don't want that on my conscience. He's my pal and he had a right to know.'

'Well, I guess it could be a bit dangerous . . .' April agreed. She knew that practically it wasn't a feasible thing for a thirteen year old to be doing, hiding out in a gypsy wagon, but secretly thought it seemed like a wonderfully romantic adventure and one that she would have loved to have experienced as a teenage girl. Though under happier circumstances than Bella was going through, of course.

'Let them sort it out. Trust me, you don't want to be getting involved,' Harvey added. 'Come on, what time is that vet of yours arriving? Don't want to keep him waiting . . . time is money and all that. Old Patrick will be rubbing his hands together in glee at this rate.'

16

Back home, and Bella had barely said a word in the van on the way and had now stomped off upstairs to her bedroom, which was nothing new. She had been like this for months now, withdrawn and sullen and touchy over the slightest thing. Hormones, his mother had said. And periods had a lot to answer for as far as Matt was concerned; his little girl had changed almost overnight when they had kicked in, and it scared the hell out of him.

Matt went straight into the kitchen and flicked the kettle on to make himself a coffee. On second thoughts, sod that, he needed something stronger. So after pulling open the fridge and locating a bottle of fancy cider that Harvey had given him, Matt pulled the cork out with his teeth and took a big swig. Ugh, it tasted like sweet shandy. Matt marvelled at the idiots who paid over the odds for this stuff as he tipped the liquid down the plughole in the kitchen sink. Moving into the lounge, he opened the cabinet and poured himself a whisky instead. This was more like it. He downed the single measure in one, and went to pour another, but stopped, hand in mid-air. *What was going on?* Matt lifted a dusty old bottle of Asti

Spumante out of the cupboard and saw that it was nearly empty! He hated Asti, so who had drunk it? And three guesses, he knew. Matt looked up at the ceiling and shook his head, wondering if he should go up there and confront her. Bella, his little girl. Only she wasn't his little girl any more. And she hated him! She was growing up fast and he had been doing his best to keep up. And what was all that about earlier? How come he didn't know she was being bullied? And how come she'd told April Lovell . . . of all people? And what was Harvey playing at? Muscling in on April like that. There was something going on between them – Harvey couldn't wait to get rid of him earlier, which was bang out of order given his track record, but so typical of him, he just couldn't help himself.

Matt took a deep breath and puffed out his cheeks as he inhaled, wondering how everything had changed so much. Bella had been such a sweet, lovely little girl, a daddy's girl some might say, which had made it easier in a way for his ex, Zoe, to abandon her . . . he guessed. Of course, none of it was Bella's fault things had gone wrong in their marriage, no the cracks had been there long before Bella came along. He and Zoe had been kids themselves when they got together just a few years after that lovely summer he had with April. And they had been happy for a long time . . . until Zoe was pregnant – because unlike him, she hadn't been over the moon at the prospect of being a parent. She'd always had a wild, rebellious streak, and had felt stifled being a mum. Ruined her life, she had said, having no freedom, and she'd felt trapped and angry with Matt as he'd always wanted to be a dad. And then when Bella was a toddler, the flings had started, the staying out all night, drinking, clubbing weekends up in London with her mates who weren't 'saddled with a baby'. He'd tried to make the marriage work for Bella's sake, sometimes turning a blind eye to Zoe's antics, but in the end a child together just hadn't been enough.

After pouring more whisky, Matt swirled it around the glass and let his mind mess with his head for a bit, wondering how things might have turned out if he had gone on to date April, properly got together with her instead. She'd taken his breath away the other day by the roadside, and then this afternoon in the orchard, with her hair all loose around her shoulders and her cheeks flushed from being outside in the country air. He hadn't dared to look at her in case he couldn't tear his eyes away again. And she had looked so concerned for Bella, kind and comforting, and quite possibly a miracle worker, seeing as Bella had actually talked to her, confided in her – which was more than he had managed to do with his own daughter in absolutely bloody ages.

Matt stood up, resolute. He'd go upstairs and try again. He'd never give up on Bella, he loved her more than life itself, but he was worried. What if she took after her mother? These signs of rebellion – bunking off and hiding out in a gypsy wagon – weren't good. And what next? He eyed the bottle of Asti that he'd put on the coffee table. Drunken tattoos after clubbing weekends in London, like Zoe? *Choose Life*. Only the tattooist must have been dyslexic as Zoe had ended up with *Choose Live* wrapped around her bicep. No, he needed to look after Bella, try to be a better dad, and somehow fill the gap created by her missing mum too.

After tipping the last of the Asti away, and dumping the bottle in the recycling box, figuring the matter was best left alone in the current circumstances – he didn't want to put even more distance between him and Bella by bawling her out over helping herself to the fizzy wine – Matt walked upstairs and tapped on his daughter's bedroom door.

'Come in,' Bella said after keeping him waiting for a good few minutes.

'Chicken curry for tea?' he said to break the ice, knowing it was her favourite, as he stuck his head round the door. Bella was sitting cross-legged on her bed, knitting, her face all blotchy from crying. And there was a small mountain of balled-up loo roll piled up on the carpet. But she managed a nod.

'Garlic naan bread?' she asked, not looking up.

'Onion bhaji,' Matt ventured, wondering if she was up for the silly old game they had played ever since he'd taken her for her first curry night at the Indian restaurant in Market Briar. It had been his birthday and Bella had only been about eight at the time, but the babysitter had cancelled at the last minute so there was nothing else for it. Bella had joined him, Harvey and few of the other blokes for a slap-up Indian banquet. They didn't have to go so far now though, since the new curry house had opened overlooking the village green, which was a result, as they did a cracking balti including naan bread for a lot cheaper than the old place.

'Pilau rice,' Bella said solemnly, clicking her needles together as she carried on knitting, pretending not to be properly interested, but he persevered.

'Poppadums.'

'Prawn puri.'

'Sag alooooooo,' he said in the obligatory daft voice and was sure he spotted the start of a smile at the corner of her lips. And then.

'Yuk!' they said in unison, both sticking their fingers in their mouths to imitate a gagging noise before laughing. Matt let out a sigh of relief as he sat on Bella's bed beside her.

'So, you going to tell me what's been going on before I go and get the grub?' Matt started, carefully moving a ball of bright red wool out of the way, knowing it would be more than his life was worth if he accidentally sat on it and squashed it.

Silence followed.

Matt waited.

'Nothing,' Bella huffed the word out in a sigh.

'OK, how about we start with the gypsy wagon. How did you find it?' Matt asked, mustering up as much patience as he possibly could, knowing if he pushed her she'd shut right down and most likely shout at him, or worse still, call him a selfish pig . . . That's what happened last time, when he had refused to give her a fiver to buy sweets, which it turned out a few days later was actually so she could get some sanitary towels, only she hadn't wanted to tell him, because, 'You just *don't* get it,' she had yelled when he caught her rifling through his wallet. Since then, Matt had set her up with an allowance . . . twenty quid, left on the kitchen table once a month to buy whatever personal stuff she needed. The rest she could earn like everyone else, doing chores around the house and suchlike. He had thought he was doing his best, but apparently *all* of the other kids got at least double that amount for doing abso-lutely bugger all! He wondered if he'd ever get it right . . .

'I dunno.' She shrugged.

'How about I tell you how I found the wagon then!' Matt said, trying to hide the weariness from his voice.

'Well, I know already. That *grass*,' she paused for maximum emphasis, 'Harvey. He told you where it was!'

'Not today,' Matt said, marshalling the patience of a saint. 'I'm talking about years ago when I was a kid, much younger than you are now.'

'What do you mean?' Bella's interest was piqued.

'The wagon has been there for donkey's years . . .' Matt started slowly, pleased to have found a hook to engage his daughter, it was a start at least. And first thing tomorrow morning he'd phone the school and find out the rest. And then he'd hunt down the little shits that were bullying his girl and clump them one . . . Just joking, Matt knew he'd never really do that, but it sure did make him feel better to fantasise about doing so. 'Me and Uncle Jack used to go to the orchard after school and dare each other to run through the apple and pear trees and go inside the wagon, but we always chickened out and went to the woods instead.'

'Wimps!' Bella sniffed, not missing a beat.

'Fair enough. Not like you though, eh? Fearless. Practically setting up home inside it.' Matt did a half smile. 'Tell me something . . .' He paused and ran a hand over his stubbly chin.

'What's that then?'

'When were you going to half-inch the sofa so you could properly kit it out? And do I need to keep an eye on the fridge? And what about the TV, I'll be gutted if that goes . . . I don't want to miss the cricket, or the rugby, or that new car programme. Please tell me you won't make me.' Matt shook his head and held it in his hands in mock desperation, risking a peek between his thumb and index finger to see her reaction.

'Daaaaaaad!' Bella clearly couldn't help herself any longer, and started laughing, nudging Matt with her arm. 'You're such a tool.'

'Now, that is charming.' Matt pretended to be put out, but inside he felt relieved that she was talking to him, having a joke at least. He wasn't stupid though, he knew this was just the start, but if he could maintain it somehow, then maybe he could keep her close. Because if the truth be told, he was petrified of losing her, of the bond they had breaking for ever; he couldn't handle that. Or what if she upped and went off to the bright lights of London like her mother had? It didn't bear thinking about. 'Seriously though, love, you can't be bunking off school and hiding out in an orchard . . .' Matt ventured.

'Why not?'

'Because you won't learn anything for starters, and then where will you be?'

'But I already know how to read and write . . .'

Matt grinned and shook his head, wondering what to say to that. 'It's not as easy as all that, Bells . . .' his daughter glared at him, 'sorry, *Bella*.'

'But April said I can go to the wagon whenever I like . . .' Bella said, studying him, as if gauging his reaction, daring, or was it pleading? He couldn't tell, but either way, she just wanted him to agree.

'Not during school time though. I'll be in trouble if you don't go to school. And there's only a week or so before the holidays start so you can go then.'

'Please don't make me go back to school!' Bella's voice faltered and Matt instinctively pulled her into him for a cuddle, but was then shocked again by how bony she was – he'd noticed it in the orchard earlier too. Oh God. He suddenly felt seriously out of his depth. His mum helped out when she could, with advice, but it wasn't easy with her living in Wales – she'd moved there years ago, before Zoe left, and had offered to come back to Tindledale to help Matt with Bella, but like an idiot he had said he'd be fine. He hadn't wanted to uproot her, and if truth be told, he'd been stubborn too . . . wanting to prove he could be a good parent on his own. But now look at the mess he'd made of it. His daughter was wasting away before his eyes and he hadn't even noticed. What if she was starving herself on purpose, dieting, and all that rubbish? Zoe had always been on a diet, complaining that her stomach or thighs were too big, when they looked perfectly fine to him.

Matt stood up and shoved his hands into his jean pockets, determined to go and get the biggest curry he could find, and with all the trimmings. Sod diets, he wasn't having his daughter getting hooked into all that money-making, brainwashing bullshit those slimming companies spewed out. And those glossy magazines would have to go, too, with their airbrushed pictures making Bella think it was normal to look like you'd had your innards sucked out.

'You have to go to school, love. I'm sorry, but we'll get it sorted, I promise . . .'

'Just tomorrow then? Can I stay at home? Or come to work with you? I can help with the horses . . . *please* Dad.' Bella looked at him, motionless, her knitting hanging from the needles as if waiting for an answer too.

Matt hesitated. He could take a day off, he only had one job on, a shoe-fitting for a mare over in Market Briar, but he'd known Howard, the horse's owner, for years, so he was sure he wouldn't mind pushing it back a day. And he'd need to call the school, go down there even, and that might take ages to sort out, and surely one day wouldn't hurt . . . it might be an opportunity for him to spend some time with her and really get to the bottom of it all.

'Oh go on then!'

Bella threw her knitting down and leapt from the bed to fling her arms around Matt, nearly winding him, just as she had used to do when she was much younger.

'Brilliant. And can we go to see April? I should say sorry, I guess . . .'

'Um.' Matt inhaled; he hadn't figured this into the 'day off school' deal. 'Maybe,' he settled on.

'That means yes! I'm going to take a big bag of grated carrots for the horses, they won't eat anything else, Dad. And you can say hello to April . . . she's sooooo nice.'

'Ahh, here we are!' Molly said. 'Just park by the lamppost.'

April looked to her left and saw an old, ramshackle wooden bus shelter, but where was the haberdashery shop?

And then she saw it. On the other side of the bus shelter was the sweetest little yarn store that April had ever seen. With 'Hettie's House of Haberdashery' in swirly gold lettering on a French-navy background above the door, it was set back from the road with a white picket fence leading up to the double-fronted shop attached to an oast house with a roundel at the far end. It was picturesque. A quintessential chocolate-box scene.

'Oh, it's amazing,' April said, switching off the Beetle's engine.

'Come on, wait until you see inside,' Molly grinned, grabbing a large flowery tote from the footwell. April was pleased that the ferret, which it turned out was aptly called Stinker, had been left at home in his cage. Molly's youngest boy had come up with the name, she had told April on the drive over here.

After locking the door, April followed Molly up to the

entrance of the shop, keen to get inside. The window display was amazing, a yarnbombed armchair next to a pile of cot mattresses draped in granny-patch blankets in a variety of bold, primary colours, one with a plump green pea balanced under an upturned corner, and all topped off with a knitted princess doll. Ahh, April got it! It was the Hans Christian Andersen fairytale, 'The Princess and the Pea'. Marvellous. April had loved that story as a child. In fact, Aunt Edie had first introduced April to it after giving her a colourful hardback edition for her birthday. And April had treasured it. In fact, she was pretty certain she still had it somewhere at home in the loft. She filed a quick memo in her head to take a look when she went home.

Molly pushed open the door and April smiled on hearing the old-fashioned jangle of the bell. It was so cosy and welcoming, like stepping inside an olde worlde sweet shop as a child, which on looking around at the numerous display shelves housing the most exquisite mountains of multi-coloured yarn, was much the same feeling that April was experiencing now as an adult. This place was incredible. An Aladdin's cave of crafting goodies. And her friends from the knitting group back home would love it. April wondered if it would be OK to take a picture to show them, so rummaged in her bag to locate her mobile.

'Come in, come in. So lovely to meet you, April. Molly mentioned that you might be joining us for this afternoon's knit and natter group.' A woman with red curly hair and a warm smile came walking towards them and held out her hand to April. 'I'm Sybs by the way.'

'Oh, um, hi Sybs.' April stopped rummaging and shook Sybs' hand, and then suddenly felt panicky. She hadn't realised. She thought they were just popping in to talk to Hettie. She didn't know if she could knit again. Not yet. What if she cried? Like she had the last time she picked up her unfinished project – a chunky Aran jumper for Gray, the one he had teased her over with the size 12 needles. The one she hadn't finished in time for him to actually wear. And for an awful moment, April could feel her chin wobbling. She swallowed hard to stave off the tears that were pricking the corners of her eyes. Not now. But more importantly, why now? This precise moment when she felt so upbeat, happy to be here in this lovely little haberdashery shop. And it was well over a year. Eighteen months and . . . April wasn't sure. And then it struck her . . . when had she last updated her diary? Crossed off another day since Gray had died? She didn't know. Certainly not since she had arrived at Orchard Cottage. No, her morning routine was different here. Now it was all about getting up and putting the kettle on the Aga to boil before pulling on her wellies to wander outside to fetch fresh eggs for their breakfast. And she hadn't even realised . . . Something had definitely shifted if she was no longer making the 'diary of doom' (as she sometimes felt about it) her focal exercise every morning. And April felt lighter for it. Calm. As if she had reached another milestone.

She took a big breath, put a smile on her face and came up with a quick excuse, because even though she had reached a significant milestone, she wasn't entirely sure if she was ready to face another one head on just yet. Knitting. April's friends from her knitting club had been very kind in visiting and keeping in touch since Gray's death, but she hadn't actually been out to the meetings, to knit in a group . . . or knitted at all, for that matter.

'Oh, I didn't realise. I haven't got my knitting bag with me.'

'No problem. I'm sure we can find you some spare wool and needles,' Sybs laughed and cast a generous hand around the shop before adding, 'take your pick.' Molly, on seeing April's discomfort, promptly intervened.

'Actually, you know . . . I'm not sure we have enough time to stay for the whole session, Sybs. I promised Cooper I'd get back to help with a big order for the Blackwood Farm Estate.' She grinned apologetically before giving April a surreptitious look. April returned the look with a grateful, but pensive smile.

'Ahh, so it's all Marigold's fault!' Sybs winked, and an older woman sitting in an armchair looked up from her knitting.

'What have I done now?' she frowned and did a very hearty laugh.

'Nothing. Only teasing,' Sybs said, and Marigold went back to her knitting while Molly quickly explained to April that Marigold and her husband owned the Blackwood Farm Estate.

'Ahh, I see,' April replied, feeling a little foolish now that Molly had covered for her, not to mention a bit mean as Molly was going to miss her knit and natter session now, and Marigold had inadvertently got the blame. Oh dear! Maybe it would be all right to try knitting again after all. If she made a concerted effort to put positive thoughts inside her head, fresh new ones with the group of women here in Hettie's House of Haberdashery and not get maudlin remembering the association that knitting used to hold with Gray . . . April looked around at all the different beautiful yarns and thought it was a shame to not at least buy a new pattern and some needles and wool . . . seeing as she was here. Then, she could see how she felt later, in the safety of her bedroom, Winnie's old room – which reminded her. 'I was really hoping to have a chat to Hettie please, if she's around?' April looked around the shop, but most of the women sitting on the various sofas and chairs were far too young to be Hettie.

'Yes, April was wondering if Hettie knows anything about her great aunt, a woman called Winnie Lovell, from years back,' Molly explained further, while April picked up a lovely chunky yarn in a gorgeous fuchsia colour.

'Oh yes dear, Edie's sister.' It was Marigold.

'That's right.' April put the yarn down and walked over to Marigold. 'Edith is my other great aunt . . . I'm staying with her and hoping to find out what happened to her sister, Winifred, who left Tindledale in 1941.'

'And you look just like her!' another voice called out. April turned around and saw a small old lady wearing a hand-knitted cardy over a navy serge dress with thick tan tights, fur-lined felt booties, and long silvery-white hair pinned up into a big Aunt Bessie bun come padding towards her.

'April, this is Hettie,' Molly said.

'Hello.' April smiled. 'It's lovely to meet you.'

'It's a pleasure to meet you too, my dear. The resemblance is remarkable.' Hettie took a small step backwards to get a better look at April. 'I was in the snug next door when I saw you through the window walking down the path to the shop, and for a moment it was like stepping back in time. I really thought you were Winnie,' Hettie chuckled.

'Ooh, well that might explain then why your aunt keeps getting in a muddle and calling you Winnie,' Molly said to April.

'You do look so very much like her,' Hettie said, studying April some more. 'What do you think, Marigold? Could have been Winnie coming down the path, couldn't it, to see what lotions and potions we had to swap? Just like the old days. Do you remember, Marigold? We used to have such a hoot going through the haul from your aunt, keen to see what treats we could change it for.'

'Yes! That's right. Such fun, we use to swap all kinds of things in those days,' Marigold told the group. 'It was at the start of the war and my aunt worked on a make-up counter in a department store – she used to get hold of lipsticks, testers mostly, but still, she gave them to me, and then Hettie and I used to trade them in for treats from the older girls in the village.'

'Wow!' April beamed, thrilled to have found some people who actually knew Winnie, her mysterious relative. 'I'm intrigued to know more . . .'

'Why don't we pop next door to the snug? I'll make us a nice cup of tea and we can have a natter. I'd like that. Come on, Marigold, you can fill in the blanks,' Hettie instructed, and Marigold wasted no time in dumping her hole-strewn knitting on a nearby table, before practically leaping up to join them. 'My memory isn't what it used to be, but I'm bound to remember some of the shenanigans that we got up to. Marigold has more of her marbles left than me.'

'But knitting isn't my forte!' Marigold explained. 'I only come for the gossip.'

'And the custard creams,' another woman laughed, and Marigold nodded and promptly helped herself to another biscuit before popping half of it into her mouth.

'Well, I have to get in quick before you polish them all off,' Marigold quipped, in between bites and they all laughed some more, including April who now felt very relaxed indeed. She loved it in here, the haberdashery shop had such a warm, cosy and relaxed atmosphere and everyone seemed so fun and friendly. It was like being in a bubble. And a very similar atmosphere to Kitty's tea room, where nothing bad happened, or so it seemed, which suddenly gave April an idea. She turned to Sybs.

'Do you have knitting groups in the evening by any chance? Or weekends?'

'Ooh, yes. Several in fact. The earliest one starts at seven p.m. . . . to give the younger ones time to have tea and do their homework and stuff.'

'Younger ones?' April's interest was piqued further.

'That's right. Taylor, from the Pet Parlour up in the

High Street, runs that group on a Friday evening. Why? Do you have a teenage daughter or son who might want to come along? We have a couple of boys too – they particularly love the yarnbombing. I guess it's sort of like graffiti, but nobody minds because it looks so amazing. You might have seen the bench in the village square . . .' Sybs smiled.

'Ahh, yes, I did. And it was magnificent. And thank you, I know a young girl who might just love coming here to knit, and hopefully make some new friends,' April said, thinking of Bella.

'Then we'd be pleased to welcome her. I'll let Taylor know . . . I'm sure she'd be delighted to have a newcomer join her knit and natter group. Although, I think they call it something far more "street".' Sybs shook her head with an amused look on her face.

'Knit, bitch and bomb!' Molly interjected, before tutting. 'One of my boys is involved. He's not so keen on the knitting, but comes along for the social element as there isn't very much to do in Tindledale of an evening unless you're into amateur dramatics – Lawrence who runs the B&B does a group in the village hall.' Molly looked at April, who nodded. 'But my boy loves the covert bit – you know, putting the knitting in situ then legging it before Mrs Pocket or someone else from the parish council spots him and gives him an earful.'

'Hmm, she's not a fan.' Marigold shook her head.

'And thinks she's the custodian of Tindledale that one. Always has!' Hettie sniffed disapprovingly.

'Oh dear,' April said, remembering the parking space

mix-up, reckoning Mrs Pocket was most likely an acquired taste, as it were. 'But I'll be sure to let my friend know about the sessions, thank you.' Bella might enjoy knitting with a group and maybe making some new friends. The tricky bit would be persuading her, but April felt up to the challenge. If she could help in some way then it had to be worth a go.

'We better get on if you need to go soon, Molly.' Hettie chivvied Marigold, Molly and April through a door and into her snug, a glorious round room with three windows overlooking the fields to the side and back and the shop at the front.

As soon as they were all ensconced on the sagging but extra-comfy sofa and armchairs with a freshly brewed pot of tea on a tray and a selection of homemade cakes, Hettie began.

'Now, the Winnie I remember was such a lovely girl. Very kind too – do you remember when her best friend died, Marigold? TB it was, terrible business, she was only a youngster – they closed the village school for the day – and then her poor mother got it and died not long after. So sad it was, as there was only the two of them, the father had already died a few years before them. Imagine that, a family gone, just like that!' Hettie shook her head. 'Ahh, what was her name now?'

'Oooh, yes shocking it was. Pauline! That was the girl's name. And Winnie took wild flowers to her grave every day for weeks.' Marigold took a sip of tea and April smiled politely.

'Yes, Winnie was older than me, but back then in the

thirties, she looked just like you, as you know, but much more groomed. She took care of herself. Always turned out nicely she was. Us younger girls were a little in awe of her,' Hettie said, staring into the middle distance as if recalling an image of Winnie from years ago. April glanced at Molly, who gave her a look as if to say, 'You look just fine, Hettie doesn't mean anything by it.'

Marigold leant forward. 'That's why she liked to swap things.'

'Yes, make-up was a luxury, hard to get hold of in those days,' Hettie took over. 'We didn't have the money for starters . . . so when Marigold's aunt got a job on the Yardley counter in Bartram Brothers – that's the department store in Market Briar—'

'It's closed down now,' Marigold clarified.

'Yes thank you, Marigold, I was just about to tell her.' Hettie gave Marigold a sideways glance.

'Jolly good, then I've saved you the bother,' Marigold quipped.

'Thank you. But I'm telling the story . . .' Hettie retorted, while Molly and April exchanged discreet looks, both amused at the two dear friends bickering like an old married couple. Just like Darby and Joan, as Harvey would relish saying, which made April smile to herself as she took a sip of tea, carefully balancing the bone-china cup on the saucer. *He's certainly growing on me. Maybe I will go on a date with him after all . . . he makes me laugh, and surely that's a good thing. Perhaps I should run it by Nancy first . . . see if she'd mind.*

'Then why don't you get on with it . . .' Marigold

muttered into her enormous slice of Victoria sponge cake after breaking off a piece and pushing it into her mouth.

'She left Tindledale during the war, but didn't come home . . . my aunt Edie mentioned something to do with a married man?' prompted April, keen to move the conversation on, if only to stop the two elderly ladies from falling out.

'That's right, my dear. But . . .' Hettie paused and put down her tea cup and leant forward. After lowering her voice to barely a whisper, she added, 'I never believed all that tittle-tattle, the gossip, you know. Married man! Baby out of wedlock! Oh no.' Hettie shook her head vehemently, her big Aunt Bessie bun bobbing about. 'Winnie wasn't like that.'

'Oh?' Molly said, making big eyes. 'What was she like then?'

'She was as straight as a die, an honourable lady and most definitely not in the least bit flighty,' Hettie stated. 'She was honest. A good girl. And an excellent knitter – she taught me the cable stitch!' They all nodded, very impressed. 'No, Winnie would never do such a thing. Yes, she liked to look nice, but it wasn't for a man. It was for herself! You know, to feel tidy and confident. She was a very progressive woman for the times. A feminist, they would say nowadays. She told me once that women could do whatever the men could. I laughed of course, because in those days I for one wasn't really interested in doing the stuff that men did. Winnie was strong. Plucky. And she spoke her mind. Utterly fearless too.'

'Yes, do you remember that time in the fields, Hettie?'

Marigold said. 'When Billy Arkwright tried to look up your dress and she walloped him one before marching him home to his mother who gave him another thick ear?'

'Yes. Indeed I do. Winnie was rather magnificent.' Hettie blushed, and then turned to April and Molly. 'He didn't see anything, mind you,' she confirmed, just in case they were in any doubt as to whether Billy Arkwright had caught a glimpse of her knickers all those years ago, which really wouldn't do. And then Hettie swiftly drained the last of her tea. And it made April smile inwardly – times really were so different back then – no wonder some people in the village had gossiped about poor Winnie. From what Hettie and Marigold said, it seemed she was a confident, courageous character, outspoken too, and that might not have been a welcome disposition for a woman in those days. But this made April even more determined to find out the truth about her great aunt Winnie. She owed it to her, and Edie too. 'It was soon after then when Winnie swapped the book. Do you remember that too, Hettie?' Marigold continued.

'Book?' Hettie's age-wrinkled forehead creased as if her brain was flipping through a Rolodex, spanning years and years of various memories gone by. April and Molly both waited on tenterhooks until, eventually, Hettie seemed to remember something.

'There were sweets involved I think . . .' She closed her eyes and inhaled through her nose, as if hypnotised.

'A stick of liquorice! That's right – I wanted it,' Marigold bellowed, startling Hettie who promptly flicked open her eyes. 'But you were more interested in the book,

Hettie, you must remember that, you had your nose in it for weeks.' She glanced at her friend, before addressing April. 'It was shortly before Winnie left. She swapped the book and the liquorice for some make-up. Lipstick testers – my aunt used to get hold of them – and a cake mascara, if I'm not mistaken . . . Dorothy Gray, from America it was. You don't see it these days, which is a pity as that stuff stayed on for ever.' Marigold shook her head in amazement.

'You know, I think I do remember!' Hettie pointed a bony finger in the air. 'I was delighted with that book. And Winnie had even underlined her favourite sentences for me. And that's why I know she would never do such a thing as run off with a married man and have his baby.' Hettie looked outraged. 'She was a sensible girl, honourable, and that's why she volunteered for the FANY.'

'Ahh, you know about that?' April asked, hopefully.

'Yes, it was a long time ago, and I was just a young girl, but I'm sure she had a uniform made especially. Do you remember, Marigold? It was a lovely moss-green colour and very well tailored. The skirt sat perfectly just below her knee.'

'I think so,' Marigold said. 'There were so many uniforms around in those days. But I do recall wondering if she might have been better off wearing those brown corduroy breeches that she had in the Land Army.'

'Why was that?' Molly swiftly asked.

'Because I'm sure Winnie was going into the field . . . to see some action, oh yes, it's coming back to me now.' Marigold paused to ponder, holding two fingers to her temples as they all held their breath and waited. 'Ambulances! She went off to a special training place to learn all about working the ambulances to help save the soldiers. She told me. And I remember feeling ever so impressed.'

'Yes, Winnie was a very magnificent girl, dear, so I can't imagine she'd have run off with another woman's husband. Oh no!' Hettie sucked in air to make a little whistling sound. 'But she did have a gentleman friend, I seem to remember. Very handsome he was in his uniform – a bit older than her he was, perhaps that's why they thought he was married. And some folk around here do like to make up the rest of the story when they don't know the ins and outs of other people's personal business, but still . . . I don't think so.' She shook her head. 'Not our Winnie.'

'How can you be so sure?' April asked, inwardly hoping the gossip about Winnie from all those years back was futile and that she could clear her great aunt's name, once and for all. But more importantly . . . find out what really happened and set poor Edie's mind at rest before it was too late.

'Because the book was about manners, etiquette, the proper way to conduct one's self. What was it called, Marigold?'

'Oh, you've got me there. I can't remember . . . something like *The Correct Way a Lady Should Behave*. Old fashioned now, but back then, as young impressionable girls, we devoured it, didn't we Hettie?'

'Hmm, *I* did. You were too busy mooning over

Lucan . . . but it did you no harm, I suppose, seeing as you married him in the end, much to your mother's delight.' Hettie smiled sweetly at her friend.

'Ha! And the old earl's chagrin,' puffed Marigold. 'He never did get over Lucan marrying me, a mere village girl.'

'Her husband is Lord Lucan Fuller-Hamilton,' Molly whispered to April while Hettie and Marigold reminisced for a few minutes. 'Marigold is actually a proper bona fide Lady.'

'Ooh,' April made big eyes.

'My father was a cow herder, you know!' Marigold then said to the group, tilting her chin towards the shard of sunshine spilling in through the window, overlooking fields dotted with buttercups and muddy-bottomed sheep. And Hettie sighed.

'I'm sure I still have the book somewhere. Shall I go and have a look?'

'Well, that would be marvellous, if it's not too much trouble,' April said as Hettie went to lift her frail body from the easy chair. 'Would you like some help?'

'Yes please dear. I'm not as sprightly as I once was . . .'

April's spirit rose as she helped Hettie out of the chair. It wasn't much. But it was something. A book. Another piece of Winnie, something tangible that had belonged to her. And even though April hadn't managed to find out yet what had really become of her great aunt Winnie, she instinctively felt a little closer to her. And there was always the general. He may still come up with something. When Deedee had come to collect Edie for this week's tea dance, she had told April that he was still on the case of the missing Winnie, and was determined to get to the bottom of it. He was taking it all very seriously, to the point of putting in a call to a pal of his in the house – the House of Lords, Deedee had then clarified, while making very big impressed eyes. It really was as if Winnie had vanished. 'Or run off with a GI. That's what I would have done. A gorgeous American. Fancy that!' Deedee had then added with a faraway look in her eye this time. But, surmising aside, April felt that she would really like to be the one to find a clue, a lead or whatever that would solve the mystery. And she was still pondering on that letter with the London postmark . . . it didn't make sense, there must be something more to know. And nothing had come of Winnie's photo that April had posted on Facebook, so that was a dead end.

A little while later, Hettie returned with a battered, musty old book under one arm.

'Here it is dear. *The Ladies' Manual of Politeness & Good Conduct* by Florence Wetherill. Published in 1932. Look, it even has the note still inside from Winnie,' she said, holding out a faded, folded letter. After carefully opening the letter, Hettie read Winnie's words aloud.

Dearest Hettie,
    Be sure to treasure this book always, for it will stand the test of time.
    Your friend,
    Winnie

18

April was in the kitchen stirring an enormous pot of chopped apples on the Aga, making her aunt's sauce – luckily Edie had remembered the recipe as if she had last made it only yesterday – when there was a knock on the front door. Edie, who was sitting on a chair at the kitchen table, went to see who it was before returning to announce, 'Winnie dear, you have a gentleman visitor.'

April smiled and wiped her hands on a tea towel before walking over to her aunt and giving her a kindly hug. The last few days had been quite confusing for Edie, with her seemingly in a constant muddle with limited moments of lucidity, apart from recalling the sauce recipe, which was why it felt quite extraordinary that she could remember it after all these years. But April had long given up on correcting her aunt, although she had put in a call to the doctor's surgery, and after a chat to Dr Ben – as all the villagers called him, according to Molly – he was coming later to see how Edie was getting on.

April went into the tiny hall and saw Matt with his head ducked down to avoid colliding with the low beams. His treacle-black curls were falling into his eyes and the moody, brooding look from that day in his van at the roadside was firmly set in place on his face. Bella was hovering apprehensively behind him.

'Come in. Please. It's lovely to see you both. Let's go into the sitting room . . . the ceiling is a little higher in there.' April smiled at Matt, and after swiping his hair away, he lifted his eyebrows in thanks. But didn't say a word.

'Shall I put the kettle on, dear?' Aunt Edie called from the kitchen.

'Yes please, Aunty,' April replied, before turning back to her guests. 'Please make yourselves comfortable,' she gestured to the Dralon settee, 'I'll just give my aunt a hand with making some tea . . . or would you prefer coffee?'

'Thanks, but we'll not hold you up,' Matt said quickly, and quite monosyllabically. 'We're here to apologise.' He flashed a glance at Bella who was twisting the handles of an old plastic carrier bag around her fingers. She didn't look up.

'Oh, um . . . that really isn't necessary. And please, there's no need to rush off. I'll make us some tea. I shan't be a second.' And April scooted next door into the kitchen to see what Edie was doing and to make sure she wasn't filling the kettle with milk, like she had last night. They had laughed about it afterwards, figuring it was no big deal, and April had quite fancied a mug of warm milk with a pinch of nutmeg on top before she had gone to bed in any case.

'Are you OK, Aunty?' April asked, pleased to see Edie had the kettle under the tap and was filling it with water.

'Yes dear. Come to check on me, have you?' she

chuckled, before popping the lid on and placing the kettle on the Aga to boil.

'No, no . . . you seem to be doing just fine without me,' April fibbed, and the two women exchanged knowing smiles.

'Well, what are you doing hiding out here in the kitchen then? I might be losing my marbles but I can still keep an eye on a pot of apple sauce while putting the kettle on,' Aunt Edie said, covertly, in a low voice. And then after stepping closer to April, she added, 'That devilishly handsome gentleman is waiting in there for you. Send the girl out to me for a biscuit if she's in the way!'

'AUNTY!' April's cheeks flamed. 'He's not waiting for me . . . well, not like that,' she swiftly added under her breath before turning away. 'And the girl is his daughter.'

'Daughter? Where's her mother then?' Edie frowned.

'She's gone away, Aunty,' April whispered now, in case Matt and Bella were listening. It wouldn't do for them to hear her gossiping, and besides, she only knew the scant details that Harvey had proffered and April had a feeling that his perception of events could very well be skewed. He didn't strike her as the kind of guy to consider the whole picture when it came to a relationship breakdown.

'Oh, he's a *widower*!' Aunt Edie's eyes lit up, but before April could correct her, she continued, 'Well then my dear, he's perfect for you.' And Aunt Edie actually hummed a jaunty little tune as she picked up the biscuit tin, pushed it into the crook of her elbow and then pulled off the lid with her free hand. 'I'll put out the best biscuits on to a plate. The Viennese Whirls. Yes, you won't want to bother him with the boring Rich Teas . . . or he'll never come back.'

And April waited, speechless, as her elderly great aunt artfully fanned a swirl of Viennese Whirls on to one of her best china plates with the sole intention of impressing Matt, who she had obviously concluded was the perfect suitor for her great niece, or was it sister? April wasn't entirely sure . . . she could very well be Winnie right now, as far as her aunt Edie was concerned.

*

'So what do you reckon, Bells?' Matt gently nudged Bella in the side with his elbow, then quickly added, 'Sorry, *Bella*,' before grinning and flicking his eyes to April who was sitting in an armchair opposite them. She smiled discreetly, admiring the way Matt was with Bella. It couldn't be easy being a single dad to a teenage girl, but he seemed to be taking it all in his stride; he was being fairly talkative, animated even, which was in stark contrast to earlier today and the time April had first met him at the roadside. And she rather liked this version of him. Gone was the mute, brooding, moodiness and in its place a charismatic, relaxed and caring man sat on Edie's Dralon settee next to his daughter . . . and those eyes. April was struggling to keep her own from staring. It was bizarre, the way Matt's magnificently moss-green eyes bore into her, as if looking right into her soul. It was disconcerting and spine-tingling, all at the same time, and April wasn't entirely sure how she should feel about it. So for now, she pushed the conundrum away, figuring it might just be easier than analysing all over again as she had when Harvey had asked her out . . .

They had been chatting for the last ten minutes, mainly with Matt saying sorry and that he would foot the bill for any damage Bella had caused, to which April said she wouldn't dream of taking his money and, besides, there was no damage – if anything Bella had made improvements to the gypsy wagon, which it turned out, via Aunt Edie, had been at the back of the big orchard since before she was born. April had then reiterated that Bella was welcome to come to the orchard whenever she liked . . . though not during the school day of course. This was punctuated by a begrudging apology from Bella, followed by a more enthusiastic thank you when prompted by Matt, at which point April had asked if she would like to try out the knitting group.

'Old habits and all that – you used to love being called Bells.' Matt shrugged.

'Yeah, when I was like *five*,' Bella huffed and rolled her eyes. April opened her mouth in an attempt to make peace between the pair, but was then surprised when Matt promptly folded his arms and pretended to sulk. He even pushed out a petulant bottom lip after doing an enormous sigh.

'DAAAAAD. What are you doing? Stop it. You're sooooo embarrassing.' Bella rolled her eyes and shoved him sharply in the ribs. And then, after trying very hard not to, she cracked up. And then April, unable to resist, joined in and laughed too. As did Matt. And then Edie, having heard them all from the kitchen, came into the sitting room and started chuckling as well, even though she had no idea what they were laughing about.

Eventually, Matt was the first to compose himself.

'Anyway, we've taken up enough of your time, April, we best get off now. And yes, my daughter,' he paused momentarily to make sure he got it right this time, '*Bella* . . . would love to go to the knitting group.' He winked, nodded and mouthed 'thank you' to April, which made her cheeks flush momentarily. She studied the pattern on her tea cup, unable to make eye contact with him. It was weird, thrilling almost, the way he made her feel.

'But Dad . . .' Bella gave him a sideways glance and then clammed up.

'What is it, love?'

'I won't know anyone there.' Silence followed. And then she quickly added, 'Will you come with me?' Bella turned to April.

'Oh, um . . .' April started, taken aback, looking quickly at Matt and then back to the tea cup. 'I'm not sure, I—'

'April's busy, sweetheart. I'll drop you off and pick you up. It'll be fine,' Matt tried, but Bella was having none of it. She resumed the twisting of the carrier bag round and round her fingers, her face contorting with anxiety.

'Please April. We could go together . . . it'll be much better with you there,' Bella pleaded. A short silence followed.

'Oh, um . . . sure, OK then,' April eventually said,

desperately ignoring the swirl in the pit of her stomach as she figured it might be all right. And, having promised the girl, she could hardly back out at the last minute. And then, who knows, perhaps she'd feel inclined to get out her knitting of an evening in front of the telly. Yes, building up to it, baby steps, was absolutely the way to go! And she did have the new needles and three balls of that gorgeous fuchsia pink yarn from Hettie's House of Haberdashery – she had bought it on the way out, unable to resist.

'Brilliant!' Bella's eyes lit up.

'Wonderful,' April said, standing up as she put the cup back on the tray, and sounding far more resolute than she felt inside. Matt and Bella stood up too.

'Please can I see the horses before we go?' Bella asked. 'I've brought some grated carrot, it's the only thing they like.' And she opened the carrier bag and held it out to show April.

'Wow! This must have taken you ages to grate,' April said, impressed. There were at least a couple of kilos' worth of carrots inside the bag.

'Dad helped me!' Bella said boldly. *Ahh, well that was very thoughtful of him . . . but why the constant gear change? The enigmatic behaviour?* April didn't get it – one minute Matt was the kind and caring dad, then the other . . . mysterious and mute, bordering on indifference.

'Then my thanks to both of you. This is perfect for them. Soft and easy to eat.'

'Is that the problem with them, then? Rotten teeth, or

most likely not been floated in years,' Matt asked, concern clouding his chiselled face. 'Bella has told me all about them.'

'Floated?' April frowned. The vet had mentioned that, but she couldn't remember what it meant. She had been so ashamed that poor Darby and Joan had got into such an appalling state that she hadn't taken it all in when he was examining them. Of course, her aunt wasn't to blame, she had enough to deal with just trying to remember what month it was half the time. No, April blamed herself. If she had visited her aunt more frequently then perhaps she would have spotted the horses before now.

'Yep. Horses' teeth don't stop growing so they have to be floated . . . you know, trimmed, the sharp corners shaved off. Much like humans, horses need regular dental checks.'

'Yes, the vet explained that some of their teeth were rotten and infected, which is why they weren't eating properly, so in turn weren't getting enough nutrition to stay healthy, so they've now ended up with all sorts of health problems, affecting their coats and suchlike.' April glanced away.

'That'll be why they have sores then.' Matt tutted and shook his head. 'And I bet they've not seen a farrier in years. Take it the vet inspected their hooves?' and the tenderness and humour he displayed from earlier seemed to have vanished now, only to be replaced with a cloud of what April feared could very well be disgust.

'Um. Yes, he did, and yes, you're right . . . But their

teeth have been treated now and the vet is going to visit regularly to administer some medicine and keep an eye on them.' April took a deep breath. 'And we've moved them into the old barn – there's a section that has been fenced off to make a kind of stable area for them. The vet said Darby and Joan will be much more comfortable in there, out of the sun, until they're feeling better and then they can go back into the orchard as long as there is a shaded place for them . . .' And the pickers had already cleared one of the smaller orchards of fruit, thankfully, so the upfront payment from the organic cider producer had come at just the right time to cover the vet's bill, which as Harvey had predicted was indeed extortionate. And there was still the cost of having a proper stable built for Darby and Joan to shelter in should they need to, not to mention their ongoing upkeep – horses were expensive. But April figured it was worth it, if only to ease her conscience at having let her aunt down.

'Mind if I take a look at Darby and Joan?' Matt asked, rolling up his sleeves to reveal the intricate tattoos again. They really were a work of art, and gave him quite an interesting and exciting edge, thought April, sneaking a look. Like the time Nancy had shown her a picture of a topless Tom Hardy, and April had never really been one for tattoos on men, but had to admit that he did look 'hot', as Nancy would say . . .

'Sure. Please do, if you have time,' April said to Matt, trying really hard not to stare at his arms now, and no, she most definitely shouldn't be wondering if the rest of his body had tattoos on. Certainly not. She coughed to clear her throat and instead busied herself with clearing the tea cups back on to the tray.

'He has the time,' Bella grinned, glancing at her dad and then at April. 'My dad is really good with horses,' she added proudly.

'Wonderful!' April said, not even daring to look at Matt. She was perplexed at how flustered she now felt. 'Shan't be long. I'll catch you up,' she managed, backing out of the room with her face fixed firmly on the tray. It had been a long time since she had felt like this. A spark ignited. Like a switch had been flicked on within her, bringing her body alive. For the last years of Gray's life, sex hadn't been possible and so April had inadvertently closed off that part of herself. They had still been intimate, she had made sure of it as she wanted him to feel loved and she had wanted something physical to hold on to after he was gone, but it happened in other ways. Cuddling up to Gray in bed – he had said he loved feeling her body spooned around him, it made him feel safe, normal, a welcome moment of respite. Then holding his hand and stroking his face towards the very end, she had wanted to feel close to him, savour the scent of his skin, the warmth of his chest against her cheek as she lay listening to his heartbeat, sometimes willing it to keep going, other times wanting to scream out loud in anger and frustration. Blame it for taking him from her prematurely. Cutting his life short so he'd never get to do all the things that he loved any more, or see Nancy and Freddie get married perhaps, have families of their own, grandchildren – all of it was snatched away from him. But that was the past, and April felt that she had come a very long way in working through her grief, especially since being here at Orchard Cottage, even starting to feel a new sense of normal, as she had once before after losing her parents. A recalibration. Not getting over Gray as such, that wasn't it. No, she didn't think that would ever happen, but more that she was learning to live without him – she must be if her interest in other men was being piqued. She had never so much as considered another man when Gray was alive. But why then did she have a sense of reluctance, a niggle, a feeling of foreboding even? She couldn't quite put her finger on it – it was as if there was still another peak on the rollercoaster of grief to get over, before she could truly let go and find a new place in her life for Gray . . . and move on.

April took a moment for herself as she went through to the kitchen and cleared the contents of the tray into the old-veined Belfast sink to wash up later. Then, after settling Edie down for a little snooze, she put the pot of apple sauce on the side to cool and turned off the Aga, before going out to join Matt and Bella in the barn.

One foot in front of the other. She said it inside her head, over and over like a mantra. It was an old habit that had seen her through the most difficult of days and for some reason it felt strangely comforting now, even though today was actually a good day.

On reaching the barn, April was shocked to feel her eyes pricking with tears, just as they had in Hettie's shop. She bit down hard on her bottom lip and pushed her hand into her jeans pocket to draw strength from Gray's Swiss Army knife, which she had taken to keeping with her at all times now.

And then she got it! That feeling inside. There in the pit of her stomach. Lingering. She felt guilty. Guilty for feeling happy. Without Gray. And potentially being happy with somebody else . . . a date with Harvey would sure be fun, he'd flirt and flatter her if nothing else. And what about her attraction to Matt? And she was growing fond of Bella. She had enjoyed being with them both in the sitting room. It had felt cosy, laughing and fooling around, and she wanted to have more moments like that.

To be perfectly honest, she felt content at Orchard Cottage. The simplicity of her life here. Collecting the eggs for breakfast. Pottering around the cottage. Doing business with the cider producer. Picking apples for the sauce. Playing rummy of an evening with a large snowball in hand. Chatting to Molly whenever she went up to the village. She felt at home. And Aunt Edie had been right. Because April really felt happy. Happier than she had in a very long time. She was healing. And all she had to try to do now was to work through this feeling of guilt. It was as if a Pandora's box had been opened and there was no closing it, whether she wanted to or not . . . April took a big breath and pressed her palms up to her cheeks as if to steady her thoughts before wandering into the barn with a big smile on her face.

19

And sure enough, Bella was spot on! Matt was indeed 'really good' with horses. It was actually quite something to watch him. In the afternoon sun, the barn provided some welcome shade, with only a shard of sunshine beaming through a hole in the roof like a spotlight on to the horse-whisperer show unfolding before April's eyes. Flecks of dust flickered all around, the smell of hay warm and evocative of the long, lazy, hazy days of summers gone by when she had been a young girl, carefree and content. April's breath caught in her throat. She pushed up the sleeves of her T-shirt, not remembering it being this hot last time she was here in the barn.

'Shuuuuuush,' Matt coaxed, wiping his sweat-covered forehead with the back of his forearm before slipping off his leather waistcoat and letting it drop to the floor as he edged slowly towards Darby and Joan. They were nuzzling each other in the far corner of the barn, their stable area clean and swept and stocked with hay. April had been making sure of it and had even called the vet several times in between visits to check that she had understood the proper way to care for them.

As he got closer, Matt's words became firmer, much

more dominant, until he was able to touch Joan and stroke her newly trimmed mane, at which point Darby dipped his head and lumbered over to get a look-in too. Matt duly paid attention to Darby by stroking his nose, yet didn't allow him to take over. It was like a dance. Matt carefully planning his next step, gauging how each horse might respond to ensure neither animal reared up or got spooked and kicked out, or worse still, trampled him.

'You can't let them think they're in charge of you,' Bella said to April who was watching, fascinated. When both horses seemed relaxed with Matt, he turned so his back was resting against Joan's body, all the while keeping his eye on Darby. Slowly, Matt smoothed his left hand along the length of Joan's back and down her hind leg until he was able to coax her enough to lift her hoof. When she did, Matt very gently swivelled his body around so he could secure Joan's hoof in between his jean-clad thighs, the tendons in his forearms flexing from supporting the weight of the horse's leg.

Sweltering now, in the stifling heart, April fanned herself with a piece of cardboard that she had spotted on the dusty old dresser stored just inside the entrance to the barn. After he had finished examining Joan, Matt turned to Bella.

'Pass me the carrier bag, will you please, love?'

'Sure.' Bella stepped forward immediately.

'And some water would go down a treat,' he said, glancing at April.

'Oh, sure.' April went to fetch the bucket hanging on a peg nearby, but Bella giggled. 'What is it?' April grinned.

'I think Dad means water for him. He looks really hot.'

Indeed.

April quickly dumped the bucket back on the peg, and after swiping her hair from her face – it was sizzling in the barn now – she dashed outside into the garden and gulped in an enormous breath of air. Happiness. Guilt. A swirl of confusing emotions tumbled right through her all over again.

'Are you OK, April?' Bella was beside her, with a concerned look etched on her young face.

'Yes. Sorry, I'm fine, I just . . . um, felt a bit faint, that's all. I'll fetch the water . . .' And April went to walk off.

'Can I come with you?' Bella called after her, and April turned around; shielding her eyes from the sun with her hand, she saw a vulnerability on Bella's face, mingled with a neediness, almost. *Poor girl, she really is in a pickle, and it can't be easy for her without a mum. Matt seems like a good dad, but I guess there are some things a girl needs her mum for . . .*

'Sure.' April smiled and waited for Bella to catch her up. And then the two of them walked together. 'And how about we have some apple cordial? Better than water, eh?' April grinned at her new young friend.

'Ooh, yes please.'

'Great. And I think there might be some biscuits too! You can help me put it all out on a tray.' April glanced sideways and was happy to see Bella with a big smile on her face as she practically skipped along, skidding her flowery Converse trainers over the grass in her haste.

'Cool.' Bella's grin widened. 'Have you got Jammie Dodgers? They're my favourite, but Dad never buys them because he says they have too much sugar inside them.'

'Ahh, well he's right,' April laughed, 'but we'll take a look in the tin and see what's there, shall we?'

Bella nodded, and then stopped skipping. 'Have you got any children?' she asked bluntly, turning to scrutinise April.

'Oh, um . . . not of my own, but I have two grown-up stepchildren. They're twins.'

'How old are they?' Bella asked in a matter-of-fact voice, and April turned to face her, amused by the bluntness of the questions.

'Twenty-two.'

Bella creased her forehead for a few seconds, seemingly deep in thought and then stated, 'Wish I had a stepmum. Someone nice like you.'

'Ahh, thank you love. But you do have a mum of your own . . .' April glanced sideways at Bella, unsure if she was overstepping the mark.

'Yes. But she left years ago. It's horrible not having a mum. What's your mum like?'

'Well, I don't actually have a mum either.'

'How come?' Bella creased her forehead.

'She died when I wasn't much older than you are now,' April said, figuring a straight answer was best.

'Really? What happened to her?'

'She was killed in a car crash. With my dad.'

'But who looked after you?' Bella asked quietly, her voice full of concern.

'My grandparents,' April replied.

'I've never met someone else who doesn't have a mum.' Bella's voice lifted slightly, and she started skipping again, as if she was happy to have made a connection with April.

'Well, now you have.' And April felt quite touched as Bella slipped her small hand into hers. A kindred spirit.

They had just reached the path up to the cottage when
Edie appeared in the doorway.

'There you are, Winnie!' Edie looked panicked, her
eyes flitting left to right. Bella flashed April a look. What
on earth was going on? 'You need to come in quickly!
There's a strange girl here in the sitting room. You need
to get rid of her. And there's straw everywhere. What
shall we do? What will Mum and Dad say? Dad's going
to be furious,' she babbled, almost incoherently. 'And
who is she? She can't come in. She might tell them it
was my fault. But it wasn't.' Aunt Edie's face crumpled
with concern, her watery eyes widened and her bottom
lip wobbled like a young child's, her fingers fiddling with
the corner of her crocheted waistcoat, over and over and
over. April pulled her aunt in close to reassure her with
a big hug, rubbing Edie's back too to help soothe her.

'It's OK, Aunt Edie. This is Bella, from earlier . . . she
came here with her dad, remember?' April paused, wondering why she had said that, as it was quite obvious Edie
was struggling to remember anything at all right now. 'He's
in the barn looking after the horses and we've come to get
some drinks. Would you like some apple cordial?'

Edie stared blankly at April. Bella stepped in.

'Lovely to meet you, Edie,' she said brightly, not missing a beat, as if she wasn't at all fazed by an old lady talking like a child. April was enormously grateful as she felt her aunt's body relax a little.

'Is he the widower? Looking for a new mother for you!' Edie said, pointing, almost accusingly, at Bella's chest. April felt her cheeks redden.

'No,' she quickly interjected, all the while shaking her head. 'Sorry, Bella, my aunt is confus—'

'My niece is a widow too! Her husband died!' Edie carried on, but it was Bella who stepped in again to ease the situation.

'Oh no, that's so sad. My dad isn't a widower. My mum left when I was little. Where's your mum? And where is the straw? I'll help you clear it up before she sees it, if you like.' April held her breath as her aunt looked at Bella like she'd just grown another head, but then miraculously, Edie moved forward and tentatively took hold of Bella's hand.

'Come in,' Edie said, 'and I'll show you.' And her whole face lit up.

'Cool,' Bella beamed, totally unfazed.

Inside the narrow, low-beamed hallway, the three of them stood side by side.

'Now, how about we all sit down in the kitchen?' April started, and was just about to ask Aunt Edie about the strange girl she had mentioned in the sitting room, fully expecting her to be in a muddle again, when the sitting-room door burst open. 'NANCY!' April couldn't believe it.

Her lovely stepdaughter was standing right in front of her.

'Yep. Surpriiiiiiise!' Nancy said, pulling April in for a hug.

'That's her!' Edie shouted, pointing her finger at Nancy now. 'I went upstairs and she sneaked in . . . I found her wandering around in the hallway. Check her pockets—'

'It's OK, Aunty,' April said quickly.

'The front door was wide open so I just came in. I did call out but you weren't here,' Nancy replied, looking worried. 'Sorry, I didn't mean to upset—'

'It's all right.' April nodded and smiled at Nancy, giving her a look as if to say, 'Let me handle this.' Then she said to Edie, 'It's OK, Aunty, this is Nancy . . . Gray's daughter, you remember her from the wedding . . .'

'Wedding?' Edie's face crumpled in concentration.

'My wedding to Gray,' April prompted. 'It was a long time ago now, but you wore a mint-green coloured dress and bought a beautiful gold locket for me to wear,' she added, hoping these details might help her aunt remember.

And then a small miracle occurred, and Edie did in fact remember.

'Yes! That's right. And I still have the dress in my wardrobe. It smells of Lily of the Valley, which always makes me think of your wedding, dear.' April breathed a sigh of relief, and filed this fact away for further use – perfume being an evocative reminder of events. 'Why didn't you say who you were?' Edie then said to Nancy. And Nancy glanced first at April and then at Edie.

'I, um . . . thought I did, but, I guess . . . maybe I didn't.' Nancy looked again at April for direction.

'Well, never mind, you're here and it's lovely to see you,' April smiled.

'Do you like snowballs?' Edie jumped in, making Bella giggle.

'Sorry,' she quickly said, slapping her hand over her teenage mouth.

'Come on, I'll make us all a snowball,' and Edie pottered off into the kitchen, leaving April, Nancy and Bella in the hallway, exchanging glances as they each smiled and shook their heads in amazement. It was hard to keep up with Aunt Edie's changing moods, not to mention time zones!

'So how come you're here?' April asked Nancy.

'Excuse me, shall I go and help your aunty, April?' Bella asked, apprehensively.

'Sure. That would be very kind of you. Thanks love.' And Bella darted off into the kitchen.

'She's a sweet kid, who is she?' Nancy whispered.

'Oh, she's the farrier's daughter . . . a long story, but we've sort of become friends,' April said in a low voice as she discreetly pulled the kitchen door to.

'Ahh, I see. The guy in the barn?' Nancy made big eyes as she leant in closer to April.

'Yes, that's him.' April motioned for Nancy to follow her to the other end of the hallway out of earshot.

'Riiiiight,' Nancy said, making April feel a little confused. She wasn't sure what Nancy was thinking, but before she could dwell on it, Nancy explained, 'I've got a few days off so I thought why not whizz here to Tindledale to see how you are. I've got a tent packed on the back of my scooter so you don't even have to put me up, I'll be fine in a field . . . as long as the cows leave me alone. I don't do cows.' She pulled a face and pretended to grimace. 'Or I'm sure I could sort something else out, I passed a lovely-looking pub in the village, the Duck and something, maybe they do rooms. I don't want to upset your aunt again . . . is everything OK with her?'

'Yes, I've arranged for her GP to pop by. It's all in hand,' April quickly said, and Nancy nodded discreetly. 'And you're not sleeping in a field, or the local pub,' she added, knowing full well that her aunt probably wouldn't even be aware, but back in the day when Edie had been fully compos mentis, she would have been horrified at the mere thought of a guest staying elsewhere. She had been very hospitable. And April fully intended on respecting that fact. Just because her aunt was old, muddled and forgetful didn't mean her wishes were to be dispensed with. 'And neither would I.' April grinned, grateful that Nancy had turned up. It was wonderful to see her.

'Well, then if you insist. I'd love to. I've missed you.' Nancy smiled, and April felt a pang of guilt for having left her back in Basingstoke. But she was here now. 'I thought it would be nice to see how you're getting on here. And from what I've seen so far . . . you appear to be getting on just fine.' Nancy pulled a cheeky face. 'When I was standing in the sitting room looking out of the window, I saw a fit guy coming out of the barn and going to fetch something from his van.'

'Oh, um. It's so lovely to see you, darling,' April said, straightening her hair, feeling flustered.

'You too. And you look amazing. The country air obviously suits you, your cheeks are all flushed.'

'Ahh, that's because I've been in the barn. It's really hot in there.'

'Ha-ha. I'll say!' Nancy made massive eyes and gave April a playful nudge in the ribs before lowering her voice and leaning into April. 'Who *is* that gorgeous creature in the barn? And I don't mean one of the horses!'

'Oh, um, that's Matt.'

'Ahh, I see . . . Maaaaatt!' Nancy lifted one eyebrow and said his name slowly as if mulling over the implications of this piece of information. 'Nice name. So tell me all about him . . .'

'What do you mean? He's just here to, er . . . um . . .' April willed her cheeks to stop burning. 'It's complicated,' she settled on.

'Really? Looked pretty obvious to me,' Nancy said, in a much more serious voice now, and April couldn't tell if Nancy was upset, cross, annoyed or whatever . . . but what she did know was that this moment right now was blooming awkward. She was thrilled to have Nancy here, but the last thing she wanted was her stepdaughter getting the wrong end of the stick and assuming that there was something going on between her and Matt, when there wasn't. Definitely not. How would that look? As if she was off meeting new men at the very first opportunity, without so much as a second thought for her late husband, Nancy's dad. No. April didn't want Nancy thinking that at all . . .

'Come on, let's go and get a drink and see how Edie and Bella are getting on,' April said to change the subject.

In the kitchen, and April knew right away that her aunt was feeling panicked again. She was crouched in the cupboard under the sink and muttering something again about needing a broom.

'Found it!' Bella said, holding up the broom as she gently patted Aunt Edie on the back.

'Well done, my dear. No time to waste. Now off we go!' And Edie went to dart from the kitchen with a very anxious look on her face, Bella close behind her as if colluding in whatever adventure Edie had planned.

'Hang on!' April interjected. 'Why don't we have a drink first?' She looked at Bella and then Nancy, wondering what was going on.

'But we can't do that!' Edie said, panicked. 'What if the whole house falls down? Then where will we be? You need to get Dad. Go and get him in from the fields.'

'House?' April repeated, a horrible sinking feeling swirling within her.

And then something clicked.

Straw.

The thatched roof.

April took one look at Bella and Nancy, before racing up the rickety little winding stairs, practically on all fours so as to negotiate them in record time. She wasn't wasting precious seconds going carefully, walking upright with her head bowed to avoid colliding with the biggest beam right under the turn as she normally did.

April made it to the second landing. The door to her

bedroom, Winnie's old room, was wide open. She put a hand over her mouth as she went inside.

'Oh my God!' Bella shrieked, coming into the room right behind April, with her hands over her mouth. They stared, motionless for a few seconds. Barely able to believe their eyes. It was surreal. Cloudless blue sky was peeping through a hole the size of a tennis racket above the beautiful Art Deco wooden wardrobe that was now covered in bits of thatched roof mingled with plaster and pulp and all kinds of debris that April didn't even want to hazard a guess as to what it was exactly. Especially as she could see a pair of prone little bird's legs peeping out from under a piece of plaster on the floor beside the pink sink.

'I'll go and get Dad!' and Bella raced out of the room.

'And I'll keep an eye on Edie, April. We don't want her wandering around up here alone. In the meantime, stay out of the room, in the doorway, in case the whole lot comes down,' Nancy instructed firmly. April nodded, figuring Nancy knew about such stuff, being a firefighter.

Moments later, Matt came charging along the landing.

'*Jesus Christ!*' He let out a long whistle and put his hands on his hips as he saw the damage. 'How long has it been like this?'

'Um, I don't know,' April mumbled, focusing her attentions on the gaping big hole in the roof, because now it was her turn to avoid eye contact. In fact, she couldn't even glance in Matt's direction, because he was topless! His smooth, sun-bronzed chest was drenched in sweat, tattoos covered his arms, he had leather chaps on over his jeans, a T-shirt slung over one shoulder and a very packed tool belt hanging from his hips. He looked like a pin-up in a calendar, especially when he pulled a band from his belt and proceeded to scoop his curls back into a bunch at the nape of his neck. And, somehow, having Nancy in the cottage, her late husband's daughter just downstairs, made April feel even more self-conscious.

'Right. Well, er . . . How precious is this to your aunt?' Matt asked, nodding at the wardrobe as he pulled the T-shirt on over his head.

'Oh, um, why?' April wished her cheeks would stop burning.

'Because I'm going to get on top of it and take a look at what is going on outside that bloody great big gaping hole that's right above it.' Matt unclipped his tool belt and slung it on the bed. 'And the wardrobe looks pretty old and rickety to me so the chances are that it might collapse . . . Better that than the roof caving in completely though,' he shrugged. 'I might be able to secure it for now – lash that old rug over the hole perhaps,' he finished, eyeing up the old threadbare rug beside the wardrobe.

'But you might get hurt. If the wardrobe collapses,' April said, sneaking a sideways glance at him. Matt gave her a look as if to say, 'Don't be daft.'

'Dad does stuff like this all the time, April,' Bella said, bobbing from one foot to the other.

'If you're sure . . .' April took a deep breath and instantly regretted it when she got a mouthful of dust which then caught in her throat and made her splutter and cough.

'Go downstairs please, Bella,' Matt instructed. 'It's not safe here for you.'

Alex Brown

'But I want to stay and watch.'

'Please love, just do it!' Matt said, sounding impatient. 'I don't want to argue, not now.' He held up a palm in protest.

'But what if April is right and you get hurt?'

'I'll be fine.' But Bella wasn't budging.

'Why can't I stay?'

'Like I said, it's not safe, now go!'

'But it's not fair,' Bella kept on, kicking her Converse against the skirting board now like a typical petulant thirteen year old. Matt inhaled and let out a long breath of exasperation.

'It's OK, sweetheart. Your dad will be all right, he knows what to do,' April intervened, hoping to defuse the tension and appease Bella, but not be seen as interfering, and she could see that Matt was getting worked up, like any parent used to doing battle on a minute-by-minute basis with their teenage child. Gray had been the same when the twins were teenagers, his fuse wore very thin very quickly, from the constant eroding of his patience. 'And I'd really appreciate it if you could go and help Nancy look after Edie – my aunt likes you, I think she trusts you because you're very kind to her.' April smiled, hopefully.

'Sure.' And Bella couldn't wait to dash off downstairs.

'How do you do that?' Matt asked incredulously, shaking his head after Bella had left the room.

'Um, I'm not really sure . . .' April shrugged, just pleased it had worked without Bella getting too upset, figuring she had enough to contend with at school.

Moments later, Matt put one foot up on the window-sill and used it to push his body up high enough to grab the top of the wardrobe, and then in one swift movement he was kneeling with his head and shoulders outside the hole in the ceiling. April folded her arms and paced around as she waited for his verdict.

'It's pretty bad, I'm afraid,' Matt said, as he brought his head and shoulders back into the room and carefully lifted himself down from the wardrobe. 'I can secure it for tonight, lash a makeshift cover over as a temporary measure,' he said, gesturing up to the hole, 'but it's going to need a thatcher to sort it out properly, the straw roof looks really old.' He shook his head. 'Sorry to be the bearer of bad news . . .'

'Oh it's not your fault . . . and thank you for taking a look,' April said, busying herself by making a start on picking up the bigger bits of debris. Anything to avoid him catching her inadvertently staring at his magnificent body, especially as he was using the front of his T-shirt now to wipe his hot face, exposing his perfectly taut abdomen.

'No problem.' He picked up his tool belt. 'And thanks . . .' he said as he went to leave the room.

'What for?'

'Well, you know . . . with Bella just now, and in the orchard too. Don't know what you said to her but whatever it was worked, 'cos she opened up to you, I had no idea what was going on. All that stuff at school. I should have known . . .' His head dropped slightly.

'Don't be so hard on yourself. I listened, that's

all . . . And you know how it is, it's much easier to talk to a stranger than to your own dad at that age.'

'I guess so,' Matt said, fiddling with his belt buckle. 'It's tough this parenting lark sometimes.' Silence followed.

'Yes it is,' April nodded. 'But you seem like a good dad to me. You love her, and you care . . . and she's a lovely, kind girl. You know, she really cares about those horses and she has a real creative talent – she's transformed the gypsy wagon single-handedly. She's a credit to you. And she's welcome here any time, I quite enjoy her company to be honest and I'm looking forward to taking her to the knitting group,' April said, and it was true, having someone to go with would make it easier for the both of them.

'Cheers,' Matt said. 'And I do try to be a good dad. But it's hard when she won't do as she's told . . . I worry about her. You know, I found a bottle of cheap wine . . . she'd been drinking. But if I tell her off about it, she'll go ballistic, that's what normally happens, but I can't just ignore it, she's only thirteen. It's illegal for Christ's sake.'

'Well, I guess nobody likes being told what to do. Maybe try asking her, and then help her make the right choices, explain the effects of alcohol . . . the dangers, and then you can guide her instead of telling her. It could backfire if you come down hard on her. She might rebel . . .' April smiled, finally managing to make proper eye contact.

'True. And that's the last thing I want.' Matt folded his arms. 'She has enough to deal with at school without me giving her a hard time!' He shook his head. 'Thanks, April. And your girl seems to have turned out fine, sensible. She was totally calm downstairs when Bella came shrieking for me to come into the cottage, so you must have done something right.'

'Thanks, but I can't take any credit, she's my stepdaughter.'

'Ahh, I see.' More silence followed. 'So, er . . . is your husband not here with you then?' he said, averting his eyes. April dipped her head.

'No.' April took a breath and then lifted her head to look directly at Matt. 'No. He passed away.' And this time she felt all right saying it.

'Blimey! Sorry. Um, I'm really sorry,' Matt said, his voice softening. 'What happened? God, sorry, it's none of my business.' He shook his head in apology.

April opened her mouth to reply, but was saved from doing so when a floorboard gave way underneath Matt's foot. April instinctively flung herself forward to help him, but missed his hand, and her fingertips ended up brushing his bare abdomen instead. She immediately leapt back and apologised profusely.

'Christ!' Matt looked startled as he tumbled backwards and his left hand touched the edge of the rug on the floor. 'We need to get out of here. This cottage is falling apart!' He yanked his boot-clad foot free and went to walk out of the attic bedroom, giving the offending floorboard behind him a filthy glare. He stopped. 'What's that?'

'What?' April looked to where Matt was pointing.

'There! I can see something right there under that floorboard. In the gap where my foot was. Here, help me shove the rug out of the way.'

After rolling the rug up and lifting the broken floorboard, plus the one next to it, which was rotten right through and almost crumbled away in their hands, they saw what looked like a small wooden box partially wrapped in a dusty old hessian sack. April gingerly reached in and lifted the parcel free. Inside the sack was an old apple box containing a number of hardback books, ledgers perhaps. She placed the box on the bed and picked up one of the books. After opening the front cover, April spluttered as a cloud of dust puffed up right under her nostrils. Carefully wiping the first page with the back of her hand, her pulse quickened as she saw the following words written in faint black ink.

Winnie Lovell
Secret Diary
Age 10 & ¾
1930

21

Friday afternoon, and Dr Ben had just arrived. April opened the door and, after shaking hands and saying hello, she ushered him into the hallway, apprehensive about how Aunt Edie was going to react, given her mistrust of doctors and modern medicine.

'I did explain that you were coming today, but my aunt's memory isn't what it used to be, doctor. She's in the sitting room, if you want to go through – I'll wait in the kitchen. Would you like a cup of tea, or a glass of water perhaps?' April said, conscious that she was talking too much and too fast, but it felt a little strange, calling the GP out to her elderly aunt, almost as if Edie were a child and she was the parent.

'A glass of water would be grand,' Dr Ben said, in a lovely lilting Irish accent as he bumped the front of his head on a low beam and nearly knocked off his black-framed glasses.

'Oh gosh, are you OK?' April quickly took a step forward, ready to assist if required.

'Yes, thanks. No damage done, happens all the time,' he grinned, shaking his head and pushing his glasses further up his nose. 'You'd think I'd be used to the low ceilings in these Tindledale cottages on my home visits by now . . .' And he turned towards the sitting-room door. 'I have all Miss Lovell's notes here, including details of the call you put in to the surgery when you made the appointment,' he reassured, patting the folder, 'so if you introduce me first, please, and then we can see if your aunt would like you to be present during my examination – it may make her feel more at ease?' Dr Ben suggested, lifting his eyebrows.

'Sure.' April smiled, starting to relax. Dr Ben was much younger than she had imagined a village doctor would be, and seemed far more down to earth than the serious, white-coated doctors in the hospitals that she had worked with as a nurse. He was wearing jeans and trainers and an open-neck shirt with the sleeves rolled up. Things sure were different out here in the countryside, far more relaxed, and she liked it.

'Oops.' Dr Ben went to push his car keys into his jeans pocket, but ended up dropping them on the carpet instead as he juggled a big medical bag and a paper file full of notes. April dipped down to retrieve the keys and saw a picture of Sybs from the haberdashery shop on the key ring as she handed them back to him.

'Ahh, I met Sybs in Hettie's House of Haberdashery . . . I didn't know you two . . .' April smiled, and let her voice trail off, not wanting him to think she was being nosey.

'Yes, my wife, she runs the shop,' Dr Ben nodded and smiled. 'And our gorgeous twin girls, Florence and Henrietta,' he added proudly, taking the key ring and turning it over to show April a picture of two curly-haired cuties.

'Oh, they're adorable. Twins are very special – I have grown-up twin stepchildren,' April smiled, starting to relax. 'A boy and a girl.'

'Then I'll be sure to come to you for advice when my wee Flo and Hettie start growing up,' he said, kindly and politely.

Having seen Dr Ben into the sitting room and reminding her aunt who he was and why he was here, Aunt Edie seemed quite happy to chat away and let the doctor carry out his examination, so April popped out to the kitchen to get him a glass of water.

'How's it going?' Nancy asked, looking up from the kitchen table where she was sitting peeling potatoes for this evening's dinner.

'Good, I think.' April glanced at the hatch to make sure it was closed, giving Edie and Dr Ben some privacy. 'Aunty seems pretty chirpy . . . she's answering lots of questions – what year is it, who the prime minister is, et cetera,' she whispered, letting the tap run to ensure the water was nice and cold for the doctor. It was a scorcher of a day and April wondered if he had a long list of home visits spanning an enormous rural area to get through, as was often the case for country GPs. 'That's not to say that she'll be getting all the answers right, but at least Dr Ben can let me know what her needs are.'

'Exactly,' Nancy said, 'and don't forget to ask about the thyroid thing. You know, I saw her tipping a bottle of tablets out into the kitchen bin earlier.'

'Really?' April filled the glass, turned off the tap and turned to look squarely at her stepdaughter.

'Yep.' Nancy nodded, looking concerned.

'Well, we can't have that, if she needs to be taking them. Thanks for mentioning it, love.' And April went back into the sitting room, keen to hear Dr Ben's diagnosis.

*

Later, having left her aunt in the capable care of Nancy – they were playing rummy and enjoying a snowball together after having an early dinner – April parked the Beetle outside Hettie's House of Haberdashery. She turned to Bella who was sitting beside her, looking petrified as she clutched the handles of her knitting bag that was perched on top of her thighs.

'Are you ready to do some knitting?' April asked, feeling nervous too, but she managed a big smile for Bella, knowing she couldn't back out now, even though it would be so very easy to do so. April inhaled and placed her hand on Bella's arm. 'Come on, it'll be fine. Let's do this together.' And Bella nodded as they got out of the car.

'You're going to stay with me, aren't you?' Bella then asked apprehensively.

'Of course. I'm looking forward to doing some knitting too,' April half-fibbed, stowing the car keys in her handbag. It was true that she was keen to see what the club was like for Bella, and if she could resume her love for knitting, and banish the bad thoughts, the negative association that had developed inside her head ever since Gray had died. The unfinished Aran jumper. The sitting together watching TV, while she knitted and he joked about the chunky needles. It was fear, all this stalling, April knew that. She was worried the memories that knitting evoked would be too painful to revisit. But then there was only one way to find out.

After looping her arm through Bella's, they walked together down the little path and up to the door that jangled to the sound of the old-fashioned, but cosily comforting bell as they pushed it open and went inside.

'Come in, come in. It's so good to see you both. I'm Taylor.' A girl with a bun on top of her head and silver hoop earrings jumped up from a yarnbombed, squishy sofa to greet them with a lovely, bubbly smile. 'You must be Bella,' Taylor grinned, eyeing Bella's knitting bag. 'Ooh, bag envy. Where did you get this from?' she asked, touching the bag.

'Um, er . . . I made it,' Bella answered warily, and glanced at April for reassurance as if bracing herself for potential ridicule from the older girl. But she wasn't at school now. April smiled and gave Bella a quick discreet wink.

'Wow! I love it. Ever thought of making . . .' Taylor paused and looked upward as if formulating a plan, 'like *loads* of lovely knitting bags and selling them on Etsy? God, I love Etsy.' Taylor fluttered her eyelids.

'Me too,' Bella said, grinning and seeming to warm up a bit now.

'Cool. Come and meet the others.' And Taylor took Bella over towards the rest of the young knitters. 'Budge up, you lot, and let Bella sit down – look at her gorge knitting bag.'

April felt pleased as the group took it in turns to swoon over Bella's bag, making her young friend feel so welcome. And the size of Bella's smile was worth bringing her here for alone, she already looked relaxed and right at home as she took off her coat and got stuck in. The beauty of being thirteen, April mused inwardly! Adaptable, resilient, and she really wished she still had more of that armour herself. Maybe she was overthinking things, worrying too much. Perhaps if she just sat down and started knitting, didn't let her mind wander back to those cosy nights in with Gray, then everything would be fine.

Still pondering, April spotted Hettie coming through a heavy brocade curtain over at the back of the shop, and went towards her.

'Hello, my dear. Fancy a cup of tea?' Hettie asked.

'Oh, yes please, that would be lovely,' April replied, relieved to have something else to occupy her while she waited for Bella. Perhaps she wouldn't do any actual knitting tonight after all. Baby steps and all that . . . She was here, and it felt like a good start . . .

'Follow me. We can sit in the little kitchen-cum-sitting-room out the back and leave the young ones to it. When Molly dropped her boy off earlier for the knitting club, she said that you hadn't done any knitting yourself for a while . . .' Hettie fixed her Wedgwood-blue eyes on April as if scrutinising her to see if she could find out why.

'Yes, well, um, no . . . that's right,' April started, hesitated, fiddled with her hair and fell silent for a moment, and then instead of getting anxious like she usually did in these situations, she came right out with it – 'Not since my husband died' – and felt much better for saying so. Hettie studied April for a moment, her papery face softening.

'I'm sorry for your loss, dear, but you mustn't let grief ruin the very things that will help you come to terms with your loss.' Hettie patted her arm and April swallowed hard, determined not to let the well of emotion that was swirling inside her right now take over. 'Come on, my eyesight isn't what it used to be . . . you can help me by reading the pattern for a sweater that I'm making for my son, Gerry. I might even let you knit some of the second sleeve if I think your knitting skills are up to it!' Hettie said firmly, as she held the curtain aside for April.

And before she had a chance to protest, let alone think about the wise old lady's stoic instructions, April found herself hanging up her coat on a hook behind the door and then sitting in a patchwork armchair with a pair of size 9 needles in her hands, and the most exquisite section of soft grey cashmerino purl stitch dangling from them. There really was no time to worry about how this was going to make her feel, and besides, April reckoned that Hettie wouldn't take no for an answer, so she just got on with it and pushed the right-hand needle down into the first stitch on the other side, wound the wool around . . . and she was knitting again! And the feeling that came over April as all the anxiety and fear that had built up inside her drifted away was utterly overwhelming in a wonderful, cathartic way.

22

A week later, and Nancy was dozing in the afternoon sun on a deckchair outside the entrance to the barn with April, Great Aunt Edie and Bella. Two days after she had arrived at Orchard Cottage, Nancy had called the fire station to see if she could extend her leave. She had loads of holiday owing to her, having preferred to keep busy after Dad's death, and being at work with the lads had helped her do just that. And it really was idyllic here in Tindledale so she had been delighted when her boss had said yes to her taking a fortnight off. In fact, Nancy was sure she had heard a sigh of relief in his voice, for he had been saying for a while now that she was overdoing it and needed a break before she became a liability to herself and the rest of the watch. Plus, they had two firefighters over from another station to do some training so it wasn't as if they were short-handed right now.

Nancy pushed her shades up on top of her head and lifted the jug of ice-cold pear cider from the upturned apple crate that was currently serving as a picnic table. Jimmy, the organic cider producer, had called by earlier with a crate of each variety – bottles of traditional pear and apple made using fruit from the Orchard Cottage crop, a lovely summery strawberry and lime and several bottles of mulled cider that April had put away for Christmas – on the house as it were, as he was so made up with the quality of the fruit. And April had been over the moon with the subsequent payment, which had covered the cost of the thatcher to sort out the roof, plus there was some left over to build a proper stable for Darby and Joan – that was happening next week. And until then they were flourishing nicely in the makeshift stable in the barn. And Nancy had been delighted too, thinking she could really get used to the countryside way of life. Free cider would never happen in Basingstoke. There she'd be lucky to bag a BOGOF deal of Smirnoff Ice in the local Tesco Express.

'More of this good stuff for you, Edie?' Nancy asked, tilting the jug towards the old lady, making the ice cubes chink and the cider fizz as she batted away a big bumblebee before it nosedived into the frothy liquid.

'Ooh, don't mind if I do, dear,' Edie chuckled and held out her glass. Nancy did the honours and poured her a generous top-up, smiling inwardly as she had come to realise that 'Old Edie' was rather partial to getting pleasantly sozzled in the afternoon sun. This was the third day in a row that they had sat in the garden gossiping and generally taking it easy. And why not? Nancy thought it a crying shame if a lady in her nineties couldn't indulge at her time of life, and she fully intended on doing exactly the same when she reached her own dotage. They had been careful of course, and rigged up a gazebo using her tent for Edie to shade under.

And Dr Ben had confirmed when he visited that Edie was indeed suffering from untreated hypothyroidism and had prescribed some more tablets which April was now in charge of administering each morning. They seemed to have given Edie back some degree of mental clarity and vigour, although he had confirmed that she had dementia too, which would account for the forgetfulness and periods of regression. But as she seemed quite content, he wasn't about to prescribe more pills or suggest she be taken off to a home. Not when her niece was here and willing to look after her, is what he had said before he left. And Nancy had felt worried about this at first. How would Edie cope when April came home? But it was becoming clearer and clearer as the days went on that April was already at home. She seemed really happy here, lighter and less burdened somehow, which was a relief, but still, they needed to talk. Freddie was going on about moving out, wanting to travel around the world with one of his mates, and Nancy wasn't sure that she wanted to stay in the bungalow on her own, not with all the memories it held of Dad being ill, especially if April wasn't coming back – she didn't want to lose her too and end up being completely on her own. But the right moment to talk hadn't arisen so far, because either Bella had been here, or Harvey the fruit farmer. Nancy had taken an instant dislike to him – he was charming enough she supposed, but there was something about him that she just couldn't quite put her finger on. And she certainly couldn't chat to April in front of Aunt Edie; the last thing she wanted

Paris. And very chic she was – always turned out nicely. Did you know that, April?'

April, Nancy and Bella all looked at Edie and smiled, knowing to treasure the rare moments of lucidity, for they were becoming less frequent these days.

'Yes, Aunty. I certainly do. Tell me about the party. What did you wear?' April asked pleasantly, and Nancy's heart softened – she marvelled at how kind and caring April was with her aunt. Just as she had been with Dad. She really did have the patience of a saint. Especially when her aunt called out in the middle of the night – Nancy had heard her and found herself feeling frustrated and grumpy at having been woken up, but nothing was too much trouble for April – and Nancy knew that she never would have coped with Dad towards the end if it hadn't been for her. He would have had to go into a hospice or something, if it had all been down to Nancy and Freddie to care for him. And if Nancy thought about that for too long, the prospect made her feel so in-adequate. She swallowed hard and concentrated on what Edie was saying, instead of letting her head run away with her. She couldn't change the past and nothing was going to bring Dad back so she might as well get on with it. Stick on a brave face as she always had. It was the only way . . .

'Oh, Winnie let me wear one of her dresses. A satin shift dress with a big red sash at the hip. I felt like a princess,' Edie chuckled. 'And after the party, we slept in the wagon. A special treat. Mind you, we didn't get much shut-eye. Winnie kept me awake for most of the night reading aloud from her book about etiquette. She was obsessed with that book in the years before she left Tindledale – Mum gave it to her for her birthday. "*It is a mark of ill-breeding to draw your gloves on in the street*"!' Aunt Edie said, adopting an especially posh voice, and the four of them laughed. 'I remember it so clearly, as if it were yesterday. And do you know,' Edie paused to point a bony finger in the air to punctuate her point, 'to this day I have never done it – put my gloves on outside of the house! Absolutely not!' Edie shook her head, making her snow-white curls swish all around.

'Hmm, and I'm sure that line rings a bell.' April put down the diary and lifted up another from the apple crate. She flicked through the pages. 'Yes, see, right here . . . in the last diary, dated 1941, right before Winnie left to go to the FANY training place. I read this one first hoping there might be some clues as to what happened to her next. Why she didn't return . . . Ahh, here we go. Look, it's one of the last things she wrote! Just there on the page all by itself.'

It is a mark of ill-breeding to draw your gloves on in the street.

'Strange, isn't it?' April commented. 'And it stuck in my head as it's also underlined in the book that Hettie gave me . . . presumably the same book that you're referring to, Aunty?'

Edie gave a polite nod and finished the last of her iced cider as a faraway look floated on to her face, making it clear that she had forgotten all about the book now – she was fading again.

'Let me see.' Nancy put the glass jug down on the dresser and leant in close to April to read the old-fashioned words written in sloped letters, and in real ink.

'What do you think it means?' April asked.

'No idea.' Nancy shrugged. 'It's a bit weird though, just written like that with no context . . . why would it be underlined in the book and then written in the diary too? What do you think, Edie?' But Edie didn't reply. She was fast asleep.

'April, can I go and groom Darby and Joan please?' Bella asked, putting her knitting down.

'Sure love. You don't need to ask . . .'

'Thank you. Dad said I have to ask.'

'Well, in that case you must,' April laughed, as Bella skipped off to the end of the barn.

'She's such a nice kid,' Nancy said, seeing how fond her stepmother was of the girl. And Nancy thought it was lovely . . . the dynamic Bella brought to Orchard Cottage, she kept things light, less heavy somehow, which was exactly what April needed. Plus, her dad wasn't too bad either. Nancy hoped he'd ask April out, it was about time she had a bit of fun, a flirtation if nothing else. Hmm, the thought lingered.

'Yes, she is . . .' April said, slowly, deep in thought. She glanced over at Edie. 'Is she still asleep?'

'Yep.'

'Good. I can show you this, in that case . . .' She flicked back a few pages and tapped her fingernail next to another paragraph in Winnie's diary. 'It's from when she was in the Land Army. Before she went off to join the FANY.'

Nancy read the words in her head as April sipped some more of her cider.

Dear Diary,

The most shocking thing happened at the weekend. I went off with Rita and some of the other girls to a dance in Brighton and got caught up in an airstrike. I could see the flames in the distance lighting up the pier. A warden dragged me to the ground as the screech of another bomb came, but I couldn't stay down as Rita had flames on her skirt and was screaming. I crawled on all fours to get to her, with fiery bits of wood and concrete coming down on me, which luckily I managed to duck out of the way to avoid, and then used my jacket to roll her in. Poor thing was in agony but I couldn't leave her there to suffer, or worse. No, I certainly couldn't do that.

I heard the next day that she didn't make it. Finch was awfully kind about it, said I deserved a medal for keeping such a cool head and risking my own life to try to save poor Rita's – apparently the warden notified him . . . I don't remember a thing really, after Rita went off in the ambulance. How I got back to base is still a mystery. I had a ride in a car, a tractor and the last transport I remember was a horse and cart. Wish I had worn my breeches and socks and not a silly dress and shoes.

'Bloody hell!' Nancy exhaled. 'Really brings it home, doesn't it? The true horror of war and what that generation went through.' She shook her head vehemently.

'Sure does. And wasn't Winnie brave? I agree with Finch – she should have got a medal for crawling on all fours under a bomb drop to try to save her friend!' April nodded. 'Yes, I'm glad her bravery was brought to this Finch man's attention, whoever he was . . .'

'Absolutely. Who is he?' Nancy asked.

'Someone important by the sounds of it. Winnie had volunteered for driving duties for the nearby army base, apparently. I read about that in one of her letters home, and made a note in my pad,' April said.

'Ahh, I see. Come on, let's read some more . . . where are you up to?' Nancy said, intrigued.

'Here.' April carefully thumbed through a number of pages until she reached a faded old envelope that she was using as a bookmark.

'Oops.' Nancy bent down to retrieve the envelope as it fluttered out of April's hand on to the grass. She turned it over, scrutinising it before going to hand it back to April. And then something caught her eye. It was faint, but there nonetheless, an imprint on the inside of the envelope, like a stamp, a crest perhaps . . . 'Where did you get this?' Nancy asked. 'Was it in the diary?'

'No, I found it in the sideboard tucked behind the pen tin, why?' April asked.

'It's addressed to Mr G. Lovell, Orchard Cottage, Tindledale.'

'Yes, that's right. George was Edie's father, my great grandfather.'

'Interesting,' Nancy said, opening the envelope and examining it some more.

'Not really. My aunt is a bit of a hoarder, there are loads of old letters and paperwork in the sideboard in the sitting room,' April said.

'Might be worth having a root through it all then, because unless I'm mistaken, I'd say that mark there looks official.' Nancy tapped the middle of the envelope to show April.

'Ahh, yes, I see it now, the outline of a crown.'

'Exactly. So whatever was in this envelope addressed to Winnie's dad might have been official.'

'From the War Office maybe!' April's eyes widened. 'Will you watch Edie while I take a proper look through the sideboard?'

'Sure. But first, read me that next bit of the diary please. I'm dying to know more about Winnie. It feels a bit naughty looking through someone's secret diary, and besides, if there is anything important in that sideboard, then it isn't going anywhere, is it?'

'True.' April turned a few more pages until she spotted the name Finch again. 'Ooh, here he is . . .' And both women read on, utterly enthralled.

Dear Diary,

I'm in love, it's true! Not that I know for sure, having never felt this way before, but when Finch pressed his lips on to mine, a glorious fluttery feeling radiated within me. Jolly good we were in the back orchard, for if we were indoors and alone, then I'm not sure I would have managed to resist him for a moment longer.

And I shall press, and then treasure the violet that he

picked for me on our woodland walk. And cherish the romantic words he said on slipping the flower into my button hole – 'It really is a hardy little heart-shaped flower, so brave to battle winter only to bloom in spring, heralding a new beginning.'

But of course, it's prudent not to take it with me, for . . .

And the rest of the words were so faded it was hard to read on until the end of the sentence.

'What do you reckon?' April asked, lowering her voice as she closed the diary, figuring the crumbled brown flakes that had fallen from this particular page had once been a flower, the precious violet picked for her great aunt by her lover all those years ago. It was romantic. And so very poignant, given that the young Winnie who wrote these words had vanished soon after, never to be seen again by her family.

'That maybe the rumours were true after all,' whispered Nancy. 'Seems Winnie definitely had a man on the go. And why would she not want to take his flower with her? Only reason I can think of is that she didn't want the other girls to see it . . .' Nancy's forehead creased as she tried to work it all out. 'Ooh, I do love an old mystery – this is just like *Cold Case*, my favourite box set.' She swigged some more cider. 'And this must mean that she had a secret! Or he did! That he was married . . .'

'Perhaps. But do you think it might be a bit of a leap? Just because Winnie thought it prudent not to take a pressed violet with her when she went off to do her

FANY training doesn't mean that the man, Finch . . . I wonder who he is? Hmm . . .' Both women pondered the possibilities for a few seconds. 'But this isn't proof that he was married, or that Winnie ran off with him and had his baby . . . she even says that she managed to resist him. And Hettie practically said the same too, that Winnie wasn't like that at all. She was a good girl – those were Hettie's exact words.'

'True,' Nancy replied, 'but you have to admit though, it's looking like the most plausible explanation. She would have come back to Tindledale otherwise, surely. Why wouldn't she? It's idyllic here and it was her home . . . maybe she didn't manage to resist Finch the next time they kissed and she ended up getting pregnant and he was married, and she was unmarried! Now that would have been a massive scandal in those days. No wonder she didn't come back home . . . probably thought it best to keep well clear under the circumstances. Her parents could very well have disowned her. It happened in the olden days, that's what they did. Or what if they had made her give away the baby? That happened a lot too! Just think of all those women on that TV programme, *Long Lost Family*.'

'OK. Well, let's not get too carried away in making up the story, and say that she did run off with Finch, aka the married man, and had his baby . . . there's still no real evidence of that.' April kept her voice very low. 'Don't you think that's odd?'

'Not really! There was a war on, who knows what paperwork got lost. And didn't you say Winnie's last letter to Edie was posted from London?' April nodded. 'Well, there you go! The Blitz. She could have died when a bomb dropped. It's entirely likely,' Nancy mouthed pragmatically, her eyes darting over to Edie as she started tidying away the empty glasses on to the dresser.

'I suppose so.' April closed the diary and placed it inside the wooden apple crate with the others before carefully stowing it on the dresser away from the hay. 'I don't want the diaries getting ruined,' she said, 'they are part of my heritage after all. My family history right there.' She grinned. 'It's most likely that Winnie did in fact die during the war. And I must find a way to explain that to Edie.'

'But do you really need to?' Nancy gave April a look and then they both glanced over at the elderly lady snoozing in the afternoon sun. Content. Her weathered face relaxed and peaceful. 'Why upset her? Maybe it would be kinder to just let her carry on thinking that Winnie is still alive . . .'

'Oh I don't know. Isn't that worse though? Letting Edie think that Winnie ran off with a married man and had his baby, without so much as a backward glance or a postcard to her dear sister in all these years . . .'

'Hmm, well, yes I guess so when you put it like that. Maybe best then to get it over with and say that Winnie died in London. And the paperwork, death certificate, got lost or something in the war. And there was no man or baby. And at least then Edie can take comfort from thinking her sister's reputation was still intact . . . because let's face it, Edie doesn't have much longer herself, so if she dies happy and at peace with her missing sister then that's a good thing, yes?' Nancy offered.

'Yes. I guess so.' April nodded and then a few seconds later added, 'But what I can't figure out, and it's been really bugging me, is, firstly, how come Winnie didn't know that her brother Sidney had been killed in action? And what was Winnie even doing in London, when the FANY training centre was near Oxford?'

'I've no idea! Having a naughty weekend with Finch?' Nancy winked and nudged April in the side.

'Stop it! You're incorrigible.' Both women laughed and drank more iced cider. 'But I'm going to pass this name, Finch, on to the general.'

'The general?'

'Yes, he's ex-army, retired, runs the weekly tea dance in the village hall. Bit of a historian,' April explained.

'Then it's worth a go,' Nancy nodded, pleased that her stepmum had the mystery of what happened to Winnie to occupy her thoughts; it was much more healthy than watching old videos of Dad in the dark. That had been horrendous, and many nights Nancy had just gone up to bed and left April to it, unable to bear seeing her like that. When Dad went, Nancy had dealt with it, it was hard of course. But it was pitiful, heartbreaking, seeing April so sad . . . Nancy swallowed hard and switched her thoughts. April seemed to be in a different place now, mentally and physically, and Nancy was glad that she had come to Tindledale to see it and that April had genuinely seemed pleased to have her here. Nancy had been worried about intruding – April was her stepmum after all, not her actual mum, and now with Dad gone, what was to say that April would carry on looking after her and Freddie? Nancy pondered momentarily, and then pulled herself together. April hadn't abandoned her, far from it, she wasn't like that, she was lovely and caring, so Nancy would need to keep that in mind – she vowed to try not to worry about it.

'And if this general has army connections,' Nancy said, focusing her mind back to Winnie's diary, 'then he might be able to find out who this Finch man was, if he was something to do with the army base that Winnie was driving for . . .'

'Yes!' April pulled out her notepad and wrote down 'FINCH', underlining it several times.

'Now, changing the subject entirely, well not totally entirely, it is kind of similar . . .' Nancy ventured tentatively, thinking now might be a good time to talk to April when she seemed so relaxed and happy. And Edie was still asleep, and snoring louder than ever.

'Go on.'

'*Weell*, talking of men!' She lifted her eyebrows. 'Tell me something – when are you going to go on a date with that oh-so-sexy, but slightly moody farrier?'

Matt had barely said a word when he dropped Bella off to go with April to the knit and natter session. Nancy thought it was a shame and wondered why the sudden change in his attitude towards her lovely stepmum, because anyone could see that he fancied her – Nancy didn't miss a thing – and the spark between them was palpable. Bella had noticed it too and they had shared a conspiratorial grin or two, which was good. Nancy figured it wouldn't hurt to have his daughter on side as well, as Nancy of all people knew what it was like when your dad met a new woman. Or maybe Matt felt awkward because Harvey had been here; he had dropped by on the pretext of seeing how things were going with the new roof, but as soon as Matt arrived, Harvey had acted as if he and April were an item, standing next to her, nodding in mutual agreement and all that . . . And Matt and Harvey *were* friends. Perhaps Matt didn't want to make a move on April and tread on his mate's toes. *You'd think they would have spoken to each other about the new woman in Tindledale*, thought Nancy, but then they were men and she knew exactly how inept they could be when it came to that kind of thing, she worked with them all day and sometimes all night long too. Hmm, well if that was the case, then Nancy knew she would have to come up with a plan! She really wanted April to be happy, and if she could help make her so, then it was the least she could do after all the love and care April had shown Dad. And Orchard Cottage was such a nice place to be, Nancy loved how she felt here, relaxed and rested, and could really see April living here. And Tindledale wasn't that far away, Nancy could always visit so it wasn't like she was going to lose April from her life completely . . .

'Pardon?' April blinked.

'You heard.' Nancy smiled playfully, and the two women sat in silence for a while, interrupted only by the soft snores from Aunt Edie. 'Oh come on, April, I can see that he fancies you, and that you're attracted to him,'

Nancy broke the silence. 'What's stopping you? Is it Dad?'

'Um, yes I suppose, and . . .' April stopped talking. 'You know, Harvey has asked me out . . .'

Nancy frowned. If her dad's widow was going to go on a date with a new man, it certainly wasn't going to be Harvey. Admittedly, she had only met him briefly, but she knew that her dad wouldn't have liked him. Smarmy. That's what Gray would have said. Whereas he would have liked Matt, she was sure of it . . . Matt seemed different, sensitive and sensible, she'd seen how he was with Darby and Joan, and caring and loyal – a single dad, just like her own had been when he first met April. Yes, Nancy thought Matt would be good for April.

'Hmm, doesn't surprise me!'

'Why do you say it like that?' April raised her eyebrows.

'No reason,' Nancy fibbed. 'So what do you actually know about him?'

'Weell,' she started slowly, 'he's a fruit farmer . . .'

'So not much then,' Nancy stated.

'And he sorted out the contract with the organic cider guy, Jimmy! Orchard Cottage would be uninhabitable if Harvey hadn't helped out with that . . .'

'You sound as if you're validating him.'

'Do I?' April looked away. 'Maybe I should go on a date with him – he has been good to me.'

'APRIL!'

'What?'

'Stop it! You don't owe him anything. Just because he helped you out . . .' Nancy shook her head and sighed. April was far too nice for her own good sometimes.

Putting others' feelings ahead of her own, wanting to keep everyone happy – she figured that was why she had fussed over Freddie for all these years, doing his washing and all that. And the thing was, he had managed absolutely fine while April had been in Tindledale.

'Yes, you're right, darling. What am I thinking?' April grinned sheepishly. 'Anyway, I'm not sure I'm ready . . .'

The implication of April's words hung in the air. And then Nancy got it. The look on April's face. She was anxious. Apprehensive.

'Are you worried that I'll be upset or something? If you go out with another man?'

April gave Nancy a look that said it all.

And Nancy took April's hand in hers.

'Listen,' she started softly, 'I can see that you're happy here. You could make a new life for yourself . . . Matt is lovely, any man that can whisper to horses like that gets a big thumbs up in my book. Why don't you give him a go?' Nancy said, putting her own feelings aside. At the end of the day, she was a grown-up, and if April moved on with a new man it wasn't as if she would up sticks and be off to New Zealand like her mum. No. Nancy took a deep breath and put a smile on her face.

'But—' April went to protest.

'Shuuuuuush.' Nancy leant in and gave April a big hug. And her blessing too – knowing that she absolutely needed it. After taking a deep breath, she added, 'Dad would be happy for you to make a new life with somebody else. You mustn't feel guilty about that!' She let April go, and that's when she saw the tears.

At last. The dam!

It had finally burst.

Nancy had known it would come. She quickly pulled April back into her and held her tight as she cried a torrent of tears, mingled with enormous, heaving sobs that racked her whole body.

that until now. Nancy explained how she had coped, put on a brave face, got on with it and tried not to worry about April . . . but had an underlying fear that she and Freddie would lose April too, which was part of the reason she had come to Tindledale. April figured everyone grieved in different ways. But then Nancy had pointed out that it seemed to her like April had done exactly the same – put all her energy and emotions into caring for Gray, then Freddie, and now her great aunt. And April agreed: it was easier, a way of getting on with it too, of protecting herself, and probably why she hadn't cried, not properly. Not in front of anyone. And they had both come to the realisation too that they'd worried about each other when they should probably have concentrated on themselves more, but at least they had come together now, and had each other to remember Gray – to talk about him, laugh about him, share mutual memories, something they couldn't do with anyone else. Like the time in a posh restaurant when Gray had shaken the balsamic vinegar bottle so vigorously that the lid popped off and an arc of black sticky liquid had sprayed up in the air before splatting him all over the head, and they had all laughed until they clutched their sides and cried happy tears. It was a miracle they hadn't been thrown out! Those were the funny anecdotes that Nancy and April would treasure for ever. And Freddie too. April had called him several times since coming to Tindledale and he did seem OK, and had started to talk to her about Gray, recalling some anecdotes of his own. And as long as they all did that, then Gray would always be with them, it would only be when they were all long gone that he would be too. That was the true essence of eternal life . . . living on in other people's memories.

But last night, there had been lots of tears, for both of them, and a fair amount of poignant laughter too as they remembered those good times. And things were definitely different now – April thought she might like to stay on in Tindledale for a good while longer. Nancy had said she was fine with it after April had categorically assured her that she wasn't about to lose her, she was her stepmother, regardless of whether Gray was here or not, and that would never change. And April could hardly leave her aunt to fend for herself. She had mooted the idea of taking Edie back to Basingstoke with her, but Tindledale was her home, it wouldn't be fair to do that, and besides, Nancy had said it might be time to see about selling the bungalow – perhaps! April wasn't sure about that yet, all her memories with Gray were there. She figured she would need to at least go back to see how she felt, see if it was possible. Even though she felt Gray's presence with her wherever she was, but still . . . his things, his shirts hanging in the wardrobe, all the physical stuff was there.

April stepped up and over the stile, curious to see how Bella was getting on with the yarnbombing. Since joining Taylor's knit and natter group, she too seemed to have turned a corner and was going to school every day now the new term had started, having made a couple of new friends from the group in the year above, who looked out for her – they had talked about it all during their knitting sessions in the wagon, which seemed to have turned into a regular event too. April hoisted her knitting bag up further on to her shoulder – the last time she went to Hettie's House of Haberdashery, she had treated herself to a new blue polka-dot knitting bag with loads of useful pockets for needles and yarn and all kinds of crafting paraphernalia. Hettie had been delighted too, when she saw her at the till. April couldn't thank the elderly woman enough for enabling her to face her fear and knit again that day in the little kitchen-cum-sitting-room at the back of the shop.

She stopped and pulled out a plastic bottle of water that was in the pocket at the end of the bag under her arm, and took several swigs. It was sweltering today, the hottest September on record, apparently. That's what the weather woman had said on the radio this morning when Edie, Nancy and April had been enjoying big bowls of Greek yogurt with porridge oats and Edie's phenomenally good apple sauce drizzled all over it. It had been too hot even at that time of the morning to have their usual eggs and soldiers, so they had taken breakfast outside and sat in the deckchairs with Darby and Joan in the barn. Edie had taken some convincing to try the yogurt, but now that she had, she had thoroughly enjoyed it too – which reminded April, she had promised to pick some pears to poach for their pudding tonight. It was Aunt Edie's favourite, with chocolate sauce drizzled all over the top.

After stowing the water bottle back into her bag, April wandered through into the next row of fruit trees in search of the best pears. Ahh, here they were, round and russet red. She picked six of the best and loaded them into an old carrier bag that she had taken to keeping in her pocket at all times, figuring it best to always be prepared for a foraging opportunity. Aunt Edie's garden and the surrounding fields were full of all kinds of produce and wild flowers. Only a few days ago, April had taken herself off for a wander through the woodland area, dappled with sunlight, with a stream running right through it that had been deliciously shaded and refreshing in the sizzling heat of summer, and came across a glorious array of wild flowers. Purple, pink and white, they had smelt heavenly and she had wondered if that was where Winnie had walked all those years ago with the mysterious man, known as Finch. Of course, it was too late for violets to bloom, but April had every intention of returning in early spring to see if she could find one to press just as Winnie had – and Finch was right, they were hardy little heart-shaped flowers capable of making it through a harsh, icy winter to bloom, heralding new beginnings. April may not be able to unravel the secret to her other great aunt's disappearance, but at least she could forge a connection to her in some other way.

April reached the gypsy wagon and was impressed to see that Bella had added two strings of jaunty bunting; hooked to the middle of the arched entrance, they cascaded outwards and were secured on two poles, creating a kind of aisled walkway. A welcome breeze made the fabric triangles flutter invitingly as April made her way to the little row of wooden steps.

'Only me, Bella. Come to see how the knitting is going.

Thought I'd join you for the afternoon . . .' April pushed a hand through the floaty white muslin curtains that Bella had also hung up, and went inside. And stopped. Bella wasn't there. Instead, on the fabric-covered bench seat where she would normally be sitting, cross-legged and knitting away while she waited for April to join in, was a large wicker picnic hamper with two crystal champagne flutes nestled next to it.

April checked her watch. One p.m. Well, that was right. Bella had popped a note into the mailbox nailed to the post at the end of the lane to ask if it was OK. April had found it when she went to collect the post shortly after nine, which was when Dave, the postman, usually called by. So where was she? And more to the point, why was there a picnic here? And a very impressive one, by the looks of it . . . April lifted the lid of the hamper and peeped inside. *Wow!* It had silver cutlery and proper china plates secured in navy criss-crossed elastic inside the lid with an amazing selection of food packed in special ice packs – pâté in a glass jar next to a selection of cheeses all individually wrapped. A meat platter. Bread rolls. Strawberries, chocolate truffles and a bottle of finest champagne. How bizarre. April closed the lid.

Figuring Bella would turn up soon enough to explain – she'd probably been waylaid on the way with checking on Darby and Joan, for she visited them daily now and always with a fresh bag full of grated carrot, which she fed to them by hand – April decided to get on with her knitting. She had managed to start a selection of simple squares, nothing fancy, not a garment for anyone with an emotion attached, as had been the case with that chunky Aran jumper for Gray. No, just plain squares to stitch on to the yarnbombed cover over the roof of the wagon.

Settling down on the seat opposite, April had just retrieved her needles from the cavernous bag when she heard a swooshing sound, footsteps through the long grass coming towards the wagon. *Ahh, that'll be her now.* April stood up and popped her head outside through the curtains.

'Oh!' She did a double take. Harvey was standing square in front of her with an extremely cheeky grin on his face.

'Ahh, so this is where you're hiding . . .' He put his hands on his hips and puffed himself up a little.

'Er, not hiding exact—' But before she could finish her sentence, he came up the wooden steps and into the wagon.

'Bloody hot one today, isn't it?' he said, more as a statement than an actual question.

'Um, yes. Yes it is,' April said, feeling awkward. Since her heart-to-heart with Nancy last night, she had decided not to go on a date with Harvey after all, and had planned on letting him know later. It wasn't right to lead him on, not when it was true, what Nancy had spotted from the off . . . there *was* a spark between her and Matt. It may come to nothing, but she'd never know if she didn't at least give it consideration.

But where was Bella? And why was Harvey here instead? And for some reason that she couldn't fathom,

April had an instinctive feeling that she had been set up somehow. But how? And why? And then Harvey confirmed it.

'Had an inkling you'd be here.' He grinned and indicated the picnic basket. 'So I thought, if you don't want to go *out*, out with me . . . if you know what I mean,' he shrugged and held up his palms, 'it's OK, I get it, Tindledale is a small place. Incestuous. And I don't blame you for not wanting people to gossip, and they probably would if they saw us together in the Duck & Puddle. Sooooo, I came up with this plan. Popped the note in your letterbox – bit cheeky of me – and then came down here to set it all up, and *voila*!' He gestured expansively around the wagon. 'Our very own private dining experience. What do you say?' He was rubbing his hands together now, like he couldn't wait to get stuck into the picnic! And April . . . given half a chance!

She dipped her head and put a hand to her face to stop the smile, born from his sheer audacity, from turning into a full-blown laugh. Incredible. And a lovely idea, the wagon did look amazing and he'd clearly made a lot of effort, *buuuuut* . . . this really wasn't what she wanted.

'Um . . . well, I'm . . .' April felt flabbergasted and quite unable to actually say anything more which was just as well as he took her hand, grabbed the hamper and went to go outside. Harvey really was something else. Not short of confidence, she'd give him that.

'Come on. Wait till you see this.' And before she could protest, she found herself tripping back down the steps after him and out into the sunshine and around the back of the wagon where a red-and-white checked blanket was laid out on the grass with a big pile of oversized cushions plumped around it. 'What do you reckon? You and me?' The innuendo hung in the air.

'Oh Harvey, this is very lovely, but I can't . . .' April could feel panic rising within her. It was too much. Too soon. Thoughts of Gray flooded her head. She could feel her chest rising and falling. Her heartbeat quickening. Hyperventilating.

'I knooooow,' he smiled, nodding slowly. 'You're over-whelmed. Don't worry, babe, I get it. Bet nobody has laid on a romantic spread like this for you before.'

April swallowed hard, her mouth felt like a sandpit, drained of saliva.

She had to get away.

Now.

And fast.

All she could think of was Gray. His face. His smell. His touch. What the hell was happening to her? Talking with Nancy about Matt. She didn't want to feel a spark with another man. All she wanted was Gray.

And all of sudden, a ferocious rage hurtled right through her, like a juggernaut with broken brakes. Out of control. Damn him for dying.

DAMN HIM.

DAMN HIM.

DAAAAAMN HIIIIIM.

'NOOOOOO.' The sound that came out of April's mouth was animalistic. Feral almost. Like an injured animal trapped in a snare.

And then she was running.

Running as if her life depended on it. Through the orchard. Up and over the stile. Through the next orchard. Tears stung in her eyes, blurring her vision, making her oblivious to the fruit trees scraping at the bare skin on her arms as she collided with the branches. Breaking them. Buffeting apples and pears all around. Desperate to get back. Back to the wonderful, cosy, familiar life that she once had with Gray.

24

'WHOA!' April felt her body brake as she ran head-long into a chest. Her face made contact with cotton fabric. Arms around her. She pulled back. Sleeve tattoos. 'You OK? What's going on?' It was Matt.

April scrubbed at her face with her palms, desperate to stem the tears and slow her pounding heart. She put her hands on her hips and bent over, in a desperate attempt to catch her breath.

'I . . . I . . . I'm sorry, I . . .' she tried.

'It's OK,' Matt said softly, his eyes scanning all around on hyper-alert, as if searching for the source of the danger, the reason for April's distress. 'No rush. Just take your time. Here, why don't you sit on this old tree stump.' And he took her by the elbow and steered her towards it so she could sit. He'd never seen anything like this. She looked distraught. Petrified. It was a good job Bella and Nancy had asked him to come and check on April in the orchard. She'd been gone ages, apparently, Bella had said, and they were getting worried about her out in this sweltering afternoon sun, so would he 'take this over to her?' And he still had April's straw sun hat in his hand. Clenched now, balled into a fist ready to strike at whatever, or whoever, had hurt her. He would give them a bloody good thump too. Terrorising women was disgusting. Maybe there was someone hiding out here after all. Harvey had thought so on that day when he'd called him over to fetch Bella, having found her in the gypsy wagon.

And where was Harvey now? He should be here helping April. Only last night in the pub, he had been going on about his big plan, another grand gesture intended to impress her. That was Harvey all over, he loved wooing the women, always had. Ever since he had rocked up in Tindledale fifteen years ago, having bought the old fruit farm for cash. For a hobby more than anything, keep him busy, he'd said. His wife was the one with the money though. She was someone important in the City of London. A QC, he seemed to remember Harvey having said – not that it really mattered, Matt had never met her. She rarely came to Tindledale. Instead, she worked hard and earned shedloads of money – married to her job, that was how Harvey had explained it.

Matt glanced at April; she seemed to be recovering now. He handed her the sun hat.

'You should put this on.'

'Thank you.' His eyes met hers, briefly, before he forced himself to look away. It baffled him. From the moment he had first seen her at the roadside in the lane, lost, he had found himself tongue-tied, like the shy kid he had been all those years ago. But he wasn't like that now. He was normally laid-back, easy-going, having grown into his own skin, as they say. He was a grown man now, but he was smitten all over again. It was stupid, he knew that. And he'd never go there. Not when she was seeing Harvey. He had been bragging about it. But the thing that Matt really couldn't get his head around was . . . why would a woman like April want to carry on with a married man? She was attractive in a way that meant she could take her pick of the men, so why settle for Harvey who already had a wife? And April was clever, insightful and kind. The advice she had given him in the bedroom that day had worked a treat – Bella seemed much less angry with him these days and was quite taken with April too, she never stopped going on about her.

But Harvey had implied that April knew he had a wife and was fine with it. Matt wasn't though. As a rule, he didn't like women like that, or men, for that matter – the bloke that Zoe left him for had known too, known that Zoe was a wife and a mum. But if Matt's head knew that, then why could he feel his heart falling for April again? He so easily could have taken her in his arms that day in the bedroom. He'd wanted to so badly, to kiss her, just like he had that day in the buttercup field. But she didn't even remember him. Admittedly, he had changed a lot, beyond all recognition it seemed, but maybe she just wasn't as into him as she had been all those years ago. He had cast his mind back, to see if he could remember much else about that summer, and he couldn't . . . apart from his brother, Jack, he had no idea who he had hung around with, so it was most likely the same for April, she had simply blanked it from her mind. He could hardly go, 'It's me, Matthew, from twenty-five

25

April was lying on the old brass bed in the attic bedroom, staring at the ceiling, at the freshly painted patch where the roof had fallen in, wondering what on earth Matt must be thinking of her. After she had got her breath back, she had stood up off the tree stump, politely thanked him for bringing her sun hat, and promptly walked off back here to Orchard Cottage, just leaving him standing there. And her cheeks were still burning with embarrassment and humiliation at having lost it like that. And what must Harvey be thinking? Yes, he'd got it so very wrong, but the picnic, the decorated gypsy wagon and everything . . . he had made a lot of effort! She had to apologise. To both men. And pronto.

April went to sit up. And stopped when the door opened slowly.

'Only me. Edie is having a snooze in her bedroom so I thought I'd come and see how you are.' It was Nancy with a mug of tea and a plate of biscuits. After placing them on the cabinet by the bed, she sat down. 'April, we never meant to upset you . . .'

'What do you mean?' April tidied her hair and sat up.

'You know, trying to fix you up with Matt – we only

289

wanted to help things along. Bella and me. Well, more me than Bella . . . she's just a kid, so please don't blame her. But she reckons her dad likes you too, and you know how fond she is of you, I think she'd love nothing more than for you to hook up with her dad. Anyway, we thought if he brought your sun hat to you, and the pair of you were alone in the orchard, and the sun was shining . . . and well, you might go for a little walk, pick a few flowers, you know . . . it might get romantic . . . just like it did for Winnie and Finch. So I thought I could create the moment, help things along a little.' She stopped talking. Silence followed. 'I guess I didn't really think at all . . .' Nancy grinned sheepishly.

'It's fine, darling. Honestly.' April placed her hand over Nancy's and gave it a reassuring pat before picking up the mug of tea. 'And thanks for this.' She took a sip and looked away.

'Well, it clearly isn't! I couldn't believe it when you came running across the garden, head down, no explanation, and straight up here. I've never seen you like that before. And look at the state of you.' April raised her eyebrows as she took another mouthful of the warm, sweet tea and attempted to tidy her hair with her free hand. 'Oh no, not like that. Please, don't start all that again – you used to do it before, worry about your appearance and all that. Do you remember on your birthday? When you thought I was criticising your hair?'

'Hmm, vaguely,' she muttered. It was true, she had thought so, and had worried about it too. But she hadn't been in such a good place then, vulnerable and sensitive, but it was OK now, and she felt so much better in herself, which was even more reason why her reaction earlier was a shock. She really had thought she was strong again, had got it together and was going forward . . . it just went to show how sneaky grief can be. How it can strike at any time. Well, she'd have to protect herself, be better prepared so she didn't panic again. That was the worst part, the panic. She'd not let it happen a second time though. No, she'd come up with a strategy and just politely excuse herself if she felt rushed or uncomfortable. Or explain! That was always an option. But then, she didn't want potential new partners feeling sorry for her, pity was an awful thing.

It was such a minefield, and she really wasn't prepared for all this. Gray had never so much as hinted at her meeting someone after he'd gone, the topic had never come up so she hadn't considered it at all, not wanting to waste a precious second of the time she had with him by thinking about all the time she wouldn't have with him.

'April, you've come so far since Dad died,' Nancy broke into April's thoughts. 'And you're blooming beautiful, do you hear me? Even if you do look shaken and your eyes are all puffy and red from crying. Please stay strong, any new bloke would be bloody lucky to have you, and this is just a hiccup. A stupid mistake on my part. I got it wrong, I rushed you. I just don't want you to be single for the rest of your life. Trust me, I know all about that, and it's no fun . . .' She paused, with a pondering look on her face, and then added, 'Matt didn't push his luck, did he? You know, try to snog you or something? He really doesn't seem the type. That Harvey on the other hand—'

'Pardon?' April jumped in and managed a smile as she shook her head. 'Nooo, no, nothing like that! I was the one who made a fool of myself.'

'Really? What did you do? I'll kill him if he turned you down. Did you make the first move?' Nancy's eyes enlarged to the size of dinner plates.

And after offering her stepdaughter a Jammie Dodger biscuit, April told her all about it.

*

'Oh my God, April. I'm going to throttle him!' Nancy exhaled long and hard, shaking her head. 'He sure is one *very* fruity fruit farmer! Laying out a blanket and all with cushions like he'd prepared some kind of lair in which to woo you. Have "sexy time" in the sun. And I bet he says that kind of thing. Euwwww!' She pulled a face and stuffed another biscuit, whole, into her mouth in disgust.

'Pleeeeease. Stop it!' April cringed all over again. 'He wasn't to know how I would react. He doesn't know about Gray – and I'm sure there are plenty of women who would love such a romantic gesture. A gourmet picnic, champagne, and he's not bad looking . . .'

'Hmm, if you say so. Personally, I think he looks a bit *Miami Vice*, and not in a cool way, with that wavy hair and all. And what's with that deerstalker hat? Please tell me he wasn't wearing it when he tried to get you on the blanket!'

'No.' April shook her head and laughed, feeling so much better now that she could see the funny side of it. She would still need to apologise of course, to explain, but it wasn't the end of the world.

'Well, that's something I guess!' Nancy smirked. 'Right. Now, are you going to wallow in bed all afternoon or are you going to get up, get a smile on your face and stay classy, lady?' She patted the bed, tilted her head to one side and petulantly pushed her bottom lip out.

'Yes, boss!' April took a deep breath and laughed some more before finishing the last of her tea. After putting the mug down, she swung her legs over the side and down on to the rug that covered the newly fixed floorboards. 'The first two I can do . . . not sure about the third one, mind you.' She rolled her eyes and made a silly face and both women cracked up.

'Good-o! Just give me a second to get rid of them in that case . . .'

'Them? What do you mean?' April said, horrified.

'Both blokes are waiting downstairs for you.' Nancy raised her eyebrows, but then instantly added, 'JOKE' on seeing her stepmum's face.

As the two women sauntered out of the bedroom and along the landing, with plans of drinking more iced cider and lazing in the sun, April decided she would call Matt and Harvey this evening to apologise. That would give her time to properly get herself together so she sounded mature and measured, instead of hysterical and irrational.

They reached the top of the tiny staircase. And it was Nancy who saw it first, through the tiny criss-cross-framed window on the landing. She grabbed April's arm and motioned for her to see too. And all thoughts of apologising and lazing in the sun drinking iced cider vanished in an instant. Both women stared at each other, their faces drained deathly white as it registered. And then they bolted out of the cottage, jumping two, three stairs at a time just to get to it as fast as they could.

26

S MOKE!
Spiralling up like a tornado from the entrance of the barn.

And the heat. April could feel the scalding intensity from the flames on her face before she had even made it to the end of the garden path, suffocating as it suffused the air all around them. But she ran, ran to the barn as if her life depended on it this time. Her heart pounding like a piston in perpetual motion. The horses. Darby and Joan. She had to get them out. And Winnie's diaries! Where were they? She couldn't remember if she had brought them into the cottage. They could still be in the apple crate on the dresser. The dresser that was now ablaze. How could she be so stupid? And Edie! Where was her aunt? April panicked, stopped and went to go back to the cottage. She had to be sure that the old lady was safe and hadn't wandered off – there had been a couple of times now when April had found her in the lane or in the meadow on the other side of the garden . . . Oh, God, what if she was near the fire? And Bella? Where was she? Oh Jesus Christ, what if she was in the barn with horses? *The horses?* She couldn't leave them to burn to death. She turned back to the barn and froze with indecision, terrified in case she got it wrong but she had to get Bella out of there immediately. Darby and Joan too. Nancy saw, and screamed in April's face so as to be heard over the din of the flames.

'Edie is OK. She was sleeping. I locked the bedroom door so she'd stay put.'

'Whaaaat? But you can't lock her in. It's not right.' April's instinct was to let her aunt out right away.

'I know. But thankfully I did on this occasion – you needed a moment to yourself. She'll be fine.'

April knew this wasn't the time to argue about it, so carried on running alongside Nancy. Thank God she was here. A firefighter. And April could see lights, blue lights flashing in the distance at the top of the lane. And then the noise. Sirens screaming, filling her head, competing with the crackling and wheezing of the flames as they tore through the wooden dresser.

*

Nancy hurdled the white picket fence and was running at full pelt, tearing off her floaty nylon but highly flammable dress, and scraping her hair up out of the way as she went. She darted over to the garden shed, searching for a tool, anything to smash with. A shovel! It would do. Grabbing it, along with a filthy old dust sheet, she ran over to April.

'Get away from here.' She shoved April hard with both hands, not caring if she pushed her over on to the grass and hurt her, better that than let her run right into the fire. And April wasn't thinking. Nancy had seen it before, a hundred times. Blind panic made people do extra-ordinary things. Dangerous things.

'But I have to get Bella and the horses out,' April yelled, her hair drenched with sweat, her face soaked in tears.

'NO! Back off.' Nancy knew she had to make it crystal clear to protect her stepmum. And thank God – April got it! She stopped moving. 'Go to the lane. Tell the crew I've entered at the back.' April stared momentarily, as if she wanted to protest, but then Nancy yelled, 'GOT IT?'

April nodded furiously, and then sped off.

When Nancy made it to the back of the barn she ripped a section of the sheet (having dunked it in a big, slime-covered water butt on her way) and secured it over her nose and mouth to protect herself from directly inhaling the hot smoke. Then she threw the rest of the sheet over her head and down her back before grabbing two corners to tie as best she could around her midriff. It would have to do. It was all she had to protect herself – having quickly assessed the fire on the run over from the cottage, she saw that the flames seemed to be confined to the front section of the barn, so she prayed that the sheet would be enough. If she worked fast. *Get in, get people and pets out, get the fire out . . . job done!* That was her firefighter's motto and she was sticking to it. She was under no illusion that she was going to get the fire out on her own, but she would blooming well get the people out. *Bella.* And then the pets out!

And with that thought firmly in her head, she grasped

the handle of the shovel and pounded it into the solid brick barn wall. Over and over until some of the old bricks started to give way. One more slam and she'd be in. But she knew she had to be fast. *Very fast*. Dislodging a section of brickwork could bring the whole thing down, especially in such an old construction like this, but there was no other way. The entrance to the barn was blocked by a sheet of flames, and even if she was able to get through there, she'd never get Darby and Joan to run out through the fire, and then stay out. Frightened and confused horses could very well run back into flames, or freeze. She knew that, having attended a fire at a stud farm one time – it had been intense, with the horses refusing to come out of their stalls, they were that scared. In the end they had to use blindfolds and strap specialist animal harnesses around them. It was a near miracle the crew managed to get every horse out and to safety with some suffering only minor smoke inhalation effects.

Nancy was in! And was horrified to see Bella trying to save the horses. Standing in front of Darby and Joan, with her back to them, she was desperately flapping a blanket in the direction of the flames as if attempting to put them out, but all that was doing was fuelling the fire further. Nancy immediately wrenched the blanket from Bella's hand and then grabbed hold of her and dragged her backwards before flinging her out through the hole to safety.

'Run as fast as you can to the lane,' Nancy yelled, gripping Bella's shoulders to look her straight in the eyes. She needed to make sure she heard the instruction. She couldn't take a chance on Bella hanging around to try to save her beloved horses. And if Nancy couldn't coax them out, then the last thing she wanted was Bella seeing such an awful scene. Bella nodded, tears pouring down her face as she turned to run.

Nancy surveyed the scene again. The fire had made short work of the deckchairs and was now consuming the dresser, all of which was at the other end of the barn. Thank God the vet had said to keep the concrete floor bare as a way of helping the horses to stay cool in the hot weather! But Darby and Joan were well and truly spooked. And no wonder – if an ignited spark flew from the dresser towards them the hay in their makeshift stable would be on fire in seconds. Pacing up and down, over and over, their eyes wide, their heads dipping and bucking back up, their hooves lifting and scraping at the ground beneath them, Nancy knew she needed to reassure poor Darby and Joan. She held out her palms, just as she had seen Bella do, and carefully but very quickly got close to the makeshift stable door.

With her back to the far end of the barn and the flames, she pulled two lead ropes from a hook and went to connect them to the horses – but how? Neither Darby nor Joan had harnesses on. Nancy panicked momentarily, and then swiftly got a grip, she did the only thing she could think of and looped the rope around Darby's neck and attempted to tie a knot, but it was hopeless, the rope was too thick and Darby was rearing up now. She looked over and saw a couple of bricks tumble down. And then to the other end of the barn – the flames were creeping closer, sparks spitting across the concrete floor. The hay near the stable was alight. It was going to be too late. She'd have to leave Darby and Joan. Or risk her own life by staying with them.

Nancy reluctantly backed away.

Then stopped.

She couldn't do it.

She rushed forward, and with her head bowed, she pressed it into the side of Joan's neck as if to say a final goodbye. Darby knew, and he nudged the back of her shoulder. Nancy turned and did the same for him. With her heart near breaking point, she backed away towards the opening in the wall, praying that they might follow her and she'd somehow coax them out into the safety of the fields all around, but neither horse did. Just as the horses in the stud farm had, Darby and Joan seemed to want to stay in the makeshift stable, apparently assuming that they were safe in their home.

Nancy had one foot over the bricks at the bottom of the wall where it was still intact, and was just about to duck her head down to carefully but very reluctantly back her body out of the barn and into the open when there was an almighty whooshing noise, followed by a spectacularly triumphant arc of water that seemed to drench the entire barn within seconds.

The pump.

Never had Nancy been so grateful to see a hose.

The crew were here at the other end of the barn and very quickly had the flames under control. A firefighter in full gear was next to her now, working deftly and swiftly to get harnesses on the horses – Nancy handed over the lead ropes and went to take Darby to safety, when she felt her legs go from under her.

What the hell? She was in the air now, slung over a shoulder with her head bobbing around somewhere near the person's backside. And she was fuming with indignation. How dare they? She had been first on the scene. She knew what she was doing. She wasn't in danger . . . well, not now the fire was contained. Not when she was a flaming firefighter herself. Nancy pummelled her fists on his back. She could tell it was a bloke. His shoulders were far too wide to belong to a woman. Besides, a female firefighter wouldn't have the audacity to sling one of their own over her shoulder, unless they were in fatal danger of course, and Nancy was most definitely not.

Outside, and in the safety of the garden, and the very minute her feet had touched the ground, Nancy threw off the stinking makeshift mask and sheet from her body and flung her hands on to her knicker-clad hips. Green slime slid down her face and on to her black bra top and she furiously swiped it away.

'What did you do that for?' she bellowed as the guy pulled off his protective head gear.

'To save your bloody life. But don't bother thanking me or anything.' He threw his hat on the floor and went to walk off towards the fire engine.

Nancy checked herself – *guess he wasn't to know I'm one of them* – and quickly went after him. She caught hold of his sleeve.

'Look, I'm sorry. I . . .' She stopped talking. April

appeared from behind the fire engine with Bella huddled close beside her, looking all shaken up but mightily relieved.

'Nancy! Thank God you're safe.' April dashed forward to give Nancy a big hug. 'But why are you in your underwear and why are you covered in green goo? Oh what the hell does it matter – you're a heroine. Are you OK?'

'Yes, yes, I'm absolutely fine. Nothing a pint of iced cider wouldn't fix, mind you.' Nancy quickly gripped Bella's hand by way of reassurance, the poor girl was still sobbing.

'Well I think we can stretch to that! What you just did was magnificent. I could never have done that . . .' April shook her head in awe as she put her arm around Bella to pull her in close for comfort.

'Ahh, horses for courses, I guess.' Nancy shrugged.

'And talking of horses,' the firefighter stepped in, 'we saved both of them too! In case you were wondering,' and he glared at Nancy.

'Oh, Pete, thank God for that too. This is Nancy, my stepdaughter – you know, I told you about her when you were here doing the garden, she's also a firefighter, in Basingstoke.'

Pete the farmer, and also a retained firefighter, stopped walking and stared at Nancy as if taking a proper look at her for the first time. His face flushed pink like rhubarb. He coughed to clear his throat, and after wiping his hand across the chest part of his firefighter jacket, he held it out to her.

'Pleasure to meet you.' *Ahh, so this was Pete the dairy farmer!*

'Hmm, likewise,' she said, clocking the twinkly eyes and stubbly chin as she shook his hand, the size of a shovel and with an astonishingly strong grip.

'And I'm sorry. I had no idea . . .' He grinned, and Nancy felt herself grinning too. He was hot in a filthy, dirty, sweaty, welly-wearing, udder-squeezing farmer/ firefighter kind of way. Older than her too, early thirties perhaps, which was a bonus as the boys her own age, like her twin, Freddie, his friends and suchlike, were mostly proper muppets.

'Don't mention it. I'll, er, um . . . get us a drink.' And she walked over to the cottage with a veritable spring in her step. Maybe she'd call her boss and see about extending her leave for a bit longer . . . as things sure were hotting up here in the sleepy little village of Tindledale.

And then she heard! And the spring in her step stopped as suddenly as it had started. Her heart sank as she listened in to the crew manager explaining it all to April.

'Yes, we're seeing more and more of these incidents. People don't realise the danger of leaving glass or mirrors in direct sunlight.'

'What do you mean?'

'We found shards of glass in the debris on the dresser – a pint glass or a jug perhaps. My initial guess – and we'll need to investigate further, but I'd put money on it – is that the hot sunlight reflected off the glass on to the deckchair, causing it to ignite and then the whole lot went up.'

'It was me!' Nancy turned around and owned up right away.

'No it wasn't, darling. It can't have been – you're a firefighter. You put fires out, that's your job, you don't start them. You wouldn't do that . . .' April immediately defended her stepdaughter.

'The iced cider jug! I left it on the dresser . . . along with the glasses. I tidied them all away on to the dresser and then must have forgotten to bring them into the cottage.' And Nancy dipped her head. How could she have been so stupid to have left all that glass outside in direct sunlight? 'And now Winnie's diaries are gone for ever. April, I'm so sorry, I don't know what else to say . . .'

'It's fine,' April said magnanimously. 'Just as long as you're safe. And that Bella,' she gave her another squeeze, 'and Darby and Joan are safe. At the end of the day that's all that matters.' But Nancy could see the bereft look in her stepmum's eyes. April was devastated. The connection, the piece of history, the link to her family, her heritage, was gone, just like that. And it was all her fault. It didn't matter that she hadn't done it on purpose, that wasn't the point. April was right, she was a firefighter, she put out fires for a living, and should have been more careful.

27

Later, after the fire-damaged barn had been made safe and then secured, and the vet had finished inspecting Darby and Joan – Matt, who it turned out was also a retained firefighter at the unmanned rural fire station, had been the one who got their harnesses on and led them out to safety into the back orchard, well away from the fire – someone suggested they all relocate to the Duck & Puddle pub garden in the village for a restorative pitcher of Pimm's, or two.

'Will you be joining us later, Matt?' April asked, hoping she might find an opportunity to apologise to him.

'Maybe,' he replied, avoiding eye contact as he put his arm around Bella and pulled her in close to him.

'Can we, Dad? Please?' Bella pleaded, looking at April and then up at Matt.

'We'll see. Think you need an early night, love, you've had a big shock today.'

'S'pose so. But you could still go . . .' Bella said, smiling at April, and then added, 'can I use your toilet please?'

'Of course you can, sweetheart, no need to ask, you know that,' she smiled, and Bella walked away.

Seizing her moment, April swallowed hard, figuring

it may be better just to go for it and apologise now in case he didn't make it to the pub later. It wouldn't be right to let it linger on. No, she needed to clear the air before he left.

'Matt, I'm really sorry.'

'What for?'

'Well, you know . . . for earlier. In the orchard. For walking off like that when you were trying to help.' She stared at the grass around her feet.

'Forget it. As long as you are OK.' Silence followed. 'And you are, aren't you?' He looked directly at her and she was sure his voice softened slightly.

'Yes,' she paused, 'and thank you. Um, I will be . . .' She still averted her eyes.

'Right,' Matt nodded, then seemed to hesitate, as if he was about to say more, but wasn't sure. 'Well, I'll, er . . . be off then.'

'Um, sure. Er, hope to see you later then.' April glanced up, feeling foolish, like an awkward schoolgirl rather than a grown woman. It was ridiculous. She felt utterly ridiculous. And wholly confused. She had panicked when Harvey had made his intentions clear, and all she could think of was Gray, but now, standing here with Matt, it felt totally different, there was something about him. April wanted him to talk to her, to be interested in her, but he clearly wasn't.

'Yep. Perhaps,' Matt said, and off he went. April watched him go for a few seconds, before turning away to walk back into the cottage. Maybe she'd get a chance later to explain to him properly. She needed to, wanted to, if only to clear the air between them. It was obvious he didn't feel the spark too, and after the way she had carried on in the orchard earlier, leaving him standing there without explanation, it was no wonder.

April went to check on her aunt. It had turned out to be a blessing in disguise that Nancy had locked Edie in, as when April had darted off to see if she was OK after the fire engine had arrived, her aunt had still been fast asleep. So, reluctantly, April had relocked the bedroom door and left her to it, figuring it the safest option under the circumstances. But she needed to let her out now; what if her aunt was awake and wanted the bathroom or something? She'd be distressed and that was the last thing April wanted, although better that than her getting caught up in the fire, which thankfully turned out to be nowhere near as destructive as they had first feared – mind you, she may need to get her aunt's hearing checked as it was a marvel that Edie had managed to sleep right through all that siren noise when the fire engine arrived.

*

In the Duck & Puddle pub garden, Molly bustled straight over to April with a pint of beer in one hand, the ferret under an arm, a wicker basket looped over the other and a flustered look on her face.

'Jesus, I just heard what happened, April. Are you OK?' She sat down on the wooden bench seat, and after putting her pint on the table and wiping the spill from the back of her hand, she pushed Stinker into the basket, gently lowered it down on to the grass and tied his little lead around the table leg.

'Yes, thank you. I'm fine. It really wasn't as bad as it first looked . . .' April swivelled her body towards her friend. 'I'm surprised you didn't whizz down to see what was going on. Did you not hear the siren or see the flashing lights?' she teased, grinning, and knowing how Molly didn't like to miss out on anything going on in Tindledale.

'Oh, stop it!' Molly guffawed, flinging her arms around April and giving her a hearty hug. 'As long as you're all OK. And such a shame about Winnie's diaries . . . Pete told me just now at the bar. Does Old Edie know yet?'

'No, she doesn't, and I can't bring myself to break the news to her. Even though her memory for the "here and now" is declining rapidly, she remembered everything in Winnie's diaries. And it was a wonderful way for me to connect with her . . . even if she did think I was Winnie.' April laughed, though she felt quite devastated, but she couldn't let it show as the last thing she wanted was Nancy beating herself up any further. 'And poor Nancy feels so bad that she's stayed at home with Aunt Edie, she couldn't face coming out – I've told her it was an accident, it wasn't like she did it on purpose, but she's being *very* hard on herself . . .' April took a sip of the delicious blackberry cocktail that Cher, the landlady, had made especially for her, saying in a cracking cockney accent, 'Get that down you, after the day you've had, you need it. And you'll feel a whole lot better in no time.'

Of course, by the time April had made it to the pub,

the whole village knew about the fire in the barn at Orchard Cottage – news really did travel like wildfire, literally, around these parts. In fact, it was one of the villagers, Ruby, who ran the vintage dress shop in the High Street, who had first raised the alarm. She'd been driving down the lane past the back of the big orchard when she'd seen the smoke billowing up into the air, so reckoned she should let Pete know, more to be on the safe side than anything, as bonfires in the countryside were a common occurrence. And then, when Pete took a look . . . well, he knew they had a real fire and immediately put the call in as he raced to the station.

'Ahh, it's a shame she's not here.' Molly shook her head and moved in a little closer to April. 'Pete was asking after her – wondered if I had seen her this evening. Between you and me, I think he was quite taken with your Nancy this afternoon . . .'

'Really?' April pondered and smiled, thinking perhaps she should treat Nancy to a little of her own medicine, fix them up on a blind date or something. Pete was a nice guy, straightforward, direct – just like Nancy, in fact. And it would be lovely for her to meet someone, make her feel loved and special – April reckoned Nancy could really do with that at the moment . . . On second thoughts, maybe April shouldn't interfere, not after what happened to her in the orchard with Matt, not to mention the disastrous encounter with Harvey.

Talking of whom, he had just arrived and was making a beeline straight towards her. April fidgeted in her seat, this wasn't exactly what she had in mind as a suitable opportunity to apologise to Harvey. Not here in front of everyone, and the pub garden was packed with people from the village – Hettie, Marigold and Sybs were seated at a wooden table near a trellis covered in glorious pink and white roses, with Dr Ben, and the baby twins. Deedee and the general were at another table – April had chatted to them on the way in, and had remembered to give the general the piece of paper that she had written Finch's name on. And then April had met Deedee's daughter, the headteacher and her partner, Dan, plus Jessie from the café who had joined them now, with her baby in a buggy beside her, and a man with his arm around her shoulders. Ahh, Jessie looked really happy with her head resting into him and a lovely, serene smile on her face. There were lots of children jumping on a bouncy castle down near the field that housed a small herd of goats. An assortment of dogs were running around on the grass. Everyone was enjoying a nice late summer's evening in the sun.

'What is it?' Molly glanced at April and then took one look at Harvey's beaming smile before muttering, 'Oh no, I didn't know . . . you never said. Not again, April, please don—' She tutted and puffed out a long breath of air.

'What do you mean?' April quickly asked, but it was too late for Molly to explain as Harvey was standing right in front of them with a flute of champagne in his hand, which he offered to April.

'A peace offering! I'm so sorry if I offended you.' And he put the glass on the table next to her cocktail.

'Oh, um, well I should really be the one to apologise . . . you had gone to a lot of effort.' April took a sip of her cocktail. 'But thank you for the bubbles.' She smiled and busied herself with stirring the cocktail, unsure of what to say next. It was awkward all over again. Then she sat upright and took a breath as she stopped stirring and fiddled with her hair instead.

'I'll leave you to it,' Molly said, going to stand up with a weary look on her face.

'No, it's fine, honestly Molly, please don't go on my account. Stay and enjoy your drink.' April looked at Harvey. 'Is there somewhere quiet where we can talk?' She wanted to be grown up about it. If she was going to be staying on in Tindledale for a while then she'd prefer to get off on the right foot with everyone. And Harvey had been kind to her, so it would be nice if they could stay friends.

'OK. If you're sure. But I'll be right here if you need me,' Molly replied. And she gave Harvey a filthy look before downing the rest of her pint.

April wavered, something was clearly amiss, why did Molly dislike Harvey? But before she could hazard a guess as to the reason, he suggested, 'There's a bench by the duck pond on the green just across the way . . .'

'Oh, yes. OK. Well, er, let's go there then.'

*

Matt had just arrived in the Duck & Puddle pub car park. He'd been busy making sure Bella was OK and settled with her knitting, a favourite DVD and a big bag of Haribo, so was running late, when he saw Harvey and April coming out of the pub and walking across the lane. He closed the van door and stood for a moment, unsure of what to do; he didn't really fancy walking right into them. He'd had a good think about everything, in particular the state April had been in when he found her in the orchard, and it was bothering him. It wasn't right and he had a hunch it might be something to do with Harvey. He knew Harvey liked to 'love them and leave them'. Perhaps that was it, he'd dumped April, played with her feelings and then discarded her. But seeing them together now . . . Harvey with his hand hovering over the small of her back, April chatting with her face turned towards Harvey, laughing at whatever he was saying as they headed towards the bench near the duck pond – well, if he was honest, it just hacked him off. And to be fair, April was an adult with her own mind, and she might not thank him for wading in and ruining things between her and Harvey if she was as into him as Harvey had implied that time in the pub.

Matt shoved his hands deep into his jean pockets and walked off into the pub. He'd stand by the bar in his usual spot, maybe play a game of darts and then head back home to say goodnight to Bella before she went to bed. She'd be disappointed that he hadn't spoken to April – he knew how much Bella liked her, and at first he'd been cross when she explained how she and Nancy had tried to fix him up with April in the orchard with the sun hat and all. But then, he'd felt pleased in a weird way, that his girl was keen for him to meet someone new, as there had been a time when Bella was dead set against any woman so much as looking at her dad and had pulled some stunts over the years to put potential girlfriends off – like the time she'd told his date he already had a girlfriend. Of course, he'd never seen that woman again. But he hadn't the heart to tell Bella that her playing Cupid hadn't worked, that April had walked off and left him standing there like a prize plum.

Matt glanced over his shoulder at April and Harvey one last time as he pushed open the door of the pub. They were sitting on the bench together now, looking very cosy indeed. April was laughing, her head thrown back. And now Harvey had his arm around her. Oh well, he figured there was nothing he could do, it was best left well alone, Harvey wouldn't thank him for interfering. And they were mates after all. It seemed that April had made her choice. He just hoped Harvey would be gentle with her, because from what Bella had said, via Nancy, April was still vulnerable following the death of her husband.

He went inside and up to the bar, but still, the niggle was there. And he just wished he could get April out of his head, because to be honest, it was doing his head in, literally. And he hadn't felt like this in ages, he was blown away by her all over again, just like he had been as that boy on the bank of the river, but it was more than that now. He loved the way she spoke, the way she was with Bella, the way she cared for her aunt, the way she had made the mug of tea that time – bloody hell, he had even loved the biscuits she had brought in all arranged nicely on a plate. What was wrong with him? Who carried on like this? He needed to get a grip, and fast. Or he'd make a right blooming fool of himself at this rate.

Fifteen minutes later, he'd had enough. The saloon bar was silent, everyone was out in the garden in the last of the evening sun, and he wasn't in the mood for all that. He finished his pint, waved goodbye to his mate, Cher's other half, Sonny, who did the pub food, and with his head down he walked out of the Duck & Puddle pub . . . and straight into April. The front of his shoulder nearly collided with the side of her head.

'Christ. I'm sorry. Didn't see you there. You OK?' He immediately stepped backwards.

'Yes, yes, no harm done, I'm fine. I wasn't looking where I was going,' April grinned as she straightened her hair. 'Are you leaving already?' she quickly added, wondering if now might be OK to apologise to him too. Harvey had really surprised her earlier when they had talked on the bench. He'd been very gracious when she had explained, told him about Gray. He had even apologised again about the blanket and the picnic and said that he totally got it but 'you can't blame a bloke for trying – fine-looking filly that you are', which had made April laugh and bat his arm as she told him off. She liked Harvey. Yes, he was very audacious, an acquired taste, and quite outrageously behaved – he had told her all about his wife in London and April had inwardly exhaled a massive sigh of relief that she hadn't got involved with him. But she was pleased that they could be friends, proper friends without all his silly flirting, although she had already warned him that she fully intended on telling him off again if she saw him trying to charm any more unsuspecting women in Tindledale. She'd call his wife if it came to it. The look of horror on Harvey's face had been such a picture that April suspected he may very well buck up and behave himself from now on. From the way he had spoken about her, he clearly loved his wife, so, joking aside, April had gently advised him not to waste what he had with her, saying 'time with the one you love is truly precious'. Harvey had then given April a hug, wished her well and said he was off to drive to London to surprise his wife for the night. And he'd promptly left.

'Yep. That's right. Goodnight, April.' Matt walked off towards his van parked in the far corner of the car park.

'Er, before you go . . . do you have a minute please?' April ventured, going after him.

'Not really,' he called out over his shoulder. April stopped walking, baffled.

'Charming!' The word was out of her mouth before she realised. Shaking her head, she stared after him. A few seconds later, Matt stopped walking. Then turned around and came back to her.

'Look, April, it's really none of my business. What you get up to is nothing to do with me. Just don't come crying to me again when it all goes wrong.'

April was flabbergasted.

And then the penny dropped.

'Is this because of Harvey? What happened in the orchard the other day? Because if so, then you've got it all wrong.'

'Oh I don't think I have . . . like I said. Each to their own. Let's just agree to disagree when it comes to carrying on with somebody else's other half.' Matt immediately looked away.

April's jaw dropped.

'Hang on a minute. I'm not like that. Matt, stop it! You've got it all wrong, what I mean is—' April said to his back, but he just carried on walking away. She wasn't having it. How dare he! And then something snapped inside her. 'What the hell is wrong with you? Why are you being like this with me? I thought we were friends, you've helped me out with the roof and the horses . . . we talked, about Bella. But now you're behaving like an overgrown schoolboy.'

Matt stopped walking. He stood stock still for a moment. April inhaled. Damn. She shouldn't have said that. No man likes to be told they're a boy. And it wasn't as if they knew each other that well. Not really. Their only connection was Bella and the horses . . . and a handful of awkward exchanges, mainly with her unable to hold eye contact and Matt doing his silent treatment thing. She sounded rude and presumptuous, but then he was making assumptions about her and she wasn't putting up with that.

Matt was coming towards her now, a thunderous look on his face. As he got closer, she could see that his eyes had darkened to an almost emerald green, his jaw fixed tight, the vein at the side of his neck was pulsing so fast, she feared it might burst at any second. He was raging. Furious. Hesitant. Nervous. She couldn't be sure.

'What did you say?' He kept his voice low.

'Matt, look, I'm sorry, it's just that you've got me all wrong . . .'

'I don't think so.'

'What's that supposed to mean?' April creased her forehead in confusion.

'OK. If I'm an overgrown schoolboy, then what does that make you?'

'I beg your pardon!'

Silence followed.

It was a standoff.

April and Matt stood opposite each other and stared, each one daring the other to talk first. It was Matt who broke the stalemate.

'Like I said, what you get up to is nothing to do with me.'

'What I get up to?' April said, affronted.

'That's right. And you know that Harvey is married, so there's no excuse!'

'Of course I do. NOW. He just told me this evening . . . after I told him that I wasn't interested in him, not in that way.'

'Then what were you doing cosied up together on the bench?' Matt flinched as the words came out. She was right. He was carrying on like a schoolboy.

'Well if you *must* know.' April was incensed now. 'I was explaining to him why I panicked in the orchard and ran off. I told him about my husband. My *ex*-husband, if you like!' She paused and took a deep breath before carrying on. 'The one who died nearly two years ago now, but who I still love very dearly. And sometimes hate too, for dying on me, yes is that utterly horrible of me? But that's on a *really* bad day though.' April shrugged and grimaced and willed her eyes not to well up. She could see Matt's eyes softening, his face folding slightly in empathy, or was it pity? She couldn't tell for sure. But what she didn't want was for Matt to feel sorry for her. No, but she was damned if she was going to carry on feeling empty, void, inadequate in a way, for having a dead husband. A widow. And all the connotations that held. She had a choice, she could carry on mourning Gray, letting the loss define her future, or she could try to find some meaning for a new life going forward. And she certainly wasn't going to shy away from people knowing, as she had done when she first arrived here. Worrying that Molly might have told the villagers. So what if they knew? It was hardly the end of the world. It had been the end of her world, for a very long time, but not any more. April was stronger now. She wasn't that same woman in the library car park, devastated because people were talking about her. '*Poor cow, and so young too*' – those words had haunted her. But no more! She refused to let them define her. If she carried on keeping what happened to Gray a secret, then people were bound to find out anyway and then speculate, feel sorry for her, and assume she was pathetic and broken. And in this very moment April felt like she'd arrived at a crossroad.

'And then I hate myself for hating him because it wasn't his fault you know.' She smiled wryly as her voice faltered. 'He got ill you see. Motor neurone disease. It was a wicked, terrible thing. And you know what, you can ignore me if you like, be rude and moody and bloody indifferent, because you'll never be the man that he was. NOT EVER!'

April became conscious that her left index finger was practically pointing in Matt's face. And then that Matt was pushing her hand away. He took a step forward. She could smell his scent, woody and earthy. She tilted her chin defiantly. And balled her fists by her sides as he glowered down at her. His emerald eyes boring into hers, which were stinging with tears now.

'You're absolutely right about that!'

'Good. Then at least we agree,' she retorted.

'Damn right we do.' And suddenly April felt his arms around her. Pulling her into him. Holding her tight. His heart hammering as she eventually let the side of her head rest on his chest.

Matt gently pulled back and lifted her chin up to his. He could feel her body trembling. Holding his eye contact as if searching to see if it would be OK. So, very slowly, he put his forehead on hers, and then waited a few seconds before whispering:

'But if you give me a chance . . . I'll show you the kind of man that I am!'

And then he kissed her. Softly and gently, instinctively knowing that she needed to lead the way. Despite her conviction, he could see that, underneath the cool,

28

Tuesday afternoon, and April was determined to talk to her aunt about Winnie and the lost diaries when she got back from the tea dance, hoping Edie may have had a precious moment of lucidity after having twirled and waltzed around the village hall with the general.

'Ahh, here's the bus now,' April said to Nancy, hearing the chug of the diesel engine as the minibus pulled up into the turning circle. Pete had done such a good job in clearing the hedgerow and filling in the potholes that the bus could actually venture all the way down the single-track lane now. Mind you, April suspected that Pete had an added incentive to visit Orchard Cottage these days – she had seen the way he looked at Nancy, chatted to her, and they had even gone for a ride on his tractor. Nancy had agreed to it on one condition: that he turned up next time with a crash helmet and let her take him for a spin on the back of her scooter. Nancy had then nearly fainted from sheer joy when he did just that – plus more, he arrived on an actual scooter of his own. Well, his dad's to be precise. It turned out that Pete's dad was a Northern Soul fan too, from the first time around in the seventies, and still kept his scooter in the shed. Pete had managed to get it working, and even made a playlist from some of his dad's rare old vinyl records, so he could take Nancy on a scooter run to the seaside for the afternoon where they listened to the music on his iPod and enjoyed a chip-shop tea on the sand. Nancy was most impressed and had been grinning from ear to ear for the last day or so. And April was happy for her, figuring it would do her stepdaughter good to have some fun, especially as she was still smarting from having left the glasses and jug on the dresser, which had been confirmed now as definitely being the cause of the fire.

But it was done now, and there was no going back. It was all about looking to the future, which was why April needed to sit her aunt down and gently explain that Winnie wasn't coming home. Not ever. And that the diaries were gone for ever too. She absolutely had to find a way to break that to her, as Aunt Edie had been talking about the diaries, a lot. Even bringing up stuff that they had read together in them dating right back to when Winnie was a young girl – Edie remembered it all, which was wonderful in a way, but April couldn't bear to see her wandering around the house in search of the apple crate, muttering about how she had them right there just a moment ago. It was pitiful and quite distressing enough just to witness, so she couldn't imagine how hard it must be for her aunt to be actually living through the heartache and confusion.

Nancy gave April a sideways smile of encouragement as they went to meet Edie from the bus. She was standing with Deedee when they arrived and the bus was backing up the single-track lane to drop the baker's sister off up at the top.

'Hello ladies,' Deedee said cheerily. 'Our Edie has had a ball! Twirling and swirling all afternoon she was.'

'Oh, that's marvellous,' April said, gently taking her aunt's elbow so as to steer her on to the garden path. Edie was getting wobblier and frailer by the day, but seemed mostly to be in good spirits . . . when she wasn't fretting about the diaries or asking after Winnie. And she seemed to have accepted now that April wasn't Winnie, but that had just made things even more confusing for her, as she had become obsessed with knowing what had happened to Winnie.

'Absolutely! Plenty of va-va-voom . . . in the young-at-heart villagers!' Deedee did one of her shoulder shimmies, making Nancy suddenly need to check her mobile, even though she knew there was no signal, just to stop herself from guffawing out loud. 'Oooh, and how are things going with you and Pete?' Deedee made big eyes and winked at Nancy.

'Oh, um, yes, he's a top bloke.' Nancy grinned.

'Ahh, young love!' Deedee clapped her hands together, clearly enthralled. 'You snap him up before someone else does, darling.'

'Sure. We're just mates . . . seeing how it goes,' Nancy attempted, but Deedee was having none of it.

'Of course you are, sweetie. But why bother "sucking and seeing" when you could just gobble him all up and go back for seconds, and thirds and fourths? Yes, get in there, girl! You can't beat a good roll in the hay.'

April and Nancy exchanged looks, both knowing exactly what the other was thinking: '*Did she really just say that?*' It was April who pulled herself together first, willing her mouth not to move into a massive smile, followed by a big belly laugh.

'Er, Nancy, would you mind . . . um, taking Edie inside?' April managed to squeak, not even daring to look her stepdaughter in the eye.

'Sure. Come on, Edie, let's get a nice cup of tea. I can't wait to hear all about your afternoon,' Nancy said kindly, as she helped Edie with her raffle prizes – a hand-knitted cushion cover, a box of Terry's jelly fruit sweets and a bottle of sherry. 'Ooh, you did well this time.'

'The sweets are for you, my dear. But don't eat them all at once, or you'll spoil your dinner.' And Aunt Edie pressed the box into Nancy's hand.

'Ahh, bless you, Aunty. Thank you.' Nancy gave the old lady a fond kiss on the cheek before toddling off with her towards the cottage.

Deedee turned to April.

'And you're a dark horse too, my dear.' Deedee smiled as she leant in to April and treated her to a whiff of her intoxicating perfume. She was wearing one of her figure-hugging bodycon dresses, which she had teamed up with a lime-green marabou feather boa trailing from her neck – the end of which tickled April's nose as Deedee nudged her conspiratorially.

'Oh, um, am I?' she replied, wondering what on earth she had done.

'You sure are. And who can blame you? That farrier,

Matt Carter, is *absolutely gorgeous*. I did hope to have a go with him myself when I first came back to Tindledale, but not a chance!'

'Ahh . . .' April said slowly, her mind boggling as it always did around Deedee, and she had been wondering how long it would be before news of their kiss got around the village. Nothing went unnoticed in Tindledale, unless it happened behind closed doors in the privacy of your own home. And even then, one couldn't be absolutely sure . . . not when front doors were left unlocked. Someone could walk in without warning, as she had on Pete and Nancy in the hallway yesterday! April had backed out quickly, but, still, the look on Pete's face – she could tell he'd been about to kiss Nancy, and she had ruined the moment. Deedee clutched her arm.

'And good for you. You make a beautiful couple, if you don't mind me saying so.'

'Thank you, but we're not a couple as such . . .' April's voice faded as she wondered what she and Matt were exactly. They had seen each other a few times since that lovely kiss in the car park, and had chatted and walked in the orchards together. Sometimes holding hands, sometimes not. They had tended to the horses together, they had even been for a cycle ride through the woods, and paddled together in the stream to cool down. Matt had kissed her again and she had felt wonderful, calm and optimistic, fizzy even. It felt nice, and exactly what she needed at the moment. She didn't want to analyse anything, preferring instead to take it for what it was right now, fun and friendship, and see what happened.

It was as if she was coming to life again, the numbness after Gray's death slowly dissipating, and she felt OK with that. She had told Matt how she felt, that being with him was wonderful, exciting, but cosy and familiar too, like déjà vu almost, in the way new couples often feel as if they have known each other for always. And he had looked at her like he wanted to say something more, but was reluctant to . . . maybe he was just being considerate; knowing how she didn't want to rush into anything, they'd agreed to let things develop at their own pace. Matt had already told her he didn't want to overwhelm her, come on too strong. Yes, that would have been it! He really was a lovely guy.

'Oh, now you're just teasing me!' Deedee winked. 'Anyone can see that the pair of you are crazy for each other. I saw the passion in the car park. Not that I was being nosey or anything, oh no.' She paused to swish her marabou boa back around her neck, nearly taking April's eye out this time. 'No, my Meg told me not to stare as we left the pub, but it's very lovely seeing two lovebirds. I for one can't help myself from going all fuzzy and sneaking a look.' April fixed a smile on her face and nodded politely. 'Anyway, I best be getting off. But before I forget, darling, the general said to let you know that he's had a bit of a breakthrough!'

'Really?' April's pulse quickened.

'Yes, I think he managed to find some information about that name you gave him, Finch, was it?'

'Yes, that's right.'

'Well, he didn't go into the specifics, but he said to

say that he'll call by after he's dropped off Mrs Godfrey, she lives all the way over near Stoneley though, so he might be some time. But if it's too late – he knows how Edie likes to take a nap in the afternoon – he'll pop in tomorrow instead. Cheerio!' And she did a jaunty wave as she sashayed off up the lane to see where the bus had got to.

*

In the sitting room, April had relayed the information to Nancy while Edie was in the bathroom. They were waiting for her to join them.

'So, are you still going to tell her?' Nancy whispered, sitting on the end of the Dralon settee.

'I'm not sure.' April pondered, and then decided. 'I should wait, at least until we know what the general has unearthed . . .'

'Yes, but sadly, the mystery could be . . . that she did run off with Finch and was still alive and died just recently . . . maybe that's why there wasn't a death certificate to be found before now.' Nancy shook her head, concerned.

'Oh God, I hope not, that would just be too sad,' April replied, feeling like a failure for not having turned up any information – she had checked at the town hall, had been online and searched through all the ancestry records, but nothing. She had found copies of the death certificates for George and Delphine – Edie and Winnie's parents – and knew that George had died in August 1943, during the war, a heart attack, and Delphine not long after, in the 1950s, which was very sad. Both were relatively young by today's standards. They were buried in a family plot in the St Mary's church graveyard in Tindledale, along with Edie's brother, Robert. Edie's other brother, Sidney, who was killed in action in December 1941, had a special plaque on the wall nearest the graves, and of course was listed as one of the many brave soldiers who lost their lives in the war on a stone memorial in the village square.

'Maybe we should wait and see what the general says . . . you never know, he might have found out that Winnie is alive and well, wouldn't that be wonderful?'

'It certainly would . . . I have an inkling though, that isn't the case. But you're right, let's wait and see what he knows. I'll only mention the diaries for now . . .' April smiled and then got up from the armchair to give Nancy a hug. 'It will be fine. She'll understand.' April patted Nancy's back. 'We can't let her go on looking for them in vain . . .'

'But what if she isn't fine? What if she cries?' Nancy pulled her top lip down over her teeth as April let her go.

'Then we will tackle that . . . *if* it happens, but let's not assume the worst. I'll go and see if she's ready to come downstairs,' April said leaving the room.

Twenty minutes later, April had finished gently explaining to her aunt, and was now waiting anxiously for her response. Edie hadn't said a word for at least ten seconds now. April glanced at Nancy, who had her head bowed.

'Are you OK, Aunty? Perhaps you'd like another cup of tea? Or how about a nice snowball? I'm sure it won't matter just this once if we indulge before we've had our dinner.'

'But I don't understand,' Aunt Edie eventually said, not responding to either of April's suggestions.

'Oh Edie, I'm so sorry.' Nancy looked up and sideways at Edie.

'What for, my dear?'

'For destroying the only link you have left—' Nancy stopped talking on seeing April shake her head as if urging caution.

'What link?' Edie turned to April. 'What does she mean?'

'The diaries, Aunty. Winnie's journals – you do understand, don't you, that they were lost in the fire?' April waited to see if it had really sunk in.

'What fire?'

April's heart sank; she was beginning to wish that she had kept her mouth shut now.

'But they can't have done. I had them just here . . .' And Great Aunt Edie tried to get up out of her wing chair.

'Here, I'll help you.' Nancy leapt up, keen to help.

'Thank you, my dear.' Once Aunt Edie had made it into a standing position, she pointed a bony finger towards the sideboard. 'There!'

'The cupboard?' April confirmed, looking at Edie and then at Nancy.

'That's right, Winnie dear.' April's heart sank further

– it really was one step forward with her aunt, followed by three steps backwards – but she smiled and did as Edie asked. 'Open it.' April pulled open the door of the sideboard.

And inhaled sharply.

'I knew they were here somewhere. Blasted memory. I put them in there for safekeeping and then forgot.' Edie shook her head as if to try to clear her mind in order to gain some clarity.

The apple crate was inside the sideboard. April beamed and breathed an enormous sigh of relief as she lifted the crate out. And Nancy promptly burst into tears before running out of the room. April wondered if she should go after her, but figured it best to let her be, give her some space.

April then felt her heart lift as her aunt told her to open the other end of the sideboard.

'That's it, dear. The old shoe box. You wanted photos. They're all in there, the box has been in my bedroom for years, ever since my mother died, in fact – it was my parents' bedroom before mine, did you know that?' Edie said, helping herself to another biscuit.

'Yes, Aunty,' April smiled, quite accustomed now to her aunt telling her stuff a trillion times.

'I put it in the sideboard for safekeeping.'

'When did you do that, Aunty?' April asked, curious to know, because the shoe box certainly hadn't been here when she had gone through everything the other day in search of the letter that might have been in the envelope with the faded crown imprint on.

Aunt Edie pondered, deep in thought for a few seconds before answering, '1971!'

April resisted the urge to laugh out loud and instead stood up and went over to give her aunt a big hug. 'Bless you,' she smiled, inwardly congratulating her aunt for having a damn good guess, even though it was off by several decades. Aunt Edie must have put the shoe box in the sideboard only in the last day or so.

'Oh Winnie, you always were such a tease, trying to trick me.' And Edie merrily chuckled away as she popped the last of the biscuits into her mouth, utterly oblivious to the poignancy and indeed humour in that precise moment. And for a second, April thought it may be a rather wonderful way to be, because don't they say that 'ignorance is bliss'?

'Open it. There are photos of you in there!' Edie prompted. April did as she was told, uncertain if her aunt Edie meant photos of her, or indeed Winnie, but by the looks of it, there were both.

After sifting through loads of Polaroid snaps of herself at various stages in her childhood – first day at school, Christmas Nativity play, Easter (with part of a giant chocolate egg in one hand, the rest of it around her mouth) – April came to a photo of herself that made her heart nearly stop. She went over to the lamp to get a better look. And couldn't believe it. She looked at her aunt, who had nodded off now so April sat down in an armchair and studied the picture before her. She turned it over, and saw the date. It was the summer before her parents died. Her palms felt tingly. Her thighs too, as a dart of adrenalin, warm and welcome, pulsed right through her. It was like an awakening . . . that was the only way she could describe it. A part of her that she thought had been closed for ever was now suddenly very much alive again. The section of her life before her parents died, before she went to live with her grandparents. And that's when she knew.

She remembered.

The familiarity.

The feeling of déjà vu.

The girl in the picture was sitting on a bike, wearing a white cotton dress.

April gasped and pressed the picture to her chest. Her first kiss. But how did she not know? She couldn't believe it. Matthew. The boy in the buttercup field. Yes! It was him. She was convinced of it now. But he looked so different then. Glasses – still those green eyes . . . yes, it was coming back to her, but he had braces then, short hair and definitely no tattoos. He had been puny too, a typical teenage boy. Sweet. Gentle. And quite different to the fully grown, muscular man that Matt was now. And then April laughed, she felt light all of a sudden, young again, a second chance, and it was incredible. But why hadn't Matt said anything?

April sat for a moment, taking it all in . . . Perhaps he had forgotten too? But then why hadn't she remembered? And she instantly knew why. April had blanked it out of her head in the confusion that was the months and years after her parents went. But it was different now, and she knew Matt would laugh when she showed him the picture from that summer. The two of them as kids, kissing for the first time. It had been intense. And awkward, in a gloriously geeky, innocent way. And she felt elated to now have the chance to rekindle a part of her that she thought had died along with Gray.

Spurred on, and eager to find more wonderful memories of her happy life before her parents and Gray died, April rummaged through all of the photos, placing them neatly on the card table after she had looked at them. She glanced over at her aunt – Edie was still sleeping, and with a contented smile on her face, which in turn made April smile with happiness.

Hang on. What was that?

April rummaged again at the bottom of the box and found some paper tucked in between two pictures of Winnie by the looks of it. One of the photos was stuck to the paper and if she wasn't careful it would tear. April carefully prised the paper free. It was a folded note, a letter of some kind. She managed to untangle the paper and spread it flat on the card table. And her eyes raced to take it all in. The crown at the top of the page. The typed words. From the War Office. Dated October 1943 and addressed to Mrs Lovell.

And then April cried. The answer had been here all along, lost or forgotten about as the decades had passed.

The tears turned into sobs, which she stifled by placing a hand over her mouth so as to stop the tears from falling on to the precious letter.

The secret, the mystery of why Winnie hadn't come

home, was revealed right here, buried underneath a pile of old photos in Edie's parents' bedroom for all these years. Winnie hadn't run off. Married man. A baby. Scandal. Not at all, it was as Aunt Edie had thought: tongues wagging, a story that had been made up from a snippet of gossip, a Chinese whisper that had gathered momentum with each person that had passed it on in the village. And for some unfathomable reason, this made April laugh . . . a sad, poignant laugh as she read the letter all over again.

Madam,

In confirmation of War Office telegram of the 24th July, 1943, I am directed to inform you, with regret, that a notification has been received that your daughter, Winifred Lovell, First Aid Nursing Yeomanry, was reported missing on the 7th July, 1943.

No further information is available at present, but all possible enquiries are being made and any further information received by this Department will be sent to you immediately. Should you receive any communication from your daughter, or should news of her reach you from any other source, will you kindly notify this office, and at the same time forward any card or letter you may receive from her, which will be returned to you after inspection.

In the meantime I am to ask you to be good enough to notify this office of any change of your address.

April sat motionless and numb. Poor Winnie. Missing. No further information. It was horrendous. And poor,

poor, poor Delphine . . . April couldn't begin to imagine how she must have felt, most likely sitting or standing in this very room, and reading this letter about her daughter. Delphine had already lost her son, Sidney, her husband, George only a few months earlier in August 1943, and now her eldest daughter was missing, and everyone knew what that *really* meant . . . April gulped in a big shot of air, conscious that she had been holding her breath. And the date: 7th July. Oh God no! Winnie's birthday. It was indescribable to think of the pain that Winnie's parents must have felt on discovering that their eldest daughter had most likely been killed on her birthday. It was enough to send a person to an early grave . . . which is exactly what it did do. Poor George died only a month after the telegram that was mentioned in the letter, dated 24th July 1943. April wondered what happened to the telegram. Had George read it and chosen not to share its devastating contents with what was left of his family? Delphine clearly hadn't known about the contents of the telegram which had led her to make enquiries after George's death. The shock appeared to have taken its toll on her too and she had died not that long after the end of the war, in the early fifties.

29

The next day, having spent a restless night going over and over the words in the letter from the War Office, April still felt bereft, but strangely at peace now that she knew. Knew that the rumours about Winnie weren't true. She was a heroine. Winnie had gone off to do her bit for the war effort and had most likely been killed by a bomb. Yes, it was disconcerting that there weren't more details, but there was a war on, maybe her whereabouts had been confidential – Marigold had said she thought Winnie was going into the field, whatever that meant, after she had finished her ambulance training at the special FANY place. But what April didn't understand was why her Aunt Edie didn't know that Winnie was missing, most likely presumed dead? Surely, she would have been told, wouldn't she? Maybe Bill, the old postman, could shed some light on it – he would have delivered the letter from the War Office and perhaps the missing telegram too. April resolved to talk to the general when he arrived with whatever news he'd managed to uncover about Finch. Yes, April would ask him if she could pop along with Edie to the next dance in the village hall and speak to Bill then. And then, when she had all of the information, she would sit down with her aunt and explain it all to her – she needed to do that soon. As Aunt Edie said . . . she wasn't getting any younger!

*

April was in the sitting room when she saw the general walking along the garden path with another man, in his sixties perhaps, wearing a linen suit and a cream panama hat, following behind. She went to open the front door.

'Good morning, April,' the general said, doing that rocking thing with his hands behind his back. 'Might we have a word?'

'Of course, come on in. I'll put the kettle on, and I have news . . . I found a letter from the War Office yesterday . . . saying that Winnie was missing, which we all know meant "presumed dead". It must have been a devastating blow for the family, but I wondered if I might have a chat to Bill, see if he knows why Edie wasn't told,' April said, stepping aside and gesturing with an outstretched arm for them to come in. But they held back. The other man seemed anxious as he clutched a briefcase. 'Is everything OK?' she asked.

'Er, perhaps we could talk somewhere in private,' the general suggested, giving the other man a sideways glance. April followed his line of vision, and then the general quickly added, 'Forgive me. I should have said . . . this is Charlie Finch. He has a family connection with this case. Charlie, meet April . . . Winnie's great niece.'

'Oh, um . . .' April said, automatically shaking Charlie's

extended hand, her mind racing. *Family connection! How? Who is he?* And for some reason, she felt quite odd all of a sudden. Curiosity, or was it fear? She wasn't sure, but whatever it was, she was intrigued. Finch. This man was obviously related to Winnie's beau. He was far too young to be *the* Finch, in the diary . . . so who was he exactly? And why wouldn't they come in? And why was the general behaving in this way? Sort of vague, secretive, sleuth-like almost, with his mention of 'this case', as if he were a policeman! *Oh God, Winnie wasn't involved in a crime, was she? Or murdered, or something equally awful?* April immediately composed herself and tried to calm her head from already writing the story, which could quite possibly be absolute fiction, she certainly hoped so. Yes, best to wait and see . . .

'Pleased to meet you, Charlie. I'm April. We could talk in the sitting room,' she offered on autopilot, as she tried to figure it all out.

'Not here. We need to talk in private.' It was Charlie who spoke now, and with a very well-to-do accent, as if he'd just stepped away from filming an episode of *Downton*, upstairs for sure.

'Um. OK. If that's what you'd prefer,' April said, taken aback by his manner. 'Can you give me a few seconds please? I'll just need to settle my aunt . . .' And April dashed inside and into the kitchen to ask Nancy to sit with Edie.

'Of course. No problem. Who is the bloke in the linen suit?' Nancy grinned.

'Charlie Finch,' April hurriedly replied in a low voice,

keen to find out more from the general as she grabbed her cardy from the chair. It was starting to feel a bit autumnal today. She pushed her arms into the sleeves. 'I shan't be long. See you in a bit. And if Edie needs the bathroom, you'll be OK to help her, won't—'

'Finch!' Nancy exclaimed and made big eyes as she put her hand on April's arm. 'Charlie Finch.'

'Yes, that's right.' Both women pondered for a couple of seconds, until April clarified, 'He's far too young to be *the* Finch from the diaries.' She laughed and went to leave. 'That would be impossible.' She shook her head, amused.

'True. But *the* Finch could be his dad!' April stopped moving and turned back to look at Nancy. 'And Winnie could be his mum!' They both took an inward breath.

'Noooooo.' It was April who spoke, with a look of incredulity on her face as her mind raced into overdrive. 'There's no way that could be, surely? Winnie went off to do her bit in the FANY, in the field, and she went missing, it said so in the letter. The official letter with the crown stamp on it.'

'Yes, but she could still have done all those things and had a secret baby. Remember that letter posted from London? Weeeell, maybe that's why she was there,' Nancy paused, took a breath, 'sorting out plans for the baby . . . you know, to have him adopted, taken care of. We know now that she wasn't killed in the Blitz, it would have said so in the letter from the War Office, surely . . . sooo, it's entirely possible.'

'OK. Unlikely though, highly unlikely, I just don't think

Winnie would . . .' But April's mind was racing again. If Charlie Finch was Winnie's son, then that would make him Edie's nephew, and her . . . second or great cousin? If there was even such a thing. April wasn't sure, she always got in a muddle when it came to figuring out family trees, and she was most likely getting way ahead of herself in any case. But, allowing herself a moment to fantasise . . . what did it matter who Charlie Finch was in relation to her if there was a chance that he was a blood relative? A member of her very own family. A living one. A part of her parents. The same DNA. And who knows, he could have an enormous family of his own. He could be a granddad with a trillion grandchildren. Imagine that! Suddenly, April was feeling very excited. And Edie would be over the moon.

'But he could be,' Nancy said, beaming as she slowly nodded her head in realisation at what this would mean for April, before promptly telling her to, 'go on! Hurry up and find out,' as she shooed her out of the kitchen.

30

An hour later, and April still couldn't take it all in. They were sitting in the gypsy wagon in the back orchard. April had suggested Kitty's café, The Spotted Pig, but the general had thought it unsuitable – 'too many ears and eyes', he had said, and now she knew why.

Charlie Finch, who it turned out, was indeed the son of *the* Finch, aka Colonel Finch, had just revealed the most incredible story. One which hadn't included the news April had hoped for, even though in her heart she'd known it was utterly unlikely, given everything she had discovered about her great aunt Winnie. No, Winnie never did have a baby.

'We'll stop talking and leave you alone with your thoughts for a moment, dear.' The general was sitting alongside Charlie on the flowery-patterned seat, and opposite April. She nodded mutely. Winnie hadn't been killed by an airstrike in the field while driving ambulances for the FANY. No, she had died a different death, and a very long way from home.

In France.

Alone.

Shot by the Nazis in one of their horrific death camps, after being parachuted in to work on dangerous missions behind enemy lines. Undercover, disguised as a French-woman, Winnie spoke the language fluently, having learnt as a child from her mother, Delphine, so she was able to pass herself off as a saleswoman for beauty products and relay coded information back to the British government using a radio that she kept hidden under the floorboards of her tiny Parisian apartment. That was her mission. She had been trained as a code transmitter. Working with the French Resistance to communicate vital and highly dangerous details of enemy troop movements, Winnie was courageous in her ability to remain undetected by the enemy for nearly two years before she was captured. By pure, fateful chance . . . she had looked the wrong way when crossing a busy Parisian street. Right first, as she would have done back home in England, instead of left as they do in France. An easy mistake to make, but people were vigilant to clues such as this during wartime and her cover was blown.

April's hands trembled as she flipped open the manila folder again.

SOE.

Special Operative Executive.

'Are you absolutely sure?' April muttered as she lifted the faded black-and-white photo, allowing her index finger to gently trace the outline of her brave great aunt Winnie's face. The uniformed woman in the photo looked just like April, albeit with a different hairstyle and a stoic, indomitable air, just as Hettie had described her. But it was like looking in a mirror too – the same eyes as her own looking back at her. And it broke April's heart as she slipped the photo back inside the folder and lifted out a bundle of papers. To think of her great aunt, Winnie, aged only twenty, younger than Nancy was now, recruited for her 'confidence, calm head, resilience and plucky persistence in all her endeavours' – April read through a photocopied document, taking in all the comments, written in old-fashioned handwriting.

Winnie had indeed gone off to do her duty, her bit for the war effort, but not to the FANY. Yes, she had gone there for a short while as part of her cover, but Colonel Finch – the man who had already spotted her potential during her driving duties for the army base when she was in the Land Army – had seen the way Winnie had handled herself when they visited the bomb site in Brighton, and then her attempts to save Rita from the flames during the airstrike, and arranged for her to go to a special training centre in Scotland, where she was assessed further for her suitability as an SOE agent and to identify her strengths and weaknesses. Then, Winnie was moved again on to a 'finishing school' in Surrey where she learnt how to lead a clandestine life, how to make contact with other agents and maintain cover stories, amongst other things, all designed to keep her safe in the field.

So it had been true, Winnie did go 'into the field' and had specifically said so to Marigold – April couldn't help wondering if Winnie had meant this message as some kind of code . . . who knows, anything was possible.

Even Winnie's ability to shoot a gun, her being a 'remark-able shot', was noted. April read through the papers in silence, keen not to miss a thing.

'There's no doubt, my dear.' It was the general who replied. 'Winifred Lovell was a remarkable lady. You should be very proud of her. The Special Operations Executive, SOE, was an elite organisation of highly trained and capable individuals that worked with local resistance movements and conducted espionage and sabotage in enemy-held territories. Highly dangerous work that only the very bravest of souls could undertake.'

'It's a lot to take in.' April slipped the papers back inside the folder and went to hand it to Charlie.

'It's yours. I had it all copied for you.'

'Thank you. But . . .' April hesitated as she folded her arms around the bundle of precious papers that contained the truth about her great aunt, utterly unsure of where to begin. So many questions were whizzing around inside her head and then her chest tightened, she felt panicky. Overwhelmed. 'Sorry, please, er, can you just give me a moment?' She stood up, put the folder on the bench and quickly left the gypsy wagon. She needed some air.

Standing outside in the orchard, April plucked a leaf from a nearby hedge and twiddled it in between her fingers as she marshalled her thoughts. She inhaled and let out a long breath as she slipped her sunglasses on and looked up at the sky. The same sky, the same view that Winnie would have seen all those years ago when she had lived here. Just a normal girl, before she became a truly remarkable woman.

April closed her eyes, imagining her aunt, Winnie, as that young girl, carefree but fearless, enjoying her youth here in the rural idyll of Tindledale, growing up in Orchard Cottage. She tried to picture Winnie, what she was wearing on the day she left, the perfectly tailored khaki-green uniform, and then . . . on the day she died. How she was then? What was she wearing? *Tidy and confident.* Hettie's words floated into her mind.

And April dipped her head, she opened her eyes and whispered, 'Oh Winnie. You poor, brave, darling lady. I so would have loved to have met you . . . to have known you.' And in that very moment, April made her great aunt, Winnie, a promise.

And then returned to the wagon.

'OK,' she addressed both men. 'Tell me everything. I want to know all that there is to know about my incredible great aunt, Winifred Lovell, the fearless Special Operations Executive agent. But most importantly, how come my other great aunt, Edie, was never told about any of this? And how come her parents, George and Delphine, died without ever finding out the truth of what had happened to their courageous daughter? And why were there rumours that Winnie had run off with a married man and had his baby?'

Both men glanced at each other.

Then shifted in their seats.

And then Charlie proceeded to tell April everything and the secret started to unravel.

31

'S o how come Winnie's parents never learnt the truth?' Now that Charlie was here, and the answers were so close, the questions flew around inside April's head. 'My aunt said she thought her mother, Delphine, had written to the War Office.'

'That's right. She did. And here's a copy of it,' Charlie said coolly, opening his briefcase and producing the letter as if pulling a rabbit from a hat, just like that. April read the words. Tears scratched in her eyes as her heart went out to poor Delphine, her words so composed and formal, as was the way in those days, but she must have been so worried about her eldest daughter, yet never got to find out the truth of how brave she was. She'd gone to her grave never knowing the secret. A solitary tear trickled down April's face before pooling in the crevice above her left shoulder blade. Silently, the general handed April a folded white cotton hanky which she took with a shaky hand.

'Thank you.' She dabbed the tear away and pressed her nails into the palm of her other hand. The old coping technique reinstated, this time for another relative. April wondered how much more loss she could bear.

'Secrecy was paramount to the SOE organisation,' Charlie started, 'and to all covert war operations.'

'Yes, I understand that, but how come you know all of this? You have copies of letters, reports about my great aunt Winnie's progress and skills during her training.' April fixed her eyes on Charlie.

'The Official Secrets Act was relaxed in 1989 so some sensitive information only came to light after that, and then of course there was my father's memoir, locked away – many covert agents and code-breakers never spoke about their work right up until the day they died.' April shook her head. 'I know it's hard, that your great grandparents never knew, but please try to take some comfort in the fact that if Winnie had made it back home, it's most likely that she would never have revealed the secret of her work during the war. Not ever.'

'Yes, of course. And at least I know now, and I can find a way to explain it all to my aunt,' April said, grateful for that at least. She had set out to find the truth and now she had achieved just that. But the victory felt hollow, given that George and Delphine never got to know how brave their daughter was.

'Absolutely. And that probably wouldn't have been possible if you hadn't scrutinised the letters, and then found the diaries and questioned everything, culminating in you giving my father's name to the general,' Charlie said.

'Maybe so, but instead, there was gossip about Winnie being a wanton woman, a marriage wrecker or whatever other labels people liked to put on women in those days.

And all the while, this "awful woman", my aunt Winnie, was off valiantly fighting to protect those very same people that were vilifying her. It's disgraceful. My great aunt Winnie should be commended. Acknowledged as a heroine. Why isn't her name on the war memorial in the village square alongside all the other brave souls who gave their lives for this country?' April pushed the papers into the manila folder and glared into the middle distance – a flower stencil on the whitewashed, wooden wagon wall behind the two men sitting opposite her.

'My dear, I'm sorry you feel this way . . .' the general started. 'If I had known it would stir up all this emotion, then perhaps I shouldn't have—'

'Please!' April held up the palm of her hand. 'Just tell me straight. I feel as if we are going around in circles. Perhaps you can start by explaining how my aunt, Edie, has a bundle of letters from Winnie, written supposedly from the FANY training centre?'

'Winnie wrote them and post-dated them before she left Tindledale,' Charlie said, giving April the straight answer that she had requested.

'So how did they get posted?'

'My father, who became Pauline—' he coughed, 'sorry . . . Dad was her handler.'

'What did you say?' April jumped in. She had heard that name before, and recently.

'I, er, meant Winnie.'

'No you didn't. You said Pauline!' April raised her eyebrows and fixed her stare on Charlie.

'You might as well tell her the whole truth,' the general

piped up. 'She has a right to know, and it's hardly going to matter now, some seventy years later, is it?'

'Yes it is!' April jumped in. 'It still matters, very much so. And it will always matter . . .' She leant forward. There was no way she was letting her aunt's memory be dismissed. Not now. Not after she had seemingly been forgotten about for all these years by the government, her country, the very people that she had sacrificed her life for. Surely, some of them were still alive, the people who trained her, the people she relayed the information back to from France, so why hadn't they made sure the whole world knew how brave her aunt was? Why wasn't there a record somewhere? A Wikipedia entry? Something?

April was fired up, passionate, and determined to find out the truth, the whole truth, because it wasn't every day that you discovered your great aunt had served as an SOE agent and played such a vital role in helping to win the war. And she needed to make sure that her aunt hadn't died in vain. That felt most important.

'Pauline was Winnie's code name,' Charlie said. 'Winnie assumed the identity of an old school friend who had died some years before, with no family left to arouse suspicion. Dad was quite specific about that in the memoir. As if he intended for this to be revealed . . . perhaps so your family would know the truth in the end.'

'Whaaaat?' April put her head in her hands moment-arily before resting her hands back in her lap as she remembered Hettie, or was it Marigold, mentioning a Pauline, a girl in the village who had died of TB, her mother too. 'But this is madness, like something out of a spy thriller. An episode of *Spooks*.' Both men nodded. 'And how, may I ask, do you know about this? How did you find Charlie Finch?' she said, looking at the general.

'My pal in the House. I asked him for a favour after you gave me that piece of paper with the name Finch on, and he did a bit of digging, got access to some dusty old government files and a match came up with both Finch and Winifred Lovell's names being linked to SO2 – that was the name of the original special operations department set up July 1940, during the Second World War. That's when I knew there was very much more to her not making it back home, but I needed to be sure before I came to you. You do understand, don't you?' the general asked, and April nodded, mulling it all over.

'And one of Winnie's letters was posted from London.'

'Was it?' Charlie looked fascinated, and seemed as intrigued as April was about uncovering the mystery. 'My father would have posted the letters.' Charlie turned to the general and added, 'He must have slipped up. The letters were supposed to have been sent from Oxford, the FANY base, so the family would think she was there. It was all part of her cover.'

'But I'm pretty certain they knew she was going into the field, to drive ambulances . . .' April said.

'Ahh, yes, that was a very common cover story, but it would have been very difficult to have engineered letters to be sent from the field while she was under cover as it may have aroused suspicion. Your aunt would have maintained her cover identity at all costs and any attempt to contact her family from behind enemy lines would have put both herself and other SOE agents in danger.'

'How do you know all this?' April asked, narrowing her eyes.

'It's all there in my father's memoirs – I've been researching his life story, hoping to publish it all as a book some day. When he died, quite a few years ago now, he left a safety deposit box key for me, with strict instructions that I was to wait a minimum of ten years before accessing the box.' Charlie paused to shake his head. 'My father was a stickler for covertness, right up until the very end. You see, I never knew about his war effort either, that he was an SOE commander, Winnie's handler. We, the family, knew of course that he was a military man, but just assumed that he had served in the regular army during the Second World War. It wasn't until I opened the safety deposit box that I discovered the truth, and then, later, by chance, an old school pal – he works for the government too and had been helping me with the research – got in touch and said that this gentleman had made enquiries about Finch, my father, the name that you had passed on to him.' Charlie turned his face towards April. 'And I'm so grateful that you did . . . you provided the missing link.'

'So you honestly had no idea?' April asked, her head spinning with it all now.

'None whatsoever, I promise. If I'd had so much as an inkling then I would have been in touch before now. But I can tell you, that towards the end, Dad talked about Winnie. A lot. And with enormous fondness. His mind was wandering and he became very muddled, meandering between muttering the name, Pauline, sometimes, then on other occasions it was Winnie. Thankfully, my mother had died some years previously, because Dad was quite vocal about Winnie being the love of his life. Saying stuff like, "I should never have let you go, my darling" and "So brave and beautiful, my precious violet"; he said that line over and over sometimes.' April shifted in her seat, recalling the words in Winnie's diary, what Finch had said to her when he gave her the flower – the true meaning, it all made sense now. And why Winnie had felt it prudent to leave the flower at home. Charlie paused, gathered himself, and then continued.

'We assumed that he was talking about an old sweetheart who had left him before he met my mother, not that he had sent a young woman into enemy-occupied France . . . I guess we chose to ignore it mostly, for Mum's sake, her memory. You do understand, don't you?' Charlie dipped his head.

'Of course,' April offered, but felt sad that her aunt's life had seemingly been forgotten, pushed into insignificance. 'But what do you know about the "married man, baby" thing, where did that come from? Is there anything in the memoir about it? Was your father married when he met Winnie? Or was it just a strand of gossip that got embellished over time when Winnie didn't make it back home, as these things do?'

'No, Dad wasn't married when he met Winnie, and there's nothing whatsoever to suggest that Winnie had a baby,' Charlie said, and April nodded, knowing that her aunt Edie would take comfort from knowing the gossip wasn't true.

'Good.' April shook her head and let out a long breath.

'I'm still trying to piece it all together, because, in Dad's typical style, his memoirs are very cryptic,' Charlie continued. 'And it's dotted with all kinds of random lines . . .'

'Like what?'

'Like, oh, I don't know . . .' Charlie's eyes moved upwards and to the right as if trying to remember. 'Ahh, yes, something about drawing gloves in the street . . .' He creased his forehead, clearly baffled. 'What's that all about? It doesn't even make sense, and Dad's handwriting was atrocious towards the end so I may have got it all wrong in any case . . . maybe he meant draw a gun instead, I've no idea.'

'*It is a mark of ill-breeding to draw your gloves on in the street!*' April recited quietly.

'YES! That's it. Extraordinary, isn't it? But how do you know?' Charlie said. Both men stared at April as they leant forward.

'Because that same line is written in Winnie's diaries.'

'Diaries?' the men parroted in unison, clearly eager to know more about this unexpected revelation.

'That's right. And Winnie underlined that sentence in an old book about etiquette, which she gave to Hettie,' April said.

'Yes, I know her . . . has the haberdashery shop.' The general nodded, straightening his blazer.

'That's right.'

'And where are the diaries now?' Charlie asked.

'In an old wooden apple crate in my aunt's sitting room sideboard,' April said, relieved all over again that they hadn't been destroyed in the fire.

'And the book? The one on etiquette?' the general checked.

'I have that too. And there's another line that's been baffling me . . .' April told them.

'Go on. Please,' Charlie prompted, pressing his fingers together to make a steeple.

'*Treasure this book always, for it—*'

April stopped talking. Charlie was on his feet now, with an incredulous look on his face and his hands on his hips.

'*Will stand the test of time!*'

'How do you know?' April asked.

'Because it's written on the last page of Dad's memoir. And it was also in the letter that came with the safety deposit box key.'

'What do you think it means?' She looked at Charlie.

'I've no idea!' Charlie shook his head and pushed his hands into his trouser pockets.

'It's a code!' The general stood up, and April did too. 'A secret! It has to be.' He put one hand on her arm, and another on Charlie's arm and then told them, 'I think that your incredibly brave relatives,' he nodded first at April, 'your aunt and her . . .' he coughed and then looked at Charlie, 'lover . . . your father, the SOE handler, left behind some clues. A way for the truth to be revealed to their families and friends in the event of them not making it back home. All we need to do now is work out what these sentences mean!'

And the three of them stood silently in the little gypsy wagon in the orchard, exchanging glances as they let this revelation sink in. April felt full of admiration for Winnie and wondered if she had deliberately given the book to Hettie in the hope that she would indeed treasure it for always, as she had requested in the note. Winnie must have done. And the line about the gloves had to mean something, it had to be a clue, why else would it be in the diary without any context? Not to mention the actual diaries themselves. Winnie could so easily have found a more secure hiding place for them; surely she would have considered that they'd be found under the floorboards in her bedroom. Why take the risk? When she could have destroyed them, or given them to Colonel Finch for safekeeping.

No, Winnie wanted her family to find the diaries, she wanted them read and for them to lead the reader to the book. It was all planned out. Of course, it could just be a romantic notion, fanciful thoughts, but the more she let her mind wander, the more April was convinced it was something more. A way for the brave, courageous Winnie to eventually reveal the truth to her family, to her great niece, April, after all. Certainly, it was a shame that George and Delphine never knew the truth, but April did and she would make sure Edie did, and the whole of Tindledale too for that matter.

*

Later, after promising to be in touch again very soon, Charlie said his goodbyes and left with the general, leaving April alone with her thoughts once more. She tucked the manila folder under her arm and walked slowly back towards Orchard Cottage, again picturing her incredible great aunt Winnie doing the exact same thing. April wondered where it was that Winnie had been kissed by Colonel Finch. And then felt an overwhelming joy that her young aunt had experienced such emotion, that true feeling of falling in love, as she had written about in her diary. At least she had that sweetness before her life was so cruelly, and prematurely, ended.

April lifted her sunglasses up on to her head and stopped walking. After carefully laying the manila folder at her feet, she stretched out her arms and tilted her head towards the sun before bringing them in close to her, wrapping them around herself, as if in a hug. A hug for Winnie. Tears trickled over April's face, but she didn't feel sad, instead she felt light, elated even, empowered and encouraged by the beautiful and so very brave woman who fearlessly gave her life for her country. Did her patriotic duty. It took April's breath away as she picked up the folder and continued on to Orchard Cottage.

Before pushing open the front door, April curled her fingers around the brass door knocker, just as Winnie would have done all those years ago, and took a moment to smile as she reflected, relishing the evocative sense of timelessness, the heritage, the closeness to the generations of her family that had lived here before her. There was a certain comfort in that. And she loved it, loved that

Springtime . . . six months later

'A re you sure you're warm enough, Aunty?' April asked, as she tucked the handmade granny-patch blanket more snugly around Edie's lap. 'Only, you can't be too careful in these draughty old castles with the stone walls and the ceilings being so high.'

'Oh yes, thank you, my dear. But where's my favourite girl?' Edie asked, her watery blue eyes scanning the atrium.

'I'm right here.' Nancy ducked around from behind the wheelchair to give Edie a quick kiss on the cheek. They had figured it the best option, given the amount of walking involved today and Great Aunt Edie could only manage a few steps now before needing a rest.

'Sit next to me, will you please.' Edie indicated the wooden bench seat beside her. 'You're such a bonny girl, and there's some sweets in my bag for you. Don't tell your mother though.' Edie chuckled as she patted her black gold-clasped bag that was looped over her elbow and resting on the blanket. Nancy grinned and squeezed in between Edie and April after she had shuffled along a little.

'What did she say?' April whispered as she leant into Nancy.

'The usual . . . little girl, bag of sweets thing again! But you're not allowed to know, remember.' Nancy gave her stepmum's hand a quick pat.

'Oh dear.' Both women stifled fond smiles. Edie was functioning now almost entirely in a time long, *looooong* gone. April reckoned her aunt was getting muddled, thinking Nancy was her, as a child, when she used to visit her aunt in Tindledale during the holidays. April had a vague recollection of her own mum asking Edie to please ration the sweets, 'seeing as our little April hates the dentist so much', but then being allowed to choose two ounces of cola cubes or sherbet lemons from the glass jars on the shelf in the village store whenever her dear aunty took her up to the High Street, which she was pretty sure was most days back then. April straightened her coat and checked to make sure her mobile was switched off; it wouldn't do for it to ring. Not that anyone ever called her on it, but Molly had teased that she would do just that right in the middle of it all.

They were all here for a special memorial service. Winifred Lovell was one of a select number of people being honoured today. And April had brought Edie along to accept the award on her sister's behalf. Posthumously. The George Cross. And April was sure her heart might burst with pride.

For acts of the greatest heroism or of the most conspic-
uous courage in circumstances of extreme danger.

That's what it had said in the official notification letter
from Buckingham Palace which April had got framed
in the bookshop in the High Street and then presented
to the parish council. Mrs Pocket had then kindly
arranged for it to be proudly displayed on the wall of
the village hall for everyone to see, and she had even
sorted out a little unveiling ceremony with curtains and
everything for Edie to open while a reporter from the
Tindledale Herald took photos to accompany the lovely
piece he wrote about Winnie's bravery, 'one of Tindledale's finest', as she had since been described. Deedee
then took April to see Bill the postman, who lived with
his daughter-in-law, Dolly, and she was very hospitable
– made them tea, and they ate cake together while Bill
told April what he remembered.

'I didn't know anything about the girls' tittle-tattling
in the village about Winnie – if I had then I'd have put
a stop to it,' he'd said seriously, a slice of cake resting
on a napkin in his lap. 'I do remember delivering the
telegram to George.'

Bill had been silent for a moment, as the memories
returned. 'He confided to me that he needed time before
breaking the news to Delphine and Edie – both had
been heartbroken when the first telegram had come
notifying them of the death of their oldest son, Sidney.'
He'd shaken his head, 'George couldn't break their hearts
all over again. No, I think he hoped that Winnie would

surface, that she'd somehow still be alive . . . but he died too . . .' Bill also remembered delivering the letter from the War Office to Delphine in the winter after George died and said that it was all so terribly sad.

April inhaled, and shifted her thoughts to the present day, hoping this would help to put right the wrong that happened back then. She had known the medal was coming, having kept in touch with Charlie – they had spoken several times over the months since that day in the gypsy wagon. And she had him to thank for making today happen – he had arranged it all via his pal in the government. Talking of whom, Charlie had just arrived and was taking a seat in one of the adjacent rows. April leant around Nancy to give him a wave and beckoned him to join them. The general had saved a space for Charlie at the end of their row next to Hettie and Marigold who, when April had invited them, had both said that they wouldn't miss this day for all the tea in China, despite London being a *very* long way from Tindledale. Both women were dressed in new pastel-coloured skirt suits with matching fascinators that kept getting tangled whenever one of them moved her head.

'Marigold, will you take the blasted thing off please? You'll have somebody's eye out otherwise!' Hettie batted a bony hand in her friend's direction.

'Shuuushh.' It came from someone sitting a few rows back.

A hush descended. Something was happening. April felt a fizz of excitement mingled with anticipation. And then a door opened. Two men in black suits with curly plastic security wires hanging from their ears walked in and down the aisle, and she swore they were scanning each and every one of the people here today. Next a group of Beefeaters arrived, looking resplendent in their distinctive red-and-gold regalia as they took seats to the side of the stage area.

And then they saw her!

The Queen.

Dressed in a royal-red dress coat. Sensible black heels and matching bag. Her silvery, white hair looking exactly as it did on the telly. April caught her breath, she wouldn't class herself as an ardent royalist, but still . . . this was a momentous occasion and seeing the Queen standing just a few feet away from her was everything, plus more, that she could ever have imagined. And any moment now, April was going to wheel her great aunt Edie over to accept the medal from Her Majesty on Winnie's behalf. April swallowed hard, and made a mental note to make sure she curtsied, exactly as she had practised earlier this morning in Winnie's old attic bedroom with its faded rose-print-papered walls. After that, April had sat on the cast-iron bed and taken out Winnie's very first diary, and next to her name on the first page had written 'SOE' before pressing the diary to her chest and saying a few private words to her great aunt Winnie.

*

After the photographer had finished taking pictures outside the palace, and a car had brought them here to the SOE memorial on Albert Embankment, April felt a little tug on the side of her coat.

'What is it, Aunty?' She bent down to hear what Edie had to say.

'Will you help me up please, my dear?'

'Are you sure?' April glanced over at Nancy who was busy chatting to Hettie and Marigold. She caught April's eye and came over to join them.

'What's the matter?' Nancy asked.

'Edie wants to stand up.'

'And walk!' Edie announced, pressing her hands on the arms of the wheelchair as if to propel herself up and forward into a standing position. April and Nancy quickly moved to either side of her and slipped a hand under Edie's spindly elbows. 'Thank you my dears.' Edie steadied herself and then told them, 'Now, help me over to the statue, will you please.'

April didn't need telling twice, so after lifting the heart-shaped wreath made by Gray's sister, Jen, the florist, from the abundance of fresh violets that now carpeted the woodland area in Tindledale, where Winnie would have walked with Colonel Finch and been presented with the violet that she had pressed inside her diary, she looped it over her arm and then carefully assisted her aunt. They reached the marble memorial with the statue of Violette Szabo on top – the courageous SOE who had also been shot dead by the Germans.

Great Aunt Edie stopped. 'Do you have the card?'

'Yes, here it is.' April quickly pinned it on to the wreath.

'Thank you.' And Edie took the wreath and held it in her arms for a moment. After kissing the palm of her hand and placing it over the top of the largest violet, she handed the wreath to April to place at the foot of the memorial. Then, in a moment of perfect clarity, April's great aunt said, 'Farewell, my darling Winnie. Fearless and brave always. Lots of love from your proud sister, Edie,' and then paused, turned her face to April and added, 'and our wonderful, kind and caring great niece, April . . . who looks exactly like you, my darling . . . and is just as brave too. In fact, your bedroom is hers now, my dear sister, and she understands the true magic of our wonderful home, how it heals, restores, makes one whole again . . . the secret of Orchard Cottage. It's such a shame that you didn't make it back home, but your spirit will always live on inside the cottage and outside too in the glorious orchards all around.'

Edie fixed her eyes on April as she clasped her hand and gave it a squeeze. April nodded, smiled and enveloped her aunt in her arms. It was true, April had discovered the secret of Orchard Cottage.

*

Later, having arrived safely back in Tindledale, Nancy was sitting with Edie, playing rummy and enjoying a snowball before bedtime, so April took the opportunity to wander outside to think about the eventful day. It was a lovely, fresh evening, with the navy night sky streaked with smudges of red, orange and gold as the sun faded over the tips of the apple trees on the horizon. She pulled her cardy in around her body and wandered towards the meadow section of the garden where the wild flowers were, along with Gray's roses. And caught her breath as she came around the corner. The sight before her was spectacular, magical, and quite romantic.

Chinese paper lanterns on metal rods pushed into the grass were swaying in the gentle breeze, each one flickering and twinkling with the light from a candle, the air filled with the heady scent of jasmine. A rustling noise momentarily startled April. She swivelled on her heel, and then clasped her hands up to her cheeks.

'Matt!'

'Sooo . . . what do you think, my love?' Grinning, he walked towards her.

'Um . . .' April was lost for words. And then she spotted the cast-iron bench placed behind Gray's glorious orange roses which were now nearly waist-height.

'Did you make that?' April walked over to the bench, and after standing behind it, she ran a hand along the top, feeling the craftsmanship, time and love that had gone into making it. Matt nodded, making his dark curls dip over his forehead and into those delicious dark-green eyes of his.

'Yep. Of course I did,' he laughed, 'and the lantern holders. I don't do just horseshoes you know.' He winked and tilted his head to one side.

'It's incredible. And very wonderful . . . just like you.' April beamed, and relished the fizzy feeling inside her stomach. They had been together properly now for a while and although it was still early days, she knew she was falling in love with Matt. Whenever she was with him, she felt relaxed, comfortable and happy . . . and it was like she had known him for ages, which she now knew she actually had.

'Well, that's handy then . . .' Matt teased, 'because I think you're pretty wonderful too!' He stepped in closer. 'And I thought it would be nice for you to have somewhere special to remember Gray for always.' And he slipped his hand around April's and squeezed it tight before pulling her into him and enveloping her in one of his enormous hugs. As she lifted her lips to his, April no longer felt lost as she had that time by the roadside. It was as if Matt, the boy who had kissed her first, had found her again and helped her find a way forward. With him. Here in Tindledale, where the secret of Orchard Cottage could sprinkle its magic all over the next chapter in her life . . .

EPILOGUE

Next year . . .

Summertime, and glorious tendrils of sunlight danced through the apple trees as they all sang happy birthday to April, who was seated at one end of the food-laden trestle table in the big orchard with an enormous candle-lit cake in front of her. Darby and Joan were shading under a large pear tree nearby, their tails swishing from side to side as they merrily chomped away on a pile of carrots. The muddy-bottomed sheep were wandering around, oblivious to the celebrations.

'Don't forget to make a wish,' Nancy said, and they all cheered and clapped as April blew out the candles. Nancy was sitting to the left of her holding Pete's hand, having recently moved in with him. After the bungalow in Basingstoke had been sold and the proceeds split three ways, Nancy had used her share to set up her own fire-safety training business, working from one of the outbuildings on Pete's farm, in addition to being a retained firefighter attached to Tindledale fire station. Freddie, after travelling the world, had settled in New Zealand, not far from where his mum lived.

April looked around and felt so incredibly happy. Everyone was here. Matt to her right, with her other stepdaughter, Bella, beside him, and quite grown up she was now too. The transformation in her after they had moved her to the new school was incredible – Bella was now vivacious and happy, and with her heart set on a textiles course at the college in Market Briar. And she had worked wonders with the horses, hand-feeding them back to health, and the gypsy wagon, over in the far corner, was a yarnbombed extravaganza, completely covered in knitwear, with a lovely outdoor seating area flanked with bunting and screened by honeysuckle-clad trellises. April gave Bella a wink as she lifted her now shoulder-length hair and dipped her head to blow out the candles. Next to Bella was her friend, Josh, with his mum, Molly (April's best friend) beside him – thankfully she had left Stinker, the ferret, at home, which April was eternally grateful for, especially as Molly had tried to sneak him along on their spa day recently by concealing him in her tote. Luckily, April had smelt Stinker before the Beetle had pulled away from outside the butchers' shop and had hastily insisted he be left at home.

Further around the table were Hettie, Marigold and Deedee, the latter wearing a bodycon boob-tube topped off with an enormous floppy sun hat. To her side was the general with his guest, Charlie, who had just published his book detailing the incredible story of Colonel Finch, SOE commander and his special agent . . . Code Name Pauline, aka Winifred Lovell. Charlie had also managed to enlist the help of an expert cryptologist who worked in MI5 to crack the codes that Winnie and Finch had devised all those years ago. It was extremely complicated, but fascinating when the expert had revealed the true meaning of the message in the letter to Hettie, something about taking the first letter of each word, ignoring the 'T's and then applying the first code, so . . . '*Treasure this book always, for it will stand the test of time*' actually meant . . . 'Pauline', Winnie's code name. And then when the second code was applied to that random line in Winnie's diary, '*It is a mark of ill-breeding to draw your gloves on in the street!*' it was revealed as meaning . . . 'my life for yours', which April thought was the most poignant and courageous thing that she had ever read. Winnie had specifically written the code in the letter to Hettie as a clue for her family and friends, knowing full well that she might never make it back home and hoping it would be discovered if she didn't . . . and she was prepared to give her life to the war effort in order to save others, her family and friends and everyone else. She truly was a remarkable woman, and April had since had a tapestry made with the 'gloves' line on, which hung in the hallway of Orchard Cottage as a reminder for evermore.

Opposite Charlie and the general was Harvey, who was pouring his very chic wife, Katrina, a large glass of iced cider before planting a big kiss on her lips, making her blush and then rest her head on his shoulder. April caught Harvey's eye and gave him a discreet nod; they had become very good friends now and she hadn't once had to tell Katrina about Harvey misbehaving, and long may that continue.

'Are you OK, love?' It was Matt. He leant in and placed a warm hand on April's thigh, the sun glinting against the white gold of his wedding ring. Last summer it had been – a simple ceremony beside the stream where they had first made eye contact, all those years ago. Him fishing, her riding her bike in the white cotton dress. They had the photo of April framed on the wall too as a memento of that precious moment in time.

'I couldn't be happier, sweetheart,' April said, giving him a kiss.

'Hey, you two . . . enough of that,' Bella chipped in, grinning as she swivelled in her seat and leant around Matt. 'Here, you haven't opened my present yet, April.' Bella scooted out of her seat and after elbowing her dad out of the way she gave her lovely stepmum a huge hug, wished her 'Happy birthday' and proudly placed a purple tissue-wrapped parcel on the table in front of her. Tied up with sparkly silver ribbon, it was gorgeous. April squeezed Bella's hand.

'Thank you, sweetheart. What is it?'

'Open it and see . . .' Bella clapped her hands together with glee.

April did, and gasped. Inside was the most exquisite hand-knitted satin white lace baby set, the bootees barely bigger than the palms of her hands.

'Oh Bella, it's perfect. Thank you.' Cupping Bella's face in her hands, April gave her a big kiss on her forehead. 'Look Matt, it's for the baby.'

'It's lovely, *Bells*.' Matt pulled a face and ducked as his daughter pretended to swipe him one. 'But what I want to know is . . . will it fit?' He turned to April. 'Are you sure we only have one baby in there?' And he picked up the little matinee jacket and held it against April's enormous baby bump. Due any minute, she was the size of a small thatched cottage, to be fair. But over the moon at this unexpected surprise, and just in the nick of time . . . April had never allowed herself to dream of having a baby at this age, but was absolutely delighted to be building a new family of her very own, especially now that her dear aunt Edie was no longer with them. She had passed away peacefully in her sleep, having finished a final round of rummy and a large snowball only hours earlier, which April had thought very fitting.

'What are you saying?' April batted his arm away.

'Nothing, my love, nothing at all.' He kissed the top of her hand, and then carefully placed the tiny jacket back inside the tissue paper.

April took a sip of her iced pear cordial. It was a new line that they were trialling with the organic cider producer, and it tasted delicious, which was wonderful given that Orchard Cottage had enjoyed another bumper crop this year, and next year looked to be just as fruitful too. Business was booming and April had used the income from the orchards to rebuild the barn and renovate the cottage, the surrounding gardens and the lane, plus was in the process of kitting Darby and Joan out with a proper paddock and stable block. And the two old horses were flourishing these days, Joan in particular looked especially beautiful since Bella had braided the scarlet ribbon from Gray's trug of roses through her bridle, making it flare out in the breeze whenever Joan mustered up some energy and got a bit of a gallop on. It was a glorious sight to see.

Smiling, April looked at all the happy faces around her, the laughter and smiles, and then raised her glass up to the sky as a toast to her dear aunt Edie, to thank her for sharing the secret of Orchard Cottage.

'Ooh, I almost forgot. Aunty Jen asked me to give you this!' Nancy rummaged inside her bag and then handed April a cream-coloured envelope.

'Thank you darling.'

April slipped the tip of her index finger under the flap at the edge, pulled out the letter and read the words.

Happy Birthday, Dear April.

Another year has passed since our last goodbye and I truly hope that you took my advice and seized every day, my darling, and that you are happy and loved by someone new. I'm sure you won't need flowers from me any more so I'm going to bow out gracefully and say thank you for loving me and being by my side through it all.

Love always,

Gray xxx

AUTHOR'S NOTE

Hello my dear reader, I really hope you enjoyed *The Secret of Orchard Cottage*. It was such an emotional and special book for me to write for a variety of reasons. Firstly, it's the first book I have written with multi-viewpoints, which was a little scary at first, but as I got into the swing of it, it was thoroughly enjoyable writing from Matt's perspective, and April's story, whilst a tragic one, was intended to be uplifting and inspiring too. And of course, Edie's decline was incredibly emotional to write at times. Dementia and Alzheimer's are something that all of us fear and through the course of my research I became aware of how harrowing these cruel diseases can be. Not only for the person living with the illness, but for the family and carers too, who do a relentless yet remarkable job in caring for that person, often with little acknowledgement or support.

However, it is Winnie's story that was the most joyous and yet conversely poignant to write. I have always felt inspired by and in awe of the many ordinary women who so courageously carried out extraordinary activities during the Second World War, in particular the Special Operations Executives. I really hope that I have managed in a small way within this book to recognize the utterly selfless courage that these women possessed. Without their sterling efforts, our world today would be a very different place, but instead, other ordinary women like us now have so much more freedom and liberty to achieve our own extraordinary things.

As a tribute to two ordinary women in particular, both SOE's who did extraordinary things during the Second World War – one being Violette Szabo who, like our heroine Winnie Lovell, was also shot by the Nazis, and Nancy Wake, who miraculously made it back home and lived to the sterling age of ninety-eight – I have peppered in a few secret references throughout the story, as follows:

Winnie Lovell is named after Winnie Wilson, Violette Szabo's best friend. As is April Wilson, our main character.

April's stepdaughter, Nancy, is named after Nancy Wake and the pressed violet flower that Finch gave to Winnie after their walk in the woods is significant for two reasons: firstly as a little clue to the name, Violette, (Szabo) and of course the violet is also the bravest, hardiest little heart-shaped flower. As, indeed, was our heroine who opens the story in the bedroom of Orchard Cottage, in the little village of Tindledale in 1941: Winifred Lovell SOE. A truly remarkable woman.

Luck and love,
Alex xx

ACKNOWLEDGEMENTS

This is my sixth novel and whilst it explores some very serious themes I do hope it warms your heart and leaves you feeling uplifted. My first thanks as always go to all of you, my darling friends from around the world, who chat to me on Facebook and Twitter, or who send emails with pictures of your knitting and crocheting, or chatty messages about what's going on in your lives and how my books have played a part in helping you through the good times and bad. You're all magnificent and your kindness and cheerleading spur me on – writing books can get lonely sometimes, but having you all is like a family of sorts and that is something very special indeed. I really couldn't do any of this without you. You mean the world to me and make it all worthwhile. Thank you so very much. xxx

Special thanks and gratitude to my agent, Tim Bates, for everything, especially for knowing when to call me and put my head straight. Massive thanks and an abundance of appreciation as always to my editor and dear friend, Kate Bradley, for having the patience of a saint, for the WhatsApp chats and being there always – the perfect team! Of course, none of the other stuff would happen without the wonderful team at HarperCollins, especially Kimberley Young, Liz Dawson, Charlotte Brabbin, Katie Moss and Hayley Camis. Special thanks to my copy editor, Rhian McKay.

I couldn't write at all without my beloved Northern Soul music to evoke the right emotions, so thank you for helping me to keep the faith and keep on keeping on.

Immense thanks always to my best friends Caroline Smailes, Lisa Hilton and Rachel Forbes. Your kindness, cheerleading and general knack of knowing exactly what to say at the right moment, is what also keeps me going. ☺ xxx

My husband, Paul, aka Cheeks, for sharing his security services expertise in code making and breaking, and my darling, QT, the bravest little girl I know – I couldn't do any of this without you both, thank you and lots of love. xoxoxoxo

Luck and love to you all,

Alex xxx

Great Aunt Edie's Famous Apple Sauce

Makes

8–10 portions

Ingredients

- 225g cooking apples, peeled, cored and chopped
- 2 tbsp water
- 15g butter
- Zest of half a lemon
- 1 tsp caster sugar

Method

- Put the apples in a saucepan with the lemon zest and water.
- Cover and cook over a low heat until they are soft and mushy.
- Take off the heat and beat in the butter and the sugar.
- Cool.

Great Aunt Edie's Favourite Poached Pears in Chocolate Sauce

Ingredients

- 6 medium-sized pears, peeled with stalks left on
- 2 tbsp lemon juice
- 450ml water
- 200g caster sugar

For the chocolate sauce

- 150ml double cream
- 200g dark chocolate, roughly chopped

Method

- Brush the peeled pears with a little lemon juice.
- Heat the water to a simmer in a large pan and add the sugar.
- Leave the sugar and water to simmer until it has slightly thickened, before adding the pears to the pan.
- Cover the pan and poach the pears for 25 minutes.
- Carefully remove the pears from the poaching liquid and transfer to six individual serving plates.
- Pour the double cream into a clean pan and heat gently, without boiling.
- Take the pan off the heat and add the chopped chocolate, stirring to make a smooth sauce.
- To serve, pour the chocolate sauce over the pears.

Winnie's Favourite
Cinnamon and Apple Crumble

Ingredients

For the filling

- 750g (3 large) Bramley apples, peeled, cored and cut into chunks
- 250g (2 small) Cox's apples, peeled, cored and cut into chunks
- 50g sultanas
- 50g light muscovado sugar
- 50g caster sugar
- I tsp ground cinnamon
- Pinch of freshly grated nutmeg
- ½ tsp ground cloves
- A little butter, for greasing

For the cinnamon crumble topping

- 170g self-raising flour
- I tsp ground cinnamon
- 50g caster sugar
- 50g light muscovado sugar
- 130g chilled butter, cubed

Method

- Preheat the oven to 200°C/fan 180°C/gas 6. To make the topping, place the flour in a large bowl with the cinnamon and sugars, mix, then add the butter.
- Rub the mixture together with your fingers until it resembles coarse breadcrumbs.
- Mix the filling ingredients together in a large bowl, then spoon evenly into a lightly buttered, 1.4-litre ovenproof dish.
- Evenly spoon the crumble topping over the filling.
- Bake for 30 minutes.
- Remove from the oven and leave for 10 minutes, then serve with warm custard.

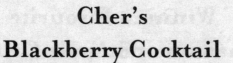

Cher's
Blackberry Cocktail

Ingredients

- 35ml gin
- 20ml lemon juice
- 1 tsp sugar syrup
- 15ml blackberry liqueur
- Slice of lemon and a blackberry, to garnish

Method

- Place all of the ingredients into a tumbler filled with crushed ice and stir well.
- Garnish with a slice of lemon and a blackberry.

Great Aunt
Edie's Snowball

Ingredients

- 100ml lemonade
- 50ml Advocaat
- Lime juice
- 1 Glacé cherry

Method

- Place all of the ingredients into a tumbler filled with crushed ice and stir well.
- Garnish with a glacé cherry popped onto the side of the glass.

DISCOVER MORE FROM
Alex Brown

The Carrington's series

'Adorable, comical and magical'
Closer

The Tindledale series

'Warm, wonderful characters
– a really lovely read'
Sarah Morgan